Erotically
Ever After

Edited by Rachel Kenley

**BLACK
LACE**

Contents

1 3 5 7 9 10 8 6 4 2

First published in the US by Ravenous Romance as *Spellbound* (2008) and
Passionately Ever After (2010)
First published in the United Kingdom in 2013 by Black Lace Books, an
imprint of Ebury Publishing
A Random House Group Company

The Random House Group Limited Reg. No. 954009

Addresses for companies within the Random House Group can be found at:
www.randomhouse.co.uk

A CIP catalogue record for this book
is available from the British Library

The Random House Group Limited supports The Forest
Stewardship Council® (FSC®), the leading international forest
certification organisation. Our books carrying the FSC label are
printed on FSC® certified paper. FSC is the only forest certification
scheme endorsed by the leading environmental organisations,
including Greenpeace. Our paper procurement policy can be found at:
www.randomhouse.co.uk/environment

Printed and bound by CPI Group (UK) Ltd, Croydon, CR0 4YY

ISBN: 9780352346865

To buy books by your favourite authors and register for offers, visit:
www.blacklace.co.uk

To Holly Schmidt and Lori Perkins,
who know the magic of a well-told tale.

Thank you for your passion and inspiration.
And to Mark, with whom I share my happily ever after.
Now and always.

Handsome and Petal

By Jo Atkinson

Once upon a time, a handsome construction worker with a serious sweet tooth walked into a neighborhood bakery near a jobsite and discovered something far more delicious than warm chocolate chip cookies and soft, miniature éclairs. Twice that same afternoon, he returned to drink in the image of the big, beautiful blonde goddess working behind the counter. On the third day, he asked her out on a date and she accepted.

She was called Lily, after the flower, she quipped, which symbolizes purity. He leaned over the counter, sinful buttercream-slathered cakes displayed in the case beneath. Chirping cartoon birds circled his neat athlete's haircut and pounding red Valentine hearts replaced his eyes. Brody never considered dating a woman who didn't slink through life in Size 2 dresses. He'd also never been in love; but when Lily filled a cannoli shell with creamy chocolate filling, wrapped it seductively in wax paper, and snuck it across the counter, on the house, he was smitten. His little petal's name might mean purity, but the image of her beautiful, pudgy hand around the phallic dessert filled Brody's head—and pants—with impure thoughts. When he attempted to stand at his full six-foot-two in height, stars replaced the chirpy cartoon birds: His cock had gotten painfully stiff.

Later that night after a fine, expensive meal and a dessert that normally would have bewitched him, Brody escorted Lily up the stairs to her second-story apartment. He was enthralled by the bounce of her breasts and the hot, round caboose he caught himself staring at over the course of the date, wondering what secret pleasures were hidden within her denim skirt. Every morning before work—and usually twice a night after first wandering into the bakery where Lily toiled—Brody masturbated to increasingly decadent fantasies of her. She was the sweetest woman he'd encountered.

"I had a wonderful time, Handsome," Lily said. Brody was the handsomest guy she'd met in her 27 years; the kind of man who stood out in a crowd. The man had presence. He was an athlete with the body of a god, a construction worker and a gentleman. She loved his magnificent twin-emerald eyes, his big, strong hands and how, when she kissed him goodnight at the open door, she felt the swell of his cock press against her.

She kissed him again, making sure to rub her belly over his boner, and heard him growl. Boldly, she touched his chest. Brody's cock pulsed, tickling Lily's stomach. "Do you want to come in?"

He nodded and grunted an affirmative through their locked lips.

She bid him to enter. A vibrant wash of color greeted Brody's eyes. Walls of butternut squash complimented by cranberry curtains, with a ruby-red-footed candy bowl filled with gumdrops on an elegant walnut credenza. The sofa was overstuffed, like a marshmallow. Everything in the charming apartment was a visual treat, good enough to eat. The air was sweet like sugar cookies.

"Lily, my Petal," Brody said.

She caressed his cheek, which showed a wonderfully scruffy layer of five o'clock shadow. "Yes, Handsome?"

"You're more beautiful than a plate of homemade brownies, hotter than hot fudge, more sinful than cinnamon." Lily blushed. His cock ached in response to the redness on her cheeks. Brody imagined similar color rising on other destinations across her gloriously sexy plus-size form.

"Would you," he said, nearly choking on the words. Charming the opposite sex had never been an issue before for Brody, who was the captain of his ice hockey team and looked hot in his tool belt and hardhat. True love, however, can overwhelm a man while transforming him with an invitation to evolve. "Would you be my gal?"

Lily tipped her chin. A happy smile spread across her face. Brody's cock jerked; ready to come in his increasingly tight blue jeans without any manual stimulation.

"Yes," she said. "And I have the perfect way to celebrate."

Lily drew a whipped cream heart over the hairy muscles of his chest and slowly licked him clean. Brody was aware of every pass of Lily's tongue. When a lock of her long golden hair fell across his neck, he seized in place on her bed. As he watched her movements, feeling like he was floating on a giant cake, she raised a candy cane to her plump lips and teasingly performed oral sex on it. Then Lily hooked the cane around Brody's straining cock and pulled his thickness into her mouth. He bit back a howl, sure he would go mad at any moment. Could a simple male experience such superhuman sex without losing his marbles?

Lily sucked Brody's cock, spread more whipped cream over his loose, aching balls, and lapped that up, too; an action that pushed Brody past the edge. He loved having that particular part of his body attended to. Lily cleaned up one ingredient, and Handsome added a different, messier variety to the festivities.

Lily's nipples were taut rosy gumdrops, capping creamy peaks. Brody pinched one while gently chewing on the other. She mewled contentedly beneath him, the sweet, sugary fragrance of her naked skin soon bringing his cock back to its full stiffness. Brody was a breast man—and a leg, thigh, ass, and pussy man. He'd never tasted so delicious a woman.

"I could eat you all night, Petal," he growled around her clit.

Lily traced the wet candy cane around her nipples. Brody lathered her breasts with his tongue and followed the sticky trail when she dipped it toward her belly. *That stomach!* Pale and beautiful, like angel cake, Brody rubbed and kissed it, playfully nipping at its roundness before dipping lower.

"I love candy canes," he chuckled, his warm breath gusting over the sensitive folds of Lily's pussy. But Brody loved honey even more and, after spreading Lily's petals, he found her wet with a woman's natural sweetness. "Fucking beautiful," he grunted. "And so damn tasty."

Leaning in, Brody brushed Lily's pussy with his tongue. Sweetness ignited across his taste buds.

The goddess' moans intensified to howls. "Yes, Handsome," she begged.

He feasted, licking Lily with slow, powerful strokes countered by quick, feather-light flicks. She writhed as Brody pressed at her clit. Lily gave the candy cane several more teasing licks and rubbed it around her nipples, tempting Brody back up to her chest. She extended the candy provocatively. Brody accepted it between his lips. While sucking, he mounted her glistening chest, briefly pinching at her cherry nipples, then lined up his cock and fucked her between the breasts.

Weeks later, Brody was sweating it out on the ice, blocking the puck, racing over the red line in his rather large skates, and scoring a goal for his team as the first period wound down. As was the case with many hockey jocks, he added to his intimidation factor by not shaving for several days before a game. Brody successfully scared several of the other team's less-rugged warriors.

While sucking down water from his bottle during the break, he caught sight of a vision beyond the boards: Lily. She was dressed in a peasant top showcasing the swells of her perfect breasts; black slacks that instantly left him hard in his hockey pants; and black heels Brody hoped would walk up and down his spine after the game. Lily carried a platter of cupcakes with pink frosting and candied cherries on top that reminded him of her breasts, worsening the discomfort of his hockey uniform. Little candy canes and other Christmas candies decorated the spaces between pastries, along with a garnish of silk poinsettia blossoms.

That's my gal, Brody thought, rounding the boards. *The most beautiful woman on the planet.*

"For you and the guys," she said.

Handsome accepted the platter in his gloved hands.

"This is enough for me, but what are the other dudes going to eat?"

She winked. Brody's cock jumped. "Later, Handsome," she said.

Brody studied Lily's tasty, round ass as she sauntered into the stands in search of an empty seat. Later, he planned to liberate her of those pants and eat until satisfied, body and soul. He started in the direction of the bench, hockey stick clutched in one hand, platter of treats held aloft in the other. His teammates swarmed around him.

"Sweet," said his buddy Denton.

"Yeah, dude—but who's the fat chick?" asked Baxter, the team's center and one of Brody's fellow construction workers.

White-hot, blinding rage surged through Handsome's blood. He put the plate down, grabbed Baxter by the jersey, spun him around, and slammed him into the boards.

"Never make that mistake again," Handsome roared into the other man's face. "That's my girl: my beautiful, perfect girl. If you ever disrespect her again, you'll be picking your teeth out of the back of your throat. Got it?"

Baxter nodded, spat, and shook free. A buzzer sounded: The game's second period was about to begin.

Brody sat in his boxer-briefs at a little breakfast nook in Lily's kitchen, sipping coffee out of her pretty demitasse cups.

"Refill?" she cooed, a sunny smile on her face.

"Please," Brody said. "You're in a happy mood, Petal."

As she poured, one of Lily's breasts slipped free of her robe, spilling completely into view. Brody had fucked her twice the night before—no surprise there, considering how horny he always got after playing sports. The sweet candy scent of her, coupled with the image of her body before him, soon had Brody ready for more. He reached for her and tugged on her nipple.

"Stop it," she protested, giggling.

"So give," Brody said, reaching down to adjust his cock and finding it painfully hard in his underwear, pinned at an awkward angle. Freeing it, Handsome couldn't resist giving his thickness a stroke. One led to two. Unable to resist, he started masturbating beneath the breakfast bar, watching as she went into the kitchen and pulled ingredients out of cabinets, sifted, measured, poured and mixed. She caught his indiscretion, but continued to work.

"I'm trying a few new recipes, that's all," she said, the slightest of smirks curling on her lips. "Cappuccino butter-cream cupcakes stuffed with a deliriously rich chocolate ganache, topped with chocolate-covered espresso beans."

Brody groaned, still stroking.

"Baking, as you know, is quite the science," Lily continued. "It is a system of precise measurements, ingredients, temperatures, and ticks of the clock absolutely unforgiving to screw-ups. It doesn't help to distract this baker when she is so focused on perfecting recipes that could help her open her own bakery."

"Say what?" Brody grunted through clenched teeth.

Lily nonchalantly crossed to the refrigerator and plucked a sheet from among the magnets, handing it to him.

"You read this," she whispered, sinking between his legs, "while I attend to this distraction."

Lily's plump, velvety lips circled the head of Brody's cock. She pulled the shaft free from his hand, handling it with upward strokes while her mouth plunged downward. Brody tried to read the sheet, but the letters ran together. A firm tug on his balls made it official: He needed to fuck Lily.

Brody joined her on the floor, licked her sopping pussy, and rolled another skin over his cock. Even Lily's brand of condoms was sweetly flavored. Brody assumed by its purple tint this one was grape. She was ready for him. He walked Lily to the sofa and slid his cock deep inside her.

"Tell me about the paper" he huffed, mid-thrust.

"I got accepted to Yum Network's big holiday competition show, 'Dessert Triathlon,'" she answered between groans. "It's rookie against a pro . . . Me up against a heavy hitter . . . Corinne Zahn . . . She's tough . . . The third leg . . . Is edible gingerbread houses . . ."

"I love gingerbread," Brody said. "And I love you. Congratulations, babe."

"Top prize," Lily continued after pledging the same in return, "is a hundred-thousand dollars—enough to open my own bakery."

"When you win," he panted, "I'll build you the best damn custom bakery shop ever, with these very hands." He rubbed her clit. Lily jumped.

"Will you come with me?" she asked.

"Come with you?" Brody parroted.

"To the competition in New York. Be my right-hand man?"

"I'll come with you," Brody gasped. And he did.

Brody strutted into Yum Network's studio on Madison Avenue behind Lily, carrying a bin containing specialty ingredients and the pans she was allowed to bring. Lily directed him toward her corner of the immaculate stainless steel setup where ovens, refrigerators and counters waited for the two opponents.

Lily had applied to the competition using her most enticing, biggest guns. For the fruit-themed first round, she submitted her recipe for her blueberry cinnamon coffee cake that had drawn rave reviews from customers at the bakery. Her cappuccino cupcakes were for the chocolate round, and a spicy, frosted edible gingerbread house for the grand finale.

Corinne Zahn was a leggy culinary legend who catered to celebrities in the Hamptons; and who'd won numerous network food challenges, including the previous Christmas cook-off. Lily recognized her instantly as the other woman barked demands at her doting assistant. Steeling herself, Lily sauntered over.

"Ms Zahn?"

Corinne's thin, sharp lips tightened in a snarl, exposing a length of white teeth. "Yes?"

"I wanted to introduce myself. I'm Lily, the competition," she offered, extending her hand for a shake.

Corinne glanced disapprovingly at Lily's outstretched fingers and laughed. "Oh, my dear, I think it's very sweet of you to consider yourself *my* competition. I appreciate the joke."

Lily withdrew her hand and backed away. Brody observed most of this from the kitchen counter at the opposite end of the set. When Lily returned to her half of the space, he asked if she was all right. She said she was, though he knew better.

Soon after, Brody went in search of the men's restroom and felt the slither of a chill across his flesh; that sense of being watched from somewhere across a room. It wasn't until he emerged that he identified its source.

"Oh *boy*," Corinne called.

She stood in a pose meant to be seductive, with one knee bent and a booted foot bracing the corridor's wall. Take away the meanness, the ugly internal toxins leaching through her pores and surrounding her in a dark cloud, and Corinne Zahn might have appeared stunning. But in that pose, and having gleaned some of what she said to Lily, she reminded Brody of a stone gargoyle leering down from an ancient European rooftop. Adding to the imagery, Brody retained enough from his two years of high school German to remember that her last name meant 'tooth'.

"If you're referring to me, I officially ceased being a boy a decade ago," he fired back.

"Yes, you sure did," she sighed, licking her teeth. Brody half-expected to see dripping globs of crimson the next time she spoke. "Sorry, it's an old habit. I call every man that, including my doorman, and he's in his sixties."

Brody's eyes narrowed. "Something I can help you with?"

"You do work for Yum, I assume?"

Brody's lanyard, hanging around his neck by a red cord, had fallen backward behind the flap of his vintage leather jacket. "I suppose."

Corinne unhooked herself from her winged gargoyle pose and clip-clopped several steps closer. Her jagged scent burned in Brody's next breath. "How about you help me with some of my needs? I have things that need to be carried in."

"Didn't you bring your own assistant?"

"*Her?*" Corinne huffed. "No, these are the kinds of ingredients that require a man's special touch and strong hands. Things to be kneaded, pulled, stuffed. I could use a man of your obvious . . . talents."

Corinne's gaze tumbled down Brody's chest to the crotch of his faded blue jeans, lower to his big feet in their old construction boots, and back up to his eyes. She snorted a terrible sound that doubled her ugliness. "I'd like you to look after my wishes. A man as handsome as you will only make me appear invincible leading up to my inevitable victory."

Face stony, Brody fished out his pass and turned

it around. "Sorry, but I work for Team Lily. And my gorgeous girlfriend's going to kick your scrawny ass back to whatever house it is that you haunt."

"Oh, fuck her," Lily pouted.

Brody, standing at the door to the hotel suite's bathroom dressed only in a towel following his long, hot shower, said, "Not with a borrowed dick. I bet her snatch has teeth."

"Fuck *me*, then?"

A lusty smile spread across Brody's freshly shaved face. Reaching beneath the towel, he gave his cock a tug and found it swelling. "Now you're talking, Babe."

Lily tossed back the top sheet, revealing cherry gum-drops stacked over each nipple and leading in a line down the center of her chest to the bright red dollop of butter-cream frosting piped in the shape of rose petals around her clit.

"I don't even want to know the flexibility required to create a design like that there," he said. "Then again, maybe I do." Brody ate his way to the flower. Lily shook in giddy delight as he nibbled. Neither suspected Corinne was several doors away, scheming to destroy them.

Corinne brooded, fingering herself. *I will destroy them*, she told herself. *I will obliterate the gluttonous pig, and stand victorious above her groveling, handsome boyfriend. That he would willingly fuck something so inferior when he could serve me, disgusts me.*

Corinne dipped two fingers into her cunt, imagining

Brody bound and bruised, bleeding from where she struck him across the lips; a broken man on his knees begging for mercy. Rubbing her clit in clockwise circles, Corinne fantasized about him denouncing the little piggy, devouring Corinne's pussy and declaring it sweet while calling Lily's as sour as salty pickles.

"Salt," Corinne hissed aloud.

Visions of forcing Lily's boyfriend to perform for her sexually didn't make Corinne orgasm, but this magic wrinkle to her plan did. Suddenly, it was all so clear and would be so wickedly easy to pull off. It wasn't the first time she'd chosen the dark side to take out the competition.

Confusing salt for sugar was a chef's worst nightmare; and such a simple mistake to make. Even simpler when, under cover of shadows, Corinne slipped to Lily's side of the kitchen set and switched one for the other.

Lily was a natural, according to the show's host Myles Cobert. He declared her a force to be reckoned with as she prepared her decadent blueberry coffee cake.

"This one's sure to be pure *yum*," the jocular, everyman's chef-lebrity said.

But all it took was one look at the sour faces of the judges to see it was anything but following the conclusion of the first round.

"I feel like I just ate a mouthful of olives and blueberries," one gasped, reaching for her water glass.

"It's an easy mistake," Myles talked at the cameras. "But it might have cost the newcomer the competition."

Corinne took bragging rights to the first leg of the

event with her caramel and apple strudel. Brody noticed the smug grin on her lips and a light went off.

"I don't think you screwed up, Petal," he said, pulling Lily aside.

She gazed into his eyes. "I did, and in the worst way possible!"

"No, I don't think it was you, Babe. I've seen you in action. I know how talented you are. I think that bitch set you up."

Brody tipped a glance toward the right side of the kitchen, where Corinne was busy organizing for the next round.

"Be careful," Brody whispered. "And remember that I've got your back."

Lily nodded and got to work.

The cappuccino buttercream cupcakes turned the tide in her favor. The pretty treats, each capped by a single chocolate-covered espresso bean, charmed the judges. They proclaimed Lily the comeback kid.

"Luscious, beautiful, and oh-so-sweet at the center, you can't help but fall in love," Myles declared. "And the same can be said about her cupcakes, too!"

Lily's cupcakes notched the second round over Corinne's triple-fudge devil's food trifle, leaving the women in a dead tie going into the final stretch.

The dreadful little porker fell flat on her ass in the first round exactly as planned, Corinne mused. The woman was disappointed by Lily's rebound. It killed Corinne to see the joy on the enemy's cherubic face, to watch her handsome companion embrace her, lifting her off the chubby turnips of her ankles and swinging her around, seemingly with ease. Corinne's only comfort came in the knowledge that his back would surely pay for it later after the cameras stopped taping and the lights dimmed.

Enraged after the results were announced, Corinne opened her oven door and slammed it as hard as she could, barely caring when the crowd gasped or when Myles Cobert commented on her outburst.

"Queen Corinne's obviously feeling the pressure," he said.

This Lily is in my way, Corinne fumed, *nibbling away at the walls of the sweet culinary empire I built from the ground up*. Corinne's first attempt to dispose of Lily hadn't done the trick. It was time to turn up the heat.

Corinne planned carefully.

She delivered specific instructions to her assistant. The young woman behind the horn rims was to knock over a glass mixing bowl the instant Lily moved away from her stovetop and toward her refrigerator. Corinne gave no further explanation and made it clear there would be no negotiating these terms. If the mousy young woman refused, Corinne would demote her. Or worse.

A symphony of breaking glass drew every eye and camera lens toward Corinne's station, providing enough time for her to sneak away. She twisted the knob on top of Lily's stove, conjuring a spark of electric blue flame before tweaking it down to the barest flicker.

The empty baking pan Lily planned to use to create

her gingerbread sat atop the burner, growing hotter and more dangerous to the touch as Corinne dropped down to help pick up the pieces and order was restored.

Brody watched Lily prepare her ingredients. Her motions through the kitchen were pure poetry, a kind of choreographed foreplay set to a delicious melody of brown sugar and cinnamon. He was hungry for her cooking, but seeing Lily waltz through the initial steps of her recipe left him craving her more than her delicious creations. Brody's cock hardened in his pants. Eyes half-closed, he willed it to soften; to lower even as Lily's gingerbread house was destined to rise. When she trounced the witch and he jumped up to embrace her, he didn't want the audience to see his erection—basic cable numbers or not.

Brody daydreamed of what would happen after: The eating and fucking; the construction of a beautiful bakery for Lily. He'd bought a ring. It was in their hotel room even now, hidden in his suitcase, the ruby center stone as big as a gumdrop. Later that evening, when Lily could focus on something other than the pressures of the competition, Brody planned to drop to one knee and ask her to be his.

A shimmer of neon blue light teased Brody's narrowed gaze. He opened his eyes fully and tracked the source to Lily's oven, just as the object of his affection reached toward her cake pan. She was clearly unaware it had cooked for the better part of a minute on top of a lit burner.

She turned toward the cake pan, intending to grease the inside.

Any moment now, Corinne thought. She fought the urge

to smile while opening her own oven. She had preheated it to 350 degrees; but to her surprise, the oven sat cold. A faint smell of gas assailed her nostrils. Corinne's grin evaporated as the situation became clear: Banging the oven door shut was enough force to blow out the pilot.

"Oh, you filthy little whore," Corinne grumbled beneath her breath. If she called a time-out and they connected her earlier outburst with the malfunctioning oven, she'd be penalized. *There isn't time to debate minutia*, she thought. *Not if I want to take home the prize*. Corinne reached for the long fireplace lighter nestled among her spatulas and whisks and leaned down.

As had happened so often on the ice with his hockey buddies, Brody's legs glided forward at an unthinkable speed. In one fluid motion, he grabbed a metal spatula from Lily's station, reached around her, and flung the pan like a puck. It sailed through the air, ricocheted off a refrigerator with a loud *ping*, and struck Corinne Zahn squarely on the butt just as she leaned down to light the pilot.

There came a flash of orange flame and a puff of smoke as the witch fell headfirst into her oven. Brody clutched Lily protectively as stagehands pulled Corinne out. The witch shrieked in outrage. Tendrils of smoke poured out of her hair. Her eyebrows were reduced to ashes. Cameras zoomed in on the terrifying image, making Corinne's ugliness clear for all to see.

The competition, the money and a bright future all went to Lily. She and her love lived handsomely ever after.

Sasha and the Seven
Rosetti Brothers

By Kelly Wade

Sasha King knocked on Jay Mirror's door, hoping he had an acting job for her. There was no answer. She walked in. The first thing she saw was a signed, framed photograph of Aiden Prince having lunch with Jay at Sardi's. Sasha stared at the picture and smiled. She remembered being 18 and watching every movie Aiden made. She also recalled the multitude of erotic fantasies she played out in her mind involving him. Sasha had taken a dozen lovers since, but never lost her heart. She was about to call out to Jay when her attention was caught by another photograph. It was Sasha's 13th birthday party with her father, Redmond on one side and Jay on the other.

Although they were as different as chalk and cheese, Jay was her father's agent for more than 20 years; even after Jay's car accident, when the part of his brain monitoring thoughts was damaged and he blurted out whatever came to mind. The injury had caused Jay to lose many of high-profile clients. But Sasha's father had a healthy ego and nothing to prove. He stuck by Jay out of loyalty and laughed at his faux pas.

Tears stung Sasha's eyes. Her father took a new bride a year earlier. Moira was a top model who had been on the cover of every fashion and gossip magazine. Having snared Redmond King, Mr Broadway himself, she pretended to love his daughter as well. Sasha tried to like Moira for her father's sake but suspected behind Moira's smiles and gifts lurked a jealous, greedy woman. But Sasha hadn't counted on Moira poisoning her father's mind while she was away studying acting at UCLA.

Sasha's father, six months earlier, left a cast party early, complaining of a headache. Moira arrived home three hours later to find his body crumpled on the black and white tiles in the hallway. Life changed overnight for Sasha. When the will was read, Redmond had left everything to his new wife, believing she would know best how to administer the estate. He took it for granted that she would provide for his only child.

Moira had her own plans. The New York City skyscraper overlooking the Hudson, which had been Sasha's home, was no longer welcome to her. Moira dumped Sasha's belongings in the lobby and issued orders that the young woman not be allowed upstairs.

The staff at the apartment complex was appalled at the callous treatment of their beautiful Sasha and muttered curses in Spanish, Russian and Greek about the witch in the Penthouse. But they had no choice but to follow orders. Sasha shuddered at the memory of that horrible night. Numb with shock at her father's blindness and betrayal, Sasha stepped in puddles, past honking traffic and jostling pedestrians to a friend's studio walkup, where she crashed on a lumpy couch. Depressed and angry, she couldn't handle anything more complicated than working at Starbucks to pay the rent on a share with four others, in a dreary area near Chinatown. She sighed. The lethargy and mindless television-watching had finally lifted; replaced by an overwhelming need to act again.

Jay stepped out of his inner sanctum, interrupting Sasha's thoughts. "Darling, it's you! Look at you." He twirled her around. "All grown up and gorgeous!" His red, simian face with slanted, green eyes and sensual lips smiled at her as he kissed both her cheeks.

"Your message said you might have something for me," Sasha prompted once they were seated.

Jay picked up an antique letter opener—one of many gifts from grateful clients—and ran a finger along the edge. "I do, Sweetie. I do."

"But," Sasha sighed. "I hear a but."

"It's a wonderful play. A small part."

"You know there are no small parts," Sasha said.

Jay sighed. "Your stepmother is backing the play."

"What!" Sasha stood up. "That's not funny." She headed for the door. Jay caught up and put an arm around Sasha's slim, resistant, shoulders. "Hasty makes wasty."

"Jay, whatever possessed you—"

"Aiden Prince signed on. He's playing opposite Moira."

"You're kidding."

"A real coupe. Aiden Prince is a huge name in Hollywood even after a two-year hiatus. And I hear he's huge in other areas, as well." Jay chuckled. "Wouldn't it be nice to find out if the rumors are true?"

Sasha blushed. "You're incorrigible.

"I know. I also know you used to have a crush on him."

Sasha turned at the door. "Moira will never go for it. She hates me."

"Of course she hates you. Look at you. You're young, sexy and talented. Those purple eyes of yours and pouty lips. Cheekbones I'd kill for."

Sasha laughed and opened the door. "You're a riot, Jay. "

"I didn't say it would be a piece of cake. But you won't be in any scenes together, and if you keep out of her way, it'll work."

"Ha!"

"I sent off a touching publicity announcement this morning to all the industry rags in town about how Moira's helping her stepdaughter by giving her a job and the pied-à-terre above the theater for the duration of the show."

"You've lost your mind."

"A piece only. Moira has dreams of acting. If she refuses, she's seen as mean and nasty by people in the industry. People who count. And you know how ugly the feeding frenzy can get when the gossip is fueled by her enemies, of which she has many. You're a shoe-in, babe."

A week later, Sasha watched the play in rehearsal from the darkness of the interior. Her eyes were on Aiden. She felt a powerful attraction to the six-two, tanned actor with the beautiful voice and deep blue eyes. Her eyes strayed to the front of his jeans and she smiled, wondering if he was as huge as rumors said. Aiden peered into the shadows as if he sensed Sasha's thoughts. She moved further back.

Moira couldn't remember her lines. The play's writers sat in the back of the auditorium moaning and clutching their hair as she massacred their work. Aiden seemed frustrated, but it was clear Moira was attracted to him. She kept tossing her blonde hair, gushing over him, touching his arm, the buttons on his shirt, ruffling his black hair.

Moira stumbled over her lines yet again. "This dialogue is ridiculous!" she exploded. Walking into a chair, she lost her balance, threw her script down, and screamed. "I almost broke my neck. Is someone trying to sabotage me?" Everyone looked away.

The director called "take five," and pulled Moira aside. Aiden walked away. Moira caught sight of Bill Hunter, who was in charge of props and stage management. "I want that man fired!" she shrieked. He's a moron." The more Bill apologized, the more abusive Moira became. Ron sighed and shook his head at Bill, who stormed off in Sasha's direction muttering under his breath.

As Bill passed her, Sasha said sympathetically, "You're doing a fabulous job."

Bill stopped and turned back. "Thanks. I need the work or I'd tell that witch where she can shove it." Sasha stepped into the light and Bill flushed, realizing who she was. "Sorry."

"No need. I totally understand. Moira can get on your last nerve." Sasha sensed he wanted to stay and talk, but one of the stage hands begged him for help and he reluctantly left.

"That was kind," a familiar, deep voice said from behind her. Sasha turned, her heart beating wildly in her chest: Aiden Prince.

"Hi," Sasha managed. She held out her hand. "Sasha King."

"Aiden Prince. I know who you are. We all read the press release and were *bowled over* by Moira's generosity," he said dryly.

Sasha grinned. "Me too!"

Aiden laughed. "I met your father once. He acted intuitively and had good judgment." Glancing at the stage, he added, "about most things."

Sasha smiled. Aiden's cologne smelled like the sea. She felt the heat from his body and an overwhelming desire to reach up, pull his face to hers, and kiss him.

Someone called Sasha's name. "I believe you're up next," Aiden murmured, brushing a strand of hair away from her face.

Sasha snapped out of her trance and made a mad dash for the stage. She gave the character a quirky, funny edge that made the other actors and director laugh. Aiden joined the throng and threw his arms around her. "Great scene!" His blue eyes crinkled at the edges as he smiled at her. Sasha smiled back. Out of the corner of her eye she saw the director frantically wave his hands in warning. The cast and crew instantly melted away.

Moira's voice, dripping with honey, placed a red-taloned hand on Aiden's arm. "Darling, I wondered where you wandered off to." Her stare was so venomous, Sasha backed up and stumbled. Aiden reached out and steadied her.

Moira leaned in and spoke in a stage whisper. "A word of advice, dear. Overacting is deadly. You want the audience to laugh *with* you, not *at* you." Sasha flushed crimson and walked off. Moira turned to Aiden, all smiles. She shook her hair. "Where did you want to have lunch?"

"I have other plans," Aiden said, peeling her claw off him. Moira watched him follow Sasha to the back of the theater.

"Lunch!" Ron shouted. He took a long pull from a bottle of Pepto-Bismol. "Everybody back at 1 p.m. sharp!"

"Don't let her get to you," Aiden said, catching up to Sasha.

"She can do it, every time," Sasha admitted grimly.

"Max's Deli is just around the corner. You want to grab a bite and vent?"

"Food sounds good," Sasha admitted.

Max's Delicatessen, crammed with autographed photos, was filled with customers. Sasha and Aiden were led to a microscopic table for two in the glass-enclosed dining area.

Like most of America, Sasha knew the cause for Aiden's hiatus from acting. Two years earlier, he took his infant son to the beach. As Aiden held the baby in his arms, a rogue wave snatched his child from him, carrying the tiny body out to sea. It was never found. Six months later, Aiden's wife ran off with the masseur, leaving him to grieve in an alcoholic stupor until he waked one day and realized he was killing himself. The grief and pain in his blue eyes was still visible underneath the charm.

Beyond her initial crush, Sasha liked Aiden. He was thoughtful, fun and actually listened when she spoke. Still, she knew it was suicidal having lunch with him. If Moira found out, heads would roll.

Moira was late again for rehearsal. It was the big love scene between her and Aiden and Sasha was sure her stepmother would be on time. For once, Aiden lost patience.

"I say we go ahead with a stand-in," he said angrily. "I've had enough." The cast and crew clapped. Ron mopped his brow. "She's only half an hour late," he pleaded, "besides, Moira refused to hire a stand-in."

"Come on," Aiden said to Sasha, pulling her on stage. "You can be Moira's stand-in."

The crew went silent. Whispers and giggles took over within seconds. Everyone could see the two had a thing for each other. Sasha had done her best to make sure they were never seen alone together, lest Moira find out.

The irony of playing a love scene with Aiden amused Sasha. Reflected in Aiden's eyes was a mutual spark of amusement mingled with desire. She shrugged. *What could happen in a room full of people?* As Aiden drew Sasha to him, she felt little shivers of desire rush up and down her spine. She told herself not to be stupid. *I'm a professional.*

Aiden pulled Sasha close. "I need you, Nina."

Sasha gasped. Pressed against him, she felt the bulge in his jeans. For a split second Sasha forgot she was on a stage. When Aiden bent over her and touched his lips to hers, her own lips parted. He glanced at her in surprise before he caught his breath, tightened his embrace, and entered her mouth with his tongue. Unable to stop herself, Sasha let out a tiny moan. Their kisses became more passionate.

One person clapped in a slow, staccato beat. "Look, Jay, I'm a few minutes late for rehearsal and already they're replacing me," Moira said coldly.

Sasha and Aiden broke apart. There was an eerie silence. Everyone held his or her breath before Ron cleared his throat.

"No one was replacing you, Moira. Aiden needed to work the scene. Since you refused to hire an understudy—"

"—Sasha stepped into the breach. How sweet. But I'm here now." As Moira walked on stage, her spike heels clicking loudly in the theater, Sasha walked off. Moira's eyes bored into her back.

"If Sasha thinks she can supplant me," Moira muttered to Jay, "she has another thing coming. She's a no-talent. And compared to me, she isn't even pretty. Right, Jay!"

Panicked, Jay snatched a half-eaten pear out of one of the crew's hands and bit down on it. He walked away, mumbling about an appointment and gesturing at his watch. Moira watched him rush off with narrowed blue eyes. She bit down on her ruby lips, breaking skin. A tiny trickle of blood oozed out of the wound and fell on her cashmere sweater.

That night, Sasha paced the floor of her apartment. *I'd be crazy to jeopardize my career and living quarters for a fling.* Sasha was a newbie. Aiden was Hollywood. He was used to seducing dozens of women. *Having an affair with Aiden isn't worth the price.* Then Sasha thought of how she felt in his arms, the way his blue eyes could be serious or full of laughter and the way his lips devoured her. Suddenly, she knew avoiding him wasn't just due to the fear of getting fired. She was in serious danger of losing her heart.

There was a knock on the door. Sasha jumped. It couldn't be Moira: She had a key and would have barged right in. Sasha flung open the door: Aiden. He carried a bottle of Chardonnay. Sasha's heart pounded.

She accepted the gift, and let Aiden in before shutting the door behind him. Sasha set the wine on a table and turned back to him. He rushed to her. Suddenly Aiden was holding her in his arms, kissing her hair, neck and lips. Without a word, they stripped off their clothes as they headed for the bedroom, leaving a trail of discarded clothing and wine behind them. Sasha felt like her body was on fire. She no longer cared what Moira thought or did. All she wanted was to have Aiden inside her.

Naked, they faced each other. Aiden lifted Sasha up and laid her gently on the bed. He bent over her. "God, you're beautiful," he said in a voice husky with desire. She ran a hand over his tanned, muscled chest and down to his engorged cock. Aiden groaned and plunged his tongue into her mouth, moving against her, his shaft teasing her clit, driving her wild with desire. He pulled out of her mouth and slowly flicked his tongue on her neck in one of her most sensitive places. The movement sent shivers of pleasure along her body. Sasha felt her knees go weak.

She eagerly opened to him and he drove his hot tongue over her slit, arousing her even more. Sasha thrashed and moaned. Aiden moved out. He lifted her up, turning her so her back was to him and she was on her knees. He massaged her breasts as his pulsating cock pressed against her flesh. He stroked her clit with his fingers. Sasha arched her back, pressing against him. Aiden entered her with a groan. The steady, rhythmic motion of pulling out and thrusting in drove Sasha crazy. Just when she thought she couldn't bear it another second, Aiden pulled out and turned her over. Staring into her violet eyes, he murmured in a voice ragged with passion, "You're wonderful. Promise me the old witch won't come between us again."

"I promise," Sasha muttered, her body trembling with desire as she slid down and took his throbbing cock into her mouth. Aiden groaned and gripped her hair as Sasha led him to the precipice. Pulling her up to face him, he entered her. Sasha gasped. "Don't stop."

He gazed into her eyes, thrusting deeper and deeper, until his final thrust sent her over the edge and she screamed out with exquisite pleasure. A second later, Aiden pulled her further onto him as he climaxed.

The theater was empty. Moira took the elevator up to the third floor, a brittle smile on her face as she imagined Sasha begging for one more chance to stay. But as the elevator door opened, Moira stopped dead in her tracks.

Cries and moans came from Sasha's apartment. Careful not to make any noise, Moira walked up to the door and listened. Sounds of sexual release floated out. Moira's pale face hardened like the mud packs she used every night until her flesh resembled grey stone. Her hands clenched into fists and the red nails dug into her palms. *Firing Sasha isn't good enough.* Moira's eyes gleamed with malicious pleasure as a new plan occurred to her—one that would destroy Redmond's little princess for good and open Aiden's eyes to see how much of a fool he'd been to turn to Sasha when he could have had Moira.

It was opening night. Sasha glowed. She was making her debut and she was crazy about Aiden. Her body was still sore from him. She smiled: The rumors were true. But Aiden was not just built—he was knowledgeable, generous and considerate in the bedroom, as well. As she stood daydreaming with a stupid smile on her face, Moira's voice startled her.

"The big night. Excited?"

"Totally," Sasha agreed, her eyes sparkling.

Moira casually glanced around the darkened theater. "Would you join me in my dressing room for a few minutes before the show?"

Sasha nervously checked her watch.

Moira smiled. "I won't keep you long. I want to apologize for my bad behavior." Moira dragged Sasha into her dressing room and shut the door. "Your father always drank one of my martinis before a performance. He insisted it brought him luck." Moira poured a light green liquid into two chilled martini glasses. "Appletini was his favorite." Sasha hesitated. Moira giggled as she handed the glass to Sasha. "It's only one drink. Bottoms up!" Moira brought the frozen glass to her lips. Sasha nervously gulped half the appletini down.

"I've got to run," Sasha said. "I haven't even done my make-up."

"Break a leg," Moira said sweetly as Sasha dashed out of the room. Moira's glass was still full as she put it down, a triumphant smile on her face.

The night was disastrous. Sasha giggled, stumbled and staggered all over the stage, slurring what lines she could remember. When she finally collapsed in a dead faint, she was carried off amid boos and hoots of derision. Redmond King's daughter had brought disgrace on the name. Everyone except Aiden avoided her. Unable to bear seeing the disgust in his blue eyes, she locked the door and refused to see or speak to him.

The moment she was fully conscious, Bill Hunter gently fired Sasha. He collected her keys and escorted her out.

Thoroughly humiliated, Sasha knew she was ruined. People detested Moira, but they would never believe she drugged a cast member. The gossip making the rounds was that Sasha had succumbed to first-night nerves and had drunk too much.

Bill glanced at her as she was leaving. "Have you heard of Rosetti's?" Sasha nodded. "My cousins own it. They're great guys." Sasha didn't respond. "I spoke to Rocco. He's the oldest and he put it to the others who all agreed. You can be the hostess and you could stay with them for a while. But I've got to warn you, the restaurant is hopping and they're always at work so the apartment is a disaster."

Sasha didn't care. When they arrived at the restaurant,

it was closing time. Even before she entered she heard someone singing an aria from *La Traviata*.

"That's Arturo," Bill said with a smile. "He trained to be an opera singer until he found his true calling as the restaurant's chef. He loves what he does, so he sings all the time."

When Sasha entered the restaurant, seven dwarfs were lined up waiting to meet her.

Rocco was the maître d' and maker of all executive decisions. Virgil took one look at Sasha, blushed, and dropped a plate. Ollie was yelled at for putting sugar in the salt shakers. Niccolo kept sneezing, whining that someone had stolen his Echinacea. Gus glared at her. "She'll probably leave her pantyhose in the shower," he grumped loudly to Arturo, who shoved him in the ribs and whispered, "Be nice." Henry yawned and seemed asleep on his feet but that was his normal modus operandi.

Sasha acknowledged the introductions as though through a thick fog. Bill led her up a set of narrow, crooked stairs. Dirty and clean clothes were tossed everywhere, including over the grand piano. There were as many books and magazines out of the bookcases as in. Two cats flew by as she entered. Catnip was strewn across the light wood floors.

"I told you it wouldn't be a pretty sight," Bill apologized.

Sasha smiled. "It's fine. I'm just so tired, I can barely keep my eyes open. Where do I sleep?"

Bill led her to the largest bedroom. "In here. Rocco made sure the linen was fresh." Bill started to straighten up but Sasha slipped out of her shoes, tossed the undershirts and socks off the bed, pulled down the comforter, climbed between the sheets, and fell into a sleeping death.

Throughout the next few weeks, Sasha found herself surrounded by seven kindly men who watched over her like hawks. Rocco insisted she start work as soon as possible. "It's good for her," he told Arturo, who accused him of being mean. "She needs to have something to get up for. A job will force her to become part of the living again."

The dwarfs were warm, loving people who appreciated everything Sasha did for them and who tried their best to make her come out of her shell. In return, she kept the apartment clean, did the laundry and shopping, and accompanied them on the piano when they sang with their friends on Sundays.

"She's okay for a woman," Gus barked. But it was practical, intelligent Rocco who brought home issues of *Back Stage* and *Variety*, leaving them on the coffee table for her to see. Sasha still cringed at the memory of that night.

"You have to get your feet wet," Rocco urged her. "You know you want to act again." Sasha took his advice and auditioned for roles in off-Broadway productions, soon winning roles and raves for her performances. Her self-confidence was gradually restored.

Arturo took Bill aside one evening. "Sasha still seems sad, but it's not just the disaster at the theater, is it?"

Under Arturo's steady gaze Bill broke down. "I think she's in love with Aiden Prince."

Arturo sighed. "I'm sorry, Bill. We all know you care for her. Did he turn against her too?"

"No," Bill admitted grudgingly. "but she insisted she didn't want to see him."

"Maybe not then, but what about now? Why don't you tell him where she is?"

"I'll think about it," Bill mumbled.

Arturo put an arm around him. "You're a good man. You'll do the right thing."

Sasha took her third curtain call flushed with excitement and pride. Four months passed since the disaster with Moria's play. Jay had come back into her life, exuberant as ever, insisting Sasha was star material. The bad memories were fading, but there was still emptiness in her heart. As she walked off stage, Sasha saw Bill talking to someone waiting in the wings: Aiden. He held a bouquet of white roses, a single red rose in the center. Sasha's heart almost stopped beating. By the time she reached them, Bill had gone.

"I missed you," Aiden said, handing Sasha the flowers.

"Ditto," Sasha agreed. "Only—" Aiden raised an eyebrow. "—I was too ashamed to face you. I knew everyone despised me."

"Not true. When I learned you had gone, I searched for you for weeks. I was worried sick." Aiden put his arms around her, pulling her to him. He looked into her eyes. "Don't ever do that again."

Sasha smiled and did her best Mae West. "Is that a gun in your pocket or are you just glad to see me?"

Aiden laughed. "You know, no one has been able to deliver that line well." They left the theater together.

He took her to a tiny, romantic restaurant uptown with flickering candles on all the tables. Afterward, they went to Aiden's sublet on the Upper West Side. They took their time undressing each other. Sasha felt suddenly shy. When they were naked, Aiden pulled her close. She shivered. When she kissed him back, the kiss deepened.

Despite their previous knowledge of each other, it felt like love's first kiss. Sasha slid her arms around Aiden's neck and their kisses turned more passionate. She could feel the heat in her lower body and a wetness as his cock nudged her. He grabbed a chair and sat on it, pulling Sasha down on top of him where he could see her face as he entered her. He gasped in pleasure and moved rhythmically as she straddled him. Sasha moaned and increased the momentum.

"Wait," Aiden whispered in a ragged breath. He grasped her legs around his waist and moved down on the white fur rug, plunging into Sasha deeply; her legs resting on his shoulders. The two climaxed seconds apart.

Sasha's unexpected success ate into Moira's soul. Aiden avoided Moira. Her spies told her he had finally located a successful Sasha, and they were dating. Breaking a nail getting out of her Rolls, Moira was livid.

Something has to be done about Sasha once and for all.

Moria's twisted, warped brain snapped. Dressed in dark glasses and a wig, she asked around the seedy bars in lower Manhattan if anyone knew of a hit man. Big Sal had a broken nose and a pock-marked face. His dead eyes were beady. He never smiled. Moira liked him straight off.

They met at a greasy diner in New Jersey and sat in a back booth. She slipped him a picture of Sasha.

"I want you to throw acid in her face. And if you break a bone or two, so much the better. Just don't kill her. I want her to suffer."

Big Sal looked Moira in the eye. "Twenty grand in small bills."

Moira smiled. *Cheaper than I thought.*

She met Big Sal again two days later. This time, the location was a sleazy bar on the Bowery. She was almost afraid to leave the safety of her taxi. She handed him an envelope. "It's all there."

Once Big Sal saw the money, he stood up. But instead of walking out, he whipped out a badge. Twisting Moira's arms behind her, he snapped on handcuffs. "You're under arrest." Three of the grubby, smelly people at the bar turned out to be undercover cops who joined in on reading Moira her rights.

As Sasha and Aiden snuggled in bed, they turned on the late news at 11 p.m. Horrified, they watched in shock as Moira King was dragged off in handcuffs screaming for her lawyer. It was alleged she had put out a contract on her stepdaughter.

Aiden turned to Sasha, a mischievous smile in his eyes. "All's well that ends well." Sasha laughed and hit him with a pillow. One thing led to another.

Windrush

By Charlotte Boyett~Compo

"Come on, Baby. You can do it. Treat your daddy right now." He slid the palm of his hand over her seat and patted her gently. Night had fallen outside. To the north, lightning whip-stitched the black velvet of the sky. The ozone smell of approaching rain tickled his nostrils.

"Just open up for me, Sweet Thing. You know you wanna purr for your daddy. Come on. Let him hear you."

He whispered soft, sensuous words to her as he slid his hand to the place that turned her on. Circling the opening with the tip of his finger, he shifted his hips and pressed into her.

Nothing happened. She sat there like a lump on a log.

"Come on, Baby!" he pleaded.

Hayver Kenyon tried twice more to get the engine to turn over, then slammed his palms against the steering wheel.

"Thanks, Babe," he grumbled. "Thanks for nothing!"

He slumped in the comfort of the crushed velvet seat, curled his hands around the steering wheel, and stared at the flashes illuminating the night. Here he was, stuck on a country road in the middle of nowhere, with a dead battery, the top down on his new convertible, and rain coming.

"I am *so* screwed!" he hissed.

Twisting around in the seat, Hayver looked out across the dark countryside. It was so quiet he could hear the cicadas and crickets revving up their serenades. There wasn't a light in sight: No farm houses, no barns, no nothing. Only the wide-open vista of soybean fields undulating in the fresh wind on a humid Iowa night.

Holding his breath, Hayver reached down to try the key one more time.

Nothing. Nada. Zilch.

Something rattled the soybeans along the opposite side of the gravel road and Hayver jumped, his heart skipping a beat. He could barely see the fuzzy head of a fat raccoon when it appeared between low branches of the plant.

"Any motels nearby, Dude?" he asked, startling the creature.

The raccoon spun around and waddled back through the beans.

"I'll take that as a no," Hayver called out.

A crack of lightning rent the air as the first drop of rain struck the convertible's windshield.

Hayver moaned. He didn't have a hat, umbrella or a newspaper—nothing with which to shield his $100 haircut. Growling, he shoved open the door, got out, then slammed it as hard as he could. The car rocked.

"Shit!" Hayver snapped, and kicked the driver side tire.

He crammed his hands into the pockets of his designer slacks, hunched his shoulders, and started walking as a gentle mist fell around him. Beneath the soles of his very expensive loafers, he felt the sharp edges of the gravel.

"You *had* to take the road less traveled," he said aloud.

To get his mind off the barren feel of the empty road and the dark night, Hayver thought about the photo shoot he'd done in Des Moines earlier that day. It was good exposure for him—or so his agent swore—to be in a layout for a magazine that any woman could pick up at the supermarket checkout stand. Not to mention the sizable chunk of cash the shoot earned him. He'd enjoyed himself, and liked the female model and photographer. The folks from the magazine treated Hayver like visiting royalty. It had been a good day until he decided to see some of the countryside, and headed over to Madison County to check out the famous covered bridges and John Wayne's birthplace.

The beans rustled again and Hayver stopped, staring into the field, the hair standing up on the back of his neck. He was a city boy, born and raised in New York. *What do I know about the critters that make the Midwest their home?* he thought. *Are there wolves and coyotes in Iowa? Do they go tripping through soybean fields late at night in search of little night snacks?*

"Knock it off, Kenyon!" he chided himself. Hayver picked up his speed. He leaned into the wind and tossed his hair, grimacing as the rain pebbled his face.

Mentally kicking himself with every step he took, Hayver wished he could go back a few days and not drive his own car out to the west coast for his next gig. He made enough money as a male model to ship the convertible. *Right now I could be on a jet with a cocktail in hand.*

"But noooo," he said, drawing out the word. "You *had* to get to know the real America." He kicked at the gray dirt.

The rain ran down the collar of Hayver's silk shirt, plastering it to his back. He was miserable. A flash overhead startled him and he flinched, waiting for the clap of thunder that would follow.

But it wasn't thunder passing above Hayver with a rush of sound. Instead, something huge flew right over his head with a single mighty flap of wings. Hayver ducked, dragging his hands out of his pockets to throw his arms up for protection. He heard a loud hiss. Then the thunder rumbled, shaking the ground beneath his feet.

He straightened and looked up, blinking against the intrusion of raindrops in his eyes. As lightning flared again, he thought he saw an immense shadow moving overhead; but the rain was coming down in torrents. Hayver's vision was blurred from all the water. He shook his head, wincing as wet strands of hair stuck to his cheek. He raked a hand through the sodden mess to push it back from his forehead.

The rush of sound came again and his heart trip hammered in his chest. Something swooped over him and he started running, digging the toes of his Italian loafers into the squelch of the cloying gray clay.

"Jesus, Mary and Joseph!" Hayver cried, falling back on his parochial school upbringing as once more the dark shape flowed above his head and a hissing sound sent shivers down his spine.

He knew there was no way to outrun whatever it was careening above him. It was much too large to be a bird. The sound it made gliding through the rain was unnerving and sounded dangerous. As it soared over Hayver's head once more, he felt its downdraft. Hayver came to a skidding stop as he caught sight of it beyond him, banking steeply as it turned to make another run. The sky pulsed bright light and in that instant Hayver got a clear look at the creature.

"Holy shit!" he said. He froze—mouth open, eyes wide, unable to move—as his winged adversary landed 50 feet away on the deserted stretch of road.

The beast was immense. Covered in copper scales that glistened in the rain against bolts of lightning, it was at least 20 feet in length from its triangular head to the tip of its thick, spade-like tail. Curved, barbed fins projected from this long tail. Its wingspan was surely twice the length of its powerful body. Hunched on the road with massive forepaws flexed and powerful haunches primed to leap, it surveyed Hayver with serpentine eyes that glowed a phosphorous green beneath a scaly eye ridge.

The monster hissed and Hayver's knees went weak with terror. He half-expected the beast to open its maw of a mouth and breathe fire on him, reducing him to a smoldering heap of ash.

"Please don't flambé me," he pleaded, ashamed his voice cracked.

The glistening muzzle twitched. Its large scalloped

ears slanted downward and rotated like a radar sweep. Two long spiny horns perched atop its triangular head tilted to the side, as though the creature strained to hear Hayver's words. Scaly pads came down over chatoyant eyes as it blinked.

Suddenly, all the hair on Hayver's body stood up. Lighting struck and speared the ground feet from where he stood. He screamed, throwing himself to the mud-slick ground as the sharp scent of sulfur filled the air. Torrential rain lashed his body as Hayver choked, his face in a puddle. His shirt was a sodden, mud-caked mess that stuck to him like cold glue. Beneath Hayver the ground shook; but he knew it wasn't from the thunder. He could hear the slap of giant paws hitting the rain-soaked ground, the scrape of talons striking the gravel.

I'm a dead man.

The claws that curled over Hayver's shoulders did not pierce his skin as he was dragged out of the mud and became airborne. He dangled like a cucumber on a vine as the beast soared through the storm, its giant wings flapping almost silently in a slow, graceful arc. It rose up to avoid the tree line, carrying Hayver higher with every sweep of the membranous appendages.

This isn't happening, he thought. *What the hell was in that diner food I had at lunch?*

From the moment Hayver got a good look at the beast, all he knew of reality had gone out the window. He shivered. He peeked down past his dangling feet and saw he had one missing loafer.

When the scalloped edges of the black mountains came

into view, Hayver could only gape at the dark, undulating line and wonder where the hell he was.

"Where are you taking me?" he shouted, craning his neck to look up at the underside of the beast. The massive body blocked out the night sky and the ripple of its muscles made Hayver realize he was probably take-out: There was no doubt a little woman dragon waiting at home with a bib-fork in one paw and a knife in the other.

Coming in low, the beast never missed a wing-beat as it swooped through a large opening in the mountain and glided along a dark tunnel that led deeper into the interior of the South Dakota cave. Lowering its massive hind paws to the cave's floor, it arched its upper body so the human would not be dragged against the rocky ground and came to a stop. It needed no light by which to see, but knew the human male was completely blind in the stygian darkness. Gently, the creature lowered its catch until the male was standing. It backed away, turned its enormous head, opened its muzzle and blew a concentrated stream of fire to light the torches lining the walls of the cave.

Hayver shrieked as the creature breathed fire and the air around him became superheated. He scurried like a rat to the farthest point of the cave and stood there, quivering.

"Hail Mary, full of grace, the Lord is with thee," he said, hands clenched together as he dropped to his knees. "Blessed are thou amongst . . ." When the dragon belched another torrent of sulfurous breath and more lights blazed to life, Hayver was afraid the next blast would include him being quick-flamed—crispy on the outside, chewy on the inside.

The dragon settled down on its haunches and regarded him, tilting its head from side to side, no doubt trying to decide whether or not it should add barbeque or teriyaki sauce to his grilling. Those enormous, glowing green eyes blinked in a way that reminded Hayver vividly of an agent he'd once dated in Paris.

"Michelle?" he questioned, then shook his head at the ridiculous notion that had come over him. *So what if Michelle Le Grand had hair almost the same shade of copper as the scales on the creature? And, yes, her thighs were a little on the thick side but . . .*

A snort came from the beast and one bony eye protrusion arched upward as though the dragon had plucked his thought from the ether and wasn't pleased by his silent observation.

"No offense!" he said, putting up a hand, palm outward. "You've got nice thighs!"

The creature made a huffing sound.

"So," Hayver said, looking around for a way to escape and finding the only exit behind the beast. He knew he wouldn't make it 10 feet before he was gobbled up. A vivid image of being crunched between gleaming white fangs and having his thigh bone used as a toothpick didn't appeal to him. "What are you going to . . . ?"

Hayver stopped—the words freezing in his throat— as the creature pushed up from the cave floor and came sidling toward him, the long tail dragging behind. A low whimper escaped Hayver and he pressed against the stone.

Claws ticking on the rocky ground, spiny barbs scraping against the cave's ceiling, the beast thrust its triangular visage with its flaring black nostrils and wisp of a reddish goatee right into Hayver's terrified face. He could smell ash on its breath, like piles of dried leaves smoldering on a crisp autumn afternoon.

"Please don't eat me," Hayver pleaded. "I may look good but I would really leave a bad taste in your mouth."

The dragon's maw opened in a fang-loaded grin. A gleam entered those glowing eyes and it turned its head, offering its jaw.

Hayver's brows slashed together. "What? You want a kiss?"

The long neck swiveled so the creature was looking him in the eye. For a moment it just stared at him, then turned its head once more.

"You want a kiss," he stated, disbelief lifting his brows into his wet hairline.

A low, purring sound came from the beast. The horny spikes on the eye ridge fluttered several times and the pale tinge of rose pulsed along bony protrusions just under the eye sockets.

Pressed against the wall, there was nowhere for Hayver to go. He couldn't get around the beast and—even if he could—it would be on him before he got very far. Just imagining being stamped down by one of those massive paws sent a shiver down his spine.

As he stood there, the creature lightly bumped its jaw on his chest. Then it rubbed its head against Hayver like a cat would its owner's leg, purring the entire time.

"Why, you little flirt," he heard himself say and was rewarded with the offer of a kiss to the scaly jaw once more. He swallowed. "And you're persistent."

Well, he thought, *I've slept with many a woman on my way to the top of the male supermodel ladder.* Actors weren't the only ones who made good use of the casting couch. Hayver's sexual expertise had been honed with power brokers and agency owners who were only one step away from being flesh peddlers. It wasn't as though he had any scruples about pleasuring homely women. *But a dragon?*

"Ah, no offense, Sweetie, but I'm not into bestiality. I—"

Once more the jaw rubbed against Hayver's chest and held there, the low purring vibrating through his body from the close contact. The paw scraped at the ground.

"Okay," Hayver said, reaching up to clumsily pat the creature's spade-like head. His hand bounced above the scales a few times before, with a grimace, he lowered his palm to the horny plate. The feel surprised him. Instead of being hard, the plain of the scales was soft, almost silky, and undulated beneath his palm. Hayver stroked the head, screwed up his courage, and lowered his lips to the extended jaw to give the beast a gentle kiss.

A loud sound of contentment came from the long neck of the creature and it moved back, its tail curling around to hook in front of its paws—vividly reminding Hayver again of a feline.

"No biting, now," he said, hoping the hot look that had suddenly appeared in the beast's eyes wasn't a prelude to munching.

A plume of lavender smoke burst from the creature's body. Hayver coughed, fanning away the thick waves of sweet-smelling vapors. As it began to clear, he realized the creature had disappeared.

"Michelle!" Hayver gasped. "It *is* you!"

She stood where the creature had perched, clad in a long gown covered in copper-colored sequins. Long reddish-gold hair rippled back from the porcelain features of her exquisite face. The sweep of long black lashes slid slowly, seductively over the sparkling green gems of her eyes. She smiled, the coral shimmer on her pouty lips revealing straight, white teeth.

"'Little woman dragon waiting at home with a bib, fork in one paw and a knife in the other?'" she questioned, coming steadily toward him on the six-inch heels of her French sling-back peep-toes. The train of her sparkling gown dragged along the cave floor.

"This isn't happening," Hayver said, shaking his head. "You're not—it isn't—" He shook his head again. "I'm going crazy!"

"'Please don't eat me? I may look good but I would really leave a bad taste in your mouth?'" she repeated and threw her head back, hair sweeping the curve of her shapely hips. Michelle's laugh was sultry. "Oh, Hayver, really!"

Long apricot fingernails pushed the wet silk of Hayver's shirt against his pecs as she pressed her body to his. She tilted her head, her smile predatory.

"What are you?" he whispered. His eyes searched her lovely face. There was no hint of a beast behind the creamy complexion, the high cheekbones, the almond-shaped green eyes and the swan-like neck.

Michelle's lips thrust out in a sexy pout. "Well, now,

let me think. Didn't you once call me a dragon lady?" She flexed her nails over his chest. "I looked that up and do you know what it said a dragon lady was, Pretty Boy?"

Hayver had one hell of a hard-on with her clinging to his body. He knew she had to feel the hard erection between them.

"A fiercely vigilant and unpleasant woman," she declared before he could answer. Her green eyes glittered as she smoothed her palms over his shoulders. "Is that how you see me?"

"Ah, no," Hayver said. "I didn't mean it in that way."

One finely-tweezed brow lifted. "And how exactly did you mean it?" Her hands moved from his shoulders down his arms and her fingers shackled his wrists, bringing them up to clamp them to her hips. Her hands slid between his arms and hooked around his waist, drawing him securely to her.

"Michelle, I'm way in over my head here. This is really bizarre, and I must be dreaming. There's no other explanation. This whole night has been—"

"—Planned for a long time," she finished. "What wasn't part of the plan was the rain, but it worked to my advantage." She ran her hands to Hayver's ass and caressed him. "Magic-wielding is a good thing, Pretty Boy. Your decisions were actually mine."

Hayver was on fire with lust: His cock throbbed; his balls tightened. Michelle's perfume spiraled around him, weaving its way into his libido. The lush curves of her body were an invitation he knew he wouldn't decline. He wanted her so bad he could taste it.

"This is like a fairy tale," he said, glancing around. "With magic and dragons and secret caves." He wished he could put distance between them so he could think straight. Idly, he wondered if it wasn't some kind of pheromone instead of perfume that was causing his body to react so rigidly to her.

"Fairy tale?" Yes, I suppose it is." She brought one hand from under Hayver's arm to insinuate it between them, sliding the palm down over the steely hardness at his crotch. She cupped him through the slacks, her fingers molding around the thickness. "It's a bit like 'Beauty and the Beast,' don't you think?" She smiled. "With you being my beautiful little stud."

Michelle's hand drove Hayver mad as she stroked him up and down. His shaft wept for want of her silky sheath. He groaned as she squeezed him.

"Still don't want me to eat you?" she asked in a breathy voice.

Hayver jerked her to him, ran a hand to the back of her head, slanted his mouth over hers, and took her lips like a starving man. He thrust his tongue deep into Michelle's mouth, lustful heat taking him over completely as he ground against her. She moaned.

Dragging his mouth from hers, Hayver grabbed a firm handful of her hair to pull her head back so he could drop his lips to the hollow of her throat.

"Yes," she groaned. "Yes, my beautiful man!"

Hayver pivoted, swinging Michelle around to thrust her against the stone wall. His hands went from her shoulders to the bodice of the copper sequined gown. Snagging his fingers in the deep V, he tore it from her breasts to cover them with his palms.

"My beast," he acknowledged her with a growl. He fanned his thumbs over the stiffening peaks, and rubbed his cock against her belly. Hayver insinuated a thigh between her legs.

"Ride me," she whispered urgently. "I want to feel you bucking against me."

He needed no urging to rip the gown from Michelle's shoulders, tug it over her curving hips, and let it pool at her feet. Save for the garter belt, black silk hose and the spike heels, she was bare to him. His hot gaze raked over her.

Forcing her legs further apart with his knee, Hayver lowered his hand to cup Michelle's satiny warmth, sliding his palm back and forth between her legs, dipping a rigid finger into her wet opening. He swept his thumb over her clit until it was hard.

"Hayver," she purred, arching her hips in invitation. She gasped when he stepped back. "No!" she protested.

"I'm not through with you," Hayver ground out between clenched teeth as he kicked off his remaining shoe. He rent the wet shirt from his chest, shrugged it down his shoulders and plucked at his belt. He shoved the slacks from his long legs and kicked them aside.

"Commando," she said, licking her lips. "Just the way I like a handsome man to undress." She reached for him but he eluded her grasp.

Hayver tilted his head down, and he looked at Michelle through the fringe of his long, dark eyelashes. "You said you can wield magic?" he asked.

"Yes," she said, beginning to tremble.

"Then make us a soft pallet." He pointed to the cave floor. "Right over there. A soft pallet covered with thick fur pelts."

Michelle's verdant gaze widened. She waved an elegant hand. The pallet appeared.

Hayver snaked out an arm and grabbed her hand, pulled her to him, and twisted his body as he took them to the makeshift bed.

"You ride me," he said, opening his legs wide. Her body dropped between the spread of his thighs. "You ride me hard, little beastess."

Michelle straddled him, sliding her warm, moist slit across the jutting steel of his erection as she knelt above him. His cock grazed her opening, flexed with need. Eyes fused with his, she lowered her body and impaled her tight, hot cunt upon his cock.

Hayver's hands slapped down on her hips to rock her on him as he thrust upward, driving deeper into her sheath—filling her, stretching her. Hayver's eyes feasted on Michelle's swaying breasts as she levered her channel up and down his slick shaft. He slid a hand to one breast to pluck at the nipple, pinch it, and mold her breast in his palm.

"Hayver!" she cried out.

Her cunt rippled around him, tight little squeezes that grabbed his cock and coated it with her juices. Before the last undulating compression ended, he bucked, turned her over, and captured her beneath him.

"My turn," he said and drove into her with hard, deep,

powerful strokes that had her tossing her head from side to side on the soft furs. With every potent lunge of his straining cock Michelle cried out until at last the jet of Hayver's cum shot hot and thick into her. He slammed into her one last time, draining his shaft, milking it of the last hot spurt, then collapsed on top of her, his mouth going to her breast to draw the nipple deep into his mouth.

"Yes," she said, stroking his wet hair. "Suckle me, my beauty. Take all there is of me."

Hayver shuddered as the last ounce of strength ebbed away. Lowering his cheek to her breast, he strove to get his racing heart under control. He felt a sharp sting and jerked, lifting his head in surprise. He looked down at his shoulder where she had bitten him. Blood oozed around the puncture wound, a drop sliding down his flesh.

"Why did you do that?" he asked.

As he stared into her glittering eyes, darkness flowed at the periphery of his vision. A great lassitude came over Hayver and though he fought it, the darkness crept steadily over him. The last thing he remembered was her husky voice.

"I marked you as mine," she said. "Now, I can find you wherever you go."

Hayver sat up with a gasp, staring wide-eyed at the tractor that lumbered past his car. The farmer sitting in the tall seat gave him a one-fingered salute as he passed.

"What the hell?" Hayver exclaimed.

Looking around him, the leaves of the soybean plants sparkled in the early morning sun. Redwing blackbirds flitted along a fencepost as a long hawk made lazy circles in the bright azure of the sky.

"A dream," he said, scrubbing a hand over his face. "That was one hell of a dream!"

He reached for the key in the ignition, turned it, and the sports car roared to life.

"That's what it was. Just a dream."

It wasn't until Hayver twisted in the seat to make sure no one was barreling up behind him before he pulled onto the road that he felt the pain in his shoulder. Pushing back his shirt, he sucked in his breath. There were two punctures piercing his flesh.

How Red Tamed Her Wolf

By Holly East

"Honestly, Ruby," Victoria sighed in her ear, "Alex Wolf may be madly in love with you, but he takes you for granted. This is the second time this month he has broken a date with you. You make it too easy for him. That's why the two of you have been going together for more than a year, and he has barely mentioned the word 'marriage.'"

"It's *your* husband he is going with," Ruby retorted. She had been looking for sympathy, but her best friend seemed to blame her for the way things were going in the relationship. "*He's* the one who invited Alex to the hockey game. Of course Alex would go with him! You know how much he loves hockey. And aren't you being left alone as well?"

"Believe me, Hunter will pay for that invitation. But it's not the same thing. He knew I was having dinner with my sister tonight. Alex never mentioned to him that you two had plans."

Ruby tried again. "But Alex *does* love me, Tori. You said yourself you can see it in his eyes every time he looks at me."

"Yes, he loves you, but he doesn't take you seriously. He even calls you 'Little Red' as though you were a kid."

"That's because I am only five feet tall. It doesn't mean anything."

"Who are you fooling? You know you hate it, but you never tell him. You're a pushover. Men like going after a prize. They don't value something—or someone—that just falls into their laps. Your Wolf needs a lesson." Tori gasped. "Lord, I'm running so late for this dinner. I'll email you a few Web sites to check out. Don't blush too hard. It doesn't go with your red hair. Then we are going to have a girls' night because we have plans to make.

"Plans? About what?"

"Look at the Web sites first."

The next night Ruby stepped out of the shower and slipped on her robe, still thinking about what she had seen on the Internet. She had never guessed those places existed. She was startled out of her musings when the door to her apartment slammed shut. "Alex?" she called.

"Who else would it be? I thought I'd surprise you. Make up for breaking our date last night." Alex wrapped his arms around her and drew Ruby into a deep kiss.

When she got her breath back, Ruby sighed. "Why didn't you call to let me know you were coming? What if I had been out?" She struggled to keep the exasperation out of her voice, and then smiled as his amber eyes raked her body in obvious appreciation.

"I told you I wanted to surprise you, Little Red." Ruby winced at the nickname. "And I knew you would be home," Alex continued. "You only go out with Tori, and Hunter mentioned they had plans tonight. Said something about being tied up."

Ruby froze, thinking of the Web sites she visited and her conversation with Tori; then Ruby's mind turned to mush as Alex parted her robe and drew her closer. His hands cupped her breasts while his thumbs flicked her nipples. As they stiffened instantly into tight pebbles, she gloried in seeing his eyes grow hot.

"That's my Little Red," he said, "always ready for me."

"I wish you wouldn't call me that." Ruby decided it was time to let him know.

"But you *are* my Little Red. When I touch you like this," one hand skimmed down to brush her curls, "your skin takes on a rosy glow that makes me want to kiss you everywhere."

Ruby arched her body closer to Alex and moaned as he slipped two fingers into her wet slit. "Tell me what you want," he growled, his fingers sliding in and out with excruciating slowness.

She moaned, unable to form words. His free hand went to the nape of her neck, pulling her closer to him. He nipped her lips and licked the sting away. Ruby instinctively opened her mouth and his tongue plunged inside, mimicking the action of his fingers. Her pussy muscles clenched in an effort to hold Alex tighter. Ruby's hips rocked in an attempt to increase the speed.

"You still haven't told me what you want," he murmured into her ear, licking the inside.

"Alex!"

"Do you want me to stop?" he taunted her, knowing exactly what she craved.

"No," she panted, urgently swiveling her hips.

"If you don't tell me, I will have to stop."

"No, don't. Don't stop, Alex." Her breath came in short bursts.

"Tell me now."

"Do more, faster!" she cried.

"Do *what* faster?"

"Fu, fuck me with your fingers." Ruby's face flamed. She loved submitting to his will, but sometimes she wished Alex wasn't always in control.

He complied, letting her ride his fingers until her release left her boneless, sagging against him. He took her hand and rubbed it against his shaft. "Come on, Little Red. It's time to let my cock come out and play."

Ruby slid the zipper down and freed him from the tight confines of his jeans. She was excited to realize he had no underwear on. Knowing what he liked, she traced her fingers up and down his shaft, gripping it at the base and then sliding her hand upward to the knob that had turned a deep red. She slipped her left hand under Alex's balls and cupped them while her right hand increased its speed.

With his arms around her, Alex backed up to the couch. Ruby slid his jeans down and kneeled at his feet. She licked the wet tip and swirled her tongue around it, fully exploring the underside and nipping lightly at the stiff ridge. Hearing his panting, she placed the knob against her lips and sucked in hard, going all the way down to the base. Alex's hands fisted into her hair and he moved her head up and down, driving his cock deeper until he exploded inside her. Ruby swallowed his cum, enjoying the hot salty taste, and licked him clean.

"You are amazing," Alex said. He pulled his jeans all the way off, picked Ruby up, and took her into the bedroom.

Ruby waked to the sound of her alarm. She automatically hit snooze and rolled over to cuddle with Alex, only to find the bed still warm with a note on the pillow.

> Didn't want to wake you. Call you later. You look beautiful when you sleep. I love you.
> A. Wolf.

Although she wished he had stayed long enough to start the day with her, Ruby giggled at his signature. He used it whenever he wanted to let her know she brought out the animal in him. She blushed, remembering the things they had done; and then worried she wasn't exciting enough to keep Alex in her bed until the morning.

As the day progressed, Ruby checked her watch every hour or so, wondering when Alex would call. She had to force herself to return to the Web page she was designing for her latest client. Twice she thought about phoning Alex, but he got annoyed when she interrupted him.

Ruby's conversation with Tori played out again in her mind. *Even my job makes things easy for Alex*, she thought. She was her own boss, and her hours were flexible. When he couldn't see her, she used the time to get more work done. If he suddenly wanted to go out, she was able to put a project on hold. *But isn't it good to be there for the person you love?* Alex had a high-stress career as a corporate lawyer. He didn't need their relationship to add to it.

When 5.30 came without a call, Ruby chalked it up to his busy day. He was supposed to pick her up at 6.30 for a dinner at a local Italian place, so Ruby dressed simply in tight jeans and a purple rib sweater that showed off her trim form. It was 7 p.m. when Alex finally knocked on the door, his arms filled with Chinese takeout. "Sorry, I couldn't reach my key," he explained giving Ruby a quick kiss on her lips.

"Aren't we going to La Cucina Italiana?"

"Not tonight. It would take too long."

"Too long for what?" Ruby wondered what part of the conversation she had missed.

Alex unloaded the cartons onto the kitchen table. "There's a big game on tonight. I invited a couple of guys from the office to join me. The plasma screen you have is perfect. I'm glad I recommended you buy it. Let's eat. They'll be here in about half an hour.

"Why didn't you call and tell me? Ruby tried hard not to sound petulant while taking out plates and utensils.

"Come on, Little Red," Alex cajoled. "Don't go all whiney on me. You can get lots of work done while we watch. Look I brought your favorite—steamed dumplings—even though I like them better fried."

"Thanks," Ruby responded automatically before realizing he hadn't answered her question. *Does he really think steamed dumplings make up for this change?*

Alex inhaled his food, checking his watch regularly. He started helping Ruby clear the table when the bell rang. "Sorry to leave you with the rest, but the guys are here."

Too stunned to say anything, Ruby continued to clean up while Alex greeted his guests. "Guys, this is my Little Red, aka Ruby." The three mumbled their hellos. "Make yourselves comfortable," Alex said while aiming the remote at the TV. "It's almost game time."

He fished a $50 bill out of his wallet. "Do me a big favor, Hon. I didn't have a chance to get beer and chips. Would you mind running out?" He pulled Ruby close, cupping her bottom and leaned into her, his tongue tracing the outline of her lips.

She knew he was trying to get around her, and she didn't want to give in but her skin heated as Alex's tongue tangled with hers. She sighed as he pulled away. "Game's starting." He bent his head for one more kiss. The heavy look in his eyes and the rapid pulse Ruby could see at the top of his open shirt reassured her he was as aroused as she was.

Shrugging in resignation, she grabbed her purse. "Don't forget dip," Alex called as Ruby stepped out the door.

Twenty minutes later she was back, panting from carrying the case of Sam Brown Ale she knew Alex liked.

"That's my girl!" Alex rewarded her with a loud smacking kiss on her lips as he grabbed the beer from her. "We have been dying of thirst."

"The chips are only going to make it worse," Ruby reminded him.

"Yeah, but the beer will take care of that."

Alex took the drinks into the living room while Ruby poured chips into a large bowl, spooned dip into a smaller one, and put a seven-layer dip into the microwave to heat.

The men grunted their thanks when she brought the food to where they sat, eyes glued to the set.

The four of them jumped to their feet as one, screaming and waving their arms wildly. Ruby saw some chips go flying. "Did you see that? That was a fucking amazing run! Holy shit! Ninety-five yards! That guy is un-fucking-believable."

Ruby felt invisible. Not even Alex was aware of her presence. "Maybe I should try to get some work done," she muttered to herself.

She booted up her laptop in the bedroom, tuning out the noise from the living room, but discovered her mind would not settle on her client's project. All she could think of was how Alex had changed their plans, not even thinking to call. Yes, he had brought dinner and had remembered her favorite, but he barely said a word while they were eating because he was in too much of a hurry to finish and get to what was really important to him: Watching the game with his friends. Tori was right.

Frustrated, Ruby decided to check her e-mail. She always felt better after reducing her inbox to a single page. Scanning down the messages, she spotted Tori's message with the subject "More Web sites." Ruby's cheeks flamed as she explored the first one, on male submission. She stared at the picture of a gorgeous naked hunk kneeling respectfully before a woman with long flowing hair, leather bustier, and pants encased in high boots. The woman held a riding crop in her hand. Only the top of the guy's ass was visible; but it was crisscrossed with some painful-looking red welts.

Ruby reflexively tightened her inner muscles, feeling herself grow damp between her legs. Her nipples hardened into peaks as she thought, *I'd love to see Alex that way.* Her thumb rubbed her mouth in pensive anticipation. Maybe Tori was right. Ruby was getting hot just thinking of the possibilities.

Opening a site devoted to gear, she was amazed at the assortment of paddles, whips, straps, canes, and other instruments of discipline. Her fingers slipped under her waistband as she looked at the array of cock rings, dildos and anal plugs. Then Alex barged in. Ruby's hand flew out as she quickly clicked to return to her home page.

"We're getting close to halftime and we've about finished the chips. Do you think you could pick up more and get some KFC while you're at it? Please?" The beseeching look he gave her was the one she wanted to see while he was on his knees gazing at her crotch. Ruby shook herself to clear her thoughts and return to the present.

"Of course, my p—love." She had to get her mind off those Web sites. Ruby nearly said "pet," and that would have started something she was not yet ready for. Putting her laptop aside, she uncoiled from the bed and slipped her shoes back on. Ruby gave Alex a quick kiss and a pat on the cheek that had him looking confused by the uncharacteristic gesture. She grabbed her jacket and purse again and set off on her errand. The brisk fall air helped cool her racing imagination. She and Tori had to have a talk.

Ruby left a brief note on her door for Alex, telling him something had come up and that they would talk the following day. She laughed to herself, thinking how stunned he would be to find she had broken a date with *him*. She had a huge grin on her face when she met Tori at the Pleasure Chest. This was her first visit to an adult store, and she hoped she could keep her blushing under control.

Tori grabbed a basket and gave another to Ruby. "We're going to fill these with all kinds of goodies. I will teach you what you need to know. Since you are new to this, we'll keep it simple. You want Alex to realize you are a mouth-watering, grown-up woman—one he has to work hard to get to. You also want to punish him a bit for his previous bad behavior, right?

Ruby felt her nipples tighten at Tori's words. Heat pooled low in her abdomen and her crotch grew damp enough to wet her panties. "Oh my God," she gasped, "I can't believe what a turn-on this is."

Tori laughed. "Welcome to the club. Someday, I will tell you how Hunter paid for taking Alex to that game without checking it out with you. He probably didn't sit comfortably for two days afterward, and, until he could, he was completely respectful to my needs. To be honest, I can't tell you which of us enjoyed it more."

Giggling while walking through the store, Ruby became more comfortable with what she was planning. Her basket had a paddle, leash, and wrist and ankle cuffs. She also added a cock ring and nipple clamps for some future fun. Tori had filled her basket with more serious devices. When Ruby picked up a cane, Tori shook her head. "You're not up to that yet. It takes more practice than we have time for." She handed Ruby a few videos that illustrated what some of the "planned activities" would look like. "Now for your outfit." She guided Ruby to the clothing section. "What do you think: Red or black?

"I like red, but it doesn't go well with my hair."

Tori flipped through an assortment of bustiers and corsets, finally settling on a black and red lace-up corset, a black thong with an open slit, and black stockings. A pair of high-heeled black boots completed the look. Ruby happily handed over her credit card while imagining the expression on Alex's face when he saw her.

"You are the best friend anyone could have."

"Well, I'm definitely the kinkiest one you have," Tori said with a smile.

"I don't know what I would do without you."

"My pleasure—and yours, and, hopefully, Alex's as well. Now we need to find the right location to spring this on your oblivious boyfriend."

As usual, the Internet proved invaluable as Ruby and Tori looked for places to go. The Web page for "Grandma's House" said it was a secluded resort for couples desiring to explore multifaceted aspects of their relationship. Ruby thought it an ironic name for an adult-oriented resort. The site showed individual cottages nestled in the woods with the main house a distance away. Meals were available there or could be delivered to the cabins. The bathrooms were huge with a separate tub and shower, each big enough to accommodate at least two people.

Ruby enlarged the picture of the shower and gasped when she saw the rings affixed strategically around the tiles. Tori laughed, "Not for your first time, but I decided that I'm booking Hunter and me in for the same weekend, separate cabin, of course. This is going to be fun."

To get Alex away for the weekend, Hunter followed Tori's instructions, and invited Alex to a fantasy football weekend that included tickets to a game. No way was Alex going to turn that down.

Ruby was ready two hours before she was due to pick up Tori. She went through her toys one more time, mentally reviewing her plans for each. It seemed perfect to bring a basket of goodies to "Grandma's House." But this time Little Red would be waiting for her big, bad wolf.

"Alex is so excited about his weekend with Hunter," Ruby said to Tori. "Do you think he's going to be furious with me when he learns it was a set-up?"

"Calm down. Between being slightly groggy from the mild knockout drug Hunter is giving him and finding himself naked on a bed, he is going to be too confused to be angry with you. And by the end of the weekend, he's going to be so satisfied, he will owe Hunter."

"Okay, remind me again. What time will Hunter arrive with Alex?"

"First you drop me at my cabin and then call him. He'll get there about a half hour later. This will give you enough time to change into your outfit. Put something over it so Hunter doesn't see. He'll haul Alex out of the car, get him inside, strip him, and put him on the bed."

"Right." Ruby breathed out slowly to calm her racing pulse.

The music to the song "Hopelessly Devoted to You" sounded, and Tori picked up her cell. "Hi, Hunter. How did it go?" She paused. "Excellent. I'll see you soon. I have lots planned for us." She ended the call and gave Ruby a big thumbs up. "Alex is sleeping like a baby. He'll be out for thirty minutes max after Hunter leaves you, so you can set the scene."

Ruby nodded, too nervous to speak.

"Just remember, you are in command. You are firm and confident. Don't let him question you. Just think of all the preparation you did, and how you are going to use your goodies."

A giggle burst out of Ruby. "I am going to make Alex sit up—probably painfully—and really see who I am."

"You go, girl!" Tori laughed.

Waiting in her cabin, Ruby threw her robe over her costume as a car pulled up. She opened the door at Hunter's knock and watched as he fireman-carried Alex to the bed. "Get his clothes off," she imperiously said, practicing her voice, "then leave."

"Yes, Ma'am," Hunter replied with a wink, and began stripping Alex.

She moved into the kitchen area so he could complete the task without her presence. When she heard the door close, Ruby came out and put her robe on a hook in the closet.

Practice paid off as Ruby cuffed Alex's wrists and ankles and attached them to the bed so he laid spread-eagle on his stomach. To create the mood she wanted, she placed candles around the room and dimmed the lights. Plucking the collar from her basket, she fastened it around Alex's neck. Ruby stared down at his beautifully proportioned body and ran her hands over his muscled ass, giving in to an urge to bite it.

It was time to remove the wooden paddle that would get the evening started. She was surprised by how comfortable it was in her hands. Ruby tried a few practice swings, noting where each fell so she would know how to position herself to give equal attention to both cheeks. Her hand slipped between Alex's outstretched legs and cupped his balls. She felt him stiffen even in his lightly drugged state.

Alex moaned softly. He was beginning to wake up. Ruby stepped back and delivered two quick strokes to his ass.

"Welcome to Grandma's House," she said, pleased to hear her authoritative tone.

"What? Where am I? Little Red, is that you?"

Ruby brought the paddle down again, the loud crack evidence of the power she'd built up in her arms working out at the gym. "I ask the questions. And it's not 'Little Red.' That's the shade your ass is now. It's Mistress Ruby, which is the color your ass will be when I'm finished with you."

Alex shook his head to clear it, rattling the links holding his cuffed wrists in place. His eyes widened as he took in Ruby standing over him.

"What big eyes you have," she breathed sensuously. "Seeing something you like?" She noted that he shifted his position. His cock was stirring. Not giving him a chance to say anything else, she struck him several more times.

"Ow! That hurts! What are you doing?"

"Start using those big ears, Alex. I told you, I ask the

questions. It's supposed to hurt. You have been a big, bad wolf, and you need a lesson." She suited action to her words.

"Cut it out, Little Red."

"Wrong form of address." Her arm swung the paddle down hard.

"Unnh," Alex groaned. He was panting now. "Please, L—Mistress Ruby, stop. It's enough."

Ruby exulted. He was coming around. "*I* decide when it's enough. You haven't begun to convince me. You have canceled dates, changed plans to suit yourself, and called me Little Red when you know I don't like it. You take me for granted, and that, will, stop. Now." She reinforced her words with a series of stinging blows. Alex's ass took on a deep rosy glow.

"I'm sorry. I'm sorry," he gasped, losing the battle to keep his voice steady. "I didn't know you really disliked being called Little Red. I'll change. I promise." His words came out between grunts of pain.

"Explain how."

Alex struggled to list all the ways he would improve his treatment of her while Ruby encouraged him with her paddle.

Ruby could feel the heat coming from Alex's ass by the time he came to a halt, unable to think of another thing. Ruby swept her tongue over her lips. "Perhaps you have finally learned your lesson. Now I have a test to see if you can *remember* it. Pay attention," she ordered. "You are to do exactly as I say."

She unlocked Alex's right wrist. "Bring this arm

underneath your other one." She cuffed the right wrist next to his left one, repeating the action with his right ankle so he was lying on his side. Ruby smiled as she watched Alex's immediate compliance. Her eyes slid down his muscular frame and thrilled to see his cock stand at quivering attention. *He enjoys this!* Swiftly releasing his left wrist and ankle, Ruby directed him to lie on his back and re-attached the cuffs.

Alex followed her commands, hissing as his abraded ass came in contact with the sheet. Ruby positioned herself on the bed between his legs. She ran her hands up his thighs, watching the muscles contract at her touch. Her breath hitched. She saw him staring at her, uncertain as to her intentions but eager for what was to come. She stroked her breast and tugged at her nipples.

"You're killing me, Lit—uh, Mistress Ruby," he gasped.

"I haven't even started." She leaned over and pinched his nipples, hard. He writhed trying to somehow touch her.

"God!" he moaned. Alex's shaft thickened and grew larger. The tip was wet with pre-cum. Ruby inserted two fingers into her dripping pussy and brought them to Alex's lips. He dutifully opened his mouth and sucked them clean.

"Now *that's* a good wolf," she breathed softly and ran her hand along his very stiff rod, licking the tip. "How delicious!" Alex thrust his hips up, seeking more.

"Not so fast." She spanked his inner thighs. "I decide when and how we continue."

"Yes, Mistress Ruby," he said between gritted teeth,

clearly fighting to control his driving need to get inside her. Alex emitted a strangulated groan as Ruby took his sac into her mouth and massaged his balls with her tongue.

Her body flushed with desire and, her breath coming in quick pants, she lowered herself onto his huge shaft. As Alex rose to meet her, she gave his nipples a twist. "This is *my* ride."

Ruby held very still, clenching and unclenching the muscles of her wet pussy around his cock. Alex's fingers bit deeply into the bed in a desperate attempt to hold himself still. She rose on her knees until he was almost outside her, and then forcefully slammed down, burying him in her hot core.

Ruby knew Alex wanted her to speed up, but tonight she was going to go at a pace that pleased *her*. She ground herself against him, feeling his cock deep inside. Gasping as her body strained for the release just ahead, Ruby increased her pace, rocking in circles, oblivious to Alex's growls until she exploded in a shattering orgasm and collapsed on his chest.

"Oh, God," breathed Alex. "That was the most incredible experience I have ever had."

"There is still one more part to this," Ruby cooed. She eased off Alex, reached for the leash in her basket, clipped it to his collar, and freed his wrists and ankles. Tightly holding the leash in her hand, she slipped off the bed. Alex, obediently, stayed where he was, awaiting her next instructions. Seeing him waiting sent another thrill through her.

Ruby tugged the leash. "On the floor, on your knees."

Alex quickly obeyed.

"Heel," she commanded. He followed her as she sat on the couch. Ruby positioned Alex between her outspread thighs, letting him inhale her scent and see her wet curls lying flat against her pussy. "And now, my big, bad wolf, it is time for you to eat me."

Alex leaned forward and slowly licked the entrance to Ruby's wet cunt. His tongue parted the folds, nuzzling them with reverent attention, then moved to her swollen clit. She gasped, digging her fingers into his hair as he stroked the hard nub, worshipping the sensitive flesh. He sucked her into his mouth, and her hips lifted, forcing herself in deeper. While his fingers played with her clit, Alex stiffened his tongue and plunged it inside her, furiously fucking Ruby with it. Her thighs tightened against his head until she screamed his name in release.

When her breathing slowed, she leaned forward and unclipped the leash. "I think my wolf has learned his lesson."

"I learned a lot more tonight, Mistress Ruby. May I take you to bed now and show you how much you mean to me?"

Ruby stood and took Alex's hand, telling him he could stand. "You certainly may, and for now, you can call me Ruby. Just know that Mistress Ruby will return if she is needed."

"Do you think we might need a Master Wolf at some time?" he suggested.

"Perhaps," she said, and smiled.

Alex enfolded her in his arms. "I have been negligent

in telling and showing you how much I love you. I think I need to rectify that. You truly amazed me tonight. May I ask a question?"

"Yes, you may," she laughed.

"Will you marry me?"

Ruby's heart sped up. "With pleasure, my big, bad wolf."

The Match
By Devin Salerno

It was terribly cold. Elle had wandered New York's crowded streets all day, mindless to the chill. She trudged on with no purpose, no hope. Graeme was gone. The void rang painfully within her.

Happy crowds thinned as the mercury dropped. Then the piercing ice shards fell, empting the street completely. Still, Elle walked; one numb foot in front of the other, the ice stinging her tear-swollen cheeks before freezing into the block of her blonde curls.

She considered going home. *I need to warm up and move on*, she thought. But she couldn't. She had no home with Graeme gone. Everything in the sparse college dorm mocked Elle's hopeless dream. *What use is there in making something of my life without the one who inspired me to make that life in the first place?* Elle cursed him for leaving her, and herself for believing he never would. She cursed her body for still craving his hands, his fingers and touch.

Graeme's family would not return her incessant calls. Elle's roommates told her to move on. Her parents told her to let go. Her heart screamed in pain. In her innocence, Elle believed high school sweethearts could survive the onslaught of the world and miles and war. She and Graeme were different. *Our love was real, eternal.* But Graeme had left her.

His love letters were a lie. Every scribbled note in the shoebox under Elle's arm was a lie. As she walked, She realized she had allowed herself to subsist on that falsehood. Graeme's statements of eternal endearments were frauds. *Why on Earth did I believe him?*

"Elle, you have to snap out of it," her roommates coaxed. "Come out with us. It's New Year's Eve. It's the perfect night to let your troubles go and meet someone else."

Elle had no intention of celebrating while still in the throws of this tremendous loss. She sat alone in her dorm with the lovingly decorated memento box, reliving the joys she thought would last forever. Soon after her roommates left, the silence taunted her with memories of Graeme.

Their first kiss when she swore she knew she would be with him forever. The first time she gave him her body, years after giving him her heart. The quiet evening before he left for basic training, when there were no words that would suit the emotions they felt.

Haunting memories drove Elle out of the confining walls and into the liberating cold to deaden her pain. Hours later, she was finally numb. Graeme's last communication was frozen in her grasp, the words cold and heartless. She didn't have the strength to put the letter in the shoebox with his other notes. So she walked with the ornate shoebox under one frozen arm, the piece of paper crushed in the other.

The wind tickled the back of her neck. She turned her head to it. Elle had wandered to a dilapidated factory building propped beside a vacant overpass, in a part of the city she had never seen. Over-achieving college seniors never went to this side of the town. Even the homeless had found better places to spend this very cold New Year's Eve.

Elle saw a barrel in the alley between the overpass abutment and crumbling brick wall. *The trash is where these love letters belong.* She marched her frozen legs over to the metallic drum. *The warmth from a small fire might even chase away the worst of this chill. It would certainly be a fitting end to all his empty words.* Elle pulled Graeme's lighter out of her pocket and looked at the inscription: *Elle, to keep you warm until I return.* He gave it to her the day before they parted.

"Liar," she sniffled. Elle lit the brown paper bag at the top of the barrel. The frozen paper wouldn't light. She placed the last letter on top of the frozen garbage. The bejeweled lid slid to the side, revealing almost a decade of love letters. Yellow, white, pink and blue papers filled the box, folds betraying their origin, and childish handwriting giving way to young adult strokes. Removing a piece of white-lined paper from the stack, Elle unfolded it. Three postcards fell out.

"Elle ma Belle," it started in a hurried, masculine hand. "This letter will be short. I don't have much time before we head out again, but I wanted to send my love. I'm getting razzed for the letters. The guys have started throwing stamps at me. I've started collecting them and will be affixing them to postcards. My love always, Graeme."

"I want you back," Elle whispered, and watched the words float away on the mist of her warm breath. A warm tear cut a course through the dam of frozen water on her lashes. Elle flicked the lighter. A flame appeared in her cold hands. She lit the bottom corner of the letter. A strangely heavy smoke enveloped her as the hot flames crawled up the letter, singeing the white paper into gray ash. Graeme's words were faintly legible on the ghostly paper. Elle felt warmer.

The smoke dissipated, and the cold returned like a million searing pin pricks. The wind blew the film of ash from her fingers. Elle picked up the three postcards. One was a fat lady holding a pumpkin. Another showed a black and white dog with a stick. The third showed mountains of dry sand. All said, "Graeme loves Elle: January 1, 2008."

"Tomorrow," she hissed. They were supposed to marry on New Year's Day. A week ago, she expected Graeme at the door. Instead she watched from her window as a dark sedan pulled up to the dorm. Two uniformed figures emerged. Elle flew down the stairs, certain the men were Graeme and his best man. She was at the door to welcome them before they had even made their way to the entrance.

He'll never be back. Strangers delivered the news coldly, with a note. Elle cracked the flame to life again.

The orange and yellow heat caressed the three thick, dry postcards Elle fanned downward to meet the licking flame. As it rose, the thick smoke returned to caress her with strange warmth. Within the smoke, Elle felt touched and safe.

She looked through the grey mist surrounding her. The cement buttresses of the overpass and crumbling brick edifice were obscured. The piercing rain disappeared. *Is the storm over?* she wondered. She saw a form; visible only by the swirling eddies of smoke.

The postcards burnt to her fingertips. Elle dropped them. The fire and smoke died instantly. The figure was gone.

Elle reached for another note. Paper still folded, she lit the corner. The smoke billowed up around her, thicker still. The figure returned: The outline of a man. His back was to Elle, and he was walking away. The figure came more into focus. He was strong, and in the patchy yellows and tans of military fatigues. He walked with a calm, slow gait. Elle knew that confidence. She knew that man.

"Graeme!" she choked. He stopped and turned. She saw his face. Elle's heart leapt to life.

"Graeme!" she cried again, stronger in the assertion.

He mouthed her name before the smoke faded. The paper was ash in her fingers.

Elle blinked at the clearness around her. The stinging rain and biting wind assaulted her. She grabbed a handful of pages with a hand that shook more in excitement than cold. She lit the muddled-up collection of paper. The flame licked the letters in her grasp.

The smoke came back thicker than before. Graeme returned.

"Graeme," Elle called, but she could not move nearer to him.

"Elle! What are you doing here?" Graeme asked,

running to her. The distance between them was gone with the thought.

"How could you leave me?" she asked as his hands touched the skin of her face. She melted into the warmth of his strong fingers. She held his hands on her face, reveling in the glorious sensations his nearness brought.

"No, Elle. I could never leave you. I love you," he said, stroking her hair with his free hand.

"But the letter? It broke my heart," Elle said, breathing in the musty smell of his uniform.

"Elle, I'm so sorry. I was trying to come home. I really was." His arms pulled her close. The rough fabric scratched her cheek. The smell of the fabric choked her. But beyond it was the familiar scent of their life of green grass, autumn leaves and warm dirt. It was a smell Elle never thought she would enjoy again. She grabbed the collar of Graeme's shirt and pulled his face close to hers. He let her go. "Graeme, I never want to lose you again. Please don't go."

"Elle, my love, you don't have to lose me. We're together now. We'll be together forever," he said, smiling.

She kissed those playful lips, tasting the sweet happiness of him. The joy invaded Elle. She felt happy. Graeme's mouth expertly explored hers. He knew just when to keep his lips soft, and went to thrust his tongue between her teeth to increase their intimacy and connection. Elle ached for that connection now, and Graeme responded to her need. His hands caressed her cheeks as he held her face. She arched her body against him, deepening the kiss any way she could.

Amid the pleasure, a pain stung Elle's left hand. She looked to see her hand was burning. She shook the fire out. With the flames went the smoke and Graeme.

"Elle don't go! Elle . . ." she heard Graeme's plea in the evaporating fog.

"Graeme!" she screamed, clawing the air he'd occupied moments ago. Panic gripped her chest worse than any cold or hurt. *The smoke will make him come back.*

Elle spied the bejeweled shoebox atop the frozen garbage. "Graeme, I'm coming!" she called. She crumpled the top few letters, and stuffed them under the stack inside the dry cardboard container. She lit the wad.

The smoke returned, congealing around her.

"Elle," Graeme breathed, warm at her check. His strong arms slipped around her again. His fatigues were gone. Now he wore the soft T-shirt and playfully worn denim she knew him in. "You felt cold. I got something for you," Graeme smiled at her.

"What?" she asked. *Just seeing him again is enough.*

Taking her hand, Graeme walked Elle though the wall of the building. She knew she should have found it strange, but instead she was thrilled to find herself in a familiar room. One she hadn't seen in years: The hotel room where they made love for the first time.

"I wanted to bring you to the place we discovered passion together."

"Graeme, I missed you so much." Elle leaned over to stroke the familiar contours of his face.

"I missed you too," he smiled into her clear blue eyes. Graeme led her to the bed and removed Elle's shoes and socks. The frozen fabric slid off like the weight of the world.

Graeme kissed her. She tasted the pleasure of his lips and the warmth returning to her core. As they kissed, his large hands caressed her body. Her skin greedily drank in the sensations. She whispered his name, giddy with the pleasure of his nearness. She never thought she would feel him again. His hands stoked down her sides, followed by his mouth. He spoke endearments between each thirsty kiss.

Graeme unwrapped her, and Elle lay naked on the silken blankets of the bed. He lay beside her. He caressed the sensitive skin of her lower abdomen. "You are so beautiful," he said. His voice was warm with love. His fingers dipped lower, searching for the pleasure spots within Elle's silken folds. He knew everywhere she was most responsive. She couldn't imagine anyone knowing her better. The gentle message sent ripples of desire through Elle. Her breath caught in her throat. His touch became focused. Her release came. The pleasure was pure and explosive, producing tears at the corner of her eyes.

As the pleasure of her orgasm faded, a different burning sensation began. Graeme, along with everything around them, began to fade from Elle's view. Before she could stop it, she had returned to standing in the bitter cold, her finger scorched, her heart longing. This time, however, she knew what to do. She leaked some of the lighter fluid on the remains of the bejeweled box and cracked the flame to life.

As she had hoped, the smoke and Graeme returned.

"I knew you'd be back," he said. He caressed a swirling lock of Elle's blonde hair.

She nuzzled his hand. "Nothing can keep me from you."

Once again, she gave him Graeme her hand and he walked her through the building. This time there was an ornate fireplace complete with a raging fire throwing off welcome heat. Elle had never been in this place before, but knew it immediately. Graeme had created the home they'd dreamed of making together. They were finally here.

"Warm your toes," he offered, lowering Elle to several large floor pillows. She breathed in the scent of the fire. It was amazing how cold she had gotten in their brief time apart.

The heat of the fire warmed her body but Graeme's touch heated Elle's core. He rubbed her feet with slow circles, kneading her strained muscles. Elle arched her back.

"I missed your foot rubs," she purred.

"Let me make up for that," Graeme said. He stroked her skin, trailing eddies of excited heat in the wake of an intoxicatingly slow advance up her legs and thighs.

"You have a lot to make up for," she warned playfully.

His brow lifted over an impish twinkle in his happy blue eyes. Graeme stroked downward pulling the stress out of Elle's toes as though he were weeding a garden.

Elle curled her toes and purred at the electric relaxation. She leaned backward in a luxurious stretch across the soft velvet pillows.

"I missed the sounds you make," he said, his deep voice thick. He kneaded the pliable muscles of her legs again, and then moved to her hips. The movements of Graeme's thick thumbs wreaked delirious havoc on Elle's senses. He moved higher up to her waist and ribcage.

Elle purred again, loudly. Graeme chuckled. She sat up slightly, wrapped her arms around him, and pulled him onto her. She teased his ear with a lick. He tasted like a sweet homecoming. They kissed until she was breathless.

"I've missed something else," she said after a deep breath. Graeme trailed a string of kisses down her long neck. Her hands toyed with the hem of his soft T-shirt, tickling the skin just above his jeans.

Graeme chuckled again. "Me too."

Elle pulled his shirt off. The muscles of his chest and arms broadcast the skill of his profession. "Where did all these come from?" Elle asked, tracing the contours of his rippled body. She pushed him down onto the pillows.

"You can thank Uncle Sam for those. But I did it all for you," Graeme said kissing her on the lips. "I love you."

Elle removed the rest of his clothes with admiration of his new, firmer shape. Graeme helped her undress, enjoying the sleek contours of her body. "There was one part of you that didn't need any extra firming," Elle said playfully, running her hands along the length of his cock. She never tired of his reaction to her attention.

It was his turn to purr, a rough grumble in his throat. She felt triumph in the sound. Elle kissed her way down Graeme's body. She heard his heartbeat against her ear: Strong alive, and pulsing with desire for her. She giggled, and kissed the firm skin of his abdomen. Her tongue followed the familiar line of hair down until she could wrap her mouth around Graeme's erection.

Elle caressed his base while her tongue swirled with all his favorite moves. His tormented groan was a heady triumph. She pumped faster.

"Elle," he moaned.

Finally, unable to wait any longer, she sat up, put one leg on either side of his body, and hovered above him. Graeme pulled her down on his length. As she enveloped the thick silk, pleasure erupted within her.

She was with Graeme, skin to skin. They were truly together. She focused on every glorious thrust, the soothing and familiar weight of him, and the tickle from the start of his stubble. They took their time. Their sweat washed the memory of their separation away.

Finally they lay exhausted, limbs entangled, sweating.

"Love you, Elle," Graeme whispered into her heart.

"I love you, too." She cuddled closer, content.

A warm light shone down on them. In the distance, church bells rang in the New Year. Today was the day.

Graeme kissed her again and helped her to her feet. When Elle looked down, they were dressed in their wedding clothes. "Are you ready?" Graeme asked, wrapping a cloak around her elegant white gown.

Elle smiled, fixing the collar of his shirt. "I've waited for today for my entire life. It's the happiest day of my life."

Graeme reached for her hand. "Mine too. Come on. Let's go home together."

"Forever," Elle agreed, taking his hand as they walked into the warm light in peace.

Letting Her Hair Down

By Ashlyn Chase

"Rapunzel, Rapunzel, Let down your hair!"

Rapunzel rolled her eyes and tossed her magazine onto the cold stone floor. She knew damn well who stood at the bottom of her tower, although she hoped beyond hope she might be wrong this time. She rose and glared out the window. Once again, it was the evil sorceress claiming to be her mother. "Crap," she muttered.

She sighed, reminding herself defiance was useless, and gathered up her tresses. Her golden locks spilled over the windowsill and down the 70-foot stone wall.

Rapunzel knew this twisted, onion-eyed freak couldn't possibly be her real mother; but hadn't yet discovered how she had wound up with her. The woman wasn't too bad as far as crazy mothers go; until Rapunzel turned 12. Then, the sorceress imprisoned her in a moldy old tower.

"Frau Gothel," Rapunzel called out the window. "Why can't you use a ladder like normal people?"

The woman stamped her foot. "I *told* you to call me Mommy Dearest! And if I left a friggin' ladder lying around, someone would surely rescue—I mean, kidnap you! The world is a terrible, dangerous place. I'm protecting you from it."

The villainous old cow grabbed hold of Rapunzel's beautiful silken strands and began hauling herself up.

"*Jeez! Ouch, oh, ow, ow, shit, damn, fuck, motherfucker, cocksucker, son of a bitch!*" Rapunzel cursed fluently, thanks to a succession of uncles who were actually the sorceress' suitors. The evil nut-bag climbed Rapunzel's hair like a rope ladder, nearly pulling it out by the roots.

"Now, now," she cackled when she finally reached the top. "Don't be rude. I brought you a sandwich."

"Bologna and cheese?"

"What else?"

"With lettuce and mustard?"

"Oops. I forgot the mustard. Well, I guess I'll just have to take the sandwich back down, slather some mustard on it, and come back."

"No!" Rapunzel coughed to cover her horror at the thought of enduring the worst case of hair pulling in history twice in one day. "No, that's all right. I'll eat it this way. I *like* stale bread covered in fat, cow parts and nitrates. Mm. Yummy." She patted her stomach.

"Oh good. Only the best for Mommy Dearest's precious one-and-only. Now, eat up."

Rapunzel took a bite of the sandwich and mumbled around it as she chewed. "So, are you ever going to tell me about my real parents?"

The pockmarked sorceress heaved a huge sigh. "Oh, I suppose so. After all, you're an adult now and you can probably handle the truth." Under her breath she added, "Besides, you're trapped here and there's nothing you can do about it." Rapunzel perked up her ears.

"As you know," Frau Gothel began, "I have a terrific vegetable garden, lush with every type of salad green, plus tomatoes, carrots, onions and celery." Rapunzel nodded. "Many years ago, in that garden grew a plant called rapunzel. It's particularly delicious in salads, and I noticed one of my neighbors coveting it. One night, her husband climbed over my fence and stole some!"

Rapunzel gasped. Having been threatened for years with all the dastardly things the skanky bitch could do to punish her if she didn't cooperate, she couldn't imagine what the poor man must have endured. "What did you do to him?"

"Oh, nothing. We made a deal. He could have my rapunzel, if I could have their first-born child. And that, my precious, was you!"

Rapunzel stood with her jaw agape. "They traded me for a vegetable?"

"I'm afraid so, dear. So, you see? You're much better off with Mommy Dearest who loves you more than a salad ingredient."

Rapunzel's knees went out from under her and she landed on the cold, stone floor. "Crap!" She lost her appetite and set the sandwich aside.

"Well, I'll be back tomorrow. Same time."

"Yes, Frau—I mean, Mommy Dearest."

"That's better," Frau Gothel patted Rapunzel on the head, climbed over the window ledge, and slid down Rapunzel's long hair like a fire pole.

"Ouch, ow, ow, shit, damn, fuckin'-a!"

When the hag reached the bottom, she called up to her. "Don't forget to eat your bologna and cheese sandwich. It has all the food groups in it. I take good care of my girl, don't I?"

Rapunzel dragged her hair back up through the window. "Yes, Mommy Dearest," She mumbled, adding "you churlish, boil-brained boar."

Then she began to cry.

That evening, as she was singing to keep herself from going mad, Rapunzel heard an unfamiliar voice. "Rapunzel, Rapunzel, let down your hair."

"Huh?"

Rapunzel rushed to the window and peered down at the ground. There stood the handsomest man she had ever seen. Okay, so she hadn't seen many men, but even if she had, she was sure this guy was frickin' lickin' gorgeous. Dressed in purple tights and some flouncy purple and gold jacket with matching bloomers, he had to be gay. *Damn.* Oh well, talking to somebody different was something to do.

"Who are you?" she called down to him.

"I'm Prince Wunderkind," he said. "A few days ago, I heard your lovely song as I passed by. 'Tis more beautiful than the birds."

"Well I should hope so. All that squawking and chirping drives me crazy."

He laughed. "Ah and you are so fair and bright. I've watched your tower, determined to return and see you when the wicked one was far away. I should like to get to know you better."

"So you've been stalking me?"

He looked puzzled. "How doth one stalk a beauty kept in an immovable object?"

"Yeah, you have a point. Okay, permission granted. Come on up." And with that, Rapunzel tossed all her hair over the window ledge, bracing herself for the man's weight. *This is gonna hurt.*

The prince pulled himself up easily. To Rapunzel's amazement, it didn't hurt a bit! *Wow, he might be lighter than he looks.*

"Fair maiden," Wunderkind said, staring into her eyes, "May I have the honor of kissing you?"

"Heck, yeah. Do you know how long I've been waiting to try all the stuff my *Cosmo* magazine talks about?"

He chucked. "You are most strange, but I enjoy your sense of humor almost as much as your beautiful countenance and lovely voice."

She shrugged and puckered up.

He swept her into his warm embrace and dipped her in a dramatic, romantic gesture. He was gentle at first, then the pressure of his lips grew firmer. At last, Wunderkind parted her lips with his tongue and demanded entrance. She opened to him and their tongues twirled, tangled and mated. He tasted of sweet fruited wine.

He held her tighter and their passionate kiss continued for what seemed like hours. At last, they broke apart, panting.

"Man, that was good! And I thought you were gay."

"Gay? But I am. I've been filled with happiness ever since knowing of your existence."

"Um, yeah, that's not what I meant, but anyway, if you make love like you kiss, I can't wait to test it out! I saw a list of positions we could try."

"Oh, my dear. To have the honor of making love to you would make me the gayest man in the realm."

Rapunzel smirked, but held in her snarky comeback.

"Let me remove your clothing for you, my darling."

"Thanks. I could use help with the corset. It's laced so tightly. I can't wait to find out what it's like to take a deep breath again."

"You are indeed amusing." Wunderkind took her shoulders and swiveled her around so he could reach the buttons and laces behind her back. One by one, they came undone and a cool breeze tickled her back.

At last Rapunzel was naked and her mysterious suitor set about removing his own clothes. She mused that clothing manufacturers who made clothing open in the front for men and in the back for women conspired to control women's sexual urges. *Only a male designer could have come up with that idea.*

When the prince was disrobed, she studied his body wide-eyed. His golden sprinkle of chest hair formed a V down his muscular torso and six-pack abs, ending in an arrow pointing straight to his engorged manhood.

"Wow, you'd better be careful with that thing," she exclaimed. "I'm a virgin."

"But of course you are, and I will be so gentle you will only feel a tiny twinge of discomfort to be followed by the most incredible pleasure I can possibly give you," he boasted.

"Sounds great. Go for it!"

"I know this is something you desire," Wunderkind said. "I heard you singing bawdy ballads."

"They're the only songs I know. The evil sorceress keeps some pretty low company. Those songs get me aroused, though."

He backed her up against the wall, his fingers laced through hers, holding their entwined hands over her head. While he kissed her neck, Rapunzel took in the spice-and-wine smell of his hair. *Does this guy bathe and brush his teeth in cinnamon grape juice?* Rapunzel wondered.

His fingers slid away from hers and found her breasts. "You want to know what it's like to feel passion. You want my hands on you, touching you, kneading you. You wonder what it's like to have a man inside you."

Rapunzel's stomach coiled and tightened. Her eyes widened. "Am I that transparent?"

He kissed her throat and licked his way to her breast, where he nipped her nipple. "Do I frighten you with my passion, Rapunzel? Or does this excite you?"

"Mm hm . . ."

The prince latched onto her nipple and suckled deeply. She moaned. Her legs weakened. "Yeah, that's the ticket."

His fingers slid away from her other breast and skated down her belly. "You're excited, aren't you? I can tell by the way you tremble against me. It's not a shiver of fear, but desire; a yearning for more." The prince found Rapunzel's mons as his mouth latched onto her other breast and sucked.

"Yes," she hissed.

Wunderkind's fingers expertly reached for the edges of her labia and slowly inched them apart. His middle finger stroked the part of her no one had ever touched.

Arching, Rapunzel's nails found the prince's back and raked down the length of Wunderkind's torso. "I want to know all the pleasures, all the mysteries between men and women," she cried. "Show me! Make me scream."

The prince's middle finger slipped inside her wet pussy and stroked her. Rapunzel moaned louder. Sensations she had never known invaded her body. Glorious, erotic fantasies took over and she couldn't wait to be fucked. "More!" she demanded.

The prince inserted another digit and finger fucked her enthusiastically. Rapunzel writhed and panted. Beads of sweat broke out on her forehead.

"Play with me, Rapunzel." Wunderkind took her hand and placed it on his cock, closing her fingers around it. "Pleasure me."

"How?"

She didn't know what to do, other than to slide her fingers along his satiny skin. He groaned and thrust his hips forward, sliding his erection up and down the length of her palm. Closing her eyes, she let her head fall back against the wall and allowed herself to feel his warmth. His mouth was everywhere—on her throat, breasts and lips. His hands roamed the contours of her body; his fingers cupped and stroked every inch of her burning skin.

Rapunzel's heart pounded in her ears. "Oh, Prince

Wunderkind, I can't wait until you take me! I want you so much!"

The intimacy of his tongue invading her mouth and his fingers stroking her clit was almost too much. In some part of her mind, Rapunzel tried to remember that this man was a virtual stranger. *He is handsome, of course,* she thought, *but is he kind? Thoughtful? Caring?*

Wunderkind dropped to his knees and parted her folds. She jolted as he began licking and teasing the center of her pleasure. *Dear Lord. He's kind, caring and very thoughtful!* She groaned in appreciation.

Fisting her hands in his shoulder-length blonde hair, she pulled Wunderkind closer. He flicked his tongue quickly and repeatedly across her clit. Powerful sensations Rapunzel had never imagined rippled throughout every nerve ending and made her quiver.

At last, the building tension reached an impossible peak and she erupted like a volcanic blast. Bucking and screaming, she rode the formidable orgasm in a dream-like state. The cresting wave seemed to last forever. White heat nearly blinded her. Whimpering when the aftershocks arrived, she quivered. The only thing left of her boneless body were ripples of sensation that marked the end of a wonderful roller coaster ride.

"Oh. My. God. I—I don't know what to say." She took deep, gasping breaths. "You've waked me to something incredible! I can't believe what a good time I've been missing."

Wunderkind stood and smiled cockily. "I know. I have that affect on lusty wenches. I have no desire to waste my talents on ladies. I've been told they just lay there and cringe."

"Really? Well, they're just stupid."

"Ah, but not you, my sweet. You're a lady and a wench in one body: The perfect woman."

"Well, thanks, I think. I can't imagine anyone not liking what you did!"

"It's called cunnilingus, my sweet."

"Cunna-what? Can't we just call it something like the horny hummingbird? I'll never remember that other word."

"Of course, my darling. We can call it anything you wish. Now, I would like to teach you how to pleasure me the same way I pleasured you."

Rapunzel stared at him, puzzled. "But . . ." She stepped back and examined the prince's cock. "You don't have the same parts. What am I supposed to do?"

"Kneel, my sweet. I'll teach you."

Rapunzel shrugged and sank to her knees onto the stone floor. "Okay, now what?"

"Put my glorious cock into your mouth."

"Your cock?" She swiveled to each side and glanced around the inside of the tower. "I didn't know you brought a rooster with you. Where is it?"

"Ha! You do have a delightful sense of humor, my love. I mean the cock between my legs."

"Your penis?"

"Yes."

"And you want me to do what?"

"Suck it."

Rapunzel tipped her head. "Are you sure? I mean, isn't that how you . . . ?"

"It is the instrument of both types of satisfying release."

She scrunched up her nose in distaste. "Well, if you say so."

"I do. Now take my manhood into your beautiful mouth and suck it."

She shrugged. "I'll try anything once."

Rapunzel inserted the rubbery head into her mouth. *Hm*, she thought, *It's not too bad.* She licked around Wunderkind's cock and found it salty, but not at all distasteful. She followed his instructions, determined to learn the art of a stellar blowjob. According to the prince and *Cosmo* magazine, that was what every man wanted.

"Push it as far as you can into your mouth, with suction."

Rapunzel sucked the head and half of his impressive shaft into her mouth before it hit the back of her throat and caused her to gag.

She let it pop from her mouth and looked up at Wunderkind with tears in her eyes.

"Oh, my love. Art thou upset about what I'm asking you to do?"

"No," she said. "I don't mind sucking you, as long as I don't choke."

"Ah, I see. Yes, I was afraid it might be difficult to take all of it. Try this. When it gets close to the back of your throat, swallow."

"Swallow? Are you kidding me? If I don't want to choke, how is that going to help?"

"Do you trust me?"

She shrugged. "I guess I trust you more than anyone else I know. Of course, that boils down to two people; and one of them has boils.

He smiled. "Then try it once, as you said you would try anything."

"Yeah, I did, didn't I?"

Rapunzel slowly slid Wunderkind's member back into her mouth and sucked it all the way to the back of her throat, then swallowed. The prince braced himself against the wall and moaned.

When Rapunzel discovered it helped both of them enjoy this new activity, she repeated the process over and over. The prince's moans grew louder and his face reddened. At last the prince begged her to stop and pulled out of her mouth.

"What's wrong? I thought you were liking it?"

"Truly, you did a marvelous job of sucking my royal appendage. I will now reward you by thrusting it into your love channel and riding you like a stallion rides his mare."

"You mean you're going to fuck me?"

"Yes."

"Finally!"

Rapunzel flopped onto her straw bed, then remembered Wunderkind wanted to take her doggy-style—or horse style, according to him. *Doesn't matter to me*, she mused, *as long as he gets the job done.*

She positioned herself on her hands and knees and felt his hand tapping her inner thighs. She parted her legs and sensed Wunderkind closing in behind her. She shivered with anticipation.

This is it. I'm finally going to know what all the fuss is about.

The prince entered her slowly. Rapunzel's walls stretched to accommodate him. Excitement, thrill and fear overtook her. The man of her dreams was about to fuck her silly.

When he was barely in, she sighed.

"Are you all right, my love?"

"Ah, yes, I'm wonderful." The feeling of his cock inside her seemed so right. She felt completed. Whole. Loved.

"Then prepare to be fully and thoroughly fucked."

"Please," she said. "I can't wait."

Wunderkind pulled partway out and inserted himself to the hilt.

"Jesus God!" Rapunzel yelled. "That hurt!" Glaring over her shoulder, she asked, "What the hell did you do wrong?"

He held her hips in place. "Nothing, my dear. I was simply breaching your maidenhead."

Rapunzel felt moisture trickling down between her thighs and glanced at it. *Blood!* Shocked, she tried to pull away. "What kind of sick trick is this? You impaled me with a dagger or something. I'm bleeding!"

"But I did not. It is only my hard cock inside you."

"Yeah, and his beak is clawing the hell out of me."

"Relax, my darling. This is natural. Only the first time will this happen. Allow me to clean you with my hat."

Rapunzel looked between her legs. Sure enough, the prince whipped off his plumed cap with a flourish and used it to wipe away the evidence. *Is this guy for real?*

"There," he said. "Now we shall fuck, and it will be enjoyable for both."

Rapunzel hoped he was right. Wunderkind inserted his cock again and rocked gently. As he increased his thrusts and found his rhythm, she relaxed and a moan escaped her lips as the pleasant sensation built. "This feel so good," she cooed.

The prince chuckled. "Do you know what would feel even better?"

"No, what?"

"This," he said.

With that, Wunderkind touched Rapunzel's clit and added a fast finger massage. "Oh!" She nearly bucked out of her skin. The sensations intensified tenfold. Her body quivered and a second later she lost control. Her climax hit so forcefully, she shook and screamed her release.

Wunderkind grunted and jerked into her a few times. At last, the two of them stilled.

"Holy cow!" Rapunzel exclaimed. "Can we do that again?"

"Oh yes. Many, many times."

And as often happens in these tales, the prince fucked her all night long. After multiple orgasms, Rapunzel and the prince fell in love.

"I simply have to find a way to get you down from this tower so I can whisk you off to my castle," he said.

"I don't suppose you have a ladder."

"Not one of this height, but I shall have the royal carpenter build one. You will be my bride. Until it is ready, I'll climb up your hair and make love to you, repeatedly, every night."

"Sounds like a plan," she said excitedly.

The prince had to leave at the break of dawn to avoid being caught by the wicked sorceress. Wunderkind kissed Rapunzel tenderly, professed his love, and gently lowered himself down her hair. Again, she couldn't believe how little the prince hurt her as he climbed down compared to the awful, nasty one, who would be showing up soon.

When the sun had chased away the last of the sunrise, the evil one stood at the bottom of the tower and called out, "Rapunzel, Rapunzel, let down your hair."

"Great," she muttered, and pushed her big pile of bed-head over the windowsill. Frau Gothel had to jump a couple of times to catch hold of the ends and hauled herself up.

"Ga!" Rapunzel squealed as the extra weight yanked on the roots of her scalp. With tears in her eyes, she let out her daily stream of curses.

"Oh, quit being a baby about it," Frau Gothel said as she slid over the windowsill and into the tower room. "What happened to your beautiful hair? It's a mess."

"Oh, I uh, I had a rough night. Tossed and turned a lot."

"I guess. Look at your bed. There's straw all over the place."

"Yes, well, I'll sweep that up in a jiffy. Sorry about that. I guess my hair got kind of matted in the process."

"Well, I'll have to comb it out."

"No! Not that! I hate it when you comb my hair."

"Fine, then do it yourself."

"I will."

"See that you do. Here's your bologna and cheese sandwich."

"Thank you, Mommy Dearest."

"That's better." The unwelcome visitor made herself comfortable on the floor and watched Rapunzel eat. "So, why did you have such a difficult night's sleep? Was something on your mind?"

Rapunzel shrugged. "Not really. I—I guess I was just wishing I could be like other girls my age. Going to balls and finding husbands."

"Well, you'll get over that."

"But why can't I do that? It's time. I'm a grown woman."

Frau Gothel scrutinized her. "You *do* look different. If I'm not mistaken, your boobs are slightly larger than I remember them. And you have this kind of rosy glow. Why it's almost as if you've—" The old woman shook her head. "Naw, that's ridiculous."

"What is?"

"Oh, nothing. Well, I'd best be off. I have evil to brew and hexes to cast. Busy, busy, busy."

Rapunzel sighed and let her hair tumble down the tower wall, cringing in anticipation of the inevitable. The sorceress grabbed hold of the matted hair and lowered herself.

"Here we go again," Rapunzel muttered.

The tension on her scalp ended abruptly.

"Oomph! Shit." A few seconds later, Frau Gothel yelled up to her. "Hey, Rapunzel. Make sure you comb out that rat's nest. It's a couple of feet short and I fell on my ass!"

Rapunzel tittered under her breath.

As promised, the prince returned the following night with news that the ladder was almost finished.

"Oh, joy!" Rapunzel could smell freedom. *Or is that me?* she wondered. She had noticed an unusual odor ever since Wunderkind left that morning. *Thank heavens the evil one hasn't noticed.* Rapunzel chalked the scent up to all the sex.

"I've been thinking about you all day, Prince Wunderkind."

"Oh, my darling, please call me by my given name. After all, you will soon be my wife."

Rapunzel sighed and gazed at the ceiling. "Princess Rapunzel. I like the sound of that." She shook herself back to reality and asked, "Oh, yeah. So, what's your name?"

"Waldeburg, but you can call me Wally."

"Hm, Waldeburg Wunderkind. That's a mouthful. Thank God you have a nickname. Now how about helping me out of this dress so we can fuck, Wally?"

"My pleasure." He unlaced Rapunzel's many layers and helped her toss them aside, leaving her gloriously naked. The cool breeze teased her skin. Rapunzel's nipples puckered.

Wally disrobed quickly and commenced sucking and stroking every inch of her body in a worshipful way. Rapunzel was so turned on, her cunt practically dripped.

"Prince—I mean, Wally, I'm burning up and can't wait much longer. Can you please get to the fucking?"

"Ah, my anxious little wench, I have something a little different to try with you."

"Different? Like what? We've done it kneeling, standing, lying down, side-by-side, and upside-down."

"Ah, but there's another orifice I want to explore." Wally wet his finger in her juices and circled her puckered anus.

"*There?* Are you out of your ever-lovin' mind?"

"No, my sweet. I assure you, I'm quite sane. But it would drive me completely crazy in a good way if you would allow me to fuck your ass."

She sighed. "I guess by my own admission, I'll try it at least once."

"Don't worry, darling. I'll help you find the pleasure in it also."

"Oh, well if there's more pleasure involved, then sure. Why not?"

The prince positioned himself behind her, then gently invaded her ass with his spike-hard cock and groaned.

Rapunzel grimaced. "I'm not feeling the pleasure yet, prince."

"Hang on, you will."

Wally had just begun to plunder her when they heard an angry voice from the window ledge.

"Rapunzel! What are you doing?" Frau Gothel yelled.

Rapunzel glanced over her shoulder and froze in shock. "Um, nothin'."

"I may be slightly cross-eyed, but even *I* can see a guy with his dick up your ass."

"Hey!" Rapunzel exclaimed as she and the prince separated. "How did you get up here?"

"I flew on my broom."

"You had the power to fly, but you hauled your fat ass up my hair every day? Why?"

"Just for this very reason. I didn't want you to know I could get up here and spy on you any time I liked."

"Mommy Dearest, you're a witch!"

The evil sorceress cackled. "And you're a slut! An ungrateful little slut."

"I am not! The prince is going to marry me."

Frau Gothel rolled her eyes. "That's what they all say. Why do you think I wanted to protect you? It was to keep you from being taken in by idiots like him."

Wally handed Rapunzel her clothes. "My dear, I am not like the other idiots. I meant what I said. I love you and I intend to marry you as soon as—"

"Argh!" the witch cried as she charged the prince, throwing him, naked, out the window.

Rapunzel dashed to the ledge and peered down at the ground. Prince Wunderkind had landed in the brambles face down, but he was moaning. *He's alive!*

"Are you all right, my love?" she called.

He waved. "Nothing twenty years of physical therapy won't fix." He struggled to his feet. Blood poured from his eyes. "Uh-oh. I may have spoken too soon. It seems I can no longer see."

"Oh no!" Rapunzel cried. She turned on Frau Gothel. "Fix him," she demanded.

"Oh, I'll fix him all right," she said, and cackled.

When Rapunzel looked down again, her naked prince was gone. She gasped. "Where is he? What have you done with him?"

"Well, now I'm not quite sure where I banished him to. I guess you'll have to look for him in every corner of the world if you want him to support the little bastards you're carrying."

"Little bas—" Rapunzel stumbled backward. "You mean I'm—"

"Yup. Good luck to all of you. Because of your condition, I won't throw you out the tower window. But as soon as I fly you down, you'd better hit the ground running. I'm thoroughly pissed."

Wouldn't that make for a terrible ending to a fairy tale! We all know the principles must live happily ever after, right? Rapunzel and her prince should be no exception. Let's give them a better fate.

After wandering blind and naked through the wilderness for a year, the prince nearly lost his mind—and not just because survival is a bitch. Wally missed his ladylove, Rapunzel.

Rapunzel gave birth to twin girls, and her life sucked too. Single parenting is never a picnic. But Rapunzel persisted, and kept singing her bawdy songs. They kept her spirits up and lulled the babies to sleep.

One day, the prince heard the voice he longed for. He pinched himself to make sure he wasn't dreaming: After all, he couldn't tell if it was night or day. He was indeed awake. Wally ran toward Rapunzel's beautiful voice, which sang a disgusting song about a sailor fornicating with a mermaid.

"At last! My darling, I found you!"

"Wally!" She put down her daughters and ran to meet

him. They embraced, kissed and cried. When Rapunzel's tears touched the prince's eyes, his sight returned.

"I can see! Dear Lord, it's a miracle!"

The prince found his castle after all, and married Rapunzel. The happy family lived happily ever after.

Schumacher and the Elf

By Chase Jeffreys

Royce Schumacher looked at the nearly empty store, drawing an instant comparison between it and his empty life. After 32 years, he had no wife, no kids, and a job he hated.

Every morning, Royce found it harder and harder to get out of bed and face another day at the brokerage firm. The fact he'd earned a small fortune since getting his MBA was of little consolation. He hated facing his over-decorated apartment each night, and social obligations with women who were only interested in his assets. Royce could see no way out of his routine.

A phone call he would have preferred not to receive came two weeks ago. Royce decided to use the opportunity to summon change.

The Schumacher & Son sign above the store looked more faded than it had five years ago when Royce last saw it. His family's business had been around for five generations, getting passed on from father to son even before coming to America from Germany. There was a long line of cobblers who had established the family name. Family legend had it the Schumachers were the cobblers from the Grimm brothers' *The Shoemaker and the Elves*.

By the time Royce was a teenager he didn't believe in magic or the shoemaking business, but he humored his father when he told the tale. Thinking of his father brought a fresh wave of sadness to Royce. He stood in front of the store, remembering.

"Royce? Can you hear me?"

The familiar voice sounded distant, like it came through a fog. Royce blinked hard. He couldn't believe what he had just heard. He didn't want to believe what the family attorney said.

Dead? Papa's dead? How? When? Why? The questions raced through his mind.

"Would you repeat that, Mr Maxwell," Royce managed.

The man on the other end of the line cleared his throat. Royce heard pain and grief when he spoke, "I'm sorry, Royce. Your father was found dead of a heart attack this morning."

Royce maintained his composure despite the anger and disbelief warring within him. It would not do to have the other cubicle rats around him sense there was anything wrong. If they did, they'd be like predators smelling blood in the water. Being a broker, you were either a shark or chum.

"Thank you for letting me know," he responded, his voice controlled. "What do you need from me?"

*

Standing there now, looking at the first Schumacher shoe store in the United States, Royce breathed in deeply and could almost smell leather in the air. The memory of his first cobbling session was filled with the warm, soft and sensuous feel of the leather between his fingers. Royce realized at the age of ten that he found the look and texture of high-quality hides arousing, before he knew what the feeling really was. He stood no chance against a woman wearing well-made leather, particularly boots. They turned him on faster than any lace or satin confection could.

"Royce? Is that you?"

Surprised at hearing his name, Royce shifted his gaze from the worn sign to the store's open door where the soft, melodious voice originated. Standing there was a slight woman who appeared to be barely 20. As with all women, her legs were the first thing he noticed—and her incredible boots. Royce's cobbler's eye instantly knew they were of exceptional craftsmanship. Black with red embroidered details, he had never seen their like anywhere. The way they made her legs look caused the subtle bulge in Royce's pants to grow more pronounced.

Forcing himself to tear his gaze away from the calf-high footwear, he took in the rest of her: Slender and petite, she was fairy-like in build. Her golden hair was pulled back in a ponytail, and her almond-shaped eyes were pale violet. He had only seen eyes that color on one other person, Elfriede. He had not seen her since he went off to college.

"Royce?" she asked again. Her eyes widened in

recognition. Excitement filled her voice as she threw herself into his arms, hugged him hard and squealed, "It's you! After all these years!"

"Elf?"

Elfriede Diefee had waited two weeks to see Royce. *Seven years and two weeks*, she corrected herself, *if I'm being honest*. He had come back for a short visit after getting his MBA; those ten days gave her enough inspiration to fuel years' worth of sexual fantasies and dreams.

Hopping from foot to foot, Elfriede stayed in the store while Royce confronted some inner demons outside. It took every ounce of willpower for her to fight the urge to burst through the front door and wrap her arms around him. Elfriede tried to ignore a burning desire to feel Royce's body against hers. Though years had passed, she recognized him instantly. Elfriede's body instinctively reacted to his handsome looks, as it had when she last saw him.

The passing of time had been good to him. Elfriede's heart beat faster. She stopped herself from fidgeting and adjusting her underwear: Thoughts of Royce always made her damp. Finally she decided she had waited long enough, and rushed out of the store, all decorum forgotten.

"Elf?" Royce whispered in her ear, his arms enfolding her. The warmth of his breath against her cheek was wonderful. Feelings Elfriede tried to bury bubbled to the surface. It felt right to be in his arms.

His bright blue eyes stared at her. Elfriede's body grew

warmer. She saw his gaze linger on her legs. His eyes moved slowly upward, finally meeting hers. She smiled.

Nobody had called her Elf since Royce left for college. Hearing him use the old nickname sent shivers of excitement through Elfriede's body. In a moment of boldness, she pressed her lips against his Royce's mouth.

His body tensed against her. A wave of doubt surged. *Was this the right thing to do?* she wondered.

Royce's arms tightened around her waist, pulling Elfriede closer to his body. He returned the kiss, his passion growing to match hers. He opened his mouth and slipped his tongue out to meet her lips. Elfriede gave him access. She savored the feel of his tongue against hers.

Elfriede's body pressed harder against his. Royce's heart beat against her chest. Her hands moved up to his head and she ran her fingers through his soft hair, marveling at how her fantasies paled in comparison to the reality.

The feeling of Elf's soft lips against his own lingered long after the kiss. Royce followed her into the store, dazed. He'd never been kissed like that before. Only in his dreams had Royce ever reacted so heatedly to her before. His mind was awhirl with emotions. Feelings of loss blended with the lust Elf's boots and kiss rekindled in him. And there was something else, a tingling Royce didn't recognize. He pushed it out of his mind.

"I'm so sorry about your father." Elfriede took Royce's hand and squeezed it. The heat of her skin against his increased his heartbeat.

"Thank you. How did you hear about it?"

A look of sadness passed over her face. "I was the one who found him. In the back." She nodded to a door.

The door Elf indicated led to the workroom. He had spent many hours there learning the art of cobbling. His eyes watered unexpectedly. "Would you tell me about it?"

"Are you sure?" He nodded. "As I was opening the store for business, I noticed light shining from underneath the door." Elf's voice quivered. "When I went to shut it off, I found him lying over his workbench." A tear rolled down her cheek.

Royce squeezed her hand. "You still work here?" He paused. "Sorry, that was a stupid question. Obviously you still work here. You came out of the store to greet me."

He looked at her under the bright store lights. With the shock of her kiss wearing off, Royce could see Elf more clearly. She hadn't changed at all in the 15 years he knew her, and still seemed to be in her 20s instead of her 30s. Royce blushed, thinking of how she starred in all his most vivid erotic dreams after his last visit.

Elf was five and a half feet tall to his six feet. Her curvy and willowy frame reminding him of a sexy Tinkerbelle. No wonder his nickname for her always seemed right. Looking into her violet eyes caused Royce to forget why he was at the store. There was fierce emotion in her gaze.

He vividly remembered working the counter, cashing out old lady Schwartz, when Elf glided into the store. She had smiled sweetly at him as she moved about the aisles inspecting shoes. Something in that look, and her appearance, triggered puberty. Royce couldn't take his eyes off her, and had to ring up the customer's purchases three times because he couldn't pay attention to what he was doing.

"What are you smiling at, Royce?"

"Huh?" He flushed with embarrassment at being caught daydreaming. "Oh, nothing. I was thinking about the first time I met you and how stunning you looked."

"Am I still stunning?" Coyness filled her voice as she batted her eyes.

Royce's face grew warm. "Yes."

It was Elfriede's turn to blush. "Why thank you, Royce. I didn't think you noticed."

"How could I not, especially with those boots you're wearing? You've got the most amazing pair of legs I've ever seen, Elf, and those boots really show them off. Where did you get them, anyway? I've never seen another pair like them."

"And you won't." Royce heard unmistakable pride in her voice. "I made them myself."

"Really?"

"Entirely."

"May I take a closer look?"

Face beaming, Elf lithely jumped up and sat on the counter. Extending her leg, she placed the sole of her foot against Royce's chest. Her spiked heel pressed on his heart.

Royce felt electricity begin where the boot made contact with him. The pinpoint of pressure from the heel alone made him momentarily forget what he was doing. He cupped the offered leg just behind the calf, his fingers touching the nude nylon stocking and the boot's soft leather upper. The combination of the two sensations further excited him.

Royce bent his head to examine Elf's boot more closely. "Very nice work, Elf. The embroidering is exquisite." He ran his fingers over the bright red thread, creating a mystical serpentine design. He was surprised by his boldness.

Royce felt Elf's calf tighten as he caressed the design. He heard her sharp intake of breath, and noticed her body shift on the counter. Glancing up without lifting his head, he watched Elf's tongue slide over her lips. The sight sent a surge of blood to his crotch, causing Royce's cock to throb. He slid his hand slowly up Elf's calf, cupping her behind her knee. She moaned.

"Yes," Elf whispered. "Yes, Royce."

He inched his hand further up to her inner thigh. The erotic texture of the stocking disappeared as his fingertips discovered bare flesh: Thigh-high stockings. Royce's heart felt like a sledgehammer being driven against his chest. Straightening up, he leaned in and pressed his lips to hers. Elf threw her arms around him, returning the kiss.

Oh yes, Elfriede thought with joy at the pressure of Royce's lips on hers. Her skin grew warmer as blood flowed faster. Where his hand was, flesh tingled. She could feel the warmth of him. It spread into her and straight to her pussy. Elfriede had longed to feel his hands all over her. She licked her lips and closed her eyes. Shifting her hips, she spread her legs a little bit, hoping he would notice the crotchless panties she wore.

Juices seeped out from between her thighs as Elfriede arched her back. The simple touch of Royce's hand on her thigh drove her nearly to the brink of an orgasm. Now that he had finally stepped forward and kissed her, she wasn't about to let him go.

Her legs wrapped around him and pulled him closer until there was no space at all between them. Elfriede's feet locked together, preventing any chance of Royce's escape. Her mouth opened. Royce responded to her clear invitation. Their tongues danced as his hand moved under her skirt, to her panties. As his fingers caressed the fabric, her dampness increased. She ground her mouth against Royce's and sighed. The sound became a moan of pleasure as his finger found the slit in her lingerie. Elfriede broke the kiss and arched her back.

"Oh Royce, you have no idea how long I've wanted you to touch me like this." Even through the haze of her pending climax, surprise at her unexpected confession was clear on his face.

"I had no idea, Elf." His finger pushed deeper into her. She tightened her muscles and closed her eyes. "But I can tell from how wet you are."

"Do you like it?" She released her hold on Royce and leaned backward, placing her palms on the counter. She gasped as another finger joined the first.

"Yes, very much."

Elfriede opened her eyes when Royce's body shifted. He slowly lowered himself between her legs. His hands pushed her legs apart. Elfriede's heart raced. He grabbed her buttocks and pulled her to the counter's edge. His breath was hot on her inner thighs. When Royce's lips lightly touched her skin around her panties, she gasped.

Royce flicked his tongue out, parting the crotchless panties just enough to make contact with Elfriede's engorged flesh. She grabbed his hair and pulled his head firmly into her.

Royce responded with more confident licks. He moved up over the opening and the hardened nub of her clit, circling the receptive protuberance. Elf ground her ass onto the counter and her hips against his mouth. "Oh God, Royce," she said as waves of pleasure coursed through her. "You're mouth feels fantastic there."

"You taste incredible, Elf." His voice was muffled against her, his lips' movement sending sensuous vibrations against her tender flesh. Elfriede's climax neared. As Royce's tongue dove between her swollen lips into her pussy, the first wave of pleasure hit her.

Royce's hands clutched Elfriede's ass as he sensed her first orgasm begin. She pressed herself forward against his mouth. Her wetness flowed out and filled his mouth. He couldn't take it all in, though he longed to. The thought of drowning in her occurred to him, and he smiled as he continued ministering to the woman who had seduced him so easily.

Elfriede gripped Royce more firmly with her thighs. Boot heels ground into his back. Their sharpness was exquisite, and he drove himself to lick her more slowly to prolong their placement there. He moved his tongue along her pussy in wide, flat strokes. He lingered at the beginning and end of each lick, savoring the taste of flesh and cum mixing in his mouth.

Royce could tell another orgasm was growing as the heels of Elfriede's boots bit deeper into him. He groaned in agonized pleasure. Moving his mouth, he concentrated his activity once more on her clit. As he swirled his tongue over it, he slipped two fingers inside and caressed Elfriede's inflamed inner walls. Within moments she climaxed again. Royce took her into his mouth once more.

"Royce," she moaned, "I want you in me. I want to feel you deep inside me."

"I would love to be inside you, my Elf," he said, looking up at her. Seeing her through new eyes, she appeared even more beautiful than before. "But I don't have a condom with me."

She pouted. "Clearly you were never a Boy Scout."

"You know very well I wasn't." He smiled and shook his head as he stood up. "But I promise I will be prepared next time."

"You think there's going to be a next time?"

Royce looked at her, trying to judge if Elfriede was playing with him or seriously suggesting he may have just missed his chance to have more of her. He caught the briefest mischievous twinkle in her eyes and decided a little boldness would go a long way. "Yes, there will be a next time," he responded with confidence. "I'm going to be in town for a while. I need to see what state the business is in."

Elfriede smiled. None of Royce's previous girlfriends displayed such joy for him, unless it was about what he could buy or do for them. He was tired of the selfish, self-centered women he dated; and had been without a girlfriend for a while because of this.

"How about dinner to—?"

"Yes," she interrupted. "Better yet, why don't you let me make you dinner? I'll make your favorite."

Elf made a wonderful dinner, but it sat like lead in Royce's stomach as he finished reviewing the business balance sheets.

"Oh, Papa," he groaned, "why didn't you tell me things were so bad?" Royce rubbed his eyes, trying to erase the numbers he had just seen from his memory.

Because you didn't care, responded the part of his brain he never liked listening to. It was the part that forced Royce to look seriously at the man he was. "I never cared about this business," he admitted, looking at the computer screen once more. "Ten stores closed. And the remaining five are in the process of closing. No wonder he dropped dead."

What do you care? the annoying voice asked. *There's no money in shoe stores, remember? The big money is in the stock market and bond-trading. Or anyplace else but here in this old, useless place.*

Royce pounded his hand on the desk. Those had been the words he spat at his father after finishing school. They stung Royce deeply now. He realized just how they must have hurt his father.

"What's wrong, Royce?" Elfriede asked.

"Elf, did you know my father closed ten stores, and was in the planning stages of closing the rest?"

"Yes." She and his father knew that without Royce to carry things on there was no chance. Elfriede understood that only with a Schumacher at the helm would the business continue, and had turned down his father's offer to take over the business. She hoped Royce would come back and embrace his legacy. And here he was; but Elfriede didn't know if he was ready to be the Schumacher he was born to be. *I pray he is, or else I will have failed the family after all these years.* She took his hand and squeezed it.

"I should have paid more attention to what was going on with him and the business instead of acting like a selfish brat," Royce said. "I was too caught up in my own life to care about this. I rarely talked to him, and when I did, it was all about me and my success. When I asked how my dad was, I never really heard any of his responses."

"I am here to help, Royce. I have always been here for you and your family. Is there anything I can do?"

"I don't know. Sales are down so much because of the economy. There's a fifteen-hundred dollar loan payment coming up at the end of the week. And if it isn't made, which at the moment I can't see how it *can* be, the bank will start foreclosure proceedings."

Elfriede kissed Royce's hand. Her heart ached for him. "You're a brilliant businessman, and a Schumacher," she said, standing and pulling Royce to her. She sat with him on his father's office sofa. "I know you'll figure out the answer. Once you put your mind to it, you'll discover a way to save Schumacher and Son."

"*And* Son." She heard derision and self-flagellation heavy in those two words. "That's such a joke."

"It doesn't have to be," she offered, snuggling in close to Royce on the couch. She wrapped her arms around him and laid her head on his chest. His powerful heart beat in her ear. "You can make it be what it once was. You're a descendant of the world-famous Schumachers. Your family has been making and selling shoes for centuries. There are fairy tales told about them."

For the first time since learning about the financial state of his family's business, Royce found himself feeling calmer with Elf lying against him. His mind cleared. Thoughts were no longer a chaotic miasma inside his skull. With clarity came the ability to lock on to something. He sat up straight and looked squarely at Elfriede.

"What did you just say, Elfri . . ." His voice trailed off as his brain put together a plan of action. He chuckled. "Elf, that's it. Isn't it? You're the elf." Elfriede's eyes widened. "Just like in the old fairy tale. I'm the shoemaker and you're the elf." He let out a hearty laugh.

He could see surprise and uncertainty in her face. He didn't care. The answer had come to him: Elfriede was the key to saving the family business. Royce was too giddy to stay seated any longer. Energy unlike any he had felt in years coursed through him. He looked down at Elfriede's boots.

"Elf, how many designs do you have?"

"What? What designs?"

"Boot designs. How many boot designs do you have?"

"I don't know." She shrugged. "I guess perhaps about two dozen."

"That's a great start." Royce pulled Elfriede up from the couch and into his arms. He swung her in a circle, kissed her passionately, set her down and slipped his coat on.

"Where are you going?"

"I'm running out to get condoms. We are going to celebrate!"

Elfriede was still sitting on the couch when Royce came back, holding a sketchpad and wearing nothing but her boots. "I don't want to disrupt your muse, if you're busy," he said.

"You *are* my muse, Royce," she said, putting down the drawing and reaching for him.

Royce's cock reacted immediately. The pressure against his zipper was excruciating. He went to her, dropping the bag with his purchase and his coat to the floor, and kissed her. Energy flowed from their lips through Royce's body. His cock hardened more, and he moaned with desire. Elfriede's hands went to his hair once again, her nails biting deliciously into his skull as she forced his mouth tighter against hers.

Royce found himself roasting inside his clothes and struggled to get out of them without breaking the kiss. Elfriede released his head, but not his mouth, and helped him undress. As he pulled his arms free from his shirt, her hands went to his belt. She grunted with frustration until her fingers opened his pants and zipper.

He sighed with pleasure at the easing of pressure against his cock. Elf slipped her hand inside his pants, rubbing his throbbing appendage. The feel of her touch sent his heart racing.

"I've waited too long to feel you inside me," Elfriede gasped. She lay back on the sofa, spreading her legs apart for him. "Make love to me, my shoemaker."

"With pleasure, my Elf." Royce removed the last of his clothes and put on a condom.

He paused to look at her. She was staring at him with passion and flushed with anticipation, her eyes locked on his cock. Royce could feel that her desire for him was beyond lust, and so different from what he had shared with other women.

He lowered himself to her, her arms enfolding him again. He kissed her, tenderly this time. Royce's hands moved down Elfriede's sides, reveling in the feel of her warm, soft skin. She moaned at his touch and squirmed beneath him as he brushed the tip of his cock against her pussy.

"Please, Royce," she begged.

"Soon, my Elf." He moved his mouth to her jaw line and continued kissing her. His hands slipped to her buttocks and squeezed them.

"Oh, yes," Elf moaned in response. "More."

Responding to the pleading tone in her voice, he thrust himself into her whispering in her ear, "As you wish, my love."

The sensation of Royce's thick cock driving into her, combined with his whispered endearment, sent Elfriede reeling to the brink of her orgasm. She wrapped her legs around him as the first wave of it struck. "Royce!" she cried. Elfriede clung to him as her body spasmed.

She couldn't prevent a second orgasm from building, even before the first fully subsided, as Royce continued sliding back and forth in her pussy.

"Yes, Royce," Elfriede moaned as he buried himself in her, keeping a slow and steady pace. His hands squeezed her ass tighter, lifting her off the sofa. The new angle allowed him deeper penetration. Her mounting orgasm grew stronger.

"Come with me, my love."

"Yes, Elf," Royce panted. He increased his rhythm, driving himself harder into her.

"Oh, Royce. Yes. Yes" Elfriede tightened her muscles around his shaft and her legs around his waist, digging her nails into his shoulders as she peaked.

"Elf, oh God!" Royce drove himself powerfully into her one last time as his own orgasm took hold. Back arched, eyes closed, he came inside of her. Elf contracted and eased her pussy muscles, milking his cock until Royce was spent.

Royce realized, for the first time in years, he was happy where he was. He didn't want to rush off or dismiss his lover, nor did he have any regrets. For Elf, he wanted to be a hero. For her, he knew he could be so much more than just another greed-monger on Wall Street. With her, he would be able to keep the family business going; and take it to a level his father had never dreamed possible.

"I adore you, Elf," Royce said leaning down and kissing her softly. "You've given me something I can hardly describe, but I have a feeling I am going to enjoy showing you."

Elfriede and Royce over the course of the next week created two pairs of boots for each of Elfriede's designs. They barely slept, and ate hurriedly to concentrate on the task at hand—and to make love as often as possible.

Royce's vision drove them forward. He knew the designs were great. Even though he hadn't worked with shoes for years, he was a born Schumacher. If he could get those drawings made, they would sell, no matter what the price. He'd liquidate personal stock to make the upcoming loan payment. It would be worth it.

He was energized in a way entirely different from Wall Street. Crafting shoes with high-quality leather was exhilarating. He'd long forgotten the joy of cobbling pieces together, creating something from nothing. And working closely with Elfriede, connecting intimately with her, was more than he had imagined possible.

Elfriede Diefee was enraptured to be working side by side with the man she had loved since first walking into Schumacher and Son. Royce's skill and natural talent amazed her. Of course, she shouldn't have been so surprised. She knew all too well the talent within his family line. Elfriede had been watching over the Schumacher family for nearly 600 years—ever since the old cobbler and his wife gave her a cute little set of clothes as repayment for making the shoes he'd been too tired to complete.

Just like then, she knew the boots they were making together would sell. Those sales would re-establish the Schumachers once again as the greatest shoemakers in the world.

Sometimes it just takes an elf to lend a helping hand, she thought. She looked up from the leather she cut and smiled at Royce. The mere sight of him, so intent upon making what she designed, made Elfriede's body tingle with wanton energy. *We'll get to work on creating the next Schumacher line very soon. After all, how can it be Schumacher and Son without a son?*

Frog

By Suzanne Elizabeth

Trudging down brick-paved Charles Street, Cassandra pulled her warm jacket tighter around her and stuffed her hands into her pockets. The icy fingers of early March wormed their way into her collar and sent shivers down her spine. Hurrying toward the Boston Common Garden, she thought it might be too cold to sketch outside. Full of activity, the Commons, as it was known, was great for people-watching, swan boats, and bridge views; but Cassandra's favorite was the frog pond, where children splashed around on hot steamy days and everyone ice-skated in winter.

Walking purposefully toward the bridge, Cassandra took the steps two at a time. She looked around at the top and breathed in deeply, enjoying the crisp cold as it tunneled through her nose like menthol. With both arms resting on the railing, Cassandra looked out at the surrounding area and watched a couple fighting. Her heart tightened in sympathy. She remembered how horrible it was when she broke up with Mark. *Love sucks*, she thought, *but unrequited love is worse.* Never again would she give her body or her heart without knowing how the other person felt.

Cassandra leaned further over the bridge and watched her reflection in the water. The pond had thawed slightly to reveal deep circles of murky green. She absentmindedly tucked her long, mocha-colored hair behind one ear. Cassandra's treasured heart-shaped locket, which had swung out from her neck, snagged on her fingers. The clasp broke. The momentum of the necklace zinged down and Cassandra gasped in horror as she watched her Grandmother's legacy shoot straight into the water.

"Noni!" she shrieked, and bolted to the end of the bridge. "Help," she called out, racing down the steps and kicking off her boots, ripping off her jacket, and lunging to the border of the pond. Cassandra paused, then plunged knee-deep into the numbing cold water and gasped, stunned by the immediacy of sub-zero pain.

A strong voice stopped her, "Take another step and we'll be fishing the pond for your body." At her stubborn silence he added, "There's a drop-off to your right that would send you into hypothermia."

"But my necklace," she stuttered as tears welled up in her eyes. Cassandra took another dangerous step forward. Her body went rigid. She couldn't feel her feet or legs. Two hands grabbed her from behind and yanked her up and out. Cassandra struggled as the man walked away from the pond, cradling her in his arms and placing her gently under a tree. "You don't understand!" she sobbed at the sharp bitter memory of Noni gifting her that locket on her ninth birthday. She shivered uncontrollably as cold and despair overwhelmed her.

"If it means that much to you, I might be able to help but . . ."

Teeth chattering, eyes wet with tears she begged "Please," clutching the stranger's shirt "I'll pay a reward. It was my grandmother's and it's worth everything to me."

The electric shock of 'Colpo di fulmine', the thunderbolt of love, brought Jason to his knees beside her. *My God*, he thought, *this is what it feels like*. In one instant his world was changed. His hand went out to comfort her, but he snatched it back when he saw how deformed it appeared. *And so*, he thought, *it begins*.

Jason's voice thickened. "If you want the necklace, you'll have to promise me something," he said slowly. "Something unusual and you may not like it."

"Anything! Anything at all, I swear, just please find it." Cassandra wiped her eyes and watched the man walk over to a large duffle, zip it open, and start to undress right there on the green. Through a wet haze she stared while he stripped down to clingy boxer shorts and pulled on a sleek, black wetsuit.

His body shimmered. Cassandra shook her head to clear the vision. Without tears clouding her sight, he suddenly looked lumpy with a greenish cast to his skin. Disheartened, she looked away, thinking he wouldn't have a chance of finding her necklace.

"My name's Jason," he said, placing Cassandra's jacket

over her hunched shoulders and handing her the boots. "What's yours?"

"Cassandra Wellesley," she responded, and glanced up into gray eyes slightly obscured by a scuba facemask.

"Where do you live?" he prodded.

"Two seventy-four Cambridge Street," she said automatically. "Do you always carry around scuba gear?"

Jason's eyes crinkled at the corners, "Only when I'm rescuing damsels in distress." He walked to the water's edge, slipped on his flippers, and plunged in.

Curious onlookers gathered and created a loose crowd on either side of Cassandra. She could see two policemen heading her way, and hoped Jason wouldn't get into trouble. The crowd began to whisper, concern growing louder as the seconds ticked by.

A stocky policeman approached her, "What's going on here, Miss?"

Suddenly Jason rose up from the depths and came toward them dripping stringy, green slime, looking classically like the creature from the black lagoon. *Ugh*, Cassandra thought.

The policeman relaxed. "Hey, Frog Man, little early to be dredging the pond." He turned to the crowd. "All right, folks, just the parks department taking care of clean-up. Move along." He and his partner strolled off with the dispersing crowd.

Jason slowly approached, stripping off his face mask and head gear. Cassandra shuddered. The cop had called it right: Jason looked exactly like a frog except, she noticed, for his expressive smoky-gray eyes. Everything else about his looks repelled her. She turned away mumbling, "Thank you for trying."

"Are you a woman of your word?" he asked harshly.

"Wha . . . what?" She looked back to him. "Are you saying . . .?" Sudden hope flared in her breast.

"You *did* say you'd do anything for your necklace, didn't you?" he demanded.

"Yes!" she repeated. He held out his soggy hand and dropped the necklace into her outstretched palm. Joyfully she whispered, "Thanks, I owe you," and kissed the locket.

Jason's lips burned. He fervently wished he could be that small piece of metal. He tore his gaze away from her sweet curving lips and the gentle hollow of her cheek, and tried to control himself. A wrong move from him now would send Cassandra screaming.

She got up and shrugged into her coat. "My father will be more than happy to give you payment for—"

"I don't want money," Jason said, walking over to his bag and starting to strip.

She followed him. "Fine. I have lots of other jewelry."

"I don't want your jewelry, either." He toweled off his chest, slipped on a hooded sweatshirt, and peeled off the rest of the wet suit.

Cassandra turned away as he pulled on his jeans. There was something about his voice that excited her; but when she looked at him straight on, he was repulsive. Frustrated but determined to keep her word she said, "Fine. What do you want?"

Jason stared at her. She felt a chill. His reptilian features unnerved her.

"I want you to get to know me. I want to take you to dinner and," he took a deep breath, "I need to lie beside you in bed."

Relaxing, Cassandra laughed and looked around, expecting to see some film crew peeping out from the dead bushes surrounding the pond. They were alone. She slowly turned back to face him. *He's serious, and I've already given him my address!* And her promise. *Why don't I just log onto a message board and post a blog for psychos seeking gullible women?*

"I'll pick you up at eight for dinner," Jason said. Seeing Cassandra's stricken expression, he added, "Remember, I said lie beside you, nothing else."

"How . . . reassuring. But I—I'm not free tonight," she said darting around him. "Sorry." Cassandra dashed away.

At seven that night, she grabbed her overnight bag and ran downstairs to the cab she called. Cassandra came to a halt when she saw Jason calmly standing outside.

"I . . . I told you I was busy."

He opened the taxi door and as she nervously got in, he said, "You gave your word. Dinner won't be all that horrible. I'm quite amusing if you get to know me. I swear, you won't have to see me after my requests are met."

"I can't," Cassandra said. She jerked the door closed, and gave the driver her friend Holly's address. As the cab pulled away, it stopped almost immediately at a red light. She saw three teenage kids walk past punching each other. One of them saw Jason and called out, "Hey, Frog Head, which one are you? Leonardo, Michelangelo, Donatello, or Raphael?" They cracked up. Cassandra's cheeks burned. *I'm no better*, she thought.

As the cab continued down the street, Cassandra wondered if Jason's demands were some sort of bet. "I need to lie beside you" he said. *Need, not want. Maybe*, she gulped, *he is going to die and wants someone to actually get to know him before he croaks*. She winced at the expression. Noni's voice drifted into her mind, "Never give your word before you think out the consequences." *Sure*, Cassandra thought, *couldn't you have thought of that a little earlier!* She sat back in the cab feeling unfairly burdened with guilt.

Later that night, Cassandra slept on Holly's sofa and slipped into a vivid dream. Lying face-down, she felt the pressure of an erect penis pressed against her ass. Someone was kissing the back of her neck, sending shock waves of pleasure through her body. His strong arms wrapped around her, lifting her slightly as hands alternately massaged and tweaked her nipples so they stood up taut and tight, aching for his lips and tongue. Pinned to the bed, Cassandra's hands dug into the sheets and she arched against him. His hot skin drove her deeper into the mattress and she felt the tip of his penis wet with desire. She groaned as he kissed and gently rubbed his stubbled chin down her back, leaving a tingling rainbow of red stripes in its path. His hands moved with him and found her lips: Hot, moist and ready. He opened them, finding her bud, stiff with arousal. Cassandra gasped. He inserted one, then two fingers inside her, and her body shivered with urgency. She squeezed her eyes shut. He flipped her over and pulled her legs apart. The flat tip of his cock pressed against her entrance, poised like a kiss, ready to ram itself straight into her. As his large hands grabbed her waist, she opened her eyes and saw Jason.

Cassandra screamed and bolted upright, shaking from the images she could still see in her mind. "What the hell," she gasped.

She flung herself out of bed and padded to Holly's bathroom. Cassandra stripped off her nightshirt and stepped into the shower. A cascade of warm water flowed over her body. It wasn't helping fast enough. She knew of one way to dampen the fires that continued to torment her.

Cassandra took down the handle of the water massage, adjusted the pulsating rhythm of the water, and leaned against the cold white tile. With her free hand she separated her tender lips to expose her blood-engorged clitoris, and aimed the jettison of water. Cassandra closed her eyes and tried only to think of her pleasure, allowing the water to vibrate against her slit. Her thighs and buttocks clenched and let to bring the heat between her legs to a sharp aching demand. She stiffened and shuddered as the waves of release rolled through her, leaving a faint reminder of the caresses from her dream and a look of passion from a pair of gray eyes.

Arriving home from Holly's, Cassandra wasn't surprised to find Jason standing beside her door. She felt her nipples harden with the memory of desire, sending pink to her cheeks. Annoyed at her body's continual betrayal, Cassandra stalked over. Jason kept his face averted.

"If you need someone to hang with," she said, "why don't you just call up one of those, um, special services that provide companionship?"

"I can't," he said dully, then looked at her. "Perhaps if you just got to know me."

There was something about the expression in his eyes that made Cassandra think of a trapped animal. His horrible features seemed to build the longer she stared so she flicked her eyes away. A vague masculine outline shimmered at his core, but when she turned to face him, the repulsive frog image leaped into view, and, much as she tried, she couldn't stop the shudder.

"Look," she said. "For a class project I have to go to the Isabella Stewart Gardener Museum and sketch her portrait. You can come along if you want."

Jason sat beside Cassandra on a long bench, watching her fingers move expertly over the page. Her upturned bee-stung lips gave him physical pain to look at when it registered distaste; but when her toffee-colored eyes were kind, he allowed himself hope. The side of Cassandra's palm and tips of her fingers were black from smudging harsh pencil lines as she worked. Jason wanted to kiss those fingers. He wanted to kiss the nape of her neck and the swell of her throat. He shifted, trying to distract himself, and concentrated on her drawing.

A young couple sauntered past, unable to take their eyes off Jason. They nudged each other and snickered between them. The woman let out a squeal of laughter when her companion nuzzled her neck and whispered "ribbit, ribbit." The pair darted out of the quiet room, laughing loudly.

"That happen to you a lot?" Cassandra asked, keeping her eyes glued to her drawing.

"I've gotten used to it," Jason admitted.

"It's odd how people's natural kindness vanishes when they see you. It's as if your strange appearance reaches out and touches their soul, awakening whatever ugliness was hidden there. I guess you get to see the truth in people, whether you want to or not."

It wasn't something Jason had ever thought of before. He didn't know how to respond. He stood up as Cassandra put away pencils and folded her pad into her backpack. "Would you like to have high tea?" he asked. "The museum does it right. Small finger sandwiches, chocolate truffles—"

"No, thanks," she said, watching his shoulders sag, "but a nice dinner somewhere in the North End would be okay." Cassandra quickly looked away.

They were both glad they had been seated at a booth in the back, safe from prying eyes. The heady aroma of garlic, oregano and tomato sauce permeated the air of Mama Maria's, an upscale Italian restaurant sparkling with candlelight and fine crystal.

During the course of the meal, Cassandra discovered she and Jason had more in common than she would have guessed. He was involved in several causes that promoted Greenpeace, was well read, and loved art. She'd confessed how she always wanted to study art abroad and volunteered at an animal shelter twice a week.

The conversation flowed as smoothly as the mellow cabernet sauvignon he'd ordered. It was an odd request, but he insisted they share each dish, including the entrees, which was fine with Cassandra. She loved variety. And if she didn't linger more than a few seconds on his face, she could listen to the lush tone of Jason's voice with pleasure. The sound sent a responsive thrill down her body. She realized with satisfaction that the dinner would fulfill two-thirds of her promise.

Cassandra never thought she'd be able to eat so much, but everything smelled and tasted delicious. The roasted fennel and scallop soup, creamy fresh buffalo mozzarella, spicy arugula with smoked bacon, and aged goat cheese were only the beginning. The leisurely pace of the meal blended beautifully with the conversation and when their entrees came two hours after they'd started, she tucked into the tender pumpkin ravioli, with gusto. At the end of the meal they sat back and sighed, too stuffed to think of dessert.

Cassandra was twirling her wine glass, feeling mellow and contemplating having another, when she sensed Jason stiffen and looked up. There, beside their table, stood the most beautiful woman she'd ever seen. Her black, shining hair waved down her back, her eyes sparkled green, and she had red ruby lips anyone would envy.

The woman stared at Jason, a thin smile pressed into her lips. "Hello, Frog."

"Cassandra, I'd like to introduce you to my twin sister, Flea," he said curtly. There was no warmth in his voice.

"Alfia, darling," she hissed, and turned her sharp gaze on Cassandra.

Cassandra smiled, extending her hand, "Nice to meet you, Alfia." On contact, she yanked it away from the cold, corpse-like grip and shuddered as Flea's gorgeous hair shimmered before her. Its glossiness seemed to turn oily and the tendrils twirled and undulated like a writhing pack of eels ready to strike. Cassandra blinked and the image returned to normal. Alfia's eyes narrowed into slits as she watched Cassandra grab her wine glass and take the last sip with shaking fingers. *I may not be comfortable with how Jason looks*, she thought, *but it is certainly better than how this woman makes me feel.*

How ironic, Jason thought. Before Flea had dabbled in witchcraft and cast this curse, he used his charm and charisma to bed countless women. But in all that time he had never lost his heart. He remembered how unfortunate it was that as handsome as he had been, his twin had grown up ugly. Full of bitter venom, she accused him of stealing all her beauty and nurtured one burning desire: To make him feel her pain.

Jason was now a condemned outsider, repellant to all who looked upon him, unable to break the curse—until he fell in love. He had to give Flea credit for being creative, and clenched his jaw when he remembered the last codicil.

"Your love alone will not be enough, brother. You must convince your loved one to share everything: Food, thoughts, desires, and," she'd said with glee, "although you will be unable to explain why, you must also share her bed!" She'd laughed a hysterical, insane laugh, which chilled him even now to remember it.

Jason resolved to ensure Flea didn't find out he'd fallen in love. She would do anything to keep the curse intact, including ensuring Cassandra's death by morning. He groaned inwardly, knowing what he would have to do next.

"Would you like to join us for a drink?" he asked, signaling the waiter.

Alfia's suspicious eyes raked over his face before she slipped into the booth beside Cassandra. "How kind," she cooed.

Cassandra, engulfed by her cloying perfume, gagged, and reconsidered another drink.

"Cassandra," Alfia started conversationally as the waiter brought her a glass. Jason poured the wine. "Did you know that Frog was once voted mostly likely to succeed by his class at Princeton? *Now* look at him." She patted his head. "He's all alone, and working as a park maintenance man."

"The outdoors and solitude suit me," he countered defensively.

Alfia smirked then turned on Cassandra maliciously. "And who, exactly, are you?" she asked, taking a deep drink of wine and licking her lips with predatory focus.

Cassandra froze, unable to answer as those green eyes skewered every nerve ending in her body. Jason's lazy reply took Flea's intense glare off of her. "Just the sister of an old college friend. I guilted her into dining with me while she's in town," he added glibly.

Cassandra shot him a grateful glance and looked away. She could feel the animosity between them, but couldn't figure out why it seemed more hers than his. Alfia was as magnificently beautiful as he was repulsive. *Why does she seem jealous?* Cassandra wondered. *What could she possibly resent him for?*

"Flea," Jason said politely, "we'd like to be alone to catch up."

A wrinkle of worry wedged itself between Alfia's perfectly plucked brows. She slowly stood up, never taking her eyes off him. "*All* elements must be in place," she spat cryptically.

Cassandra was glad to see her go.

Watching her retreating back, Jason knew he had only a small window of time before Alfia guessed how close he was to having the elements in place. When he looked across at Cassandra, who seemed lost in her own thoughts, he was overwhelmed with longing. The sexual need for her pulsed strongly within him, but the overpowering urge to protect won out. *Although*, he thought, *if I spend the night with her, I will be more able to protect her.*

Jason comforted himself with the knowledge that if he were successful, the power of the curse would reverse multiplied tenfold, and Alfia would be rendered harmless. *But how could this work with someone who can't even look at me?* He knew if he didn't move quickly, before he got Cassandra to agree to sleep beside him, Flea would come for her like the relentless nightmare she was. He would have to take some risks.

"Home sweet home," Cassandra said nervously as she walked out of her bedroom with blanket and pillow, plopping them down on the couch beside Jason. Oddly enough, because of the strange interaction between the twins, she had told Jason he could stay the night. She hoped this would take care of the last third of her promise. Keeping her eyes averted, she continued to focus on his voice and forget what he looked like.

"I need to lie beside you," he gently reminded her.

"Why?" she asked for the tenth time.

"I can't . . ." Jason stuttered, frustrated that he couldn't answer. He was close to shattering the curse and disabling Flea, but had to make a decision fast. "Would you like me to leave?" The softening of her rigid shoulders and relieved expression told him what he needed to know. He got up from the couch. "Thank you for a lovely evening."

So, he thought, *this is what love is. It demands sacrifice even to one's own detriment.* As he walked to the door, he looked in the mirror hanging beside it and saw his ghost-like image imprinted beneath his froggy face and body. Dark blonde hair, gray eyes and aquiline nose blurred a few times, then came into focus. *I need to escape.* Watching Cassandra shrink away from him was like a physical blow. But more important, Alfia could never suspect how close Jason had come to ending the curse

Cassandra felt a wave of emotion assault her as he opened the door. *He is willing to put my comfort before any promise I made.* Something in her shifted. "Wait," she said. "I have an idea." She felt compelled to allow this intimacy. Cassandra spread a comforter out on the floor. "If it means that much to you, can we lay together, in the living room watching TV?" Nervously she cleared her throat, "Would that fulfill your request? It's not my bed but I fall asleep out here sometimes."

Jason's eyes narrowed as he thought about it. He must have decided her suggestion was acceptable: He abruptly beamed a radiant, dazzling smile of joy.

Cassandra sucked in her breath. *I must be lightheaded from the wine*, she thought. She could have sworn she saw Jason morph into the most handsome man she had ever seen. Noni used to tell her that the good in people shone through. Cassandra shut off the lights so they could see the television more clearly. As they traded comments on the show they watched, she forgot about his looks and was lulled by the beautiful sound of his voice. It caressed her more lovingly then some men's hands. She moved closer to him, putting her head on his shoulder as she drifted to sleep. She felt comfortable and happy with him.

From nowhere, a cloying sweet perfume enveloped her. Cassandra coughed violently. Opening her eyes, she stared at a greenish, lumpy reptilian. *What the . . . ?*

A swirling vortex of wind plumed straight up inside her living room. Stunned, Cassandra sat up and watched the whirling configuration. A screech of outrage shot out from the funnel and Alfia's face wavered inside it. Her green eyes spit sparks of fury as she saw them together, and then blackened to orbs of obsidian. She let out a bark of laughter, "You pathetic little toad. That won't work."

"I love her, Flea," Jason said tightly. Cassandra gasped beside him.

Alfia looked startled, then slowly turned her glittering hate on Cassandra. Protectively, Jason shielded her with his body. "I'll leave and never see her again if you don't hurt her."

That's when it all fell into place for Cassandra. She couldn't believe how blind she had been. Perhaps it was her old fear of getting hurt that prevented her from noticing what was truly in front of her the whole time. Now she could see clearly.

The wind whipped around her as she grabbed for him. The fearful face of Alfia looked from Jason to her. "No!"

Cassandra dove into Jason's arms and raised her face to his. "Kiss me! Kiss me now!"

He pulled her to his chest, encircling her with arms no longer short and misshapen, but muscled and strong. He kissed her. Cassandra felt all the pent-up passion he had been hiding. Jason's lips hungrily found hers. She shivered with arousal and kissed him back.

Her eyes opened and watched as the visage of frog was yanked with tremendous force into the vortex. Alfia shrieked as the two images circled, picked up speed, then tore through the window, splintering glass and wood. A scream of violent rage howled outside the building. Moaning and squeals of pain filled the room, then faded to a final croak of despair as it dragged itself away.

Jason kissed Cassandra tenderly, then more urgently, demanding her willing response. His gray eyes bore into hers. As she took a deep breath, she noticed Jason's hair and skin smelled deliciously like clean linen, fresh air and sunshine. She stroked his chin, raspy with stubble. *He is magnificent*, she thought. *And he loves me*. She was overwhelmed with emotion.

He picked her up, walked to her bedroom door, and kicked it open. Their hungry mouths kissed deep with longing and Cassandra felt her body flush with desire. Jason drew back, his gray eyes darkly hooded with yearning, and put her down. She felt his hardness pressing against her. "Tell me what you want," he said. "I won't do anything you don't—"

Cassandra led Jason to her bed, stripping off clothes as she went. "I dreamed about us once," she admitted. "I'd like to be awake this time." She smiled and helped rip off his clothes.

Jason wanted to be inside her, to feel and watch her explode with passion. He stroked her neck and breasts, and watched Cassandra's eyes squeeze to tiny slits of pleasure. Her nipples stood up and his hands slid down, finding her slick with longing. She put her hands out and grasped Jason's shaft. He groaned. One hand stayed on her pussy, manipulating her clit, and his other pulled her to him. His warm, wet mouth closed down on a rigid nipple. Cassandra groaned, grinding her hips into his hand. Her own hands were busy as she cradled his sac and slowly massaged his balls.

Jason's arousal was feral and demanding, but he wanted to taste her first. He thrust Cassandra down on the bed and fell on her like a starving man. She squirmed with desire, digging her fingers into his dark blonde hair. Jason's hot breath blew against her stomach and she shivered as his tongue tasted her skin. He worked his way down to the silky V below, and licked the swollen crease. Cassandra's hips rocked with frustration as Jason separated her labia and teased her hardened clit, sending electric sparks through her body.

Her body screamed with hunger, forcing her up and surprising Jason by pushing him back. Cassandra grasped his cock as he fell against the pillows and she mounted him, rubbing the tip of his hardened rod with her juice. Jason groaned and shuddered. He watched as she teased him, then eased his shaft deep into her hot canal. He let out a yell of pleasure and pulled her to him. He twisted Cassandra around so he was once again on top and thrust himself to the hilt, watching her cry out.

Jason reached down with one hand and, with every plunge of his hardened cock, rubbed her clit faster and faster. She whimpered for release, and knew he felt her body arch and stiffen as he reached his own violent climax. They shuddered together. Cassandra sensed his heart pounding in time with hers through sweat-drenched skin.

As they lay wrapped in each other's arms, Jason still warm and inside her, Cassandra marveled at the change in his looks. But it was his eyes shining with unconditional love that was more beautiful than any feature she had ever seen. *No more unrequited love for me*, she smiled.

Jason's affluent family welcomed Cassandra with open arms. The couple toured Europe on their extended honeymoon, and Cassandra was able to study art to her heart's content. Jason left his maintenance job and started working for an animal-rights group.

And they lived happily ever after.

Free Falling

By Victoria Lake

Peter took a deep breath and stared out into the space before him, focused and alert. Leaping off the small platform, the sensation of freefall was short lived. He was caught by the safety net, and thrown ten feet back up. Peter tucked into a somersault and landed feet-first on the net. He bounced a few times and smiled, his piercing brown eyes capturing everything under the giant tent. The platform loomed 50 feet above the ground and 40 above the net.

Applause echoed through the cavernous space. Peter fell back, letting the net capture his fall. Springy steps jostled the net and someone flopped down next to him.

"Hello, Wendy."

"Hey, Peter."

"To what do I owe this visit?"

"Just seeing what you do in your off time. I thought you'd be practicing or off in a bar someplace causing mayhem with some adoring female fans."

Wendy was the only female Peter adored, but he wasn't

in a position to tell her. Peter rolled over on to his belly and cradled his head on crossed arms. "Just had an urge to jump off the platform. Can't explain it."

"Sometimes I think we can fly when we're up there," Wendy said. "Nothing between us but air. Nothing to save us but each other and a lot of trust. Hoping that a pair of strong hands will rescue us from falling."

"No one falls," Peter reminded her "not anymore." Wendy pushed her curly blonde hair from her eyes and tucked the stray strands behind her ears. Peter watched as she ran her eyes over his toned body. He let her hand hover inches from his thighs. "We should get ready, Wendy. Hooke hates it when we're here, and he's not involved."

"Bastard is probably in his trailer dreaming of ways to take advantage of more people."

Peter said nothing, although a hundred comments ran through his head. It was hard watching Hooke have the run of the Second Star Circus. Unfortunately, until he could prove otherwise, Peter had to continue to play the part of the simple employee.

He rolled over and met Wendy's eyes. Brown stared into green. He looked at her full lips and stroked her cheek before kicking up into a standing position and offering her his hand. Wendy took it and allowed Peter to pull her up. She went to the edge of the net and flipped over. Peter followed, watching the effortless grace of his shadow as his feet hit the ground.

"See you in a few hours?" he asked. Wendy nodded and watched him walk off, out of the flap in the canvas.

"Nice tent," she whispered. He stopped in the sunlight, smiled, shook his head and walked away.

Peter locked his ankles and leaned back on the bar. The chilled metal dug into the back of his knees as he swung. He clapped his hands together. Talcum from his heavily taped appendages fell to the floor like pixie dust. Stern concentration crossed his face, brown eyes focused straight ahead to the other platform. Michael and John, Wendy's brothers, held the trapeze while she prepared herself. He nodded, and she jumped.

The creak of her taped hands was heard through the tent as she swung into the air. Peter watched Wendy's legs pump to gain height and momentum. Their eyes locked and he smiled. Their swings became timed, caught in a pattern known only to high flyers. Wendy nodded, her eyes filled with strength and trust. Then she let go. She tumbled through the air in a triple somersault. The crowd stopped breathing as they watched the stunt, frozen in time.

Peter's strong arms caught her as applause and cheers roared through the circus. Wendy looked up at him, relieved, and mouthed the words: *Thank you*. He smiled at her. On the next swing, her hand slipped. A gasp exploded from 50 feet below. Peter tightened his grip. She had slipped less than an inch, but the fear of falling was always there—with or without the net. Peter swung her up hard and she landed on the platform, caught by his sister Belle. Wendy looked back to see Peter pull himself up into a sitting position on the trapeze.

Peter extended his arms and slipped off, landed on his legs, bounced up, and stood bowing to the crowd's applause. The brothers John and Michael were next, doing their own stunts to get to the ground. Belle slid down a rope. Peter stared at Wendy's body as she leapt into the air, caught in the spotlights: The firm calves, curve of her hips, and the fullness of her breasts. She tucked into a ball before plummeting to the net and bouncing.

Wendy reached for the handle of the trailer. The air was stale and reeked of sweat and old cigarettes.

"One minute there, Missy. I don't think our business is finished yet."

"Any business we had was over years ago, Hooke."

Hooke stood from his chair and pressed out a cigarette into an overflowing bowl. Tendrils of greasy black hair spilled over his shoulders as he stepped toward Wendy. The trailer had been an apartment, and was now converted to the circus' business office. Wendy knew an old cot was behind the curtain at the very back of the trailer. Hooke was here every moment he wasn't in the big top. The desk, once a magnificent antique, was cluttered with stacks of paperwork and scarred with cigarette burns. It had been Peter's father's.

"You like your job here? You like flying through the air and seeing all the hot men in their tights, hearing the applause night after night?"

"For a reminder, I'm related to two of those men. You're disgusting. How many times are we doing this, Hooke?"

"As many times as it takes for it to sink in. You are only

here because of me. Never forget it. I can snap my fingers and have a whole new flock of high flyers in a week. Then you and your two brothers are out of work again."

Wendy's fingers tightened on the door handle. She turned slowly.

"What do you want from me?" she asked, knowing the answer. Hooke stepped closer and loomed over her. His fetid breath cascaded over Wendy's neck. He advanced again and slid his long fingers over her shoulders. She gasped from revulsion and fear.

"You know what I want, Wendy. What I've always wanted. I will never be satiated." He leaned in close to her ear, his moustache prickling her lobe. "Meet me by the bear cage in four hours. After the show, don't shower. Make sure you're still sweaty." Wendy shivered and bolted out the trailer door.

She paced in her dressing room. The sound of her slippers scuffed across the floor. It was a communal dressing room for the women, laden with costumes and make-up stations with lighted mirrors. Wendy wiped the make-up off her face and tightened the tie on her robe. She was still in her costume, flesh-colored tights under a bright blue tunic, and not much else under that. Despite the chill night air seeping in, she was sweating.

"You can do this," she whispered at her reflection. "One last time until the contracts are renewed." She dabbed at the dampness forming in her eyes and sighed. The thought of Hooke on top of her and, worse, inside her, filled Wendy with such revulsion she retched into the trashcan. Gagging at the taste, she rinsed her mouth with a glass of water and wandered outside.

Later, Wendy walked out from behind the empty bear trailer used for parades. It normally housed Kaos, their trained black bear, upwards of 20 years old and twice as crotchety. The cage door was lowered and rested on the ground. A large blanket was spread out inside across the floor. Wendy shivered with the thought of the lumps under the blanket and hoped they were hay.

"I love a prompt woman." Hooke stepped around the corner, riding crop in one hand, megaphone in the other. His elbow-length leather gloves were still on from the show. He stepped into the cage and lay down on the blanket, then tapped it next to him. She inched forward.

"Don't make me do this."

"One last bang for the show? It's almost contract renewal time," he reminded her needlessly. Wendy stepped forward. "Getting closer, prolonging the agony, I like it."

"You're such a bastard."

"And if you don't get in here, you're going to be unemployed," he hissed. He checked his watch, the face an alligator with moving arms.

"What's the matter, Hooke? Got a hot date?" Wendy jumped at Peter's voice. Hooke bolted up on the cage, banging his head on the roof. "I thought I had seen all the slimiest things, until now."

"Mind your own damn business, Pan." Spittle flew from the edge of Hooke's mouth and caught on his moustache.

"I'm making this my business," Peter replied. Hooke slinked out of the cage. They watched the glint of metal coming from a hip sheath with a large dagger in it. Hooke reached for the jeweled handle. His fingers tickled the hilt before he skulked off into the shadows.

"Contract time is coming," he yelled over his shoulder. "I won't forget."

"I could have handled it." Wendy tightened her robe, obviously flustered and embarrassed.

"You shouldn't have had to. Hooke is a dirtbag."

"I owe him."

"No, Wendy, you only think you do." Peter grabbed her hand and gave it a squeeze. She ached for so much more, but couldn't bring herself to tell him. *Not here. Not now.*

"Please, Peter, this is something I have to deal with."

"You know where I am if you need me."

Wendy stood on tiptoes to kiss his cheek and walked off.

Michael and John held the trapeze while Wendy prepared for flight. She grabbed on with one hand, holding the other high above her head. Across the big top, Peter was already in motion, hanging upside down by the knees, waiting for his special arrival. Wendy grabbed hold of the bar with both hands and jumped off the platform.

She kicked her legs up high while the spotlight tracked her movements. Peter kept his eyes fixed on her speed and positioning, never letting his mind wander. Their eyes met. When Peter swung back he saw Hooke skulking in the shadows.

Another pass, a glint of reflected metal where it shouldn't be. Lying on the floor beneath the safety net was Hooke's dagger. Peter looked hurriedly around and saw the lines to the safety net, one partially hacked at. When he stared back again, he saw Hooke looking frantically for something at his hip and bolting off. Wendy swung out again, higher this time, her hands and wrists getting tired from the exertion. Her grip slipped coming back toward the platform. Michael and John got ready to catch her.

She swung out again. This time Peter was ready, but before he could signal her not to release, she tucked her legs up to her chin and began her revolutions. Peter was not in position and knew it. The lights followed Wendy and then captured the concern on Peter's face as he fought to swing out to catch her. She came out of the roll with her arms extended. Peter was almost there. She started to fall. Peter knew the net was compromised and slid down to his ankles, catching his feet between the bar and cable.

He caught Wendy by one wrist and swung back toward his own platform. She was too low to make it safely, and there was no knowing if the net would hold or not. The crowd gasped when Michael leapt to catch his sister's trapeze. He dropped down to swing by his knees, extending his arms.

Get ready, he mouthed. Wendy nodded. Peter swung her backward and high. Michael caught her easily and swung her up onto the platform. Held in place by John, she looked out to the center ring where the unplanned show was going on. Peter reached out and kicked off the bar. He felt Michael's hand and grabbed on. Two strong swings and Peter was on the platform next to Wendy. They hugged tightly and Peter could feel the sobs coming from her. John started down the pole slowly to make room for Michael to land safely.

Michael touched down on the platform, with Wendy

and Peter grabbing at his wrists for support. Wendy hugged her brother and while the three descended the pole, a pack of clowns came out with trained dogs to take the attention away from the aerial acrobats.

"That was too close," Peter said, holding her to him. "And it's not going to happen again."

Wendy walked into the men's dressing room and stood next to Peter. He was shirtless, just out of the shower. She had changed earlier to a pair of jeans and a comfortable shirt. Peter pushed out a chair with his foot. Wendy took the seat. She leaned forward to meet his eyes, but all she could concentrate on was his clean-shaven face and soapy scent. She could never fight her attraction to him, even when she was able to hide it.

"It was Hooke," Peter said. "Some kind of retribution for the other night."

"Please don't do anything drastic."

"He tried to kill you and kill the crew."

"I know, but I need to protect my brothers."

"They're grown men now, Wendy. Maybe you should start thinking of you."

"I can't do that, Peter," she breathed, turning away.

"Why not?"

"Because I'm too busy thinking of you," she said with an unexpected honesty.

Peter smiled and took Wendy's hand. "How do you feel about surprises?"

"I love them. As long as it's not while I'm fifty feet in the air."

He pulled a long silver scarf from his pocket and tied it over her eyes. "No peeking."

Peter rested a hand on Wendy's back and eased open the flap of the big top. He slid the scarf off her eyes and waited. "Okay, open your eyes slowly so the light doesn't blind you." Wendy gasped at the scene before her, like some secret fantasy come to life.

The safety net was strung up, a large down comforter spread across it. Candles traced a path on the floor. The trapezes were loose. Silver and blue ribbons hung from one, a large wicker basket from the other. The main spotlight of the circus trained on the blanket.

"I don't know what to say."

"Just say yes."

"Yes."

Wendy looked deep into Peter's eyes and kissed him. Their lips parted and tongues explored. Wendy felt his strong hands on her waist, moving slowly up her torso to her back. Peter pulled her in to him, allowing their bodies to mesh. She pulled back and licked her lips to savor his lingering taste.

"Do you know how eagles mate?" Peter asked.

"Tell me."

"They interact in mid air, coupling in a death dive, falling faster with each passing second and thrust. Then at the moment of orgasm, they pull away and fly off. Sometimes they're so impassioned they crash into the ground and die."

"You have the sweetest bedroom talk."

Peter smiled and took Wendy's hand. He led her to the

support pole and lifted her to the first rung. She climbed onto the net and waited. Peter wasn't far behind. They bounce-walked to the comforter and collapsed on it. Wendy stared up at the ribbons, caught in a stray breeze and reflecting the light.

"This is amazing, how did you do all this?"

"Sometimes I have a lot of spare time on my hands." She raised a knowing eyebrow at him. "All right, Belle helped me."

Peter looked deep into Wendy's eyes and ran a hand through her thick curly hair. He leaned in and kissed her, first on the forehead, then the nose, and then on the lips.

"I used to dream of you at night, Peter, alone in my trailer. Thinking about your arms and your legs, and how you never dropped anyone. I've seen shows where people fall."

"As long as you're here with me, Wendy, you'll never fall." She leaned in and kissed him gently. "I want you to trust me," he continued, "on and off the trapeze. I will never let you fall." Wendy kissed him harder, tasting Peter's breath and tongue. She rolled on top of him and smiled at the pressure of his erection against her abdomen. Peter slid his hand up her ribs.

Wendy sat up, straddling Peter, and let him slip her shirt off. He ran his strong hands over her bra and squeezed her breasts before sitting up and reaching around for her bra straps. She smiled and looked down.

"So old fashioned." With an easy move, Wendy released the catch on the front of her bra and watched it float through the safety net to the floor below. Peter buried his face between her breasts. A small cry escaped her lips. He kissed each orb, letting his tongue dance over the areolas and nipples. Wendy reached down and pulled his shirt off.

"I tried to rig the trapezes with safety harness," he grinned wickedly. "I thought that could make for some fun."

"Next time," she said.

Peter kissed Wendy's chest and slowly worked his way down her abdomen. She smiled at him, already feeling the familiar contractions starting. *At this rate I'm going to come before my pants are off*, she mused. Peter deftly unbuttoned and unzipped her jeans. She rolled off him as he slid the material away, raising each leg to free her of the denim. Peter kissed her toes, then continued upwards, massaging and licking her calves, stopping at her thighs.

Every instinct and emotion in Wendy ached for him to tear off her thin panties. She could feel the dampness already. Peter knelt down and gently spread her legs, slowly lifting the corner of the white cotton bikinis and running his fingers through her blonde thatch. Arching her back, Wendy's breath caught in her throat when Peter slipped two fingers inside her and worked gently, teasing and playing until he took a first tentative taste of her juices.

With an animalistic growl Peter tore the panties free. One finger still probing her, he started to lick. No fantasy Wendy had came close to what he made her feel. Alternating between the flat of his tongue and the tip, Peter touched every part of her. She opened her legs wider. His skilled tongue, combined with her own intense need, brought her climax all too quickly.

When he didn't stop, Wendy reached down and wove her fingers through Peter's thick hair. He continued to lick at her clit as his fingers reached deep inside of her. Finding a spot she had only previously read about, Wendy shuddered and bit her lip to keep from screaming as the second orgasm raced through her. *Now this*, she thought, *is flying*.

Peter raised his head from her sex and looked at her. Wendy never felt more beautiful. Her nipples were still hard, and he licked each one before lying next to her.

"Did I wear you out?"

"Not even close, Peter. I'm just getting warmed up." Wendy rolled on top of him, letting her hands travel down his sculpted abdomen to his pants. The heat coming through the jeans was like a furnace. She unzipped him and slid her hand in. Peter pulled her into a fierce kiss. Wendy rubbed the front of his boxer-briefs, giggling at the pinpoint of moisture soaking through. She pulled off the pants along with his underwear.

Wendy cradled Peter's balls and slowly stroked him. Peter moaned and grabbed a handful of her curly hair. She licked the tip of his erection, then the shaft, letting her tongue travels its length before taking him into her mouth. Peter groaned in ecstasy and thrust his hips to meet Wendy. She kept with his need, never allowing him to slip out, except when she paused to run her tongue along his shaft.

"You'd better stop, Wendy, or the rest of my plans will be spoiled." Peter pulled her up to his chest. She listened to his heart hammering and relished his need for deep breaths. His chest was warm against her cheek. "There's a little something for you in the basket," he said.

Wendy reached up into the flat basket hung from the trapeze and took out a condom. "Unlubricated," she noticed. "Were you expecting something?"

"Hoping, and they were the first ones I saw in the store." She unwrapped the condom, slipped it between her lips using her teeth for a barrier, and crept down his body again. Using her tongue she slipped the condom over the tip over his cock and then took him into her mouth until it was snug.

Wendy climbed on top of Peter and eased down his length until he was deep within her. She rocked with him and let the motions of the net help carry them. The springing movements of the net drove their thrusts deeper until they both reached that moment of perfect synchronization, as they did each night when they were on the trapezes flying through the air.

From the spotlight in the corner, their shadows danced across the walls of the tent as they moved together. Their bodies knew each other so well that this final intimacy was as natural as it was powerful. They thrust against each other until neither could last a moment longer. Their moans blended as they came. Peter sat up and put his hands on Wendy's back. She continued to rock with their quaking orgasms. She bent her head to his. They kissed passionately as their pace slowed and the net stopped swaying.

They lay intertwined on the comforter, both still naked and glistening with sweat. Peter reached into the basket and withdrew a bottle of wine and two plastic cups. He pulled the loosened cork out and poured them each a glass.

"How did you think of this?" Wendy asked, looking over the rim of her cup.

"Call it a long-time dream." She smiled and kissed him, tasting wine still damp on his lips.

"And what about Hooke?"

"Now *there's* a mood killer. Leave him out of this."

"I'm sorry, Peter, I didn't mean to." She looked away, finished the last sip of wine, and reached for her pants. "I can't."

Peter put out a hand to stop her. "Let me worry about him."

"You don't understand. I have to look out for my brothers."

"No, *you* don't understand. Hooke is *my* problem, *our* problem, but not for much longer. I have another surprise, but I can't tell you until tomorrow. You have to trust me."

"Does it involve safety harnesses?" Wendy dropped her jeans and reached into the basket for a second condom.

Wendy closed the door to Peter's trailer softly so she wouldn't wake him. They had spent the night there, curled in each other's arms. She planned to catch a ride into town for bagels, coffee and fresh orange juice. Wendy finished pulling on her shirt as she was going down the small set of stairs to the ground. A gasp escaped her lips when the shirt cleared her face and someone pulled her hair free.

Hooke stood there, an evil grimace smeared across his face. The muffled rumblings of Peter waking up came through the thin metal walls. The door opened. Peter stood in the morning sunlight staring at Wendy, who was still staring at Hooke.

"What can I do for you, Hooke? You get a good earful?"

"That's it, the both of you." Hooke's hand slid down to the hilt of the blade he always kept there. "I can rid myself of two problems now." He reached for the knife, his hand closing around the grip. Peter's hand connected with the side of Hooke's head before the blade was removed. Another blow hit Hooke's midsection, and finally his nose. Hooke howled and grabbed at his face to stop the bleeding.

"You're both fired! Get out now!" Hooke's face was beet red, more so from rage than the blood gushing from his nose. "Pack up your brothers and your sister." He spit out a mouthful of his venomous blood. "You two can go work the carnie circuit."

Wendy and Peter watched Hooke slink off. Neither moved until they heard the slam of his trailer door. Wendy laced her fingers with Peter's and put her head against his shoulder.

"What do we do now?" She was trembling and on the verge of tears. Peter cupped her chin and brought her face up as a tear slipped free. He kissed her and smiled. "How can you smile?" she asked. "Everyone is fired. Everything we've worked through and done is worthless. You don't know what I did—"

"I *do* know, Wendy, and I'm sorry it went on for so long. I made some phone calls the other day after he tried to cut the net and I have something to tell you. When you're a third-generation performer, you pick up a few tricks along the way."

"You have some super secret bank account to support my brothers and your sister?"

Peter took a deep breath. "No, but I may have controlling interest in this circus."

"How is that possible?"

"The circus never belonged to Hooke. I had some suspicions, but didn't follow through until a few days ago. Seeing you with Hooke made me realize it was time to grow up and take responsibility."

"What are you saying?"

"Thanks to some helpful lawyers, the circus is now mine. My father never gave up ownership, just control. He transferred it to me about two days ago. I have the faxes in my trailer. Hooke doesn't know. Yet." Peter watched a smile spread across Wendy's face. "Hooke is a figurehead, nothing else; but as long as my father was an absentee owner, the power fell to him. The truth is, he can't fire anyone. All he really does is run the bookings. He couldn't fire an ant if it crawled across his stinking hide."

"You'll need a new ringmaster."

"My dad is considering coming out of retirement."

"So what's next?"

"You want to help me fire Hooke?"

Wendy pressed her face against Peter's chest and nodded. They walked toward Hooke's trailer, hands locked, eyes never wavering from their destination ahead.

Legs

By Rachel Kenley

Every step she took was agony, but any discomfort was worth it to finally have legs. She felt strangely exposed without her tail. It was hard to decide what was more awkward: The sensation of walking, or the sand beneath her new bare feet.

She left the comfort and familiarity of the sea for the dry land of man in the hope of finding a pleasure and connection lost to her in the fathomless ocean, while living with her father's limited ideas of acceptable behavior.

If her father knew she had been to visit the Sea Trader, her punishment would be severe. His wrath was doubly worse than the paper she signed. While the Trader's clause resulted in her death, her father would let her live—and only *wish* she were dead.

I will make it to that rock before I try to rest, she thought, starting to walk again. The pain had begun to ease by the time she reached the boulder. She was sturdier on her limbs. She pushed herself up to sit more securely on the rock and looked at her legs for the first time.

They appeared so slender and frail compared to the wider expanse of her absent tail. It was no wonder they were difficult to use. She leaned forward to touch the tiny feet and laughed silently when it tickled. She watched in awe as her toes wiggled and the muscles moved beneath the skin. Slowly she allowed her hands to travel up to her ankles and calves, smiling at the sensations her own touch created.

She reached her knees and marveled at how they bent to allow movement. Her tail did not need the ability to do that. When she touched the skin behind her knee she experienced a new thrill: A tingle that started where her fingers were and ended someplace else. She moved her hands away and the feeling faded.

Curious, she thought, placing her hands back and restoring the sensations. She gasped. *This is worth the Trader's price.* She had never used her voice anyway. Mermaids communicated telepathically through the dense water. The silence of this world was one of the first things she noticed. *Other than my legs, of course.*

Wondering what other surprises she might find, she continued to work her way up, now reaching her thighs. Here she found more muscle, somewhat similar to the strength in her tail. Nothing here created the pulsing sensation of the other place, so she moved further up and almost fell off the rock when she discovered a small patch of soft hair.

What is that doing there? she wondered, leaning forward to look at the fine blonde hair covering the juncture. She'd asked for legs. *Did the Trader get something wrong? How can I walk among humans with this on my body?* The only hair she had came in long waves starting at her head and reaching her waist, the same color as this new find.

Deciding it needed additional exploration, she put her hands gently on the hair and searched for the skin beneath. The earlier thrill returned, stronger. She gasped and moved her hand away. The feeling stopped. Immediately she touched herself again.

The flesh was magnificently sensitive and her breathing sped up while she stroked the skin more firmly. As she continued, she found a small cleft in the skin and allowed her finger to trail between the folds. The increase in pleasure was breathtaking. Her eyes flew open and she had to squint against the sunlight.

Never before had she experienced such an exquisite rush. Her finger traced lower and she found a small swollen bud. Her hands fisted as a jolt of pleasure surged through her. It was unlike anything; yet once she felt it, she couldn't imagine how she had lived without it. She thought nothing could be better than the sensation of walking. *I was wrong. Walking doesn't compare to this.*

She stretched out fully on the rock, the breeze caressing her as she allowed a second hand to touch what the first had discovered. She continued to massage the tip that was responsible for such joy while her other finger moved lower. There she felt wetness—her first since leaving home—and an entrance surrounded by more sensitive skin. One finger, then two, slid in. She was certain she was going to explode.

Something built inside of her. And although she

couldn't say what it was, she knew it was different from anything she had felt before. Waves grew within her; not unlike the ones she grew up playing in, and yet nothing at all like them. She could hardly wait to experience what was about to arrive.

Her heart raced as she reveled in each added sensation. A flood of wetness escaped. She hastened her movements to match the increase in pleasure. Her body reached to meet a peak rushing toward her.

"*There* you are!" a deep voice startled her and her hands fell to the side, taking the bliss with them. "Everyone at the shoot is waiting for you. What are you doing out here by yourself?"

The sun was behind him and she saw nothing except the outline of a tall body with broad shoulders. As he got closer her breath caught. He was her first human, and he was gorgeous. Large dark eyes stared questioningly at her from a tan face. He had full lips and pearly white teeth. His deep brown hair was wavy and slightly long, and she could see sparks of red where it caught the sun. Her eyes wandered down his body. He was nearly as naked as she, although she saw a small piece of clingy material covered his waist. She thought she noticed something move behind the covering, but it stopped before she could be certain.

"We've been wondering if you were here," he continued. She had no idea what he was talking about, but liked the sound of his voice. "We're set up on the other side of the beach. You must have been given the wrong directions. I'm glad I found you."

So am I, she thought.

"I'll walk back with you so you can check in, and we can get to work. By the way," he held out his hand, "I'm Logan Merrain. And you are?"

She put her hand in his and tried to answer. Nothing, of course, came out.

If he didn't know better, Logan would have sworn he'd come across a beautiful woman masturbating. But she couldn't have been. She must have been enjoying the sun and sea breeze; although someone with such fair skin probably shouldn't lie out for too long. Particularly not someone whose paycheck depended on his or her looks.

He'd been modeling for more than six years and knew what it took. He had one of the best reputations in the business and commanded the salary to go with it. Logan prided himself on being professional, dependable, and not letting on that he was bored out of his mind. For the last year none of the benefits of his career outweighed the unending tedium of each shoot.

Finding a naked woman on a rock was admittedly a nice job-related perk; especially after the last model walked out the day before in a snit. Something was not quite right with this one, either. She seemed unable to tell Logan her name—or anything else, for that matter. Too bad, because she was stunning; and for him to respond to that was rare. In addition to her gorgeous skin, she had light blonde hair she wore long and wavy. Her lips were the palest pink and matched her nipples. Logan couldn't help but notice. Light blue eyes added to her beauty.

"Can't talk?" he asked. "Laryngitis? I've never had it

myself, but I've heard it's a bitch. Don't worry. It's not as if this work requires us to talk." She was still holding his hand and without thinking he pulled her toward him and started walking. She seemed unsteady, so he kept his pace slow. He hoped she wasn't drunk. "Let's go before our photographer Ivan has a cow. He's tough to deal with even when he's in a good mood. At least his end results are worth it."

Logan turned and smiled. She returned it. "Why haven't we worked together before?"

She shrugged her shoulders, lifting up her small breasts and hardened nipples. He felt an immediate urge to stop and lick them, but tapped the need down.

"Boy, am I glad we get to be near one another for this job." She nodded in agreement. Something in Logan stirred. "It's a great location for the product line they're launching. Have you ever been here before?"

She shook her head.

"Me either. My understanding is they wanted a place that looked untouched. I think they chose well."

She nodded.

"Can I admit something to you?"

She cocked her head to one side. He stopped and gazed at her.

"I wasn't looking forward to this job, but now that you're here, I have a much better feeling about it. Whatever brought you here, I'm glad."

She took the hand he wasn't holding and brought it to the side of his face in a gentle caress. He was taken aback by her kindness.

"Perfect!" a loud voice called out. She jumped behind

Logan as a man walked rapidly toward them. "That was an exquisite shot. I have no idea when or how I am going to use it, but it was gorgeous nonetheless."

"Glad to hear it, Ivan."

"I see you've found our wayward model."

"Yes, the agency sent her to the wrong part of the beach." He looked at her and gestured to the man. "This is Ivan. Ivan this is . . ." He didn't know how to finish the introduction. Before he could say anything, Ivan grabbed her hand and pulled, causing her to stumble and fall against him. Logan had a flash of inspiration while being glad the photographer was gay. " . . . This is Grace."

"Not the best choice of names for you, my sweet, but if you photograph as beautifully as I think you will, I wouldn't care if your name was Ralph. Come, we have work to do." Ivan took Logan's hand too, and dragged the two of them to the set.

Grace, she thought happily. It wasn't even close to the name her family called her, but she didn't care. The wonderful man named Logan chose it for her and that was all that mattered.

She was nervous about what a shoot would be, but it didn't seem to involve pain; just a lot of people hovering around, putting stuff all over her body. She was glad she could see Logan from where she sat. As long as she could spend the day close to him, she didn't care what modeling was.

No one seemed to mind she couldn't speak. Ivan, in fact, was thrilled. "A mute model. That's perfect! Why didn't I request one before? Darling, you are the answer to a photographer's prayers."

It was nice the energetic man was so happy, but it was Logan's smile and his "See you in a little bit" that made it possible for her to sit through all this attention to her face and hair.

When she couldn't wait another minute, Logan stepped into view and held out a hand. "Ready?" he asked. She jumped up, letting the towel fall to the ground. She joined him at the water's edge.

"No false modesty for our Grace," Ivan said as they walked to where he pointed. "How about you, Logan? Care to strip out of that Speedo?"

"Not for you," he said, and whispered in her ear. "But perhaps I will with you later."

She looked at him and smiled. He winked, which startled her at first. She enjoyed his laugh when she tried unsuccessfully to imitate him.

"Enough with the lovey-dovey eyes. Save it for the camera."

"Come on, Grace. Let's go make Sea Foam Cleansers the sexiest product launch in history. We'll give them pictures they'll never forget."

She didn't have a clue what a product launch was, but knew sexy equaled Logan. Her instincts told her to stay with him. As for never forgetting, she understood that only too well.

She had only three days to find the ultimate pleasure or the Sea Trader would return for her soul, leaving her to become nothing more than a memory to those who knew her. She would become less than the sea foam he mentioned. She shuddered at the thought.

"Are you cold?"

She shook her head, glad she couldn't say more.

"Don't worry," he said. "I'll warm you up."

I believe that completely.

The first part of the job was easy. She and Logan were required to play in the water, splashing and jumping. He lifted her and spun her around until she had her first experience with being dizzy. Then everyone was in a rush to get them ready for the next set of pictures, which had to be taken at dusk. Logan pulled her close and held her against his body.

"You're incredible," he said in her ear. His hot breath sent a shiver through her. The sensation ended with a tingle at the top place on her legs.

As are you, she thought, leaning her head back to gaze into his eyes. Instinctively she raised her hands to run them through his hair. As she did, his forehead came forward and touched hers. She moved her head to the side to breathe him in.

"Brilliant," Ivan yelled. "That's the spirit."

"You don't care about what he says any more than I do," Logan said.

She shook her heat against him and felt his cheek move against hers in a smile.

"Pretend he's not there. Pretend this sunset is just for us."

She moved to look at him. *How could the world hold more than us?* she thought, wishing he could hear her.

Logan chose that moment to lean in. With gentle lips, he kissed her. Her heart leaped for joy. She stood on tiptoes to bring her mouth closer to his. He moaned in pleasure, and she ached to make the same sound to let him know she was feeling what he was.

When his tongue touched her lips she opened her mouth to receive him and reveled in the new feelings this created. His arms came around her and he pulled her closer, his touch traveling down her back.

She almost stiffened when he got to the place where her tail would have started, then remembered she no longer had one. When he touched what was there now, her body reacted strongly and she gave a small jump in his arms.

"Okay, kids, save that for your trailer or the movies. You could earn an X-rating with a kiss. We're done today, people. Good work. Everyone needs to be here early for the sunrise shoot tomorrow."

Logan smiled at her as an assistant helped her into a robe. It was heavy and confining. She didn't like it. "Join me for dinner?"

She nodded enthusiastically and gave him her hand.

"Home sweet trailer," Logan said. Normally he requested and received luxury hotel accommodation for his jobs, but had asked to stay on-site when he saw the hours required and the assignment's location. "It's not much, but it's all I need. I'm tired of the familiar rooms I'm always put in. Do you know what I mean?"

She nodded and took a spot on the bed. Logan would have taken it as a come on, but there were few places to sit beyond the two chairs at a table.

"I also wanted to be able to hear the ocean when I fell asleep and woke up. Have you ever enjoyed that?"

She nodded again.

He laughed. "You're easy to talk to."

She smiled and blushed, looking down at her hands.

"Oh no," he said coming to sit next to her. "I didn't mean anything by that. I'm sure your voice is lovely, and I look forward to hearing it, but I have to admit something. It's nice to have someone who listens to me. On the job and even away from it, everyone thinks I'm nothing more than a pretty face." She put out her hand to caress his cheek. "Rarely is anything I say taken seriously. Except of course when I tell my family I want to leave this business. Then not only do they listen, they panic."

She gave him a quizzical look.

"My work supports my parents and some of my siblings. I've always contributed to the family, but when I started modeling, the money was so good that almost all the responsibility fell to me.

When she gave him a nod, he continued.

"The responsibility has become pressure. I can't leave because I'm concerned about what it will do to the people counting on me."

Her eyes opened wide at that comment.

"You understand my situation."

She nodded quickly.

"Family can be challenging."

This time she rolled her eyes when she nodded. He laughed.

"Yup, looks like you understand completely." On impulse he kissed her. "I don't know how or why you ended up in my life today, but I am so glad you did."

She closed her eyes and leaned into him. He accepted the invitation and kissed her again, more deeply this time.

A voice in Logan's head reminded him he had only met her that day. He didn't want to be a gentleman, but also didn't want to scare her off. "You must be starving. I don't have a lot to offer—some cheese, crackers and fruit—but I think it will be enough for us."

They walked three steps to the kitchen area and Logan took out food and bottled water. She seemed enchanted by the meal, especially the fruit. Her expression of enjoyment at each bite shot straight to his cock. He'd never witnessed a joy more pure.

"Where did you come from?" he asked dreamily.

She touched her throat and pointed out the window.

"Sorry, forgot for a moment. I suppose it doesn't matter. You're here now," he said, and took her hand.

Not for long, she thought, aching to tell him. She was allowed only two more sunsets. If she didn't find the ultimate pleasure by then—no, she wouldn't think of that. Instead she focused on Logan. She loved listening to him and was fascinated to learn he had limitations and family frustrations too.

A strange sensation came over her. Her ears felt odd and her mouth opened involuntarily as she inhaled deeply.

"Oh no, a yawn," he said. "Either I'm boring you or you're falling asleep."

A yawn. How interesting. With her hands she tried to

indicate she was tired. She couldn't imagine being bored by him.

"I know it may seem forward of me, but since we've spent most of the day nearly naked, I'm hoping you will consider staying here and spending the night with me."

I'd love to, she thought as she nodded again. *Nothing could be more wonderful than being in his arms.* Logan quickly turned off all the lights and led her the short distance to the bed. As he pulled down the covers, she took off her robe.

"Oh my, you are exquisite," he said, turning to look at her, "but if you sleep nude I am never going to be able to keep my hands off you. Then Ivan is going to yell because we both look exhausted. I'm blathering and making ridiculous rationalizations, but if I don't I am going to ravish you."

She blinked, trying to take in his rapid words. She could tell he was uncertain. Talking his hand in hers, she tried to reassure him. *Don't pull away from me*, she thought.

"How about a T-shirt?"

She cocked her head to the side. *A what?*

"I'll get one for each of us." He pulled a container out from under the bed and withdrew two squares of material which he shook out before handing her one.

She started at the pretty blue thing and watched as he put it over his head and face. His arms poked through two holes in the sides. Repeating his movements, she managed after a few false starts to get the covering on.

"Damn, you still look completely sexy," he said.

So do you, she thought and put her arms around him.

He reciprocated and held her. Another yawn took her by surprise.

"Come to bed, my Grace," he said. He climbed in first. She curled against him and looked into his eyes hopefully. He leaned forward and kissed her. The warmth between them astounded her.

"Thanks for filling in and doing such a great job today."

You're welcome.

"And I know it wasn't completely by choice, but thanks for listening to me. It may sound crazy, but with you, I don't feel like a brainless object."

You are so much more than that. Look at the kindness and thoughtfulness you've shown me. She ran her hand over his chest, stopping at his heart.

"You've touched my heart, too."

I'm glad. You deserve that. She kissed him and put her head where her hand had been.

"Good night, Grace."

Good night.

A banging outside the door woke them both. It was still dark.

"Wake up, Logan!" someone yelled. "They want you in makeup in fifteen minutes. And I hope the girl is with you 'cause no one knows where she is otherwise."

"She's right where she belongs," he murmured. He hugged her close, although she had been by his side the entire time.

She had never slept with a man before and found the experience exciting and relaxing. Stretching out, she flexed from her arms to her toes, marveling once again at the experience of legs.

"As much as I would like to linger, work calls."

Something in his voice bothered her. She pulled him back as he started to get up. *What's wrong?* she tried to ask with her expression.

He figured it out. "I'm tired."

She looked at the pillow and at him.

"Not that kind of tired. I've been modeling for a long time and it's not fun anymore. Each job is harder and harder to give what I'm supposed to. I want out, and I don't know how."

I understand. Intimately, in fact, and she was sorry she couldn't tell him or offer him comfort.

"Come. We'll make today great together."

Absolutely.

She let the hovering people "fix her face" again, although she didn't know what was broken. Ivan and his camera started clicking rapidly as the sun started coming up.

The day's pictures were sexual. From sitting in Logan's lap to lying on his chest, she spent hours naked and pressed against him. The tingling she experienced on the rock was back, full force.

"That's a wrap until afternoon," Ivan called.

Logan took her hand and helped her up from the sand. They stood there staring at each other as assistants splashed warm water to wash the sand off and handed them towels.

"I need you alone," he said when the crew walked away. "I need you now."

Yes, her body screamed, and she was glad she was steady on her legs because they couldn't take her fast enough into his trailer.

They dropped their towels the moment the door closed and were in each other's arms with the next breath. She had been close to him all day. It hadn't been close enough.

Logan took off the clothing he'd been wearing and she saw his complete body for the first time. It was more unusual than hers and she reached for the place between his legs that was different.

"Oh God, that feels good."

She smiled, pleased to have done something right, and continued to explore the rigid skin and the area around it.

"Before my knees give out, let's get into bed." He picked her up and placed her in the center of the mattress. "I love being near you, touching you."

So do I. She showed him by touching him more.

"No one's ever been so attentive to touching my cock before."

Cock. Interesting word, she thought, glad to know what it was called and more pleased that he enjoyed her actions. She let go of him for a moment, however, when he slid his fingers into the place between her legs.

"Your pussy is so wet, my sweet, so ready."

Now she had a name for the part of her where all the sensations were concentrated. He continued to touch her there and she found her legs parting of their own volition.

"You want more?"

She nodded, not knowing exactly what the more could be. Logan started kissing his way down her body.

She missed the feel of him against her lips, but when he got to her pussy she experienced a thrill that was beyond anything she had enjoyed so far. He licked her gently, using only the tip of his tongue. She saw stars behind her eyes.

"Oh yes, Grace, that's it. I love seeing you respond to me." She could feel the warmth of his breath against her skin and it added to the pleasure. He lapped again. "And I love the taste of you, like sea water and honey."

His touch was incredible. When she felt him push a finger into her, her hips lifted off the bed, increasing her reaction and pleasure. Everything he did was more amazing than the last. As his tongue stroked the skin at the entrance to her body, she felt something begin to build. *Oh please*, she thought, *don't let it stop.*

"You're close, aren't you," he murmured against her. "I can see from the way you're grabbing the sheets, from how wet you are, from how swollen your clit is."

When he said the word *clit*, he flicked his tongue briefly, too briefly, over a point on her that shot fire through her blood. She didn't know what she was close to, but knew she wanted to get closer. She pushed herself toward him to try to tell him how she felt.

"Yes, my lover, I know what you want. Let me give it to you."

Logan touched her clit again and continued to suck and lick at the spot. A wave of pleasure built inside of her. She knew there was no stopping it. And although it scared her a little, she craved it more. His strokes continued, his tongue moving faster.

This is it, she thought. *Any moment I will reach—* and then she did. Pleasure spiraled though her body, concentrated at that magical place at the top of her legs. As another peak began to crest, she grabbed Logan's head and opened her mouth.

"Yes!" she screamed as the sound poured from her mouth and repeated over and over. She couldn't stop saying it. Hearing the return of her voice was nearly as wonderful as the passion he created within her.

When she stopped calling out, they both heard an ear-splitting yell that rattled the windows and made everything in the trailer shake.

Logan stopped what he was doing and lifted his head. "Did you hear that scream?"

"You mean the one other than mine?"

He looked at her and did a double take. "You can talk?"

"Because of the pleasure you brought me." She reached for his hands and pulled him up to her. Running her hands along his skin, she told him the story of her bargain with the Sea Trader. "I gave up my voice for the chance to come here and experience the ultimate pleasure. Once you had given that to me, my voice was returned."

"Do you have to leave now that you found what you wanted?"

She kissed him. "No, Logan, that scream we heard was the Sea Trader disappearing forever."

"Then you'll stay with me."

"Of course. The physical pleasure you've given me was magical, but it is only a part of what I receive from being with you. Being on land wouldn't be worth it without you.

I want to stay here and help you build whatever life you want, with or without modeling."

"One question then."

"Yes?"

"Will you tell me your name?"

She smiled, "Out of water it is nearly unpronounceable. Besides, I always want to be your Grace."

"And I always want you to be mine." He found his wallet in his pants pocket, pulled a small package out, and slipped something rubbery on his cock.

"What's that?"

"I'll explain later. Right now, I want to be inside of you."

"I want that, too." She opened her arms to him and he was above her, touching her pussy, wetting her again before slowly sliding into her. Wrapping her legs around him, she decided that this was their best use so far. He reached a barrier. She looked at him, puzzled.

"Of course! This is your first time. Oh, my sweet love. Forgive me for the moment of pain, but trust me about the pleasure to follow."

"I do," she said.

He kissed her deeply and pushed himself deeper. He was right. It hurt for a moment, but her cry was caught in his mouth. He caressed her until she relaxed and then continued to move within her.

"You're all right," he asked.

"More than all right. Don't stop," she said because she had the feeling that something even better was about to be part of her life.

The Thirteenth Fairy

By Kristabel Reed

One hundred years to the day, and still none breached the impenetrable walls of her curse. Morgannia, feared by many despite the passage of time, stood on the deserted turret to survey the prison she'd created. Once her castle danced with life and beauty; once splendor had graced this land. No longer. Now it was an empty, silent tomb. And her graceful castle stood guard, stood as an eternal warden over the one across the valley.

Across the verdant, rolling hills, her gaze rested on the suffocating briar encasing the structure in living death. A testament to betrayal. Her curse crushed every living thing that dared navigate its vice-like grip.

Another, Morgannia noted with a peak of interest as a solitary rider galloped across the hills. *Another princely fool come to hack into my prison of thorns and his way into a slow, agonizing death.*

With an irritated narrowing of her eyes, she inquired of her devoted servant, "A distraction. What number will this make, Ratha?" She breezed down the stone steps into her bedchamber.

"Several hundred, Milady," Ratha responded in an emotionless tone. "The thorns have consumed all the corpses."

"I'll have to see that they consume this new corpse immediately."

Morgannia stopped in front of the long, gilded looking glass. She undid the ties of her dressing gown and allowed the heavy, rich velvet to tumble to the floor. "I do not want any unnecessary interruptions this evening."

The looking glass told her all she needed to know. A hundred years of bitterness had not marred her eternal beauty. Ratha stood behind her, the deep blue of Morgannia's velvet gown now waiting in the servant's gnarled hands. The newest prince's arrival triggered an impatience to wake her sleeping lover.

And wake him she would.

The king of that once thriving, abundant land would see all his actions wrought during his one hundred years of sleep—his kingdom in ruins, his lineage forgotten. He would wake in the skeletal arms of the woman he chose to replace her. The daughter, the child he longed for, still in her perpetual slumber. This evening he would taste the ripened and cold revenge she had served him.

Morgannia took one more long look at her reflection. Fiery red hair fell about her shoulders in a riot of curls. Her emerald green eyes still sparkled, but there was no kindness left in them. Her breasts and form were the envy of any woman, and her naturally red lips were full and eager to give the king of that cursed land a last kiss.

A light knock at the bedchamber's door echoed through the room. Ratha slid the dressing gown onto Morgannia's shoulders and went to attend to the interruption. Morgannia turned to face the door, curious as to who dared disturb her, today of all days. All her attendants knew what today held.

"Milady," Ratha began, waving away the manservant, "there is a visitor who requests an audience."

"Pardon?" She spun to face Ratha, incredulous. "Who is this *visitor* that he should approach my door, much less request an audience?"

"The king, Milady," Ratha stated. "He claims to be the king."

Perturbed, Morgannia stared at her servant. *The king?* She nearly laughed, but curiosity had her tying her gown closed and stepping into her slippers. Leaving her hair loose around her shoulders, she went to investigate her mysterious guest.

It couldn't possibly be her king, her old lover. None had broken free from her curse, but who else would dare?

The anteroom where this king waited lay in darkness, the only source of light coming from the fireplace. He stood straight, eschewing the chair and spare repast laid out on the table. He was tall, dark brown hair cropped close to his head, light brown eyes steady as they watched her approach. A handsome man whose confidence was evident in his stance. He didn't flinch, even as she stormed into the room, magicks crackling around her.

"Who are you to disturb me?" she snarled. "What lies have you told to enter this place?"

The man offered a low, sweeping bow, elegant with no hint of fear. "I'm Lukas, King of the Northern Lands. It is my son who is the next to attempt to breach your thorns."

Morgannia laughed, a low, wicked sound. "Then I suggest you plan his funeral."

Lukas walked forward, clearly not intimidated by her threats. She laughed again and said, "Or perhaps he is a son you don't wish in your kingdom."

Angry now, he narrowed his eyes. "The prince will be the next king in my lands, make no mistake. And he will possess the beauty and riches purported to be locked away in that cursed castle."

Intrigued, she studied the king before her. By rights, he should be cowering, begging for his son's life. Several had done as much before, only to share the same fate as their foolish sons who attempted to rescue the sleeping beauty.

"You're a bold man," she allowed, eyeing his crown, "Perhaps you truly are a king." But then she dismissed him with a flick of her hand. "You've sent your son on a fool's journey, one that will result in his death."

Something in Lukas's face relaxed, and he offered a slow, erotic smile. Suddenly wary, Morgannia braced herself. She was positive this mere mortal could not harm her magickally, yet the way he looked at her, the way he was not cowed by her sparked through her veins.

A warning? Or was this . . . desire?

"All our lives," he said, "we have heard the tales of the castle and its riches. Of the young beauty sequestered high in the tower, slumbering for eternity. Those tales have captured the imaginations of kings, princes, and noblemen."

Impatient, she waved him on. This wasn't anything she hadn't heard before. In fact, she made sure that rumors of the riches in that castle spread far and wide.

"But not I," Lukas said, surprising her. "It was no tale of sleeping maidens that captured my imagination." He stepped closer and Morgannia couldn't look away. "'Twas the tale of the redheaded fairy, her legendary beauty, and the passion that drove her to place the curse that captured my boyhood dreams."

He raised his hand, but Morgannia stood enthralled with his words and did not smite him as she probably should have. Lukas stroked her cheek, the pads of his fingers rough on her skin. Her breath caught, and for a heartbeat she froze. Shaking the seductive spell from her mind, she leaned closer to the handsome king.

"You're a clever one," she whispered, voice harsh in acknowledgement of his ploy. "Or believe yourself to be. Coming here with absurd tales in an attempt to distract me and allow your son a chance to breach the thorns."

But this king, this *Lukas*, merely closed whatever remaining distance separated them. "Look into my eyes," he commanded, "and tell me you do not see the desire I hold for you."

Before she could respond, he tugged the ties to her gown. The material fell open, exposing her to his heated gaze. The fingers of one hand traced the tops of her breasts. Morgannia was shocked to feel lust pump through her veins, surprised this Lukas could elicit such a reaction in her cold body.

"You don't know what today is," she spat, swatting his hands from her body. She made no attempt to cover herself, but did move back enough to snarl at such presumption. "You don't know what significance this date holds. You arrogant mortal. Today your son will be torn to shreds, and I shall see my vengeance come full bloom."

His laugh was the same heated sound as before. There was no begging in Lukas, no fear, only erotic passion focused entirely on her. "I know precisely what significance this day holds," he corrected. "I've waited for today, for this moment, since I was a lad."

He stepped closer once more, and Morgannia found she couldn't move away.

"On the anniversary of the hundredth year, in spite of the memory of that other man, you will have just me. My hands on your skin." His tone sounded possessive when he said, "My lips tasting your sweetness. I do not fear you." His look seared through her, dominant. "I have no fear of you, but do you have fear of me taking you?"

Wetness flooded her pussy, and Morgannia reflexively swallowed. She hadn't felt this kind of passion . . . ever. Even with her lover, even after being scorned by a man who promised her eternity, she'd never felt such clawing need as she did with this strange mortal.

"Relinquish your anger and the memory you cling to," he coaxed, his finger slowly circling her hardened nipple, "for I am also a king, and what I've come for is you."

She tossed her head back in challenge. "You hold

yourself in high estimation. Are they just words? Or do you possess the stamina to prove it?"

Prince Phillip dismounted his horse and focused on the task at hand. He spared a thought, but not a glance at the castle on the opposite glen, for his father and what the other man did at this moment, then drew his sword. This was what he'd strived for his entire life, a moment to define him.

The thorns throbbed with life, with hatred, and pulsed around him. Philip swung his sword and with one blow, cut the vine in half. Did the fairy feel it? Did she know he sliced through her briars?

Nothing took its place. Phillip glanced over his shoulder. Perhaps his father had been right and this distraction would be his salvation. With a deep breath he carefully stepped forward. Slashing another thorny vine, he continued on.

"You have the softest skin, Morgannia."

Lukas stroked a finger along her cheek, memorizing the softness, the curve. Slowly, watching her as he did so, he lowered his head. She didn't move, had stopped whatever magicks she used against him. Her lips were cool when they met his. Cool and open, and her eyes held his as they kissed.

He'd often imagined what she tasted like, how she'd react, and wasn't disappointed. Lukas savored her, the tang of her, the darkness. *Morgannia*. He was finally before her, and for however much longer he lived, he'd never forget that.

"Lukas," she breathed when he released her lips. They were swollen from his kiss, her eyes dark and heavy. She was flushed, nipples hard, chest heaving. "You may regret this, mortal," she said. But she didn't pull back, and he knew she was aroused.

"We all have regrets," Lukas acknowledged. "But I doubt this shall be one of mine."

With fingers that were steady and feeling more sure about this than anything he'd ever done, Lukas pushed her gown off her shoulders and let it pool on the floor. Morgannia stepped out of the material, proud and not the least embarrassed.

"Why?" she asked.

Before he could answer, she quickly undid the ties of his doublet and dropped it to the floor.

"I'm being impulsive, Morgannia," he murmured against the side of her throat. She tasted as spicy here, he was pleased to note. Her skin was soft and untainted by perfume. Only her scent invaded his senses, and he was overwhelmed. Exhilarated. Aroused. She shuddered beneath him and he smiled. "For once in my life I'm going to take what I want. I'm going to feel. Do the one thing I haven't planned, plotted, or thought through to the very last possible outcome."

Her breasts fit his palm perfectly. She gasped and arched forward, but her eyes remained open and aware, boring into his. Lukas had never wanted anything as he did her. It scared and thrilled him. He wanted to lose himself in her.

"Then do so," she said, as if she'd read his thoughts.

Her voice was clear, but he could hear the passion there, the control she held over herself.

Determined to snap that control, Lukas quickly sucked on one nipple, biting down hard. Morgannia's knees buckled. Not unaffected at all. One arm banded around her, holding her to him as the other toyed with her neglected nipple.

"I'm going to make you scream my name," he promised.

Her fingers tangled in his hair and she looked at him with eyes that glowed. "And I shall make you scream mine."

Prince Phillip continued to hack the ever-encroaching vines. He made progress, he knew, and yet the slumbering castle seemed no closer. Still, the newly cut thorns receded from his path.

Did his father also make progress with the last fairy? Swinging his sword again, Phillip moved steadily closer to his goal.

Morgannia kissed this delectable king with all the passion she felt. He met her equally and demanded more. His body was hard and muscled, and she wrapped her hand around his stiff cock, stroking it lightly, teasingly. Giving herself over to arousal, letting her body dictate her will, she nearly let go of her control.

It was then the niggling weakness made itself known.

She pulled back, looked at Lukas, and smiled a slow, sensual smile. "You believe this will let your little prince live?"

His face darkened but he didn't deny it. Just as well:

She'd know he was lying. But there was something more to his look, an emotion she couldn't place. While she was attempting to figure out what that emotion was, Lukas thrust two fingers into her.

Clenching her teeth for control as a climax washed over her, Morgannia awaited his answer.

"He'll fight his battles," Lukas said, "but I shall win mine."

Still stroking his cock, she looked at him and purred, "Will you?"

Her lower back hit the table. Lukas shoved plates to the floor, his mouth rough on hers. It was then Morgannia realized she didn't care. She'd take care of the little prince soon enough. Now she'd enjoy King Lukas.

Pumping his fingers in and out, his mouth pleasured her, teeth biting down and she rode the wave of pleasure. Again he built her up, again she allowed the climax to envelop her.

He spread her legs wide, thumb making slow circles over nub, watching her for just a moment before thrusting into her. Morgannia's breath caught, and she wrapped her legs high on his waist, bringing him deeper into her body.

Lukas pounded into her, offering no quarter, and Morgannia required none. She met his every thrust, clawing his back until the scent of blood filled the air.

Phillip moved through the vines with ease. Thorns pricked through his armor, and he knew he bled from dozens of places, but they lessened now. Whatever his father did, it affected the fairy. Gasping for breath, he moved forward. The castle was within view, and he knew it was only a matter of moments now.

The sleeping beauty was within his reach. He could not fail.

Lukas watched Morgannia. Her wild red hair spread like fire over the table, eyes enticing him. Bewitching him. His fingers found her nub again, and he encircled it, watching her chest heave. Still, he continued to pound into her willing body. He was close but would not lose control before she was completely sated. He wanted to watch her orgasm again, wanted to see the pleasure overtake her.

"Yes," she hissed and arched her hips.

Then she came. Lukas was right—it was beautiful. She was glorious in her unbridled passion. Releasing the thread of control he barely held over himself, he climaxed.

Breathing hard, he fell to the table beside her.

Phillip could see the open courtyard, and victory surged through him. Just as he swung his sword, the brambles tightened, encircling him, biting his legs, pressing hard against his armor.

Struggle as he might, he couldn't move. The castle faded from view as more brambles grew, thickening over his vision.

Morgannia stood from the table and reached down for her dressing gown. Slipping it on, she turned to Lukas. He, too, stood and began to dress. His magnificent body moved with a grace she'd rarely seen, and she took a heartbeat to admire him.

A bare heartbeat, for her anger returned as she felt the prince within her thorns.

"You've failed. Your prince is trapped," she snarled. "And like all the others, he'll wither and die on the thorns."

"Have you ever had a king," he demanded, crowding her against the table, "attempt to break through your cursed thorns? My son will not die in your prison."

"No," she said through gritted teeth, tightening the thorns around the prince. She could all but feel his body dying. "You both will."

So saying, she turned away, dismissing the king. The most pleasurable sex of her very long life or not, he was insignificant compared to her vengeance. She heard the knife unsheathe, but turned a fraction of a moment too late.

Lukas caught her hand and sliced her palm. Blood welled up and fell to the stone floor.

"The thorns will give way now," he said confidently, quietly. No boasting coated his voice. "You've lost, my queen."

Glaring at him, one hundred years of hatred rising within her, Morgannia acknowledged the trick. "Clever, my dear Lukas. Perhaps you'll enter that castle. But who is to say *you* will ever leave it?"

"You." The word cut clearly through the anteroom. Honesty and truth rang in that single syllable, and Morgannia froze. She couldn't have said why, but Lukas's conviction was so strong it gave her more than a moment's pause.

"For my intention," he continued, "is to return to you. My son shall have his princess and all her father's lands. But *I* shall make you my queen."

She was touched by those words, though she refused to accept them even though a warmth quite unlike the heat of arousal moved through her. Dismissing it, she laughed, a harsh sound that echoed in the room. "You'll not come back for me," she said confidently. "This is merely another of your clever tricks. You wish me to believe you'll return to my arms." She spread her arms out, a mockery of a touching gesture. "But all you care for is escape."

"Test me."

Again she paused, considering him. Morgannia sensed no falsehood in Lukas, but neither did she believe him.

In the silence of his words, he finished dressing. Lukas bowed deeply to her and left without another word.

Lukas rode hard across the glen. Morgannia's scent clung to his skin. He could still taste her delectable lips. He'd meant every word he said to her. He'd return. If for no other reason than to prove he was not like the sleeping king in the castle before him. His entire life, Lukas wanted Morgannia. Now that he had her, one afternoon would not be nearly enough. But first, he had to save his son.

Dismounting, Lukas unsheathed the bloody dagger and hacked at the thorns blocking his path. He could only hope Phillip moved straight from where he'd tethered his horse. Easily breaking through the briars with the dagger, Lukas quickly made his way to his son.

Phillip stood bound by the thorns, struggling to break

free. Morgannia's curse encased his son. With renewed energy, Lukas attacked the briars, hacking them until they retreated, freeing Phillip.

"What are you doing here?" Phillip gasped. "Did your distraction not work?"

"We still may not escape this cursed place," Lukas warned, ignoring the questions. "Let's find your princess and not stay here a moment too long."

Easily breaking through the rest of the briars, Lukas let his son race ahead of him. Together, they climbed the steps to the highest tower. Outside, Lukas waited while Philip knelt beside the sleeping beauty's bed and gently kissed the woman. It was a tender moment between strangers, and Lukas looked away.

He stood outside the door, examining the dagger. The blood had dried, and when Lukas attempted to scrape it off, it wouldn't be removed. Permanent, then, the blood of the last fairy. A whispered conversation drifted to him, a low murmur of sound, and he walked down the stairs to the landing.

Across the glen he had an unobstructed view of Morgannia's castle. The tower stood high enough to look over the still-pulsing briar patch. Breaking through hadn't stopped the curse. More likely, Lukas admitted, Morgannia's will kept the thorns where they were, waiting for his exit.

Phillip carried the princess down the stairs, and Lukas trailed him. He couldn't hear the sounds of the castle awakening as the curse broke. It remained as silent as ever. He was tempted to see the king of this no longer significant kingdom. See the man who engendered the wrath of Morgannia.

"I don't understand," Phillip said, the princess standing weakly by his side. "Shouldn't the curse have lifted?"

"That was what was prophesied," the princess said, her voice hoarse after her long sleep.

"It's not the curse itself," Lukas said. He swept his gaze around the sleeping great room. "It's her."

His son looked at him, but Lukas didn't elaborate. There was no time. He understood why Morgannia let him leave. Why he'd been able to cross the glen, cut through the briars, why Phillip found the princess.

Morgannia allowed it.

"We should return immediately," Phillip insisted, and Lukas had a feeling his son had said more that he hadn't heard.

He led the princess to the still gaping hole in the thorns, and with one last look at the castle, Lukas followed. Behind him, the castle still slept. Before him, with every step he took, the thorns receded.

Phillip helped the princess onto his horse, ready to leave. Lukas took a moment to study his son and his soon-to-be bride. Phillip turned and waited expectantly. He was a fine boy and would rule the Northern Lands well. Of this Lukas had no doubt. From the time the lad could speak, Lukas ensured he knew the proper workings of the kingdom.

"I'm going back," Lukas said. "It's not the promise I made to the fairy that draws me back to her. Nor is it a bargain for your life. It's my desire. It always has been."

"Father," Phillip began but stopped.

Lukas swung into the saddle. There was much to say, but he couldn't find the words, didn't want to say anything before the princess. After a moment, Phillip nodded.

"Cross no fairies, my son," Lukas said with significant irony in his tone. More seriously he added, "Rule with the heart I know you possess."

Morgannia watched father, son, and princess from her tower. Her fury grew with every beat of the horses' hooves, and she prepared to strike all three down. She could still entrap them in her briars, keep their rotting bodies there for all to see. *This is what happens when one crosses the last of the fairies.*

Lukas had betrayed her.

She should have known it was all a ploy, yet she'd given him a chance, offered him this opportunity. Now he'd die with his son, and that kingdom would never wake. Perhaps she'd include Lukas's kingdom in her curse. Revenge for—

He veered off.

Puzzled, Morgannia halted the ever-expanding thorns and watched as he separated from his son, heading toward her castle. She watched until there could be no doubt. Was he coming to gloat he'd beaten her curse? Or . . . to return?

Sharply turning, she descended the steps and headed for the main entrance. On her way, she barked at her servants to leave, and they obeyed at once. Standing in the main doorway, the empty courtyard stretching before her, Morgannia waited.

Hope welled in her, even as she cursed herself a fool for such anticipation. But he didn't come. Had it been another diversion? One to allow his son and that damned princess time to escape? Did Lukas truly believe her powers could not reach to the Northern Lands?

Then she heard his horse. Adopting a cool expression, Morgannia crossed her arms over her breasts and waited. Horse lathered, Lukas galloped into the courtyard. Before she fully had time to register his presence, that he had returned, Lukas dismounted, strode across the yard, and pinned her to the wall.

"You didn't think I'd return," he said.

Morgannia didn't have a chance to reply. His mouth descended, locked firmly on to hers, hungrily as he tasted her. Devoured her, more like. The kiss made her dizzy and disoriented, and knocked every thought about why he was there out from her head.

His hands ripped open her dressing gown, fingers rough as they tweaked her nipples, pinching them until Morgannia thought she'd come right there. He pulled back to look at her, hands cupping her breasts, thumbs still rubbing her nipples. Mouth far too dry to speak, Morgannia wondered why he did it. Why he'd returned.

"I told you I would," Lukas said as if he'd read her mind.

He didn't wait for a response before bending to her breast, latching on to her nipple and sucking greedily. His teeth scraped the sensitive peak, making her legs weak.

In the back of her mind, Morgannia knew she had to reassert control over herself and the situation. In spite of all that, she couldn't help but moan. Her nipple, her entire body, was so sensitive, more sensitive than she could ever remember being. The wet heat of his mouth felt far too good to resist.

"I wanted you yesterday," Lukas stated, kissing the sensitive spot below her ear. "I wanted you today." His mouth moved along her shoulder, up her neck, exploring until he found a spot that made her shiver. His touch moved down her body, and he tugged the gown until he knelt before her. Looking up at her he said, "I've wanted you my entire life, Morgannia."

A small, small part of her believed him.

She gazed down at Lukas, watching his dark eyes gaze at her, his fingers doing wonderful things to the inside of her thighs. Morgannia stepped wider, needing him within her, touching her.

One finger entered her, then a second, pumping hard within her. His tongue tasted her, teeth nipped over her nub. Harder, faster, and she came. There was no purchase on the wall, no place to anchor as her climax crashed through her. Lukas was relentless, driving her again and again. Morgannia clutched his shoulders, grinding down against him. Screaming his name.

She shook, knees weak by the time Lukas pulled away. It took long moments for her mind to function again, and even then it came back to her slowly. The silky sensation of his hair beneath her palms. The feel of the stone against her back. His hands on her hips, holding her steady as he slowly stood before her.

Her name came out as a cross between a whisper and a growl, and he repeated it between each lick and suck of her skin. Morgannia felt herself being lifted, knew with an eagerness that had her body straining for his that he was going to take her against the wall.

"Let go, Morgannia," Lukas coaxed as he guided her onto his hard cock.

When had he undressed? It seemed unimportant as he settled her onto him. Her body shivered in orgasm. The sound she heard was her own whimper.

He buried his face in her hair and inhaled deeply. "I have always been meant for you," he sighed.

Carefully, Morgannia wrapped her legs around his hips, her breasts brushing his chest, nipples aching for more than that brief touch.

Lukas thrust into her, pounding her against the wall, mouth on her neck, relentless. His cock stretched her, delicious inside her. He bit her skin savagely, muttering things she only half heard. Fisting her hands in his hair, Morgannia brought his mouth back to hers, kissing him with equal ferocity. And promising herself that as soon as she could think again, move again, she'd take the time to drive him as wild as he did her.

His fingers found her nub, working her body, and she felt another orgasm coil within her. She panted something, his name? And dug her nails into his shoulders as he built her higher and higher. If she didn't come soon . . .

Every muscle in her body locked, and she used the last bit of breath she had to shout Lukas's name as her orgasm smashed into her. Everything went black.

When she could open her eyes again, Morgannia realized they lay on the flagstone floor. She was half atop him, curled around him as if it was the most natural thing in the world. He still breathed hard, and his arms were bloody. Only some of the blood was from her nails; the rest was from the thorns he braved to save his son. Very gently, feelings swirling within her she had no wish to dissect at this moment, Morgannia plucked a thorn from his arm. The wound instantly healed.

Lukas lifted his head and looked at his arm. Staring at the smooth skin, he tore his gaze away to look at her. Still he was silent. His dark eyes bore into hers and Morgannia swore he could see right through her.

"I'm uncertain the remainder of my life inside of you is long enough," he finally said. His lips pressed soft kisses along her neck and shoulder, arms tightening around her.

"We'll have an eternity," she promised.

The castle slowly woke, coming back to life. The king stretched, clearing the fog from his mind. What had happened? He couldn't remember but had a troublesome feeling he should. That he needed to.

Jerking his head to his right, he turned to his queen-wife and recoiled at what he saw there. In that woman's place lay a skeleton, her clothes ragged strips hanging off her body. One bony hand gripped a golden goblet, the ruby ring she wore lying on its side next to her hand. Her face, devoid of all flesh, grinned at him in a mockery of joy.

The curse.

Morgannia. She'd placed the curse on his daughter, his beloved only child, in revenge for his taking a wife.

"You don't understand," he said to the dead body of his

wife, but talking to his former lover instead. "I'd always planned to return to you."

Around him his great hall woke. He heard the questions and wonders, the exclamations and curiosity. What of his daughter? Had the spell lifted? Was she safe?

He rose to see to her, to discover what happened.

Before he could do more than straighten, he felt it. As if a slow wind swept across his body, he felt the life leach out of him. Bit by bit, breath by breath. There was no time to rail at Morgannia, to curse her as she had him before he was dust.

Morgannia, head resting on Lukas's chest, smiled. Her revenge was complete. Strange, how she'd kept it close to her heart for one hundred years, and now, with the introduction of one man into her life, she could release it.

But then again, she thought as she shifted to bite his shoulder, rousing him, Lukas was hardly an ordinary man.

Boots and Her Pussy

By Holly East

Grandma Miller was dead, and Bina, whom everyone called Boots because of her fondness for shoes, was inconsolable as she clutched the pussy she inherited to her chest, seeking comfort from its warmth. It was clear Puss liked the position, as he began purring and kneading her breast in a way more arousing than soothing.

"You have to stop that," she murmured into his ear, "before I embarrass myself." The rather large purebred Abyssinian, smelling amazingly of sandalwood, gave her a knowing look and then settled himself into her lap for what should have been a quiet snooze, if only his front paws weren't resting so perfectly on her mound. Fortunately, the layers of her dress and petticoat kept his position from completely distracting her as she listened to her grandmother's solicitor review the contents of the will.

The old gentleman who had served her wealthy grandmother for many years cleared his throat. "I realize that this distribution seems grossly uneven, but your grandmother was very wise, and I am sure she had her reasons. Her will is solid, as you would imagine. Lucinda inherits the house, the land it sits on, and a rather large trust fund. The major portion of Mrs Miller's wealth goes to her partner, whom she prefers not to name at this time, in accordance with an arrangement they set up long ago. Bina"—he smiled at her before continuing—"is entrusted with her grandmother's beloved cat, Puss, as well a small carriage with a horse, and this packet, which contains directions she is urged to follow scrupulously." As he rose to leave, he added, "Boots, you know she loved you deeply and only wanted you to have your heart's desire."

"Obviously, Grandmother Miller thought your heart's desire was to have a cat." Lucinda laughed unkindly. "Clearly she didn't love you as much as you thought. She must have seen I am far more capable than you in managing her wealth, and I intended to enjoy myself. I'll wager you are sorry you turned down the few proposals of marriage you received, for the room you thought of as yours is now mine, as is everything else here. I suggest you pack quickly since I want you on your way within the hour."

The cat hissed as though he understood Lucinda or at least her tone of voice. Boots hushed him, petting him from his back to his tail, which stood erect as she stroked, making her think of another appendage. "It's quite all right, sister. I do not wish to remain here. It was hard enough returning for the funeral. I certainly do not wish to strain your hospitality."

Clutching the cat and the packet, Boots hastened to the

room she once loved and carefully folded her few garments into a travel bag. Although Lucinda's words stung, Boots didn't regret her previous rejection of marriage. Better to be on her own and poor than tied to a boring idiot of a man. "We should be on our way, Puss. Lucinda has a nasty temper, and I don't want to extend our time together." The cat meowed loudly, scraping his claws on the ribbons tying the packet closed.

"Thank you for reminding me. I shouldn't leave without finding out what Grandmother wished me to do." Boots opened the packet and removed several pages in her grandmother's handwriting along with an envelope. She tuned to the letter first.

> *My darling Boots,*
> *If you are reading this, I have died. I am sure you are surprised by my will, but if you follow my directions, I promise you will receive what I want most for you. The envelope, which I am sure you have not opened as yet, contains sufficient funds to take you on the journey I have planned. Do not tarry. I am sure Lucinda is of the same view.*
> *Take the carriage I have left you and travel to Midlands. As it is the next town, you should get there before dark. Please stay at the best inn there. Do not read the next page until the following morning.*

"It's all most peculiar, Puss, but I have always trusted Grandmother. So I guess we are off to Midlands." Puss jumped lightly off the bed and strode to the door, waiting expectantly. "You are the strangest cat. It's almost as though you understand everything I say." Puss just mewed.

The journey to Midlands was uneventful, except for Puss's insistence on sitting on her lap and moving in such a delightful way that it was hard for Boots to concentrate on the road. Her hand kept straying to his soft fur. Every now and then he would turn, inviting her hand to stroke his belly, which seemed much tougher and firmer than one would expect in a cat. He must be exceptionally muscular, she mused.

No sooner had she made her way to her room at the inn when the innkeeper himself knocked at her door. He gave her a large package, which he explained had been awaiting her arrival. "I received directions to give this to you and to tell you to open it after you have dined below. You are the honored guest of Sir Marcus Carabas, and he orders only the best." He bowed his head to her and left.

She wanted to open the box but decided to follow the instructions she was given. "I am sure you know how irresistible curiosity can be, Puss, but Grandmother seems to have planned something of an adventure for me, so I suppose I should do as I was told." The cat caught her long skirt and made an effort to climb up. She scooped him up with a laugh. "I guess you are hungry as well. Would you care to dine with me?" Puss rubbed his head under her chin and licked her neck. "You are the most affectionate cat I have known. Let us go downstairs and see what we have for dinner."

Boots had a hearty appetite, but it met its match as course after course was presented with much fanfare. Her sense of the ridiculous made it difficult for her not to laugh at all the fuss, but Puss's presence kept drawing her attention away from the flamboyance so she was able to manage a serious demeanor. The cat stayed in her lap throughout the dinner, delighting in eating from her fingers.

When the several desserts finally came to an end, Boots rose, carrying Puss, who had one paw on her breast and his other paw stroking her ear. She shook her head at his antics, amazed at how quickly he had become such an important part of life. Once inside her room, she undid the package to find a beautiful robe lined in rabbit fur and a message written in a masculine hand. She read:

> My honored Lady,
> I hope you enjoyed your dinner. I chose my favorite foods in hope that you would share my taste.
> I beseech you to wear this gift to bed tonight— and nothing else. It would give me great pleasure to have the granddaughter of one I called friend wearing something soft and comforting after what has been a long and difficult day.
> With great anticipation for your decision, I remain
> Sir Marcus Carabas

Boots fingered the fur as the cat stared at her. "I suppose I shall do as this Lord Carabas asks. I suspect it is all part of a scheme of my grandmother's." She started removing her clothes as she normally did but found Puss staring at her almost lasciviously. A bit embarrassed, she continued in a more discreet manner, putting the robe around her as soon as possible and then slipping the remaining garments off with her back to the cat, who emitted a sound something like a growl.

She climbed into the bed and blew out the candle. Puss jumped up and settled himself between her legs. "You really shouldn't be doing that," she murmured as his nose rested near her clit. She thought of pushing him off, but it felt wonderful, as did the luxurious feel of the fur next to her skin. Nestling in, she fell quickly asleep.

And awoke just as quickly. The moonlight streamed into the room, and a candle on the bureau was lit. *I doused that*, she thought. *I must be dreaming*. The sound of breathing close by startled her. She opened her mouth to scream, only to hear a deep voice that sent soft rumbles through her body say, "Hush, Boots, I am not here to harm you."

"Who are you?"

"I am your midnight lover. You can live your wildest fantasies, because it is all a dream. I am here to serve your desires, for they are mine as well." She tried to see his face but he was mostly in shadows. Only his golden eyes gleamed as did the brilliant white of his teeth as he smilingly untied the sash of the robe. She heard the intake of his breath as she felt his gaze travel over her naked breasts, the creamy swell of her belly, and the dark triangle between her thighs. "You are perfect. More beautiful than I could ever have imagined." He lowered his head and drew one taut nipple into his mouth, biting it just hard enough to cause a mixture of pain and pleasure that went straight to the juncture of her thighs.

Boots had a fleeting thought that, dream or not, she shouldn't be permitting him such freedom, but it felt so delightful. The light scent of sandalwood permeated the air, and a soft moan slipped from her lips as his mouth moved to her other breast before he began trailing licks, nips, and kisses slowly down her body. He seemed to be learning every inch of her with his mouth even as his hand moved lower still, enticing his lips to follow.

She fisted her fingers in his hair as he exhaled over her swollen nub, and groaned as he left it to explore her sensitive inner thighs. "Please," she gasped.

"Please, what?" he asked teasingly.

"I don't know. Back where you were. I need . . . I want . . ." She gave up, not knowing what she needed or wanted—just more.

Murmuring "All in good time," he resumed his leisurely exploration of her legs. He licked the back of her knees and continued down her calves. He sucked on her big toe, letting his tongue circle it while his hand strayed higher to the tight curls, wet with her growing desire. He cupped her, kneading the soft lips as his thumb artfully stroked her clit, moving in circles and adding pressure.

Boots was writhing, her breath coming in short gasps. When his mouth replaced his thumb, she screamed, her hands tightly clutching the sheets as her body bowed upward straining to reach a height just out of reach. His tongue delved into her hot channel, flicking upward to touch the sensitive walls, and then she did explode, splintering into pieces.

"That was a good beginning," he said.

"Beginning? I don't think I can move."

"We shall have to find out." He bent his face to hers, his tongue tracing the outline of her lips, sliding inside as she moaned in pleasure.

Following an instinct she couldn't explain, Boots reached between them, her hand seeking the hard cock she could feel pressed against her stomach. Her fingers circled it below the head, and she was rewarded as he moaned into her mouth. Liking the feeling of power it gave her, she began sliding her hand up and down his shaft. As she increased the pressure, she felt him grow harder and impossibly longer. The tip became wet and she used the moisture to lubricate her movements.

"Lady Boots, you are killing me," he growled.

"I believe that is only fair," she said, laughing to let him know how much his reactions were pleasing her.

"We shall see about that." He slid his throbbing cock into her, burying himself to the hilt in her wet channel. With each thrust he went deeper still, his balls hitting her ass as her legs instinctively wrapped tightly around his waist. She screamed her pleasure once more as he roared his own and rolled her on top of him. She could feel the rapid beat of his heart thudding against her breast.

"And now, my passionate one, you need to sleep. Dawn will soon be here, and your day tomorrow will be long." Boots felt him slip out from under her, and although she didn't want him to go, she was too tired to hold him.

She awoke fully refreshed but sore between her legs. Her nipples were puckered and tender. "That was a very strange dream," she said to Puss. "It was so real. And my midnight lover seemed almost familiar, but I can't imagine who I thought he was." The cat just padded over to her, nuzzling his head under her chin.

The innkeeper knocked softly. "I have breakfast for you and for your cat as well. I will leave it outside your door."

Boots scrambled out of bed and dragged her breakfast inside. She piled the dishes for her meal on a table and left the food intended for Puss on the tray. "Perhaps if you are occupied with eating, you won't be staring at me while I dress." She washed rapidly and began pulling on her clothes, but the cat still managed to sneak numerous glances her way.

Relieved when she was finally presentable, Boots dived into her breakfast. "I am so hungry," she told the cat. "I promise to share some of this with you. You do love eating from my fingers." Puss watched her as she savored the food. When the juice from the strawberries trickled down her chin, he leaped up to lick it away, taking time to thoroughly clean her face. "Puss," she exclaimed, "I have a napkin. I don't need you doing this."

Leaving a few morsels of her breakfast, she opened the packet from her grandmother, eager to see what the next page of directions would bring.

I am sure yesterday was a most interesting day. I hope you and Puss are becoming good friends. For today, I would like you to continue down the main road until you come to Southdale. It is not far, so you can be more leisurely on your journey. Again, stop at the best inn in the town. Be yourself on your travels and believe that dreams come true.

Don't go any further in your reading until tomorrow morning.

"We are off again, Puss. I suspected as much. I wonder what Grandmother would say if she knew what I dreamed last night." She laughed lightly as the cat rubbed against her leg underneath her long skirt. She scooped him up and marched downstairs.

The innkeeper told her the carriage was ready, and he sent someone for her baggage. When she tried to pay him, he informed her that Lord Carabas had taken care of everything.

"I wonder who this Lord Carabas can be and why he is being so kind," she said, more to Puss than the innkeeper. "Ah well, this is already a most peculiar journey. Perhaps I will meet him in the future and will thank him then for his generosity." Puss purred very loudly.

Following her grandmother's directions, Boots let the horse set the pace. Before long she noticed vast fields on either side of the road. Workers were busy sowing but called jovially to one another and seemed to be enjoying themselves. Curious, she pulled the carriage to the side of the road, got out, and hailed the closest worker.

"Whose fields are these?" she asked.

"They belong to Lord Carabas," the man replied.

"He would appear to be a very lenient master as I see no overseers, and you all, while busy, do not seem to be overly worried about showing how diligently you work."

"The master is the best I have ever heard of. We all have our own land and give a small portion of the crops to him in rent. He markets it for us and gives us a fair price for what we grow. Since we also earn a portion of what he makes on his own land, we don't need anyone to tell us to work hard. What is more, if we come up with a way to increase the yield or handle a situation on our own, we are rewarded with additional land."

"You are indeed fortunate in your master," Boots told him. "What does he give you if you bring a problem to his attention?"

The man scratched his head. "Nothing, my lady, but no one has ever thought to ask him about this. I would think that noticing a situation before it became a big problem would be as much, or possibly more, help than fixing something. I guess I will have to ask him."

Boots got back into the wagon and placed Puss beside her. He jumped into her lap, his favorite riding spot, but kept staring up at her face with his golden eyes as though wondering about her.

They weren't far down the road when she saw a loaded wagon with a broken axle. A man sat beside it, his head cupped in his hands in despair. Boots pulled the carriage to a halt. "May I help you?" she asked.

"I doubt whether a lovely lady can fix the axle, and I am far too late to get to the market and sell my produce. I had been counting on the coin for my family."

"You are right that I can't fix it, but just a little ways up this road, there are workers in the field. I will get some of them to help." She turned the carriage around and brought back the promised assistance. She opened her purse and took out a goodly amount of her precious money. "This should cover the cost of your produce. Please deliver it to the inn at Southdale where I am staying the evening. I am sure the innkeeper will be pleased with the quality."

"My lady, I don't know how to thank you."

Boots smiled and said, "I ask only that in the future you help someone else in distress. That is all the thanks I need." Puss stared up at her, his golden eyes unblinking.

The remainder of the day was uneventful, and the evening at the inn in Southdale was much like the night before. The innkeeper was exceedingly attentive and presented her with a fine dinner of partridges accompanied by another letter from her mysterious patron.

> I hope you find the partridges to your liking. I trust your day went well. Enjoy the wine, which is one of my own vintages. You deserve only the best. Please wear the robe again tonight.
>
> Tomorrow, I hope you will break your journey at my estate where, I assure you, you will be an honored guest.
>
> Most sincerely,
> Sir Marcus

"I see we have become more familiar. He signed his first name," Boots said to Puss, gasping slightly as his kneading paws found that spot in her pussy that caused heat to pool between her legs.

Although she wasn't very tired, Boots went to her room. Puss's ministrations were apt to attract unwanted attention as other guests might notice the flush on her cheeks and the way her breast were rising and falling. She undressed, ignoring the cat's continued interest in her dishabille, having become accustomed to his ways. No sooner had she donned the robe and gotten into bed than she fell into a soundless sleep.

When her midnight lover appeared in her dream again, Boots was not surprised. She raised her arms welcomingly and drew his head down to her face. Imitating his actions of the night before, she outlined his mouth with the tip of her tongue and slipped it inside as he parted his lips in response. She explored its moist recesses and teased the roof of his mouth. He caught her tongue with his own, and they twined and danced together.

His hands tweaked her already puckered nipples that pebbled into painful hardness, kneading and pinching them until she moaned. As she arched under his ministrations, he moved to her ear, his tongue finding a new way to delight her before he licked her jawline and nipped, kissed, and suckled his way down her neck to her breasts. She could feel the hot wetness dripping from her cleft and hoped he would hurry only to change her mind a moment later and hope he would take his time and prolong this sensual agony.

To her surprise, he flipped her over, his fingers working their way down her back, slipping underneath to cup and caress her breasts. And then his mouth trailed down her spine. Her face heated as a knot of desire coiled in her nether region when he licked her between the twin globes of her ass. She was bucking frantically, wanting to be able to touch him as his talented tongue reached her dripping pussy.

When he allowed her to turn, his hard cock covered with her own wetness stroked her swollen clit. Determined to give him the same pleasure he was giving her, she reached down and cupped his sac in her hands. She pushed him lightly so he would lie on his back. When he was in the position she wanted, she replaced her hands with her mouth, rolling his testicles on her tongue as she stroked and sucked. His groans increased her sense of power and added to her own growing need.

Struck by an idea, Boots took the tip of his shaft in her mouth and enfolded its length between her breasts, slowly moving up and down to add friction. He slid his hand down, inserting one then two more fingers into her cleft before he lifted her so she was positioned over his thick erection. At first he guided her rhythm but she soon found one that suited them both. Erupting to the sounds of his hoarse cry, she dropped bonelessly over his chest.

He kissed her deeply and said, "Sleep, my love. Tomorrow will bring answers to your unasked questions and you will discover something better than a midnight lover."

When Boots woke the next morning, the musky scent of lovemaking hung in the air. She felt sticky between her legs but decided she was just reacting to her dream, although that wouldn't explain why her nipples were swollen and tender. She stroked Puss who sleepily purred and rolled over on his back with a strange meow. Boots blushed as she recalled what she did when her midnight lover was on his back, but hurriedly went to wash and dress before the thought could take hold.

Breakfast was a hurried affair, but Boots did stop to read the final page of her grandmother's letter.

Today I trust you will be stopping at the estate of Sir Marcus Carabas. You have some startling information to learn, but I know you will use your wonderful mind and tender heart to accept the truth and forgive an old woman for her meddling. I hope you will be as happy as I want you to be.

Your always loving grandmother

Boots couldn't wait to get underway. Much as she enjoyed the journey, she was eager to reach its conclusion. Her grandmother's message was a mystery that she wanted to unravel.

Throughout the day, she continued to pass fields and orchards all tended by busy workers who assured her that she was coming closer to the home of Sir Marcus Carabas. By mid-afternoon, she could see the top of a large home set on a small hillside rising above tall trees. "I think we are approaching our destination," she said to Puss. He meowed in obvious agreement.

Boots turned her carriage into the wide driveway flanked by tall trees. It seemed to go on forever but eventually she came to beautiful manicured gardens and a circular drive that curved in front of tall double doors that opened at her approach. A smiling elderly gentleman came out along with a number of what appeared to be household staff who lined up in two rows facing each other.

"Greetings, my lady. We have been expecting you. I am

Horace, butler to Sir Marcus. The staff is here to serve you." Boots smiled and nodded to them all as they bowed and bobbed curtsies.

Puss trailed at her side as she walked up the three steps leading to the entrance, but she had no sooner gotten inside than he disappeared.

"A footman will bring your bag, and a maid has been assigned to unpack and tend to your needs." Horace beamed at her. "Once you have had a chance to refresh yourself, I hope you will come down and have some light refreshments before dinner. The master is eager to speak with you."

Boots found herself eager as well, She allowed the maid to assist her bath and dress so she could return downstairs as quickly as possible. The footman opened the door to the dining room, and Boots' breath caught in her throat. A man was seated at the end of a long table. His face was shadowed but he rose as she entered, walked the length of the room, and took her hands in his. A light hint of sandalwood filled the air around her.

He kissed her hand, but as he raised his head she could see his golden eyes were twinkling. "I am delighted to have you in my home. I am Sir Marcus Carabas."

Boots surveyed his handsome form. Her mind quickly reviewed all that had occurred in the past two days. "I am pleased to make the formal acquaintance of my midnight . . . visitor. And shall I also call you Puss?"

Marcus laughed heartily. "Yes, you may, my clever Boots. When I despaired of finding a wife who was intelligent and compassionate with a loving, passionate heart, your grandmother assured me you would be more than I dreamed possible, and she, as always, was correct. When I saw the portrait she had of you, I knew you were beautiful, but for the rest, I must admit I was skeptical. Not only did you see through my subterfuge, but I saw your intelligence when you questioned the men in my fields, and your compassion shone through when you helped that poor man despite your own limited funds. I can only hope you find me as desirable as I do you. But before you answer, I have a final letter from your grandmother." He handed her a sealed sheet of paper. "I trust she supports my suit, but in truth, I don't know what she wrote."

Boots sat on a nearby settee, broke the seal, and read,

Darling Granddaughter,
Your journey has come to an end. Marcus has long been my mystery partner. His business acumen is unmatched, but I grew tired of his complaining that all females (excepting me, of course) were empty-headed ninnies and he would never find a fitting wife.

I know you, too, have given up your dream of a marriage that would include passion and partnership. I watched as you rejected many suitors for fear of being tied to a tyrant who would want you to be a non-thinking brood mare interested in nothing more than the latest fashions.

It seemed you and Marcus were made for each other, but you had to find it out for yourselves somehow. It is his ability transform into a cat that

gave me the idea for this scheme. You must get him
to tell you how he does that.

Whatever your decision, know that the portion
of my estate that supposedly went to my partner is
actually yours. You are a wealthy woman, free to
make your own choices. Trust your heart and your
dreams.

I will watch over you always,

Grandmother

Boots looked up, tears sparkling on her lashes, as she
smiled at Marcus, who was alternately pacing and stopping
to stare at her. She loved seeing he was not always as
assured as he was in her bed.

When he saw she had finished the letter, he hurried
over and knelt before her. "I apologize for deceiving you
and will never do so in the future, if only you will do me
the honor of becoming my wife."

"I am now a wealthy woman and I should not be too
hasty in my choice of a husband. I must see if you are
as good as my midnight lover who pleased me greatly,
although I never saw his face. I will give you my answer
afterwards."

"I will rise to the challenge, my lady," said Marcus
scooping her up in his arms. He raced up the stairs carrying her as though she weighed nothing and brought her to
his bedchamber. After setting her on her feet, he lit every
candle in the room. "I want to be sure that you see everything."

"Then I want to see all of you. Let me be your valet,"

she said impishly and proceeded to remove his jacket and waistcoat, slipping her fingers between the buttons of his shirt to touch his flesh before opening it. He hissed as he drew in a breath. Her tongue darted out, licking the corner of her lips in concentration. Marcus tried to capture it in his mouth, but she darted away.

"Nay, my lord. You did say I was to be able to see everything. I have a big decision to make." She gazed down at his cock straining beneath the fabric of his trousers and corrected herself. "A very *big* decision."

When she saw he was going to let her have her way she slid his shirt off and slowly walked around him, appraising his magnificent form. Standing behind him, she ran her fingers over his massive shoulders, one hand trailing down his spine while she moved in to nip at the tempting skin. When her seeking hand reached his trousers, she inserted two fingers just to see how his muscles tensed, and then returned to face him.

"Let's see. What shall I do next? I know, your boots must come off." She pushed him lightly and he complied by sitting on the bed. Kneeling at his feet, Boots pulled off his boots. She couldn't resist mouthing the large bulge straining against the buttons of his trousers. His groan let her know she was becoming as good at tormenting him as he was with her.

She tugged his arm, signaling she wanted him standing. Once more she circled his body, touching him, delaying what they both wanted with increasing desperation. She could feel her juices trickling down her legs and was sure he could smell her arousal. But loving the power, she resisted speeding things up. Her fingers dipped into his waistband and felt for his cock. Taking pity on him, she opened the buttons, letting him free. She bent to lick off the milky liquid that leaked from the tip of his shaft, and then knelt and drew him fully into her mouth.

It was only moments before he growled, "Enough! If I allow you to continue, I will embarrass myself and disappoint you." He grabbed her and fell with her onto the bed. His fingers circled and pressed her hot nub and then entered her channel, which was dripping in readiness for him. He raised himself over her and slid his shaft deeply into her, seating himself to the hilt. She screamed his name for the first time as his thrusts took her over the edge. With great effort he held himself back, using his fingers to once again bring her to the edge before his hips began pistoning against her as he sought his own release. "Marcus," she cried again. He roared as he spilled himself inside her, and she splintered as she contracted in waves of intense pleasure.

He rolled on his side and held her close. "Well, my lovely Boots, how did I fare?"

"I would say you more than rose to my expectations."

"And what is your answer to my question?"

"Yes, my Lord—Puss. You are truly the companion I have always wanted, and I will be honored to be your wife."

The Frog Princess

By Carolyn Heaven

Long ago, a beautiful princess with eyes of blue and long, flowing, golden hair was to wed the most eligible bachelor in the land. Alas, the fair princess did not love him. The prince claimed the title of most eligible man in the land, as well as the reputation for being the biggest rutting boar. He arrived to claim his prize, the Princess Fierra.

Sure, many would consider the prince a fine specimen of male, all brawn and brash and undeniably lacking a shortage of bed mates—a fact Princess Fierra discovered as she stumbled upon the long line leading to his bed-chamber on the second night after his arrival. Fierra refused to be among them, which did not make the prince happy. The sweet princess dreamed of true love and could not bear the thought of marrying this man.

Her father, the king, allowed her many years to find true love, but she never found that elusive beast. Now, an altogether different beast found her instead.

In the receiving room, she found her father and betrothed present sitting on the thrones. The prince was seated in the queen's throne. Fierra was glad her mother was otherwise occupied.

"Father, may I have a word with you in private?"

"My dear, the prince is to be your husband. Whatever you wish to say can be said in front of him for there are no secrets between man and wife."

"Father, I really must speak with you alone."

"Nonsense, Fierra. Out with it."

She already tried pleading with the lout she was promised to on the first day he arrived. Her words might have had more effect on a brick wall. He had no need of her heart. Her lands, titles, and wealth ensured him a rich future. Her beauty was merely an added tribute to him. "Father, please. I do not wish to marry this man. I wish to marry for love, and he does not love me. He only cares for our wealth and to become king."

"Daughter, marriages are made to increase wealth, and someone must take my place as king. Besides, it is past time you married. It is time you let go of foolish fairy tales and behave as the future queen. You will grow fond of each other in time just as your mother and I have developed a deep fondness for each other."

Determined, Fierra stated, "Father, I will not marry this brute."

"You will do as I say." He stood and walked toward the hall leading to his private study but looked back when he found himself unaccompanied. "Are you coming, Prince?"

"In a moment, Your Majesty. First, I would have a few words with your daughter."

"Very well, you know where to find me." The king continued down the corridor.

Once the king was out of sight, the prince grabbed Fierra by the arm and pulled her to him, growling, "This kingdom is mine. You are mine. If you do not tell your father you wish to marry me, then I shall introduce you to my witch, who has a spell to turn people into frogs."

"I am a princess, and for my people's sake I will not bow down to any threat. How dare you try to intimidate me. A frog indeed. I should call the guards this instant. Just suffice to know you will never own me."

"I'll own the part I desire most, and that's all that counts, Princess. Mark my words, if you deny me to your father, you'll live out your days in a golden cage. Able to hear, able to understand, and unable to tell anyone what happened to you."

Fierra slapped a hand over her mouth to cover a gasp. "You can't!"

"I can and I will. You and this kingdom belong to me." He pulled Fierra to him to grind his lips against hers in a punishing kiss meant to prove his dominance over her. Tears of anger and rage spilled from her eyes. Finally, she could take it no longer and bit his lip . . . hard.

The prince released his hold at her vicious nip and licked at the blood on his lips. "Perhaps I was hasty with my words. I will find a way to make up for my behavior. Meet me tonight, and we shall discuss an arrangement."

Fierra, not trusting herself to speak, nodded before the prince left down the hall to follow the king.

That night she joined him in a private alcove where a

small table was set with fruit and cheese. An old woman served them wine. As they drank, he offered arrangements for their marital bliss. His ideas were absurd and self-indulgent.

"I do not wish to marry you. I will marry only for true love," she said.

"Then you never shall. Now, witch."

The servant—a witch who hated the prince—chanted her spell. Pink smoke filled the room. Princess Fierra morphed into a small green, spotted amphibian who was placed in a golden cage just as the prince had said. Unknown to the prince, however, the witch altered the spell, allowing true love's kiss to break the curse.

Wanting to get Fierra away from the prince, the witch carried the princess through the early morning fog to the crossroads where she found a caravan. There she explained the tale and spell to an old gypsy matriarch and paid her to care for Fierra, imploring her to never let the prince find the frog. The gypsy queen was moved and vowed to take care of the cursed princess.

The gypsy queen was as good as her word. To keep Fierra safe, she sold the frog princess to a king in the desert, where the amphibian would be considered exotic and special. She told him of the curse, and told him of how a kiss and love could break it. The sultan was pleased with the prize, and for many generations the frog princess lived a life of luxury in the harem as a treasured pet.

It came to pass that a sheikh desired grandchildren to ensure his family line, and decreed whichever son married first would have the throne. A grand party would be held so his sons, Malik and Aasim, could choose a bride from the ladies in the land. Sultan Jalal, the sheikh's brother, knew the elder son, Malik would be detrimental to the kingdom and its people. He had to be certain it was Aasim, the second son, who married first. Fortunately, the sultan also knew something Aasim had yet to acknowledge, and it would save the sheikhdom once Jalal could convince Aasim to believe in the old tale.

Aasim readied for the gala while speaking to the frog his uncle gave him on his eighteenth birthday. Fierra was the only one he could share his dreams, aspirations, and concerns with. Speaking to her was like talking to an old friend, and he often forgot she was simply a pet.

"My father is dying, Fierra, and I must choose a bride soon or be forced to live under my brother's rule for the rest of my life."

My poor prince, thought Fierra, wishing she could comfort the man she had come to care for deeply.

"And far worse, my people would suffer with Malik as their ruler. I suppose it was foolish of me to put off marriage, wishing for love."

Never, my prince. Fierra understood his pain and need, for time had not changed her wish to wed for love. Unfortunately, there was no way for her to tell Aasim the truth of her situation and how deeply she felt for her friend.

Not long after she was given to Aasim, her affection for her kind owner grew like well-tended flowers. His mind, voice, and heart made her yearn to have a true conversation with him. At times, she almost believed he understood her croaks and ribbits. He would speak, and his words were enough to drag her gaze away from his lush lips. When he wasn't speaking to her, she couldn't keep her eyes off the man's body. Soon, the flowers blossomed into more than simple affection.

For years she watched with a growing hunger as he dressed and bathed. The times he ran late and rolled out of bed neglecting a robe were among her favorite mornings. Her cool skin burned on the nights he pleasured himself and she imagined it was her bringing him to release—him groaning into her ear rather than his pillow. She ached for her human form to give to her heart's desire.

"At this party, I am to find a wife, Fierra, and duty supersedes love."

Fierra wanted to cry for her prince, for herself, and for the people she knew Aasim could not abandon to his brother. Her heart wrenched at the thought of losing him to another, but all that came out was a feeble croak.

Aasim sighed at the hopeless sound, "Yes, but you are not a woman, my friend, for if you were, my duty would equal my desire." When he spoke to her like this, Fierra could almost believe she was a woman, and at the same time felt heartsick for what she could not give him. "Now, no more of this. I will wed and you shall be the most pampered pet in the sheikhdom." He stood before his mirror in formal attire, then turned to her. "How do I look?"

Delectable as always, she thought, then nodded to him in approval.

He smiled in understanding. "Wish me luck."

Fierra gave him a half-hearted happy ribbit, wishing she could be the woman he needed.

As the royal guests dined at the feast, Malik sought his bride in the throng, anxious for his chance to lead, but Aasim could not bring himself to search among them. This was not the way to choose a wife, no matter the political ramifications. He would try to reason with his father. Malik would never stop laughing if he knew Aasim would rather be talking to a frog than the women of the court.

Following dinner he sought to speak to his father, but Sultan Jalal pulled Prince Aasim toward the gardens. "Walk with me, nephew."

Aasim respected his uncle enough to follow. After several moments of silence and checking for eavesdroppers, Aasim asked, "What can I do for you, Uncle?"

"Do you still have the frog I gave you on your eighteenth birthday?"

Taken aback at the odd question, he responded, "Of course. I take care of her myself and speak to her everyday as you told me."

"Good, so why haven't you kissed her as I instructed?"

The prince stared at his uncle as though he had lost his mind before gathering his wits to respond to the sultan, "I thought you were joking."

"The story I told you is true. She is a princess without a kingdom, whose lands have fallen to the sands of time. You need a wife, and I've provided you with one. If you have been good to her, then you may enjoy her tonight, and in the morning you shall wed." The sultan lost his smile.

"Your father's health continues to fail, and the last thing we want is that conniving brother of yours trying to take over the sheikhdom."

Aasim nodded. "I agree Malik is the last ruler my people need." He grinned weakly at his uncle. "So, this princess you have waiting for me, is she aware you've arranged a wedding for us at first light?"

Sultan Jalal smiled indulgently. "The tale says this princess is the most beautiful in all the land and believes in true love, a trait you both share. Go back to your room and tell your frog what I've said. Once you've shared everything, kiss her, and your princess will appear. By morning, you will have the love you seek and a princess to wed."

Upon returning to his chambers, Aasim told Fierra every word of the conversation with his uncle, the kiss he had to give her, and about them being married in the morning. At the end of the conversation, he opened her gold cage, lifted her out, and asked if she was ready. She responded by hopping to the front of his hand and pushing her little froggy lips toward his.

He puckered up and placed a gentle kiss to Princess Fierra's lips. Immediately, thick pink-colored smoke filled the room. Aasim felt Fierra struggle in his hand then leap free. Aasim remained in place not wanting to step on his poor frightened frog.

"Fierra," he called. "Stay where you are until the smoke clears. I don't want to hurt you, so stay out from under my big feet."

"I'm more worried about your big cock than I am about your big feet, Aasim."

He drew his sword out of reflex from years of weapons training, but lowered it as the meaning of her provocative suggestion overshadowed his concern for the frog and the sound of her sexy voice made the aforementioned organ twitch with excitement. "Who are you? How did you get past the guards?" The prince thought for a moment. The guards outside his chamber were loyal to Jalal. "Oh, my uncle. You must be the woman Sultan Jalal sent. Before we go any further, help me find Fierra, my frog. She is very important to me."

"That is very good to know," the woman said.

Fierra's heart swelled for this gorgeous man who befriended a lonely frog. His generous, loving nature and magnificent body had her heart and body melting at the sight of him bent over to look for her. She couldn't help checking out his backside with him in such a tasty position. His wavy, dark-chocolate hair, warm brown eyes, and olive skin had fueled her fevered dreams. She knew this man. She loved this man. Somehow she would reassure and convince him she was the frog.

Fierra looked down to first see her pert breasts and was pleased to realize her appearance was perfectly preserved from the time the witch cast her spell. She only hoped her prince would be pleased as well.

"Aasim, your frog princess is safe." She was careful with her wording so as not to lie to him. "I have her with me." After so many years, she knew the frog would always be a part of her.

The smoke cleared completely, and the prince strode

straight toward the woman with his hand out to retrieve his friend. "Let me have her."

She smiled slightly and put her hand in his. "I will let you have every part of her once you let me explain."

"If you harm her, I will not marry you."

"I wouldn't harm her for the world."

The prince nodded curtly.

"Look at me," Fierra said, "and tell me what you see."

The prince openly stared at her, reaching out to touch her hair and shoulders. She saw his breath quicken and looked down to see his cock thicken, lengthen, and press against the front of his pants.

"I see a golden goddess. You are the most beautiful woman I've ever seen, princess. Once you give Fierra back, I'll spend the hours we have until dawn showing you how beautiful I can make your body feel."

Fierra shivered at his words and pressed her thighs together, causing moisture to dampen her folds. Her clit hummed at the thought, and she fought to make him understand. "Aasim, look at my dress. Does it look anything like current fashion?"

"No, but that does not change how lovely you look. Hopefully in time we will come to care for each other."

The princess grew frustrated, even as she ached to simply melt into his arms and show him how much she already loved him. "Aasim, I'm your frog."

"Do not play games with me; we both know that is not possible."

"Ask me something you've only told your frog."

"Who did I dream about last night?"

She smiled, answering quickly, "Fierra. You often dream that I am human and able to make love with you. I heard you moaning in your sleep, and this morning as you dressed you told me about it. You said you dreamed I was in your arms as we woke after making love for hours. I am here to make your dreams a reality. I am here to help you save your people from your traitorous brother, but most importantly I am here to love you."

"The stories are true," he said with wonder in his voice. "No one but Fierra knows this fantasy." Taking her in his arms, he walked her backward to his bed and laid her down gently. His raging erection pressed against the juncture at her thighs. She was tall and their heights were well matched. The thought of how perfectly they fit had her grinding herself against him, needing the warmth of contact.

Fierra groaned at the sensations. Wet heat flooded her nether lips. Her back arched, thrusting her breasts toward him and forcing her pelvis into his to press them closer together. Physical sensations flooded her body while emotions tethered her heart to a safe port. She loved this man, and she knew he would love her. "Make love to me, Aasim. I need you."

He caught her lips in a fiery kiss. She opened to him on a gasp, and his tongue entered to explore. Their tongues danced, sliding sensuously over each other, heightening their desire. His hands roamed her body, gliding over every inch he could reach. Desperately, he rolled them to the side and began tugging her skirts up. Fierra moved to help him. She wanted this, needed this fiercely.

Once her gown was a puddle on the floor, she tugged at his belt and growled in frustration as she fumbled with the unfamiliar clothing. He chuckled before assisting her. Soon, clothes were no longer a barrier to their passionate exploration of each other.

Her hands glided over his flesh until she found the part she wanted to discover further. Fierra slowly pushed her way between Aasim's spread legs, kissing his lips, chin, and jaw as she longed to do for years. Firm but gentle kisses trailed down his throat to his chest until she came to his nipples. With only her tongue, she licked her way around an areola, then placed a soft kiss on the sensitive flesh. He shivered, and she reveled in his response, wanting more.

As Aasim lifted his knee, Fierra straddled and rubbed it against her aching mons. She moaned, then returned her attention to his nipple, teasing and sucking before repeating the actions with the other. She wanted more of him in her mouth and slid down to engulf as much of him as she could. She brought her tongue into play, licking the sensitive spot at the base of his cockhead, tickling it back and forth rapidly, all the while applying suction. Up and down she began to bob. She fondled his balls, pulling the sac, rolling his balls, and lightly tickling the fine hairs there. Fierra enjoyed the texture of his smooth skin, his slightly salty taste, and his bliss-filled responses.

"If you don't stop, I am going to embarrass myself," Aasim said hoarsely. "Your mouth is incredible, but I want to be inside you when I come. So, my precious desert flower, let me taste your sweet nectar and return the pleasure you are giving me. Let me hear you scream your release."

With no other warning, Aasim grabbed Fierra, pulling her up to straddle his shoulders, and drove his tongue between her dripping lips as she braced herself against the headboard. Fierra squealed in delighted surprise and wriggled her hips atop his face.

In the harem, Fierra saw the women giving and receiving pleasure in every conceivable way, but she had never experienced it for herself. She also knew this first time would hurt, but couldn't seem to care. She wanted Aasim more than she had ever wanted before and enjoyed the pressure building behind her clit as she moved faster atop him. Now, she could barely catch her breath. She was sure this was what the women called an orgasm, but neither had she experienced this.

He added two fingers, working them into her tight sheath, adding to her pleasure. She stiffened slightly, then instinctively leaned forward, allowing him better access. She was tight, and when his fingers were finally in, he realized he had aleady breached her barrier. He paused, but it was too late.

"Aasim," she called to the heavens, then collapsed forward, taking care not to smother him. She rested there trembling, catching her breath.

It was the loveliest sound he ever heard, as his beautiful, virgin bride-to-be screamed his name in her ecstatic cry of release. As he brought her to his side, he knew he couldn't take her virginity like this. She was too tight. He'd hurt her, and he didn't want that. He took his aching member in hand, ready to tend his own needs.

Seeing what he was doing, Fierra stopped him and

said, "My love, I want the rest of your fantasy." She moved above him again, this time sliding her still-slicked skin down his body to connect with the tip of his cock. He immediately moved it away, unintentionally sliding his crown through her wet folds to bump her clit. She cried out at the exquisite sensation from the sensitive area. "More. I want more."

He grinned at her. "It pleases me to know you enjoy my touch"—he looked serious—"but we can wait until after the wedding to make love if you wish. Your first time will hurt."

Fierra closed her eyes at his words and grabbed his thick cock to hold poised at her entrance. "You will love me through the hurt."

At that moment, he knew he would love her through anything. As she brought herself slowly down the length of his rock-hard cock, conscious thought fled. Aasim gritted his teeth to allow her body time to adjust. She hesitated, then pressed down hard against him as he raised his hips to meet her. Her body shook in silence, and he saw the combination of pleasure and pain flicker over her features.

"Focus on me, Fierra," he said while caressing her cheek. When her eyes met his, he ran a finger down the side of her neck, circled her breasts, rolled both nipples, chased away her pain, and found her clit. There he stroked circles around the hard bud until she felt the urge to move once more. The faster he stroked, the faster she lifted and dropped herself. Up and down she rode his length, and after a few moments he knew the pain was gone, and was hopefully replaced by that same building pressure she experienced earlier. The sounds she made were making his desire burn, driving him closer to completion.

Her face was a mask of near bliss, and he could barely hold back for her. "Hold on, Fierra."

He flipped them while still deeply situated inside her. Aasim could have stayed like this forever, but the tingling in his balls told him he wouldn't last much longer. Pulling her hips up to him, he thrust into her fully. They groaned together at the change in sensation. He drove himself into her until they exploded in unison, vowing their love for one another. The last remnants of the curse broke with their vow of love—and a puff of pink smoke.

Dawn's first light found them in each other's arms, covered in blankets with the sultan and a man to marry them at the foot of the bed. After Fierra and Aasim were wed, Sultan Jalal took Malik to work in a far-off land where he could not harm the new couple or the people they ruled with love, compassion, and strength.

And the couple, of course, lived happily ever after.

Ride

By Kristina Marqué

As the heavy, weathered door slammed behind her, Jocelyn jumped in surprise. This was not where she expected to end up when she fled the ballroom.

She was making small talk with her parents and their friends at the Marlborough Country Club, but as she glanced across the room, her eyes caught the stares of the notorious "princes" of the club, both born with silver spoons in their mouths. Their reputation was for getting any girl they wanted, bedding them, then casting them off when they got bored or a better offer came around. Now they had their sights on her.

Jocelyn ignored her mother calling her as she made a beeline for the door to the kitchen at the back of the room. There she stood silently among the bustle of dishes clanging as they hit the metal prep shelves.

This is so not *me*, she thought to herself. She wasn't someone to run from a situation, but just this once she decided to escape rather than deal with a conversation she could practically write out in advance. As she surveyed the kitchen, anxiously looking for a way out, her eyes caught those of one of the head waiters. He motioned to her left as if he read her mind and sensed her need to escape. She followed a maze of hallways and passages. Over twenty years coming here with her family, and never had she passed these walls before. One quick turn to the right, and she almost walked straight into the door. With a strong shove, it flung open.

As she stood catching her breath, she saw a beautiful trellis covered in white jasmine blooms. She walked closer, breathed in their sweet smell, and noticed a cobblestone path at its base, which led past the lush lawn. She followed it as if invited, snaking in and out of oak and pine trees. When it ended, she stood admiring the setting sun casting a hazy orange glow over everything. Breathing deeply, she closed her eyes.

"You're trespassing," a voice boomed.

Jocelyn turned and faced him. An unfamiliar man stood in the shadows, his presence alarming. "Excuse me?" she said.

"You're trespassing," he repeated, "which could get you in a lot of trouble."

As the wind blew, it drew her dark hair across her face, framing her deep green eyes and perfect pink lips. Seeing her took Alan's breath away. As her eyes pierced his, he felt it in his heart—and not for the first time.

Their paths had crossed a month ago, although only from a distance. She was the type who was noticed everywhere she went. More than her beauty or her family's money, people spoke of her wild spirit. He watched in secret as she kicked off her heels and played hopscotch with two young girls, much to the distain of her parents. The girls cheered her on, and her smile sparkled as they call laughed. She may have been called a princess, but it was as much true inside as out. He lost his heart in that moment.

Thoughts of her haunted him. All of his deepest desires included her. As he drank his morning coffee he would picture her there with him, sharing breakfast. His showers lasted forever because as he lathered his hair, he closed his eyes and imagined her warm arms wrapping around him from behind as she joined him. The bubbles would slide down his neck and chest, waking every hair on his body. His cock throbbed while he imagined her lips gently brushing across his back as her hard nipples pressed into him, her slippery body rubbing against his. Images of spinning her around and pressing her against the shower wall filled his thoughts. His hands would glide down to her beautiful ass as he sucked on the back of her shoulder. His cock would press between her legs, gently moving against her. Lost in his fantasies and surrounded by the steam of the shower, his hand would find its way to his shaft and slowly slide up and down. The combination of the lather and water offered him a tease at the sensation of being inside her drenched pussy. The fantasy would continue with him spreading her open and running the tip of his cock over her swollen lips, waiting for the arch of her back to show him she was ready. Then he would dive into her, driving his cock deep until his balls pressed against the insides of her legs. While his hands would furiously stroke himself closer to coming, in his mind he would take possession of her hips gliding her body back and forth over him. He could hear her echoed moans filling the room, her begging to have every inch of him. When he pictured his hot cream deep inside of her pussy, his balls would tighten and throb releasing his want for her into his own hand. She was his dream.

And now she was standing in front of him as if conjured.

She approached him cautiously. "I was just . . ." Her voice trailed off.

"Trespassing," he repeated. "Read the signs."

Don't blow this, said a soft feminine voice in his head. He turned and walked away from her.

As he walked away Jocelyn noticed his shape outlined in the setting sun. His hair was dark and longer than the other staff members were allowed. His gray T-shirt lay tight across his chest. Some kind of tribal-inspired tattoo banded his arm and peaked from the edge of his shirt. His faded jeans were white with numerous worn spots. And he had a seriously nice ass. She wondered if his abs were as chiseled as the rest of him.

She chased after him, wanting to explain. "I was just trying to get away from the crowd," she said as if to defend herself.

"You mean run away," he said as he continued to walk in the opposite direction.

"Hey, I've never run away from anything in my life," she said.

He paused and turned. "Whatever you say, princess," he said with a slight smile on his lips.

Jocelyn did not appreciate his sarcastic tone. This conversation was *far* from over but it was getting more difficult for her to follow him in her damn heels. They scraped each edge of the stony path as her pace quickened to his. "Oh, crap, I'll just take these off," she muttered to herself.

As she rounded the edge of the lawn, she saw him swinging a muscled leg over the seat of a motorcycle. Though she wanted to explain herself, it was the motorcycle that called to her. Looking only at the machine, she walked closer, drawn to it as if spelled.

Alan was thrilled when he saw her eyes shift from looking at him to staring at the motorcycle.

More than three months ago he had walked around the junkyard looking for anything that would occupy his time for a while. When a reflection of blue light blinded him, he had to investigate. There in the farthest part of the yard under a few pieces of sheet metal and rusted gears was a beat-up motorcycle.

The chrome seemed in decent shape, and although it needed some new leather and a few parts were stripped, it was a sound bike. On closer inspection he was intrigued by a small antique lamp engraved into the body. As he cleared the scraps away and rubbed the image, a tingle entered his fingertips.

When bike rose onto its wheels from the rubble of its own accord, his heart beat faster. He lifted his leg to straddle the seat and melted into the frame, electricity filling his body.

Hello, handsome, said a soft feminine voice from the

recesses of his mind. *I've been expecting you. That gentle rub of your legs against me . . . Mmmmm . . . Make your wish. It will come true.*

And so it began. Alan worked feverously to restore the bike—Genie he called her—to perfection. When he needed to escape life, he jumped on and rode, and the world seemed to go his way. He knew the bike had magic inside it. He could feel it, but he also knew that while Genie kept offering him wishes, he needed to save them for the things he wanted most.

Seeing Jocelyn standing a few feet away, breathless from chasing him, he knew his chance had arrived.

She will be yours, whispered Genie. *This is your golden opportunity. Go for it, sweetness.*

She walked closer and read the license plate aloud. "L-ADIN3 . . . Aladdin three . . . What's the three for?" she asked.

"Three magic wishes. All you have to do ride with me," he said.

"Does that line actually work for you?" she asked.

He simply smiled. "Anything is possible if you believe in it. Besides, you are the one running from something, wanting something else." He continued to gather his belongings together, putting them in the bike's storage areas.

He could tell she wanted to make a clever retort, but she couldn't. Wanting her to feel comfortable, he decided to lighten the conversation. "'You don't know what we can find. Why don't you come with me, little girl, on a magic carpet ride?'" he asked. He tried not to smile too much as he recited the lyrics from an old Steppenwolf song. Her smile said yes, but for the wishes to work, he needed to hear the words from her mouth. He continued, "'Close your eyes girl, look inside girl . . .'"

"'Let the sound take you away,'" she said, finishing the verse.

Time to make your move.

"Come for a ride," he beckoned. He offered his hand to her. "Make your first wish and trust me."

She hesitated slightly as her heart skipped a beat. She laid her hand gingerly into his. "I trust you," she said. "I wish to take a ride"

You've got her, baby . . . Now ride. I'll do the rest . . .

As he raised his right leg and straddled the machine, the jeans against his skin tightened and she couldn't help but notice the outline of his ass staring back at her. The shredded holes in the pants seemed to widen and split open.

She threw her heels into the grass as her black dress moved in the breeze, flickering above her thighs. Her right leg rose over the bike as he steadied her, her dress sliding up to her hips and exposing her lower ass.

There was something about him. Him and this bike.

"Hold on," he said.

She grabbed the belt loops of his pants and raised her feet up to the footrests.

Before she could take another breath, they were racing into the night. Her thighs clenched the bike tightly as her clothes vibrated with the wind. He opened up the throttle a little more. The machine between her legs began to hum and the vibration sent chills up her spine. The feeling was incredible.

She leaned her body into his, pressing her chest deeply into his back, and the sensations continued to excite her. Wetness flowed from her, soaking her tiny panties as the cycle buzzed along. She rolled her hips forward, exposing her clit to the pleasure between her legs. She knew he could feel her warmth as she inched closer and closer to his body.

For the moment she was lost in time. The beautiful countryside flashed past her, and with it went all her worries and despairs. She forgot who she was and about everyone else. The only one she knew was him. And she didn't even know his name.

Their speed and her pleasure increased, and her legs began to shake. Jocelyn was wet with excitement. Her hands made their way around to his legs, grabbing at his hips. With every turn of the road she melted into him. As they continued to ride she sensed his excitement. Her hands stroked his legs and almost touched his rock-hard cock. The excitement was so erotic and she longed for her skin to touch his. She edged herself back and forth over the bike's seat, attempting to press her full nub into the strong vibrations. He suddenly went full throttle as they climbed the tallest hills. The intensity was too much, and suddenly she came, there on the bike. Her legs quivered against the heavy machine. She was unaware her hands grabbed at his thighs, hungrily kneading them with her fingertips. She exhaled and closed her eyes.

Suddenly they came to a stop and she lifted her head from his back. She was surprised to see the country club. As she stood, her body stuck to the seat and a mark of wetness lingered. She said nothing to him as she brushed her hair away from her face.

"Until we meet again, princess," he said. "For your next wish." He revved the engine a few times and drove off into the night.

Her body seemed to glow against the night sky. As she walked unsteadily back to the party, she looked over her shoulder to follow his headlights into the dark. Somewhere deep inside she believed she would see him again. He'd granted her first wish. She couldn't imagine what her next might be.

The next few days were filled with her mother's unending questions about what Jocelyn would wear to the next party at the club and other mandatory social engagements. She didn't want to go. A life all planned down to the very last detail, just like her mother's? No, this was not her wish at all. She wasn't going.

She planned it out well, claiming exhaustion, a headache and chills. All that really bothered her was her hunger for him—and perhaps that second wish.

A soon as her parents left, she sprang from her bed into her closet, sliding on her favorite jeans and a little white tank top. She jumped in her car and drove, not sure where she was going but trusting she would end where she needed to be.

She spent hours driving around town, looking down every dark alley for the blue glow of his motorcycle. She scoured every parking lot, every back street she could think of. He was nowhere to be found.

"This is crazy," she thought. "I'll never find him."

She was on the verge of giving up when a faint blue light caught her eyes. Her heart raced. His bike was parked out front of the dimmest bar in town. She parked her car and walked up to the door of the bar. As she passed his motorcycle, she swiped her finger across it. It seemed to burn her fingertip. She entered and every head turned to see her. A few whistles exploded in the air.

"Oh God, what have I gotten myself into?" she whispered to herself.

As she continued to walk toward the bar, she could feel their stares burning through her. She sat down on the stool and tried to pretend she was comfortable being there.

"You lost, sweet thing?" the bartender asked.

"Just looking for someone," she said.

"You lookin' for me, sweet baby girl?" the bartender asked as he inched forward toward her.

"Looking for the owner of the blue bike out front."

The bartender chuckled slightly. "Hall," he shouted as his eyes never left her face. No answer. "Hey, Hall!"

"Yeah," a voice responded.

"Someone here to see you." He turned and walked away.

From the back room a familiar shape edged its way from the darkness. There he was. Same ripped-up jeans that seemed even more inviting than before, and sexy blue eyes more visible in the light. A smile crept over his face.

"Princess," he said, his voice deep and soft.

She hesitated. In that moment she didn't know what to say, how to say it, or how to say anything. So much for bravery.

He'd been dying to see her, to have her near him, ever since their last ride. When she pressed herself against him, his cock rose, aching to be touched by her. And making it very difficult to drive.

It was Genie's voice that held him back. *Not yet, baby. Don't rush. You have to make her wait . . . make her want you.*

Tonight he knew what to do, what to say. He rounded the bar and slowly walked behind her. He leaned over her shoulder and whispered into her ear. "'You don't know what we can see . . . Why don't you tell your dreams to me . . . '" His breathy whisper pierced her ears.

Jocelyn turned to look at him. "'Fantasy will set you free.'" She completed the verse again.

"Come for a ride," he continued.

"Let's go," she said. "I wish for the night with you."

It was darker and colder than the evening of their first ride, but every part of her body warmed with delight. He straddled the bike and looked at her as he started the engine. Before he had a chance to offer his hand, she grabbed on to his shoulders and hopped on the back, immediately pulling her body into his.

In a flash they were off, wind singing against their bodies as they sliced the night.

"This is what you want," Genie whispered to him. *"She's wished for you. Now is the time for your wishes."*

As they continued to ride, she reached her arms around his body, sliding her left hand up his untucked shirt, tracing her fingers over the outline of every muscle of his abs. She slid her right hand up and down his thigh, allowing her fingers to explore the worn holes in his jeans. The gentle touch of her fingers sent intense pulses to his cock. It was awake and hungry for her.

"Wish her to touch you," Genie said.

Touch me, he thought.

Her hand found its way to his throbbing cock, stroking him through his jeans. He sensed the pre-come seeping from the tip and soaking into his jeans. Is this really happening?

"Stop doubting me, boy. Just ride."

Her hands made their way to the button on his jeans. With one quick tug it was undone. She slid down the zipper and into them went her cool, wind-kissed fingers. He couldn't stop his sharp inhale and moan.

They raced faster, throttle full open, and Alan knew she must feel the intense vibrations against her clit again. She moved against him, lifting his cock out of his pants and slowly stroking it as the night breeze blew against it.

"Your hands are so soft and they feel damn good." He knew she couldn't hear him, but it needed to be said.

"Would you like to hear her thoughts?" Genie asked.

"Yes," he said.

"I need to have you in me," her thoughts demanded.

"See? Now is the time, baby. Take her for the ride she really wants."

He slowed and turned down a narrow dirt road. His

cock was slick with his wetness as her hand moved up and down his shaft, her index finger stopping at the head to circle it gently. He lowered the bike stand and turned off the motor. For a moment neither of them moved. Her hand remained wrapped around his cock. He turned to face her. Her eyes reflected the light of the moon back to him.

He took her face into his hand and captured her lips with his. Breaking the kiss, she whispered, "Are you a fantasy or real?"

He was silent for a while before whispering, "Can I be both?"

In an instant, his mouth was on hers, his tongue hungrily exploring hers. His hand tangled in her long, dark hair.

"It's time. Wish her to be yours," Genie said.

I want to make you mine, he thought.

He pulled her mouth off of his as he got off the bike, his erect cock still in plain view. She followed, then kissed him once more before she moved lower. She took his cock into her mouth and twirled her tongue around its head. His low moans clearly enticed her. As she pulled down his jeans, his cock slid deeper into her throat, reaching the very back as she licked his full balls. They ached and tightened. He was too close already.

"Come here, princess," he ordered.

She was happy to follow his command and rose to stand before him. She helped him remove his shirt and lay it on the ground.

He kissed her again before descending to his knees. He pressed his face into her body as his hands wrapped

around her hips. He gently licked her stomach. As he
unfastened the button to her pants, she ran her fingers
through his dark hair. He slid her jeans down to her ankles,
exposing her tiny black panties, and rubbed his nose in
their wetness, soaking in their scent. It was intoxicating.
While kissing her hips, he lowered the scrap of fabric. She
lifted her feet out of them.

"*Tell her what you want and she will do it*," Genie said

"Lie down for me," he requested.

She did.

The reflection of the moonlight highlighted her body.
He pressed against her as his hand slid between her legs,
parting them. Her lips were swollen with anticipation. He
ran his finger lightly against her pussy and felt the thick
wetness of it. Her moans were sexy but soft. He slid down
her body and opened his mouth for her. His tongue moved
against her swollen clit and she groaned with pleasure.
Then he entered her as he tasted her for the first time.
His mouth worked her hard button as she raised her hips
to meet every movement of it.

"Take all of me," she beckoned.

He slid his pants off and lay upon her, the head of his
cock poised at the entrance of her. As quickly as he could,
he sheathed his himself with a condom. "You are mine,"
he said.

And with that he plunged into her. Her eyes widened
and her hands grabbed his ass as he slid into her, pulling
him in deeper. He moved in and out of her as his mouth
found hers. Their breath and their bodies became one.
With each stroke his cock swelled, and for a moment he

feared hurting her, but her cries of pleasure urged him on. Their sounds filled the night as he filled her. Every response she made drove him closer to the edge. He had to slow things down—at least temporarily.

He rolled her on top of him. She sat with her hands against his chest. He paused to drink in the sight of the moonlight against her perfect breasts. Even her belly button was beautiful to him.

He ran his tongue across her erect nipples before meeting her mouth with his. His fingers ran through her hair, down her back, before he grabbed her hips. He moved her back and forth, keeping his eyes locked on hers, willing her to not look away.

The pressure of his body between her legs intensified. His cock could not go any farther into her. She swore he grew harder inside her as he filled her with each stroke. The shaking build-up of an orgasm began deep inside, followed by that unforgettable tingle that stole through her body. Her moans grew louder together with his. She was close. He was close. They could not stop the pleasure they created together.

"Now . . . now," she begged.

As he held his breath, he released every drop of come deep inside her pussy. His cock and balls pulsed within and against her. His climax triggered hers, and she came with a fiery intensity while continuing to move her pussy and grip his cock in with every pulse. Her body fell on top of his in exhaustion. He kissed her deeply. She was afraid to look in his eyes as a small tear rolled down her cheek. She struggled to fill the silence of the night and the confusion in her heart.

"You are amazing, my princess," he told her. He kissed her once more.

Logic returned, screaming inside her head. Was this real? Was this just one night? She had so many questions, but she didn't want to break the magic.

They lay together until he kissed her tenderly and said, "We should go."

They dressed and started off on the bike. Before long he stopped at her car and offered his hand to her, but she didn't take it. All she could do was look at him. His eyes sparkling in the night were not enough to quell her sudden sense of panic. Why was she acting like this? What was it about him that made her forget reason? Did she want more? He took her face in his hands and kissed her gently. Her heart raced with mixed emotions.

"Until we meet again, princess," he said. He revved the engine a few times and drove into the night.

She sat in her car wondering if she should have said something different. How was it possible to feel so desired and cared for by a stranger? Not knowing how to find the answers, she drove home.

Days passed into weeks without seeing him. She wanted desperately to find him and worried if she missed the chance to say what she felt. She had no way to find him— no phone number, no address, only the name "Hall." And passionate feelings that wouldn't go away.

Her parents, seeing her edginess, finally convinced her

to come out for a night at the club. There was a party for the new owner and she deserved a fun evening. Jocelyn agreed, hoping it would take her mind off her stranger for a little while.

Once she was there, however, she knew she'd made a mistake. She attempted to make small talk with friends and to smile though the emptiness that shook her to her core, but found herself hiding in the bathroom when she could not contain the tears that welled up without warning. She was ready to run again when she overheard the announcement of the new owner entering the room. Leaving would be too conspicuous. She hoped the presentation would be quick so she could escape.

Everyone gathered around the stranger with eager voices and quick handshakes. She couldn't see his face through the crowd that surrounded him, but noticed expensively tailored pants and matching suit coat. As he moved though the mass, she finally caught sight of him, his face sleek and smooth. His dark hair perfect, if a little long. His smile beaming. Time ran in slow motion as his blue eyes looked past everyone—and straight at her.

It was him.

She stood frozen watching him as he worked his way toward her. As people tried to stop and talk to him, he easily put them off till later. He walked up to her with a mischievous smile.

She held her breath.

"Princess," he said softly.

"I thought you weren't part of this scene. I thought you

couldn't possibly be." She couldn't believe he was here of all places.

"Like you, I'm more than where I go or what I wear. You now that. Anything is possible if you believe in it," he said. "And wish for it enough."

"I'm Jocelyn," she said.

"I'm Alan."

He offered her his hand, and as she took it this third time, she grabbed it tighter than ever before. Everyone was staring. She couldn't have cared less. "You know, you are trespassing. You could get into a lot of trouble," she said with a slight laugh. "So do I get my last wish?"

"My apologies. I was selfish and used the last wish myself," he said.

"So you wished to own a country club?"

"No, I wished to be with my princess." A smile crept across his face and his eyes sparkled. "Come for a ride," he said.

"Even if my wishes have come true?" she asked.

He leaned in closer to her. "Absolutely. Let me take you away," he whispered, "and we'll think of some new ones."

The Vibrating Pea

By Rachel Kenley

"If I don't have an orgasm soon, I'm going to go insane," Hannah Christian said as she paced the luxuriously appointed hotel room. "I'll give it to myself if necessary."

"If you do, you might lose everything, including—and most importantly—the man you love."

Hannah sat on the sofa with a thud. She could feel the leather material against the backs of her legs, and it wasn't helping her keep her composure. Being near Jason, seeing him daily, was revving up her sex drive to breaking point, and the buttery material against her bare skin was making things worse. "This is completely unfair."

"I agree. Nevertheless, you know what must be done if you want to succeed. It will all be worth it. I promise, sweetling."

Hannah sighed and nodded at the older woman as she accepted a hug. Normally she wouldn't have conversations about orgasms or masturbation with a woman old enough to be her grandmother, but Celeste had proven herself to be an invaluable confidante and, truthfully, nothing had been normal for the last few weeks

It had been nearly three weeks since she found herself at the employee entrance of the New York Palace, the jewel in the crown of the biggest chain of residential hotels in the United States. She was wet and bedraggled from the rain, tired, and in need of a place to sleep after being evicted from the apartment she shared with her now ex-best friend and said friend's ex-fiancé. It was Celeste who found her, brought her in, and gave her a job and a place to stay.

"You need to finish getting ready," Celeste said, bringing her back to the present. "I'll be back in a while to help you."

As Hannah sat at a vanity table staring into the mirror and thinking about the night to come, she was fairly certain fate was playing a horrible game with her. Of all the places she could have ended up that night, she found herself on the doorstep of the first man she loved and who, no matter how long she tried to make it otherwise, was still the one she craved.

Hannah met Jason Palace when she was a junior in high school. She transferred to the bigger school after her father's job took him from rural western Pennsylvania to Philadelphia. She was used to knowing everyone around her having been in classes with them since kindergarten. Now she felt lost and completely alone.

Jason saw her standing in the middle of the central hallway and offered to walk her to her class. A senior, he was the sexiest guy she ever met and, as she found out later, popular and well liked on campus. He stood nearly six feet tall with an athletic build, wavy dark hair, and deep brown eyes that made her melt.

Their paths might never have crossed again, but she ran into him—almost literally—on a Thursday night after coming out of a showing of an independent film at the local art house. Lost in thoughts of the characters and their lives, she discovered she left her gloves in the theater. Stopping and turning around quickly, she plowed directly into Jason. He kept her from falling over by putting his hands on her upper arms, sending a tingle through her. He smiled and asked if she was all right, and everything inside her warmed. When he asked her out for coffee, she could only nod her agreement.

Hannah called her mother to tell her she'd met up with friends from school and would be home later. Her mom was so happy Hannah was connecting with her peers she didn't set a curfew. They ended up going for hot chocolate—she hated the taste of coffee—discussing the movie and why they were both there alone. For her it had been a choice, a way to get out of the house for a little while. He came because he broke up with the girl he'd been seeing an hour before the start time and he'd bought the tickets in advance. They stayed until the café closed and he drove her home. She'd never allowed herself to be kissed on a first date, but she was more than ready to make an exception for him.

When his lips met hers, it was everything she'd dreamed about since she first started to notice boys. He put a hand on her cheek and leaned forward slowly, giving her plenty of time to back away, which she had no desire to do. His touch was warm and firm on hers, and as she stepped closer to deepen the kiss, he slipped his tongue into her mouth. It startled her, but having read about it in the romance novels her mother gave her since she was 14, she chose to enjoy the new sensations it created.

They kissed until Hannah was certain her legs wouldn't hold her up any longer.

"I guess I should go," Jason said.

She nodded, not completely trusting her voice.

"See you tomorrow at school?"

"Yes," she said, hoping he meant more than just passing in the hall.

The next day he was waiting for her when she arrived, took her hand, kissed her cheek, and offered to walk her to her class. They were inseparable from that time forward. Hannah was instantly accepted, immediately popular because of her association with Jason.

The summer after he graduated, they spent as much time as possible together. Jason was going away to Boston University. She hoped he would be closer, but they made plans for her to come up for a weekend by train in October.

For all they did together during his senior year, the one thing they didn't do was have sex. Hannah didn't feel ready, and he didn't want her first time to be in the back of a car or any other uncomfortable location. She was grateful for his understanding. Their parting at the end of August was emotional, and she counted the days until her trip.

The weekend got off to a rocky start. Things were fine when they were alone, but she was forced to watch him flirt with a bunch of other girls when they went out with a group later that first night. When she mentioned it, trying to keep the whine out of her voice, he explained it wasn't serious, that everyone acted this way in college.

She hoped he'd be more like his old self when they returned to his room, but instead the kisses became more heated, Jason pushing for them to be more physically intimate. When she told him she wasn't ready for sex, he said coldly, "You need to stop being so naïve, Hannah. We're not kids anymore. It's just a way to share how much we love each other."

Somehow it didn't feel to Hannah as though it were about love at all.

Jason tried again on her second night and again she refused. She told him he'd changed and she didn't like the person he was becoming.

After writing a hurried note, she left early Sunday morning while he was still asleep, although she hadn't planned to leave until late Monday. A few hours later he called, but she didn't respond. Whether it was out of cowardice on her part or disdain for him, she didn't know. They never spoke again.

Over the years she followed his life, both social and professional, in the papers as his hotel chain grew and succeeded, and never stopped missing him. Now she was living in the same building and wondering if there was finally a chance for a future with him.

Hannah knew when she started working at the Palace she might see Jason, but Celeste assured her if she stayed in the room service office, she would be safe. Rationalizing that he was busy running his business, traveling, and doing exciting things that he'd never make time to come down, Hannah took the job and the guest room in the older woman's suite. She planned to stay long enough to get her life together before moving on.

It didn't work out that way. He came down to the room service office only a few days after she started, and all the old feelings returned. She didn't want to still care about him, but her heart clearly had different ideas. She accepted his requests for dinners, movies, and in no time her heart was his again. Still, she couldn't stop the doubts that crept in when he wasn't around. How could she possibly hope that a man of Jason's position and success would want his childhood sweetheart back? And why did she want all of this anyway?

Tonight would decide everything.

Jason Palace stared at the small silver object nestled in the red velvet. Tonight he was going to put it to use, no matter how strange a test it might seem. His thoughts drifted to the conversation he had with his father when he first received it. "You want me to use a vibrator to choose my wife?" Clearly the old man had lost his mind.

"It worked for your mother and me," Harold said, sipping his coffee and looking very pleased with himself.

"Oh, Lord, that is way more information about you and Mom than I ever wanted," Jason said, horrified, shutting the box with a snap.

Harold laughed. "I won't go into the details."

"Thank goodness."

"But you have to trust me when I tell you that the woman who can respond to that finger vibrator is a woman of great sensitivity and deep responses, two things I know have been lacking in your relationships."

Jason wanted to give a clever retort, but his father's comment hit too close to the truth for him to come up with anything. He'd been married in his late twenties and divorced shortly before his thirtieth birthday. His wife hated the hours he worked and the time he was away from home. She wanted a quiet life with lots of children. He wanted someone who would travel with him until he was ready to build a more permanent home. They parted quickly and amicably.

His next two major relationships led to engagements without marriage. Thank goodness. In the first case, he discovered his fiancée cheating on him, which he thought was the ultimate humiliation until he came across his second fiancée while she was masturbating. It was exciting to be a voyeur, and he planned to join her, until her climax hit. As she moaned and arched her back off the bed, it was clear to him from her response she'd faked every orgasm she had with him. The fact that she whispered, "That was wonderful, Captain Jack," as she relaxed didn't help. He knew he was no Johnny Depp, but he didn't need to know who his future wife was fantasizing about.

Neither of those engagements ended amicably. There were screams, lawyers, and gossip-column postings. Ultimately, he was left alone wishing he could have the kind of loving, supportive relationship his parents still had over 40 years after their wedding.

Which was why he starting taking his father's suggestion seriously about the tiny vibrator. He stared at the object, wondering if it was powerful enough to do any good. He asked his father, who simply said, "It does a great deal to the right woman."

Jason suddenly had a horrifying thought. "This isn't the same one that you and Mom . . ."

"Oh, no," Harold laughed. "Of course not. This one was made for you."

That was a relief. Sort of. "I'll consider it, Dad. Thanks."

"I hope you do, and you're welcome."

After receiving the vibrator, Jason put it in the top drawer of his desk, where it sat forgotten for a few days. The next time he took it out, he had—if possible—a more embarrassing experience. After staring for an hour at the same report on the construction of the newest Palace Hotel, he needed a break. Remembering the vibrator, he removed it from the drawer and its box. It was a simple device, worn by slipping it over the index finger. At its tip was a small silver ball, no bigger than a pea, that when pressed vibrated intensely. Sensation wouldn't be great, but it would be directed.

He was still listening to it hum and wondering about using it when, unfortunately, Celeste came in with his dinner. As the head of room service at the New York Palace, she ran the twenty-four hour service, winning raves from critics and customers alike. She was also his grandmother.

Six years ago, as the Palace chain of hotels was growing, Celeste's husband, Jason's Grandpa William, died. A few

months later, human resources passed him her application
when she came in for a job.

"Meme Celeste, what are you doing?"

"Trying to keep busy," she answered as if it were the
most natural thing in the world. "I am not going to sit in
a chair and rock myself into an early grave. You know me
better than that. I have years left, and I plan to enjoy them.
Now, do you have a place for me here or should I apply to
one of your competitors?"

Celeste started the next week as a room service captain
and was managing the department a year later. Because
the hotel was half residential, the division was always
busy with requests, whether someone didn't want to cook
and needed dinner brought up or was having guests and
needed a larger meal. Celeste hired world-renowned chefs
for limited stays to impress guests and residents as well
as discovering several promising local chefs, helping them
to gain experience and a reputation. There were at least
four restaurants in New York alone that owed their start
to Celeste and the Palace. She was an asset Jason could
never have imagined.

She also had a knack for knowing everything going
on both with her family and in the hotel. "*Oh shit,*" he
thought as she wheeled in a cart. There was never a hole in
the earth to crawl into when you needed one. Fumbling,
he managed to turn the vibrator off and put it back in his
desk, but by that point she was in front of him, and his
cheeks were on fire.

"What's for dinner?" he asked, trying to sound in
control.

"I think dessert is your main interest," she said with a smile and a wink. "I see your father gave you the family heirloom."

He was surprised for only a moment that she knew what he was holding. "It's a copy, but yes."

"It's about time. I have fond memories of that little toy."

Jason was grateful he didn't have anything in his mouth, or he would have choked. "You know about . . ." He let the sentence trail off, unable—and unwilling—to be more specific.

"Of course, silly boy. Your grandfather was the first to use it." She waited a second for that information to sink in. If Jason thought he couldn't be more embarrassed or uncomfortable, he was wrong. "It brought us together, as it did your parents. You've been alone too long, which is why I'm glad your father finally had yours made. Trust me when I say you'll be pleased in more ways than one."

She came over, gave him a quick kiss on the forehead, and left his meal without saying anything more, for which Jason was grateful, although he hoped he didn't run into her for the next several days.

He threw out that hope little over a week later when he went to meet the new operator Celeste had hired. Something about her voice captivated him, and for days he called the department more than necessary, ordering enough coffee to keep him awake for a month all to be able to talk to her for a few minutes.

"Good afternoon. Room service. How may I help you?" she said when she answered the phone. Every time he heard it, his blood heated.

He wanted to answer with, "Let me take you to bed," or "I want to know if your moans sound as lovely as your voice," but he was always professional. And it was killing him. Finally, he decided he would go down, place his lunch order in person, and introduce himself. After all, he rationalized, it was perfectly normal for a company executive to meet his employees.

Of course, if she was anything like her voice he wanted to know her intimately. It took him nearly a half hour to get to the main room service office since he was stopped every few feet by someone who wanted his attention, a reminder of why he tended not to leave his office and preferred to have things brought to him. Eventually, he made it there. Standing in the door, he listened to her for a few minutes, with her back to him. Something about her was familiar now that she was close, but he couldn't quite place her.

He knocked on the doorframe to get her attention. She turned around, startled by the interruption, only to look even more so when she met his eyes. He assumed his expression mirrored hers.

"Hannah," he said when he found his voice. "It can't be? Is it really? What are you doing here?" He wasn't certain any of his sentences were cohesive or even complete, but he didn't care. How could the woman he most regretted losing be sitting there only a few feet from him? And how long had she been in the hotel without him knowing?

"Hello, Jason," she said. He hated that she sounded calm even if she looked shocked. "Yes, it can be, it's really me, and I'm working."

A thousand more questions flooded his already muddled brain, but instead of choosing one, he said what he was feeling. "It's great to see you. You look wonderful."

And she did. Her hair was long rather than the practical bob she wore in school, and pulled back into a careless yet somehow completely sexy ponytail. He wanted to reach out and release it from the elastic, watch it fall over her back. Her preferably naked back.

It was hell getting through that first conversation with her. He kept wanting to ask her out, but he knew if he didn't find a way to control himself, he would blow it with her again, and he wasn't going to lose her twice.

He made certain they saw each other in and out of work, always carefully avoiding the sexual chemistry and desire building between them. She was as funny and smart as he remembered, and he loved every minute he spent with her.

The waiting had to end. Tonight he was going to use the tiny vibrator with the woman who had been his first love, the one woman in his life he regretted letting get away. He could only hope his patience—and the use of the toy—would pay off.

As the days passed and Hannah accepted that she still loved Jason, she tried to make her interest clear. She flirted, touched him, and kissed him with everything she felt for him. Still he held back from her. One night she mentioned her frustration to Celeste, who told her about the vibrator.

"You must come for him when he uses the vibrator or he cannot marry you."

Hannah thought the woman was kidding, but when it became clear she wasn't, Hannah knew that no matter how many fantasies she had about Jason, she needed to let the sexual tension build between so she could show him her desire and love when the time was right.

It was killing her.

Fortunately, the wait would be over one way or another tonight. There was a huge party being held for the staff, congratulating them on receiving a prestigious hospitality industry award, and Hannah was dressed for seduction.

The party was in full swing by the time she arrived, which wasn't a surprise, since Celeste wouldn't let her go for the longest time. She was talking to friends when Jason walked over to her and brought her out onto the floor for a slow dance. Being close to him, breathing in the scent of his cologne was making her wet and weak with longing. He caressed her cheek and she turned her face into his hand, looking into his eyes and hoping he could see all she felt.

He kissed her, slowly and deeply and she thought—she hoped—she tasted hunger.

As the song ended he said, "I need you alone, and I need you now," as he licked the outside of her ear and gently bit her lobe.

"Lead the way," she said. Three more words than she thought she could manage. People in the elevator kept them from causing a scene, and it seemed like forever before they were alone in his apartment.

He took her hand and led her into the suite. "Welcome to my home," he said as they walked into his living room.

She heard other employees talk about how lavish the owner suite was, but nothing prepared her for the gorgeous room and stunning views. The door hadn't clicked closed before he was pulling her to him for a kiss she felt in every part of her body. Her hands ran through the soft waves of his hair as she relished every touch, every sensation he gave her, and the anticipation of every one she hoped to cause.

Taking a deep breath for courage, she reached behind her and unzipped the dress. With a few shrugs it fell to the floor and she stood before him wearing nothing but her black bra, panties, and thigh-high stockings.

"You take my breath away," he said, sweeping her into his arms and carrying her to the bedroom. It was dimly lit, which made her smile. It made her happy to see that he'd anticipated tonight too.

He placed her in the center of a large bed with dark gray linens and a matching quilted headboard. "These aren't Palace standard issue," she said, smiling.

"A guy needs to get away from business somehow, especially if he lives were he works."

"Makes sense," she said, reaching for his tie and using it to pull them closer before undoing it. "You're wearing too much."

"I agree." He took off his coat as she started on the buttons on his shirt. Her hands trembled and it was harder than it should be, but she loved seeing his chest, his skin bare to her touch. He pulled his belt free as she reached for the waist of his pants.

He undid the catch as she unzipped him, the sound raising goosebumps on her flesh. She stroked his cock through the cotton material of his briefs as Jason shed his pants and socks at the same time.

Stretching next to her, he teased the skin at the edge of her bra cups, sending shivers through her body. If this is how she responded to his gentle touches, she was going to be a quivering wreck before the night ended. She could hardly wait.

He brought his mouth to hers in a heated kiss, and she ran her hands down the back of his neck and across his shoulders. She loved having him so close. Too soon he moved away, but he continued kissing her as he moved down her body. He kissed between her breasts before unhooking her bra and sucking her nipples to hard, sensitive peaks. She shimmied out of the straps, then returned to caressing him, wanting to touch as much as be touched. The heat of his skin felt so good and helped her believe this was finally happening for her, for them. It wasn't another erotic dream.

Giving a few last licks beneath her breast, he kissed his way lower, and her body hummed in anticipation and need. He stopped at the material of her panties and nipped at her skin. She moaned softly as her body trembled and liquid heat rushed between her legs.

He continued to tease her, running his fingers along the edge of the fabric covering her pussy, but never touching there. Her legs opened wider to show him what she wanted, but he continued to torment her.

"Please," she finally whispered.

"Please what?"

"Jason, touch me." She was surprised at the demand in her voice.

"Like this?" With no other warning he slipped a finger under the thin fabric and into her wetness.

"God, yes," she called out as she melted over him.

"You are so sensitive," he said softly, his breath whispering over her skin.

"You do that to me," she said honestly. She couldn't remember responding to any other man the way she did to him.

"Take off your underwear, Hannah," he said.

Without thinking, she reached for the flimsy panties, lifted her hips, and slid them down. It was exciting seeing him watch her strip away this last piece of covering. She wore nothing but her stockings, which made her feel more exposed, more vulnerable. It was thrilling.

"You are stunning," he said, and before she could think of a way to reply, his mouth covered her pussy and his tongue teased her clit in the barest hint of a touch. Her body responded immediately and she cried out with the pleasure, certain her climax would rush upon her if he continued.

She gripped the sheets until her knuckles were white, trying to get herself back under some semblance of control. Jason must have noticed, because he gently pulled away.

"Not so fast, my beauty," he said. "There is something I want to do to you, for you."

He reached into his nightstand and pulled out a small box. When he opened it she saw what looked like a small silver tube the length of half a finger.

"What is that?" she asked. Celeste told her about the vibrator but never described it—or mentioned how small it was.

"Something I hope you will like," he said. She saw him cover his index finger with the tube as he spread her legs wider and once again began teasing and tasting her.

Hannah's body returned quickly to a state of heightened excitement, aching for a release she'd wanted for days. Unexpectedly she heard a faint buzzing sound, but before she could ask what it was, a current of pleasure ran through her body as Jason gently touched her clit with the tip of the tiny vibrator. Her back arched off the bed, giving him more access to her and increasing her bliss.

"Oh my God, Jason," she said. Her whole world was focused on where he touched her.

"You like?"

"An understatement."

"Then I will continue," he said and used his mouth and his fingers together with the vibrator to build her to a fevered peak.

"Jason," she cried, "I can't hold back."

"Then don't," he said against her skin.

A breath later her climax hit her with an intensity unlike any she'd ever experienced. She shouted his name and a series of "yes" and "oh God" until she was babbling. Every muscle in her body was trembling with the energy of her orgasm. She thought her ears might be ringing.

He gentled his strokes, caressing the lips of her pussy with the vibrator, easing her down from her peak. As her breathing neared a more normal state, the buzzing stopped. He kissed his way up her body, creating delightful aftershocks of pleasure. When he reached her lips, he claimed her mouth and she surrendered to the love she always held for him

"I need to be inside you," he said.

"Not yet," she replied. "I think there is more we can do with that lovely toy, or more specifically, more I can do." In the dim light she could see his confusion. She held out her hand, and he gave her the vibrator. "Lie back and let's see what this does to you."

Kissing her way down his body, Hannah reveled in her growing power over him. The orgasm she experienced with him was like nothing she'd ever enjoyed, and for the first time in her memory, what she wanted most was to give her lover the same pleasure.

With the toy on her index finger, she pressed on his nipple, bringing it to vibrating life. Jason's quick intake of breath was just the right sound of encouragement.

Jason's heart had soared when Hannah climaxed powerfully for him, but it nearly stopped completely when she took the vibrator and caressed one nipple while drawing deeply on the other. Blood rushed to his already engorged shaft, and he wondered how long he could stand this delightful torture.

Mimicking his actions, she kissed her way down his body. Then she paused when her mouth was near his groin, and he wondered if she was going to stop. Instead, she took off his briefs, then teased him at the base of his cock with gentle licks and kisses. Finally, as he thought he would scream, she took the head of his cock into her mouth and placed the vibrator against the skin behind his balls.

If he thought he couldn't get any more excited, she was quickly proving him wrong. The combination of her warm tongue, the suction of her mouth, and the pulsing of the toy was incredible. He swore he became harder as she took him deeper, bathing him with her pleasure.

"Hannah, my love," he managed. "I want to come inside you, and if you don't stop, neither will I."

She released him and gave him a sexy and wicked grin before sliding smoothly up his body until they were face-to-face. "Then take me," she said.

He rolled her on her back and reached for a condom in his nightstand drawer. He covered himself quickly and without hesitating sheathed himself within her warm pussy. His cock surged forward eagerly, and he almost lost his control, her cry of joy nearly undoing him. Wanting to make this last, he forced himself to breathe slowly. "You feel amazing," he said. "So tight."

"I'm swollen and sensitive from the orgasm you gave me."

"How about another?" he asked. He took the toy from her fingers and placed it on his again. Pulling back slightly, he turned it on and touched her clit.

"Oh, Jason, yes!"

"Holy shit, I can feel it too," he said. The quivering in her pussy traveled to his cock, heightening the pleasure for them both. "I can't hold back."

"Good, because I'm going to come again," she said, and as her second orgasm built, she lifted her hips, taking him deeper. His balls pressed up against her entrance as his climax ripped through him. He yelled out her name and looked into her eyes as years of yearning and regret melted away. He belonged with Hannah. He always had.

When his body stopped shaking, he gently pulled out of her and rolled to the side, drawing her close, needing her near.

"That was better than every fantasy I've ever had about us," she said, kissing him. "You are everything I've ever wanted. Everything I've always wanted."

"I have loved you forever. Will you marry me?" he asked.

Hannah looked at him and smiled. "And live in your palace?"

"As happily ever after as I can make it."

As she whispered her answer, she sealed their promise with a kiss.

The Lucky Duckling
By Soleil d'Argent

"Wow." Charles breathed the word, stopping in his tracks outside his bedroom door while buttoning his black dress shirt. Juliana thought he looked quite sexy himself, especially clean shaven with freshly combed hair. She rarely looked at him that way, but he was clearly looking at her that way. It was delightful.

He was showering when she let herself into his unlocked house. The isolated little cottage overlooked a pond Charles was quite proud of, complete with a small flock of ducks and a mated pair of swans. Charles never locked the door when he was at home. As she waited, Juliana stood at the end of the upstairs hallway, in front of the full-length mirror, and took off the safe outfit she'd put on over the slinky black one she planned to wear to the club that evening. The tailored shirt and long skirt were just in case she lost her nerve.

She stared at her reflection, thinking, *I'm too old to pull off this look. Forty-year-olds do not dress this way.*

The dress she wore was nothing more than a slip

clinging to her muscular but slightly too thin build. Sheer black stockings worn under fishnets and a pair of black leather lace-up heels completed the look. She wore no makeup and very little jewelry. As she fussed with the dress, self-consciously inspecting the outfit in the mirror, she heard him utter the single word as barely more than a breath.

The simple word had the power of an exclamation.

Turning to see her friend of more than three decades standing at the other end of the hallway, she asked, "Was that a good wow, or an I-can't-believe-you'd-even-consider-wearing-that-out-in-public wow?" Taking her long blonde hair out of its French twist, and combing her fingers through it, she walked to him, her heels clicking gently down the hardwood hallway.

"That was definitely a good wow," he replied. Pleasure softened his usually stony face. "You look"—he paused, then added breathlessly—"amazing!" He sounded almost surprised. No, perhaps it was stunned. She liked it. "What are you trying to do to me, Jewel?" he said, playfully swooning.

She smiled and blushed, thoroughly enjoying both the flirting and the compliments but certain he was overreacting. "I guess I overshot," she said.

Before she could continue, he interrupted, saying, "You were just hoping to keep me from walking out?" His smile reached his eyes as he paraphrased a movie quote from *As Good As It Gets*. They'd recently watched it together, and he knew she'd get the reference, especially as she'd just quoted the movie herself. It was a game they played often.

She never realized, however, he was such a flirt—and a rather good one at that!

"Actually," she said, "I was going for easy on the eyes, and hoping not to embarrass myself."

"I'd say you definitely succeeded." His gaze changed quickly from playful to serious. A muscle clenched along his jaw as he approached her and gave her a hug followed by a quick, uncertain peck on her bare shoulder. His lips were soft and sensual, yet firm. It was barely a glancing kiss, but it was the one and only time he kissed her in all the years they'd known each other. The realization produced a warm glow to her chest and a rush of exquisite heat between her legs. It also brought the awareness that things seemed to be changing in their relationship. A realization both terrifying and exciting.

Charles never forgot meeting Juliana Gordon. It was one of the most vivid memories of his childhood. Self-confident little Juliana was eight years old, and the school bully, Karl, shoved her down during recess again because Juliana refused to let Karl kiss her, yelling "Never!" just before she struck the ground. One of her long blonde ponytails was yanked askew and her tear-stained face was covered with sand. As she struggled to sit up in the sandbox, Charles came to her rescue punching Karl with a strength he didn't know he had.

Charles was small for his age, and his sharp nose was a little too large for his face. He was slightly bow-legged and therefore walked with a swagger, which, in a child of his size, unfortunately looked more like a waddle. Charles knew he was better with animals than he was with people. Animals were easier to deal with. Karl dubbed Charles Goslin "Chuck the Duck" or "Ducky" for short, and the unfortunate nickname not only stuck, but it caught on with many of the other kids as well, and prompted much teasing of "ugly little Ducky".

Charles stood over the older and larger bully, who was sprawled in the sand clutching at his stomach. Turning to Juliana, Charles asked proudly, "Are you okay?" and offered Juliana his hand, which she took, as he helped her up off of the ground. He carefully and very gently brushed the sand off of her cheek, noticing her long eyelashes sparkled with jewel-like teardrops in the afternoon sunlight. Her clear blue eyes were rimmed with red. "Juliana, right?" he asked. "I'm Charles, but you can call me Charlie, if you want." It was hard to keep eye contact. He was self-conscious to begin with, and much more so around her.

"Yes and no," she replied, removing her hand from his and brushing sand from her jeans with one hand, while rubbing a still-tearing eye with the other.

"No? I thought your name was Juliana. You take dance classes with my sisters" he said, confused. Unlike Charles, his triplet sisters were born with a natural beauty and grace. Much as Juliana had been, thought Charles. Anyone who saw the girls dance in *Swan Lake* last year could attest to that.

"Yes, I'm mostly all right, but no, not entirely. I've got sand in my eye." Juliana replied, sounding more than a bit annoyed. "And yes, my name is Juliana."

"Oh, we should get you to the nurse," he said. He gently

took her hand and led her to the school nurse's office to have the sand washed out.

From that day on, they were birds of a feather, best friends—but only friends. Never more, no matter how many heated fantasies Charles enjoyed over the years. And there were many. Tonight, however, he was taking the risk to change that and trusting he wouldn't lose her forever.

Juliana agreed to go to the club with Charles in spite of, or perhaps because of, the fact that the friends who planned to join them cancelled for various reasons. It would be Charles and her tonight. She hadn't been to a club since college and she thought it might be fun to people watch if nothing else. Charles told her there was a woman he expected to see and wanted to talk to, but hadn't taken the opportunity to ask out. Juliana knew no matter how successful Charles was in his veterinary practice, he continued to have difficulty approaching a woman. To make it easier for him, Juliana said she'd be his wing-man. Charles wasn't sure a woman could be a wing-man, in fact, he was pretty certain that she couldn't be, which he told her as he pulled on his black cowboy boots and gathered up his wallet and keys. Still, she needed to get out there for herself as well. Since the end of her last relationship she'd become far too reclusive. She hoped tonight could be a new start.

Charles was thrilled he and Juliana would be alone tonight, especially since seeing her in that devastating black dress. It was the sexiest little thing he ever saw—accent on the little—and it was absolutely stunning on her. He had exactly what he wanted for the evening, and more than he'd hoped. The most beautiful woman he'd ever known was standing at his side, holding his hand, as they headed for his car.

On the drive into Boston, they talked, laughed, and joked about everything imaginable, even that they got a bit turned around when it came to finding the place. Charles paid for them at the door, and their hands were stamped as they entered the loud club. They stopped at the bar and he bought them drinks. Then, arms draped about each other, they stood at the edge of the dance floor, people watching and pointing out other club-goers.

"Check out the blonde in the red dress . . . three o'clock." Juliana stood very close and spoke into his ear, her warm breath tickling his neck. It never bothered him to have her show him other women since they'd done this for each other for years.

Tonight he ignored her recommendation. Leaning in, he asked, "If you're done with your drink, do you want to dance?"

"Sure," she replied, "but I thought you didn't like to dance. In fact, I could never get you to dance with me when we were younger." He couldn't tell her he was terrified of getting an erection while dancing with the prettiest girl he knew.

Juliana took Charles by the hand, and he led the way as they cut a path through the crowd onto the floor itself. It was almost as crowded as the perimeter, forcing them to dance very closely, something Charles didn't mind at all.

It was a slower song, and Charles took the opportunity to wrap his arms around Juliana's waist, occasionally letting his hands drift just a little lower than the small of her back, cautiously exploring her gentle curves with his fingertips, wondering how much he could get away with.

When the music changed, she turned her back to him, pressing up against the front of him, and moving to the rhythm of the music, wriggling her tight little ass into his groin, bending at the knees, while keeping her back straight and pressed firmly against his chest and sliding her backside down the front of him, and back up again.

"Do that again!" he half-begged, half-ordered, after she completed the move, his breath hot and urgent in her ear.

As he leaned into her, Juliana enjoyed the heat radiating from his body, the feel of his muscles as they pressed against hers. And she did it again. He groaned with pleasure and stiffened against her body. Well, she felt his cock stiffen against her—the rest of him seemed to soften and melt a bit. Damn, she was enjoying this far too much. The pleasure-filled noises he made got her instantly wet. Much more of this, and she'd be tempted to find a dark corner and have her way with him right there in the club. She pushed the thought away. She couldn't—wouldn't—risk losing him as a friend. She had almost lost him once before, and she'd be damned if she'd lose her lifelong best friend now.

At the end of the song, Charles asked, "Is it hot in here? You ready for another drink?" Taking Juliana by the hand, he led her toward the bar without waiting to hear her reply.

During their return to the bar, Juliana couldn't help but notice how sexy and tight Charles's ass looked as he swaggered ahead of her. With Charles wearing those boots, watching his determined swagger, Juliana couldn't help but think, *ride 'em, cowboy*. The thought was quickly followed by, *God help me, I'm in trouble*. She couldn't decide if she desperately needed another drink or if she shouldn't be drinking at all. The decision was taken from her when he handed her a cold glass. She finished most of it before they danced some more, after which they switched to ice water in preparation for the drive out of the city.

Charles rested his hand on Juliana's knee, as he usually did, on the drive back to his house, but it seemed to Juliana he had a lot of trouble keeping it there. It kept wandering higher on her leg. Juliana pretended not to notice.

Charles stood in his driveway and opened the passenger side door to let Juliana out. "Stay the night," he said. "It's late and you have a long drive ahead of you. Better to make the drive in daylight. And I'd like your company." There, he'd admitted it. "I promise I'll be a perfect gentleman, but only if you want me to."

"I think that sounds like a smart idea," she said. He wished he knew what she was thinking.

Her graceful, swan-like neck and soft ivory shoulders beckoned him, but he didn't dare give in to the urges too quickly. She was strong, kind, and the most beautiful woman he'd ever known, and completely unlike any of the women he dated, the women his therapist referred to as the "broken birds" he kept trying to fix, much to his own detriment. His therapist strongly suggested he restrict his avian rehabilitation to the ducks and swans currently residing in his pond and those brought in to his veterinary clinic. Charles was ready to learn from his mistakes.

This time, he thought, it would be different because she was different, special.

He did the gentlemanly thing and offered Juliana his bed, then started preparing to sleep on the sofa. "Charlie, where are you going?" Juliana looked at him questioningly and beckoned, patting her hand on the bed next to her. "This is your bed. You can stay in here with me." He loved the sound of her voice, the sight of her every movement. He always had.

She took off her earrings and placed them next to a cup that sat on the small antique writing desk next to the bed, which contained beautiful quill pens Charles crafted of feathers from his swans. Her shoes were next, and she tucked them neatly under the desk.

He paced from bedroom to hallway and back as he seemed to wage a serious argument with himself, although it felt more like an epic battle. "Are you sure?" he asked. "I mean, I was hoping you'd say that, but I didn't want to assume anything or give you the wrong idea." *Wrong idea, right idea*, he thought now. Who cared? Charles had lots of ideas regarding Juliana at the moment, most of them wonderfully, spectacularly wrong. He grinned and blushed at his thoughts. It was time to stop the internal debate and move forward with this risk.

How had he missed her removing her stockings? *Damn.* Juliana sat bare legged on the bed, wearing nothing but the black dress. "How long have we known each other? How many times have we slept in the same room or in the same bed together over the years? Sleep here with me," she said, smiling, patting a delicate hand on the ultrasoft blanket next to her.

Juliana had bought the blanket for him as a gift when she noticed all of his blankets were in tatters. Charles had always taken care of others, animal and human alike, but no one ever bothered to take care of him other than his family and Juliana. And Juliana had taken care of him as well as any family member ever did.

Taking only his black cowboy boots off, he climbed onto the bed next to her. Her body was slender, her hips slim, and he was having trouble trying to find a safe place to rest his hand while they lay on the bed and talked, winding down from their evening out. Juliana told him that she couldn't remember the last time she had been out until almost two in the morning. Every time he rested his hand on her gently-curved hip, he moved closer to pulling her hips toward him. He settled on awkwardly playing with her elbow as her blue eyes sparkled with amusement. He began to wonder if she had figured him out.

His profile was rugged and somber and his strong features held a certain sensuality she was surprised she'd never noticed before. The awkward young boy was gone, all but the boyish twinkle in his brilliant blue eyes, and in his place was this amazing man. When had her duckling turned into such a magnificent swan? His prominent nose now fit his face. He had truly grown into his features. Though, at the moment, he still didn't seem particularly comfortable in his own skin. She liked the smile lines around his eyes and the way they crinkled a lot when he looked at her.

She giggled and asked, "Okay, what's up with this sudden fascination with my elbows?"

"Elbows are safe," he smiled, then added, "Honestly, I'm having a really hard time resisting the urge to take you in my arms."

"Oh," she said softly, understanding what he was actually saying. For the first time in decades of conversation, there was an awkward pause. Before she could think of a way to end it, Charles leaned forward, hesitantly at first, then with intent, and kissed her. His lips were everything she loved from a man. She closed her eyes and accepted the kiss.

He pulled back, looking ecstatic. "I can't believe you let me do that," he exclaimed, his smile registering his surprise.

Her mind raced, conflicted. She smiled almost as broadly as he did, but she worried this could be the swansong of their friendship. She was terrified of losing him. But the gates were opened, and there was no going back. She reached up and returned the kiss, slipping the tip of her tongue between his lips, enjoying the feel of him, the taste, before slowly pulling away. He smiled warmly down at her and took her into his arms in a deep and passionate embrace. She never experienced this with any other man, feeling immediately trusted, protected, and loved. How could she possibly resist? She couldn't. She was going to have to trust it would be worth the risk.

She was finally allowing herself to fall in love—and in lust—with her best friend.

Holding her tightly, Charles buried his face into the side of her neck, kissing her there, and deeply inhaled the scent of her skin and hair. It was intoxicating, and hearing the primal moan that escaped him made Juliana melt inside and out as she pressed her body tighter against him. His erection was hot and hard against her thigh. He pulled his head back and captured her lips again as tongues and breath intertwined.

He found the hem of her tiny dress and pulled it up to her slim waist. He ran his hands under her satin panties, down over her buttocks, and when his fingers found the hot, wet cleft he was in search of, he dipped a finger into it in a teasing manner. Juliana moaned and wriggled in an attempt to get him to go deeper; then she wasted no time freeing his erection from its nest of fabric. Charles changed focus and had his pants off and onto the floor in record time and pulled Juliana to a straddling position on top of him.

There was only one way to go from here.

He liked that she felt as light as a bird. Charles watched intently as Juliana peeled her slip of a dress off over her head, tossing it across the room, then set about unbuttoning his shirt as he fondled her perfect little breasts appreciatively. She straddled his full erection in her satin panties, rocking her hips against him slowly. "Condoms?" she asked. Apparently Juliana didn't have any hidden in the tiny purse she carried tonight.

Charles attempted to stifle a noise of frustration, and he said, "Actually, no, it's been a while." It had been well over a year since he kicked his last girlfriend out of his house, and there had been no one since then. "If it helps to know, I've been tested for everything. I'm clean." He didn't take any chances after the disastrous way his last relationship ended.

Juliana grinned at him. "That makes two of us. And, I'm on the pill, so I guess we'll have nothing between us?"

"How appropriate," Charles said, and with a devilish grin, he flipped her onto her back and stripped off the last thing standing in his way, the tiniest black satin panties.

He lowered himself gently on top of her, supporting most of his weight with his arms, fearing he'd crush her delicate form. When she breathed, "I ache for you, Charlie," into his ear, it was the sexiest thing anyone ever said to him. There was no way for him to hold himself back.

She was hot and dripping wet, beyond ready for him, which was a good thing, because while he planned to be gentle, passion changed his intentions. He dived into her body, sheathing himself completely with none of the usual first-time awkwardness. They both gasped in pleasure as he thrust into her hard and hot. Her warm, wet folds were even softer than her satin underwear.

He filled her as though they were made for each other, a perfect fit. He rocked into her wave after wave, burying himself to the hilt, unable to get enough. As she moved with him, he knew he couldn't hold back, much as he might want to make it last. "I'm going to come."

On hearing that, Juliana arched her back and changed the angle of her pelvis, taking him deeper. "Hope you don't mind if I help that along," she said.

"Not at all, but turnaround is fair play." He slipped a hand between them to find her clit. "God, I'm going to come now," she said. She grinned and gasped, and he watched as her entire body convulsing in orgasmic pleasure along with his. Charles moaned in ecstasy as he emptied himself into her.

"Wow," Charles said, breathing heavily.

"Wow," Juliana said, also out of breath. "That seems to be the word for the evening."

"I didn't hurt you, did I?" Charles asked, cradling her neck in one hand and stroking her face and hair with the other.

Juliana smiled. "You can rest assured, those were definitely moans of pleasure."

Charles was sorry their first time was so quick. And while Juliana insisted he had nothing to apologize for, she gladly took him up on his offer of a do-over. She never imagined their relationship would take flight like this, but now that it had, she couldn't imagine them being any other way. This felt so very right.

Juliana plucked one of the quills from the desk and ran it softly, lightly, over Charles' lips and along his strong jawline before tracing it down his neck, the center of his chest, and the line of hair pointing to his almost fully erect cock. She was impressed and quite pleased by his ability to recover after a short time of kissing, touching, and snuggling in each other's arms. She continued stroking and tickling his nipples, belly, cock, balls, and the area behind them with the feather until he was fully hard again.

"Who knew you were so perverted?" he asked as he took the feather from her.

"Excuse me?" Juliana said. "I am kinky, not perverted."

"Tomato, tomahto, it's the same thing. You're too beautiful when you're naked to be arguing semantics," he said, grinning.

"Nope, I have it on good authority that kinky is tickling your lover's arse with a feather, whereas perverted actually requires using the entire swan." Juliana grinned and winked at him, kissing him repeatedly while she rolled over and straddled him.

"I'll never get tired of kissing you, Jewel," Charles said.

Juliana beamed at his words. "Glad to hear it. Now, give me your tongue."

"What?"

She enunciated more slowly, unable to resist being a smart-ass, "Give . . . me . . . your . . . tongue." He smiled and did as she commanded, sticking his tongue in her mouth. She sucked on it as if it were a Popsicle—or his cock. He moaned in pleasure as his erection swelled between her thighs.

"Climb on," he said. Juliana ignored the instruction and instead pulled back and took his cock and balls into her hands. The featherlight touch of her hands seemed to excite Charles even more than the erotic tickling had. She realized if she wasn't careful, he'd explode in her hands.

Gently grabbing her wrists, Charles pulled Juliana

down to him. Juliana whispered, "take me and do with me as you will," then spent the next half hour enthusiastically taking direction from Charles until shuddering, sweating, and spent, they collapsed into each other's arms, breathless, smiles beaming.

"Well, we now know we're also sexually compatible!" she said, snuggling closer to him under the blankets. It was a wonderful piece of knowledge.

"Very." Charles held her tightly. "You are the most precious thing in the world to me, Jewel. You always have been, always will be." He cupped her face in his hands and gazed deeply into her eyes.

The love and honesty she saw had her pulse racing. "My dearest Charles, I love you. A piece of my heart has always belonged to you and only you. You're the pulse of my soul," Juliana said, eyes glistening. "I never let myself imagine that my sweet duckling would turn out to be such a brilliantly handsome swan. I'm sorry I . . ." Her voice broke, and Charles kissed the awkward moment away.

"It's okay, Jewel, you've always been the one, my swan. It's just taken me a while to accept that I could have you in every part of my life."

"In and out of bed," she said.

"Absolutely." Charles added, smiling, "You do know swans mate for life?"

"Yes, Charles, I do."

Alice

By Amber Kallyn

Alice loved her strange dreams about the world she called Wonderland. She always woke back in her college dorm room remembering the people and creatures populating the lands. Most times, Alice would roll over and turn her iPod on, wishing she could be back in that most unusual place.

But this time, Alice woke beneath a purple and yellow striped willow tree, its long fronds gently moving in a cool breeze. She knew something was different. The fact that she was also naked and entwined with two men further enhanced this belief. Sitting up, Alice pushed tangled blonde hair from her face and surveyed the scene. The scent of sex hung heavy in the air. And sweat. And lusty males. Mixed in was the aroma of sweet perfume, jasmine, and roses.

For the life of her, Alice couldn't seem to remember how she'd gotten there. Or who the men might be.

A callused hand rubbed her hip. A dark-haired, orange-eyed man peeked at her from beneath incredibly long lashes. His tanned body, lanky but with a hint of strength, stretched out beside her, his leg tangled with hers.

Rising on one elbow, the man said, "Morn, sweetie." His raspy voice sent chills skittering down her spine, directly to her pussy. Wet heat filled her.

Trying to ignore her rising desire and figure out if she was dreaming, Alice asked, "Who are you?"

The man laughed, his hand playing across her hip and onto her thigh. "You don't remember?"

"He's the Hatter." A deeper voice came from her other side.

Alice looked at the other man, as light as the Hatter was dark.

"I'm Ches. We've met too." He rose, reaching to cup her breast. One smooth thumb flicked over her nipple, sending shocks of pleasure through Alice. Her nipples tightened into hard buds. "Many times, we've met."

Ches grinned. A ghostly, toothy grin that pulled at Alice's memories. They drifted away before she could fully grasp them. Hatter slid closer, his foot rubbing along the top of hers. The raspy hair on his thigh tickled her leg. He trailed his hands over her skin, his fingers teasingly brushing her clit.

Though Alice knew she should be concerned with the situation of things, she couldn't quite bring herself to care. Not with the heat racing from her breasts to her throbbing clit, the sight of both men's jutting cocks seducing her further into the acceptance of this strange situation.

When Hatter leaned over and replaced his rough fingertips with smooth, hot lips, Alice gave up wondering completely.

Ches ran his hand up her back, grasping her shoulder

and pulling her back down to the bed of moss. He tweaked her nipple, pinching and tugging in the most delicious way.

Hatter licked his way up her thigh, then pressed his burning tongue against her clit. Alice's hips jerked, and a moan escaped as his fingers worked their way inside her pussy. He stroked in and out while his tongue torturously slowed. Alice relished the pleasure. Especially once Ches took her nipple into his mouth and sucked greedily. The intense double pleasure nearly drove her over the edge.

Something wrapped around her ankle, soft, furry, rubbing up her calf. Alice lifted her head to look, only to find a pink and purple striped cat's tail. Leading to Ches.

"What?" she asked, a bit startled.

Ches lifted from her breast and glanced down uneasily. "Sorry, the furry one sometimes tries to take over. Don't worry, beautiful. I won't shape-shift while we're making love."

Then he returned to her breast, drawing more of her nipple into his mouth, using tongue, lips, and scraping with his teeth. Ches lifted her hand, guiding it to his hard, velvety cock, and stroked it, his hand clasped over hers.

As if jealous or feeling left out, Hatter grabbed her other hand and moved it to his own, much larger cock.

Alice stroked them both, guiding her hands up and down, changing momentum every few times. The men writhed in the moss, though their mouths still worked hungrily on her body.

Hatter's fingers fucked her faster, keeping time with her hand on his cock. Alice felt herself coming to the brink, gasping as his mouth licked her, as his fingers brought the orgasm so very close.

Hatter and Ches pumped their hips, one lavishing her pussy, the other sucking and licking her breasts and throat.

The rippling explosion coursed through her, her pussy clenching around Hatter's fingers. Ches leaned back, his cry hoarse as he spilled hot come over her hand.

Hatter kept up his work with his tongue and hands, sucking her clit, all the while his fingers slid relentlessly inside her. Already, another orgasm was building.

Ches licked at her lips, then pushed his tongue inside her mouth. She met his kiss. His hand grasped her breast, playing with her nipple, gentle, then tugging hard, then gentle again. Alice felt herself rising to another peak. As Hatter rubbed her clit with his thumb, moving in fast, hard circles, she was pushed over once more. She screamed into Ches's mouth.

Hatter glanced up from his position near her hip. "Faster."

Alice stared into his eyes, still orange but turning blue, as she moved her hand up and down his cock. Following his direction, she hurried her movements, wanting to bring the man to his own pleasure. With her free hand, she maneuvered to reach down and cup his balls, rolling them in her palm.

His eyes clenched shut and he grunted, coming.

Alice stroked him a few more times, loving the way his body shuddered, then lay back. The breeze picked up, drawing cooling air over her body. Minutes passed in silence as their breathing slowed.

Ches leaned over her. His purple eyes were mesmerizing

as he asked, "So, Alice. Do you remember anything yet?"

With her body so sweetly satisfied, all Alice wanted to do was go back to sleep. But she thought over his question, trying to figure out where she was, who these men were, and how she'd gotten here.

Slowly, the memories returned. Wonderland. Hatter was the Mad Hatter, a man obsessed with his tea times—though he did brew a wonderful pot. Ches . . . was a shape-shifter. He could change form from man into an overgrown cat at will. He could also disappear like a ghost, which Alice sometimes found a little creepy.

And for the past three days, they had been running from the Queen of Hearts, searching for a caterpillar who could show them the way to overthrow the cruel woman, once and for all. As the knowledge hit her, sounds of armored soldiers crashed through the forest. Alice jerked up, searching for her clothes, only to find a ragtag pile of pants, shirts, and finally her dress and underwear.

She looked to the men, who seemed unconcerned. "Are we going to run or let them capture us?"

Ches and Hatter exchanged glances, then shrugged and began to dress. Alice led the way from beneath the willow, crouching in the wispy yellow grass, which grew four feet high. They were near a towering mountain to the left and facing a long, barren field on the right.

"Which way?" she asked, keeping her voice low.

"Absalom is near the mountain at evening tea," Hatter said, blinking wide eyes, his irises now the color of the bluest sky.

Alice looked to Ches for clarification.

"Sunset," he gruffly replied.

Which, if her limited knowledge of astronomy meant anything in this wild place, was only about an hour away. Alice didn't know if they could make it in time, especially not with the sound of the queen's guards coming closer, but they had to try.

Because besides needing to be rid of the queen, she needed to get home. Finals were coming up. She only had one semester to complete before finishing her nursing degree. And while that paled compared to the adventures she had here, no matter how much she longed to stay in this place, she never managed to achieve it.

This time she'd been here a few days. Unfortunately, she'd accidentally come across a beautiful sapphire ring sitting on a toadstool, and though she knew better, she'd picked it up.

The ring clasped around her finger and refused to come off. The queen appeared, saw the ring on Alice's finger, and started shouting. Not that they'd ever gotten along. Alice had found the best course was to stay out of the woman's way. When the queen demanded the return of her ring, Alice, unable to take the damn thing off, ran to the two men she knew could protect her until she found a way out of this fix.

Alice crept away from the willow, searching for the guards she heard.

"Up," Hatter calmly said.

She looked up, only to squeak at the sight of a battalion of armored guards riding through the air on their mounts, creatures that looked like small dragons.

Grabbing both Hatter and Ches's hands, she darted into the wild grass, racing for freedom.

"Halt in the name of the Queen!" came a shout from above.

Hatter tugged his hand free, then reached into the bag he always carried. He pulled out a tea saucer and sent it whistling through the air. It hit a guard, shattering. The man didn't make a sound as he slid from his steed and fell through the air to the ground.

Ches and Alice jumped over the unconscious guard, racing on while Hatter kept up behind them, pulling more saucers and striking guard after guard. Soon, the flying creatures pulled back, a few men still seated, the rest asleep in the grass.

After what seemed like eternity, the three made it to the foothills. Ches stopped, sniffing the cool air. A moment later, he nodded.

"This way." Tugging Alice along, he headed right, only to stop a few yards away from a tall mound of earth.

"Absalom?" Hatter called.

No answer came.

"Be right back," Ches said with a wink. The air around him shimmered. In seconds, he stood thigh high to Alice as a colorful striped cat. With a purr, he rubbed against her leg before padding to the mound. After turning three times, Ches lay down and smiled.

First, his tail disappeared. Then his hindquarters, legs, and finally his head.

"Show off," Hatter replied, pulling Alice against his chest.

"Are we supposed to wait?" she asked.

"There's nothing else to do. Unless you want some tea?"

"No," she said, loving the way his strong arms wrapped around her, making her feel safe. "When you hold me I can recall my dreams of this place from when I was younger. And of why we are on the run today: I pissed off the queen."

"Again," Hatter added, but he softened his word with a smile. His eyes were a strange, swirling combination of orange and blue.

"But," she asked, "how did we come to be beneath the willow tree?"

Hatter pulled her tighter to his hard chest, running his hand down her hair, then tipping her head to the side so he could place kisses down her neck. A shiver worked down her spine as the stubble on his chin tickled her skin.

"Alice. Darling, beautiful Alice. Do you not know Ches and I have waited years for you to be ready?"

Enjoying the caresses, Alice asked, "A woman, you mean?"

"Of course." Hatter's hand moved over her belly and up her ribs to cup one of her breasts. His other hand gripped her hip, pulling her against the hardness in his pants. "Absalom showed us a vision long ago of you at this age. Of the things we will be capable of doing together."

"What do you mean?"

"This day has been foretold. The day when the three of us will be able to vanquish the Queen for eternity and free Wonderland from her cruel control."

"So the lovemaking?"

He sighed, cupping her cheek. "You are so hard to resist. And the way you have been looking at Ches and me. So hard to resist."

"But how did we get beneath the tree?" she asked again as Hatter's hand slipped along her hip, tugging her dress higher, then moving to caress her clit through the silkiness of her underwear.

"Because," he whispered, placing gentle kisses along her jaw as his fingers rubbed harder. "It was time for tea and love." She never did understand him completely.

The large mound of dirt in front of them shook, and a line appeared as if the earth was opening to swallow them. The high pile of rocks, dirt, and leaves grew smaller, smaller, until it disappeared. Pebbles bounced over the ground as the dark line grew into a wide, circular hole, dark and deep.

Hatter pulled her toward it. "Let us go." He glanced back and winked. "Fear not. Soon it will be time for tea and love once more."

Alice felt herself getting hot, wet at the promise in his eyes.

Then they jumped into the hole. Time seemed to stop as they fell, sometimes fast, the wind rushing past and whipping her hair and clothes. Sometimes slow, as if they were barely moving at all. During one of these times, Hatter pulled her into his arms, pushing her dress down her shoulders so he could lick her breasts, nibble gently on her puckered nipples. His hand impatiently ripped at her underwear, freeing her pussy for his fingers to play.

He untied his pants, letting his cock spring free.

Then, other hands were on her shoulders, drifting down her back, over her ass. Ches whispered, "You're supposed to wait for me."

Hatter replied, "I figured you would catch up."

Alice couldn't stop the moan as Ches's slickened fingers slipped between the cheeks of her ass to rub against her entrance. Hatter's fingers delved between her pussy lips.

"Are you finally ready for us both, our beautiful Alice?" Ches asked.

"Yes," she replied, remembering how as a teenager, growing into womanhood, she'd had so many fantasies about these two men. And now they were finally coming true.

Hatter pulled her closer. The wind breezed past them, soft, soothing, enflaming her sensitive skin. It was as if their descent had slowed so they could have this time together. Hatter slid the tip of his cock against her clit, then lower, pulling her legs apart. Staring into her eyes, he kissed her deeply, his tongue plunging into her mouth as his cock pushed into her pussy. Shocking pleasure raced through Alice. She could only moan incoherently as he pumped deep inside her.

Then, Ches slid his cock between her cheeks, probing her hole. He snapped his fingers and a bottle appeared, falling beside them. Dipping his fingers into the clear, glistening substance, Chess rubbed the creamy oil down her ass and along his cock. Then he slid inside her slowly, in such contrast to Hatter's plunging dick.

Alice felt herself stretching almost painfully. Ches bit

her shoulder, bringing the pain there as well. But it was a delicious pain. A welcomed feeling.

Still, he slid deeper into her ass.

Unsure she could take any more, Alice let her head fall back, only able to relish the sensations these men brought her. Then, Ches was fully sheathed.

Hatter stopped, and for a moment they fell, unmoving, both men's cocks filling her. Alice thought she might burst from the pleasure. From the feeling of being exactly where she'd always wanted to be, where she belonged.

She felt complete for the first time in her life.

Ches whispered something that sounded like words of love. Then he slapped her ass. As if it was a cue, both men jerked their hips, fucking her hard and fast. Alice had never experienced such wondrous feelings. It was heavenly, but surely something this devilishly exquisite couldn't be allowed there.

They were entwined, legs rubbing, hands roaming. Ches licked her back, her neck, nibbling everywhere he could reach. Hatter kneaded her breasts, playing with her nipples, kissing her with a frenzied urgency. Alice wanted it to last forever.

They moved inside her, their cocks plunging in and out in tandem.

Soon she felt the orgasm reach a screaming peak. Both her pussy and ass clamped down, spasming around their cocks. They shouted in pleasure and increased their rocking, making Alice come with a scream.

Still, they fucked her, until she came again. And a third time.

Dizzy with pleasure, Alice was hardly aware when they stopped falling. She only noticed when the men, their breathing hoarse, fast, interspersed with moans, cried out as they came inside her.

When Alice came back to herself, she didn't want to leave the warm arms of the men surrounding her. With a sleepy, satisfied smile, she said, "When can we do that again?"

Hatter grinned. "Any time you want, my love."

Ches took her hand and helped her stand, while Hatter relaced his pants, grumbling about shape-shifters and conveniently appearing clothes.

Firmly on the ground, it was time to continue their quest. They headed down a dark, rocky tunnel. The only lights were flaming torches sporadically placed along the rough walls. What seemed like miles later, they emerged into a cavernous room. On the far end, another mound of dirt lay, surrounded by wispy smoke.

"You must go alone," Hatter said, his blue eyes sad.

"Yes, darling. Alone," Ches agreed. He, too, seemed sad for some reason.

Alice felt unsure, but she trusted them and did as they bid. She stepped into the smoke, her skin itching as it grew darker. Looking back, she couldn't see the men behind her. The air stirred, opening to reveal a path leading to a large mushroom growing on the mound of dirt. On top of it sat Absalom, his pipe pumping more fragrant smoke.

"Ah. Alice," the caterpillar said as she approached. "How have you been enjoying Wonderland now that you've come of age?"

Her face heated at the knowing look in his eyes. "Very well, thank you."

"And Hatter and the Cat? Are they to your liking?"

"Yes," she replied, certain her cheeks were a bright red.

"Good." He blew another ring of smoke, which wavered into the shape of a heart. "You are back because you turned 21."

"A few days ago." She shifted her feet, clasping her hands behind her back. "What does that have to do with anything?"

"It is destiny, as is everything."

Damn cryptic caterpillars. "Which means?"

"You have bested the Red Queen before. But do you want to know the only way to truly defeat her?"

"Yes," she whispered.

Absalom waved his hand and the ring on her finger slipped off, floating in the air in front of her.

"You must choose to remain," he said.

Alice stared from the ring to the caterpillar. "But I can't. I try, but I always wake up back in my own world."

"Ah, but this ring will allow you to stay. And when it is with you, the Queen of Hearts loses much of her power. Every time you are here, she weakens. If you keep this ring and stay in Wonderland, Alice, her power will drain and she will never be able to harm anyone again."

"Stay here?" Alice's mind spun. It was all she ever dreamed.

"Forever," Absalom added, his words cautious.

"And my real life?"

The caterpillar coughed laughter, the strangest thing

she'd ever seen of the many strange things in this place.

"This is real life too, my dear."

A picture of her family flashed in her mind. "And my mother? My sister?"

Absalom nodded. "Sadly, you will most likely never see them again. It is a difficult choice. But know there are people here who have loved you from afar, even if only recently they managed to get their hands on you."

The caterpillar winked and disappeared, the smoke with him. But his voice whispered to her. "Choose, but make sure you are ready. For once the ring claims its spot on your finger, you will never be able to go home."

"This can be home," said two voices behind her. Alice turned to stare at Hatter and Ches. She felt their arms around her, keeping her safe. Their hands on her body, bringing her more pleasure and comfort, and the feeling of homecoming, than she'd ever experienced in her life. Recalling Absalom's words, she could see the love shining from their eyes. Inside, her heart expanded. She had always loved them too.

"Yes," she whispered. "I want to stay."

The ring whirled in the air, then disappeared. Alice felt her heart crack, until the ring appeared on her finger once more.

Taking the first step toward the men waiting for her was hard, but before long she was running, then throwing herself into their waiting arms and kissing first Hatter, then Ches.

After a moment, Hatter stepped back, staring into her eyes. "Are you sure you want to stay?"

"Are you both going to keep loving me? Keep fucking me so sweetly?" she asked with a grin.

"Oh yes, love," he said.

Ches added, "Any time, any way you want."

"Prove it." Alice pulled her dress above her head, standing naked before them. Soon their clothes were shed and spread on the ground.

Ches laid her down so sweetly, covering her body with his. Hatter bent over to kiss her, but that wasn't what Alice wanted.

As Ches pushed his cock inside her, she pulled Hatter to her mouth and slid her tongue over his length, teasing the swollen tip with her teeth stopping briefly to ask, "Always?"

"Always," they both replied.

Hungering for Nia
By S.D. Grady

One

Cain Hastings knocked back the last of his Coors draft. He scratched at the daylong growth of beard and took a slow perusal of the Deep Dark, his favorite honky-tonk on the outskirts of Tulsa.

Still early on Friday night, the band banged around as they set up their mics and drum set. A few booths that lined the far wall boasted groups of giggling girls—not his type. Too young. Too eager. Too slim. Not that he was truly on the prowl tonight, but one never knew. Besides, after a week behind the wheel of his tractor-trailer, he could use a little bit of pleasant female company—somebody to take the edge off the hum of the highway.

Yellow light from the parking lot spilled in the doorway as a crowd entered the dim, dusty dancehall. Cain nodded at a few other drivers from Kenilworth Transport. He smiled at Brad, who held Lila from accounting close to his side. His partner, Curly, tried to capture the laughing

Steph's hand. The gang headed toward one of the long tables near the stage.

Cain began to spin his stool back to the bar, when a tight pair of jeans hugging a sweet, soft ass nudged past. He paused.

She trailed behind the others, clearly the extra wheel, tiptoeing in her cowboy boots. Her shoulders hunched with each solid click of her heels. Long dark curls skimmed the tooled leather of her belt. The white-collared shirt hid her upper curves. He hoped she would turn around for a better glimpse.

One of the other girls snagged their heel in a crack on the floor. A pocketbook fell. The mystery woman stopped to pick it up and executed the wished-for spin as she handed it back to its owner.

No shit.

Cain swallowed hard. No way. That could not possibly be Nia Gordon. Her husky voice chased his tormented soul across the country as Kenilworth's dispatcher. When he stopped in the office, she always sat in the back, headset stuck to her ears and chewing on a pencil. She didn't speak. She didn't move, laugh, or even dress—

Where in the hell did she get those jeans?

She looked around the open-beamed barn while she stuffed her hands into her front pockets. Hazel eyes skimmed the forty-foot bar and skipped over his sorry ass.

She stilled.

Cain stood up, remembering at the last moment not to fixate on her generous breasts.

She looked back at him.

He dipped his head, winked, and wished for a moment he'd dressed for dancing tonight. That first smile always worked better with a hat.

Abject terror raced across her features before she skittered over to the table where her friends waited for her.

Cain felt the beast in him wake up. Miss Gordon needed to watch her tail tonight, because he was going to grab it if he could.

"No, seriously, Lila, scoot over!"

"Why?"

Petunia Gordon, Nia to her friends, scowled while her heart continued to beat out of control. "Because! If you don't, then I'm on the end and then . . ."

"Hi guys!"

Jesus freakin' Christ! Not tonight. Nia froze before pasting a smile on her tired features and turned to greet . . . him.

Nia firmly believed there are people placed on this planet just to make the world look better. Cain Hastings totally belonged in that category. Every time he stopped by the office, she had to clean her fingernails so she wouldn't stare at his six-foot-two-inch muscled body. She already felt the betraying blush sear her cheeks. "Hi, Cain."

God, that sounded lame. She felt lame. Tonight was lame. She eyed the exit door, a mile away from her on the other side of the hall. He snared one of the chairs, spun it, sat down and leaned on the curved back. Nia tried not to lick her lips as the veins in his forearms danced under bronzed skin.

Right, don't speak and don't move and you'll be fine, she reminded herself. Following years of solid advice, she escaped to the other side of the table and sank into the empty chair at the end. The huge ceiling fans overhead sent ticklish drafts of air down on her neck. Chilled and overheated, she shook and removed her nail file from her purse.

"Hey!"

Nia ignored the overly loud whisper.

Steph tried again, this time jabbing her in the side.

"What?"

The older woman exhaled. "I did not squeeze you into my best pair of jeans so you could do a manicure!"

Nia took a deep breath to tell her friend all the reasons why this night was a really bad idea, when the lights lowered and the band struck the opening chords of a two-step.

"Can I have this dance?"

His hand hovered in the edge of her vision.

Oh God. "I . . . uh . . . I . . ." What could she say? "I don't know how." She suppressed a smug smirk. That should stop him. Maybe she rarely spoke to Cain beyond a friendly good-morning in the last six years, but that didn't stop her skin from breaking out into goosebumps every time she did. Dancing? That would be suicide.

"That's okay. It's been years since I braved the floor." He waited.

Just long enough that Nia felt compelled to look up. Blue eyes—sparkling blue eyes—and lips that looked warm and soft and strong and . . . *Oh God.*

He bent closer. The heat of his breath stirred the curls

by her ear. "We'll remember how to do it together."

Every muscle in her body locked. *Shit. Fuck. Oh* . . . "Okay."

She managed to stand and place her hand in his.

Cain pulled her soft body closer to his as they followed the beat. Not only was his blood pounding in his temples, his cock strained for release. Her floral scent rose between them as she stared at his Adam's apple. He could feel the tension in her every fiber. Each time he managed to capture her curious glance, she trembled.

With great restraint, he loosened his grip on her waist and held out his hand for a spin. She followed with natural ease. Maybe she hadn't danced in years either, but she knew how. He knew why she lied. He could see her doubts chasing back and forth in her expression. Lust fought for supremacy with fear.

He ran his hand up her back, bringing her close to him again. Muscles tightened, then eased with each pass. Her breasts pressed against his chest, creating further havoc in his groin.

Long years of seducing women on lonely Saturday nights told him he ought to be chatting, asking her about the workweek and why she chose that particular blouse, but all those words stuck in his throat. Instead, wild images of Nia's curls splayed across his living room floor mixed with phantom groans and tastes of sex—tantalizing his senses and igniting his imagination.

He flexed his fingers and tightened his grip on her hand and hip.

Something in the movement drew her attention up. She swallowed twice. "What is it that you want?" She still shook.

The need and desire that swamped his body urged him to answer, "I want you."

She skipped a step. They spent a moment finding the beat.

She stared at their boots for a moment. "You *are* holding me."

"No, I want you naked . . ."

She gasped. Her eyes dilated.

"Naked, under me, around me, and screaming for me . . ."

"I need you to take me home now." Nia swiped at the tears on her cheeks. She spared a quick glance at the dance floor where he stood, arms crossed over his chest and a black scowl on his face.

Lila rose to her feet. "Are you okay?"

"I'm not feeling well. I don't think I should drive." She sank to a chair as her legs gave out.

Her friend began collecting purses and keys. "Did something happen? Are you hurt?"

Nia wanted to stamp her feet. "No! Nothing happened. I just . . . have a headache." She squeezed her eyes shut. Her body still felt like it belonged to an alien. Sparks raced up and down every limb. Her gut felt twisted and hungry. And her throat . . . She fought the impending sobs.

"Did Cain do something to you?"

Nia turned away. Lila was just being nice. Nia hated

lying, but if she said nothing had happened, then maybe the girls from the office wouldn't take her home and then he'd come back and . . . "Yes. I want to leave."

Little was said on the way home. Lila and Steph tried a few times to get details from her, but Nia just stared out the window.

Lila pulled up in front of the modest three-bedroom ranch and put it in park. "Should I come in?"

Nia shook her head. "Thanks. My mom's home. I'll be okay." She crawled from the car before she realized. "Steph! Your clothes! Mine are still at your house."

"Hey, honey, I'll just bring them with me on Monday. Deal?"

Nia nodded, faced with the new difficulty of getting past her mother. "Monday. Thanks."

She entered through the kitchen. The TV flickered in the living room. With any luck . . . She kicked her boots off and started to tiptoe down the hall.

"That you, Petunia?"

"Yes, Mom." Nope, luck wasn't with her.

"You're late, tonight."

She stayed in the shadows. "I went out to the Deep Dark with the girls."

"That's the honky-tonk out on State 51?"

This wasn't going well. "Uh, yeah."

The recliner creaked. "Did you meet anybody?"

"No!"

Her mother appeared around the corner, her gray hair tied back in a long braid. "Good. I knew I raised a good girl. Them new clothes?"

Nia pulled at the pointed collar. "Steph from the office lent them to me. What do you think?"

The wrinkled nose said everything. "I think you're forgetting that a good woman doesn't flaunt her figure for men to ogle."

Or touch, Nia added in her mind. "I'm sorry. I won't go again."

"See that you don't." Her mother walked down the hall and closed the door to her bedroom.

Nia leaned against the wall.

Touch . . . He touched and held and caressed and whispered, and for just that one moment, Nia wanted to know what it would be like. Even a hug would've been nice. She stared at her mother's closed door. She had never been hugged.

Two

"Hi, Nia."

She jumped and dropped her headset. His eyes danced with mischief, damn the man. "Good morning, Cain. Got your assignment for the week?"

He propped his chin on the top of the cubicle and hung the manifest over the edge. "All local stuff. Know what that means?"

She fumbled with her computer, straightened a few gnawed pencils, and answered, "No, what does that mean?"

"That I can take you out to supper tonight. Does Trattoria sound good? Do you like Italian?"

She pushed a curl behind her ear and tried not to scream. "I'm busy."

"Really?"

How dare he? "Yeah, really."

She typed in the first few manifests into the system. She thought she could hear the toe of his boot kicking the other side of her cubicle.

"I know what you're thinking, and I'm not mad."

Her fingers clicked over the keys. "No? Why not?"

He began swinging his paperwork back and forth in front of her face. "Because you want me as bad as I want you."

Her fingers curled into fists while she closed her eyes. This was so not happening. Not in her lifetime. Not this way. "Would you please excuse me?" Without looking at him, she snatched her purse and headed to the ladies' room.

The door swung closed behind her. She grabbed the edge of the counter and bit back the cry of frustration bubbling beneath the surface. When she opened her eyes, she squeaked. "What are doing here?"

His reflection towered behind her. His dirty blonde hair curled just above his dark blue T-shirt collar. He didn't smile. In fact, with his arms crossed over his chest and a gleam in his eye, he looked almost . . . hungry.

"It seems we need to talk, even though I'd much rather be doing something more satisfying with you." He let his voice drop. The suggestion lingered in the air between them. His hand appeared at her left.

She shrank away even as he let it settle on her arm and began a soothing motion up and down.

"I have no intention of hurting you, Nia. I just want to kiss you."

Nia began to shake her head.

"Maybe touch you, lick you, taste you . . ."

"Stop!"

He did. "Why should I?" His hand hovered over her flesh.

She felt her skin pucker beneath it. Her nipples tightened. "I've . . . I've never . . ."

He grinned. "Still a virgin? At what, 25? That's okay, we'll go slow." His fingers resumed the torture of her arm, traveling up over her shoulder to the small patch of bare skin by her throat.

"No, not a virgin." God, these were things she didn't even tell herself late at night in her cold bed. "I've never loved anyone before."

He stepped around her and hitched his jeans-clad hips on the counter, apparently settling in for a good chat.

Nia glared at the door. Seriously, what if somebody came in?

He just shook his head. "Tell me how you've lost your virginity, yet never *loved* somebody?"

She ran some water and splashed it on her face. "I was 16. He was too. And an ass. We . . ." The enormity of the confession locked itself in her chest. She turned her back to him again. "I didn't like it."

He laughed, the bastard. "Then you didn't do it right." His hands snaked around her waist while his chin rested in the crook of her neck. He enveloped her. His strength and scent . . . and a very obvious erection.

Heat and longing mixed with a dark twist in her belly. Nia wished she could understand what it was her body was doing. Her breasts felt heavy and tight. She wanted to burst from her skin, and all because of a hug.

"Hey!" His arms tightened. "Am I that bad?"

Nia felt the world close in on her. She tried to hold back the sob, but she couldn't hide the shaking.

His lips caressed her neck.

"Stop, right now."

She felt his heat abandon her. Before he could try to lure her back in, she escaped through the door.

* * * *

Cain adjusted his painful grip on the steering wheel for the tenth time. Now he was just pissed.

What was eating the girl? Not him, that was for sure. All he did was give her a little nuzzle, and now he had human resources breathing down his neck. Funny how all his local deliveries for the week were suddenly reassigned and he found himself climbing the high plains of Colorado on his way to Montana.

He'd tried calling her house, but he only got some irate lady who hung up on him every time he asked for Nia, saying, "Nobody lives here by that name." What the fuck?

Nia Gordon, the hot little woman hidden in the back of the office under heavy sweaters and khakis lived at 48 Washington Street, and he knew her number. What, had she skipped town just to avoid him? That was hardly complimentary.

He eyed his cell phone. Well, he did know one place he could catch her. At the next fuel stop, he dialed the office.

"Dispatch." Her throaty purr zinged straight to his crotch.

"Nia?"

"Leave me alone." The line went dead.

He redialed. This time it rang four times before the office manager answered. "Is that you, Hastings?"

"Yes, Ma'am. May I speak to Nia?"

"I thought HR told you to stop harassing her."

"I can hardly harass her from Denver! Put her on the line." He chewed his cheek while he listened to the hold music.

Moments passed before her familiar voice came on. "Dispatch."

"Dinner. Just dinner. I can wait . . ."

Her husky voice lowered into a whisper. "Wait to rape me?"

"Oh, honey! With the fire between you and me, it won't be rape. It'll be . . ." He groaned. *How do you describe anticipated ecstasy, especially to someone who seems so scared of it?* "Hot, baby. So hot. I'll make sure you are screaming with pleasure. I'll . . ."

"I don't want to be hot or anything else you have to offer. Just leave me alone."

Cain watched the fuel pump total up his diesel purchase. "Nia, if there's one thing I know, it's when a woman trembles in your arms, the last thing she wants to do is walk away. You like it when I hold you. Just imagine how an entire night spent in my bed would feel." He waited a few more seconds, smiling when he heard her breathing deepen. "I wouldn't ignore a square inch of your body. I'd kiss your neck, your breasts, your nipples. Did you know, when I twist your nipples, the sensation will shoot straight to your pussy?"

She gasped. He waited for the line to go dead again. But it didn't.

"That's right. I can't wait to run my tongue through your wet, tight pussy. I can almost taste it right now."

"Oh, jeez. Cain, they record this line!"

He laughed. "They'll only check the recording if you go crying wolf again." He could picture her brown sweater rising with her panicked breathing. "Should I continue?"

He barely heard her "Yes."

He took a breath, looking forward to describing her sweet ass and how it would feel when he spanked it.

"No! Cain! Beatrice is back. I gotta go."

For the second time, he listened to a dial tone, but that was just fine. He would be stopping for the night in another five hours, and then he'd call again. By the time he walked into the Kenilworth office Friday morning, he doubted she would be hiding in the ladies' room anymore.

Three

As she finished her jog, Nia lowered herself onto the massive boulder, every muscle in her legs screaming at her. Nothing seemed to help, not since Cain reappeared on Friday, dropped a gift box on her desk, and vanished just as fast. She left the red baby-doll negligee in her car.

Mom would have a heart attack if she found that in her underwear drawer. But the four-pack of condoms included with the card had *her* hyperventilating.

He wouldn't stop. She knew that. She felt like a rabbit in its hole, waiting for the big, bad wolf to go away, but Cain persisted.

She rubbed her neck, stretched her legs in front of her, and touched her head to her knees.

"Flexible too. That's always a good thing."

Fuck. He hunched down next to her. She opened her eyes to see his jeans and boots carefully balanced. His hands played with a tall blade of grass, pulling it apart. "It means I can open you up more. Bend you. Provides for better penetration."

She sat up and met his happy expression. "Do you have no shame?"

He shook his head and looked back over the water of the reservoir. "I never found shame to have much use. Can I ask you something?"

"You mean instead of saying something crude . . ."

"And sexy?"

Impossible. "Yes."

"Yes, I always say something sexy, or yes, I can ask you something?" He started to chew on the grass blade.

She drew her knees to her chest and rested her cheek on them. "Both."

He leaned back and sat down. "I'm making progress. Here, I've been talking to you for a whole minute and you haven't run away."

"Do you have a point?" The familiar anger and panic

were beginning to stir in her stomach. She blushed as he studied her.

"Is that a mother-approved jogging suit? She must not be a complete loss."

She crossed her arms over her chest, covering the red spandex tank. "No. I bought it yesterday when I decided maybe working out might . . ."

"Might what?

It was time to go. This was going nowhere. She stood up and turned to jog back to her car.

He blocked the sun. "Might what?"

She looked to her left and then the right.

His hand took hold of her chin and directed her gaze back up to his. "There's nobody here to run to, Nia." His other large hand sneaked around her waist, drew her in. Trapped her. "Answer the question. What did you hope to achieve by running?"

"I . . ." Flashes of conversations dashed through her mind. He spoke of bites, licks, fingers . . . orgasms. She tried to back away, but his grip firmed. "I'm afraid."

"Of me?" His lips caressed her temple.

She felt it all begin to fall apart. Maybe that began at the Deep Dark, but now, with his hard muscles holding her to his wide chest, she crumpled. She closed her eyes as his fingers pushed her hair out of her eyes, lingering in her scalp.

"No, not of you." His knee nudged her legs apart, setting fire to . . . her pussy. There, she said it, maybe not out loud. In her mind. Part of her body ached and wept. Part of her wanted. "I need so much, Cain." She looked up.

He studied her, no glint of amusement in the depths of those eyes. "What do you need?"

She wrapped her arms around his waist and buried her face in his shoulder. "Hold me, and let me believe you care."

Cain gritted his teeth. His entire body howled for relief, and instead of begging him to take her to bed, all he had managed to achieve was a hug. Christ, she was driving him crazy.

Soft breasts with hard nipples pressed through that tight top and rubbed him all the right ways. Sunshine mixed with her sweat and that light floral scent he identified as Nia. And his knee still rested between her thighs.

Ah, man. Long, lean legs encased in tight jogging pants. He wondered how much hugging this final step of seduction would take.

She sniffled and wiped her nose on the back of her hand. *Crying?* What did he do that made her cry all the time? "Hey." He cupped her cheeks and helped to dry her eyes with his thumbs. "It's okay."

She drew a second harsh breath and attempted to smile.

Lost, he smothered her trembling lips with his and swallowed her surprise with his kiss as triumph roared through his chest. Her tongue tried to evade his conquest, but failed. He swept forward and drank of her flavor. Vanquished her fear. Drew her in.

He pulled her closer; his arms encircled her shoulders. There would be no escaping this time.

Lust fogged his brain and sent urgent signals to his cock. He widened his stance and hoped that there would be a little more room in his jeans for the pressing problem.

She whimpered.

He drew back.

She reached up, sank her nails into his neck, and licked at his lips. "More, Cain. I want more."

Ah, sweet victory.

The line of her back stretched and arched in to him. Lean muscular arms, coated with a light sheen of sweat, wrapped around his waist.

The kiss lingered. Hot, needy, and hungry. He skimmed her hips with one hand, up her rib cage, and when he reached the swell of her breast, he sucked hard on her tongue.

Her right leg wrapped around him. He cupped the swollen flesh. She gasped. His thumb flicked over the nipple. When she cried out, he transferred his teeth to the taut line of her throat.

"Hey! Get a room!"

She broke free.

He tried to reach for her, but had some trouble ripping his gaze away from the lovely cleft of her cleavage. Full, ripe, soft, and inviting. He could eat at those tits all night long.

The jogger who interrupted was now all the way down the path and already disappearing. She ran her hand through her hair and pulled on the long braid that swung down her back.

"Well, Nia, which will it be?"

She nibbled at her lips and let her eyes skim over his body. He felt his cock harden more as she lingered at his crotch.

"Well?"

"Well, what?"

He needed to figure out how to distract her like this all the time. "Your place or mine?"

She paled. "My mother would kill me."

He grabbed her hand and headed toward the parking lot. "My place."

She hung back.

His patience strained. "What is it now?"

"She *will* kill me."

He counted to ten, a difficult endeavor at the moment. "Only if she knows."

"Oh, she'll know. She knows eve—"

"Nia."

"What?"

It was a challenge to see such innocence in a woman he had so many nasty intentions toward. "How old are you?"

"Twenty-four."

He pulled her to him and held her head steady. "Then by all that's holy, your mother has no business prying into your bedroom. That privilege belongs to the man you give it to, which in this case is me. Just me."

When he released her lips minutes later, he gave a satisfactory grunt. No hint of worry remained in those hazel eyes. "My place."

Four

He didn't stop. His tongue danced over her shoulders. Her rib cage. Belly button. Her stomach rippled as his hair tickled the lower curve of her breast. It felt wonderful and decadent and urgent. Her heels dug into the silk sheets.

Periodically she opened her eyes, but closed them in shock as her eyes met her own in the mirrored ceiling. If she had time to think . . . A hiss ripped through her teeth. *To hell with thinking.*

Never, ever in a hundred thousand years had she thought it possible. His tongue burned a path through the aching folds of her pussy, yet missed something key. Her hips rose off the mattress, seeking . . .

Sparks shot through her mind when that wet, curious part of his mouth landed there.

"Like that, Nia?"

How could he talk? Her throat fought to form words, but failed when he touched that magic spot once again. She groaned and moaned and ripped at the slippery sheet with her nails. "Again."

"My pleasure."

His fingers held back her folds. His tongue swiped over and over.

Suddenly, a sharp pain twisted through her nipple and shot straight through her stomach to join in the torment between her thighs. Trying to catch a breath, she slapped at air when the intriguing pleasure-pain combination attacked again.

Everything throbbed. Just as he said it would.

"I'm eating your clit, Nia. That's the word. Will you say it for me?"

He placed a full-mouth kiss over it and sucked.

Nia suppressed a keening cry. "My clit. Oh God. You're eating my clit."

"Should I stop?"

"No. Never stop."

Hot. So hot. And tight. Her pussy clamped around nothing. "Inside, Cain. I need you inside."

His finger penetrated her channel, touching nerves never before truly awakened. "Can you take me, sweet?"

She nodded several times before muttering, "Yes. Oh, yes."

Her muscles fluttered. Her back arched. His finger set up a rhythm and tugged deep inside.

"But not yet, I think. You're so close, sweet. I can feel you clamping down on my finger."

The movement inside didn't stop. She didn't want it to stop. A little faster, a little harder.

"Will you come for me?" His tongue tickled.

Her mind blanked.

All that remained were the buck of her hips, the sting in her nipples, and the pulse in her womb. The desire swamped her body.

She dimly recognized his shoulder holding her hips down. His teeth grazed her clit, which felt far too big. It ballooned in her mind. Beating. Hungering. Twisting. Needing.

When he gave one unending suck to that tortured bud, her mind flew away.

Was it her voice that roared a guttural moan of release? Muscles contracted and weakened.

He kept sucking.

She shook and leaned into the divine sensations.

When she thought she might drift into a land of mist and down, something huge and hard thrust its way into her overstimulated body.

"Oh God, baby. So tight. So tight. Don't move." Cain felt the sweat trickle down his cheek.

She lay beneath him, her hair splayed across his bed. Passion-slack eyes fluttered open at the intrusion. He wrapped her legs around his hips. Perfect.

And between them, he watched the muscles of her pussy quiver as she struggled to accommodate him.

"That's it, Nia. We're gonna ride together. Ready?"

Her swollen nipples rose in the bright light. He had made them red. Their sweet taste called to him even as he continued to lick the cream of her release from his lips.

"What was that?" she wondered and shifted her hips.

Cain leaned forward, groaning and fighting to stay motionless within her trembling vagina. She still hadn't loosened her grip on his cock. Soft, wet, hot . . .

He rocked forward.

She rose to meet him.

Withdrawing, he waited a moment before returning.

She sighed.

"That was your first orgasm, sweet. Ready for another?"

"I don't know. It was . . ." Her eyes glazed over when he seated himself fully in her depths. "Wonderful."

"Good, then you'll think this one is amazing."

He breathed across the hard buds crested so nicely atop her firm, round breasts. They puckered, earning him yet another groan of satisfaction from her. He licked. Then drew one inflamed nipple into his mouth and rolled it back and forth.

Responsive and eager, she skimmed her nails over his back and reached for his buttocks. When he growled, she sank them deep into the muscled flesh.

He picked up the beat.

She flowered beneath him, her musk mixing with his own. He kissed the hollow of her neck and savored the sharp flavor of her skin. He relished the sensation of his balls tightening and the firm caress of her on his cock.

Together they reached the plateau where the slip and slide of skin rocked into never-ending bliss. His hands roamed every soft curve, lingered just beneath her ear, and rubbed a bit harder when she proved ticklish behind her knees.

"Cain?" her voice punctured the haze of lust.

"Uh-huh?"

"Could you . . . oh . . . could . . ."

He paused in the thrust and retreat. "Could I what?"

She trailed a finger down his chest and circled his flat, hard nipples. "I want . . ."

He bruised her mouth with his. "Anything you want, baby, you just ask for it."

She studied him for seconds too long. "Harder."

He bumped her hips with his own and chuckled. "Harder?"

"Oh, yes. Again."

Cain obliged.

Her cries rose with his. His hands and cock beat at her. Her wail widened.

He felt her inner muscles flutter. "Ah, baby. That's it." He reached up to flick her nipple, then reached between them and pressed her clit hard.

His orgasm gathered in his balls, raced up his spine, and exploded.

She gasped to catch her breath as she came down. "Cain?"

He rested his forehead against hers. "Yeah, baby?"

"You were right."

He leaned away to discover she was laughing. "About what?"

"I wasn't doing it right . . . when I was 16. Can we do it again?"

He laughed, gathered her to his chest, and rolled to his back. "Not right now, but I promise, Nia, I'm willing anytime you are."

He felt her body loosen and begin to melt into sleep. "Good. 'Cause now that you caught me, I'm not gonna let you go."

Cain stared up at the ceiling and smiled. The reflection of their entwined limbs nudged something very primitive deep in his soul. He patted her bottom and sent a low howl into the night.

Cold Kiss

By Michaela March

Bound in a web of silken cords, Psyche writhed in mingled terror and anticipation of her coming ordeal. It was the only way to save the life of her dying husband, because his plight was all her fault.

Six months earlier

Psyche hurried from the women's quarters, heading for the tiny reception room on the other side of the courtyard in her home. She should proceed at a more dignified pace, but she was afire with curiosity at the summons.

Who could possibly be visiting her? Not any of her female friends—they would have come straight to the women's quarters. And as a respectable virgin, she had no male friends.

She halted at the entrance, remembering at the last moment to drape a corner of her linen shawl over her head, and was disappointed to find her visitor was only Uncle Demetrios, her late father's younger brother and her titular guardian. Mother sat next to him, looking simultaneously worried and elated.

"Ah, there you are," he said around a mouthful of the honey-glazed almonds that Mother doled out sparingly to guests.

Psyche gave him a wary nod. "Good day, Uncle."

"Congratulations! You've received an offer of marriage, my girl." He waved a folded sheet of parchment at her as he shook the foundations of her world.

"W-who?" Who could possibly want to marry *her*, the dowerless daughter of an impoverished widow? Reeling, Psyche frantically reviewed the past month's visitors, trying to remember if anyone stood out. Had anyone with eligible sons come to call upon Mother? Any widowers?

"It's a very generous offer." Her uncle's bluff, hearty manner could not hide his disquiet. Mother's hands were in her lap, clenching handfuls of her gown.

Psyche swallowed, trying to moisten a suddenly dry throat. "Who, Uncle? Who makes this offer?"

"Ah—" Uncle Demetrios looked away, at the flaking plaster of the wall, which had once been painted with fine frescoes. A leaky roof, still not fixed, had ruined them.

"It was Lord Amor, a visiting scion of the Erotes," Mother interjected softly.

"*What?*" Psyche was horrified.

Everyone knew of the Erotes, mysterious traders in perfumes, medicines, and erotic aids. They never revealed their features and were rumored to be hideously deformed creatures who corrupted youths and maidens with depraved carnal pleasures before devouring them.

Psyche remembered the oddly bulky shape of a cloaked and veiled figure plying his trade in the sanctuary of Aphrodite just last week, and shuddered. She stared at her mother and her uncle, neither of whom would meet her eyes. Shock rapidly gave way to a feeling of betrayal. "Mother, how could you even consider this?"

Her mother shook her head mutely, gaze fixed on the worn straps of her sandals.

Uncle Demetrios cleared his throat, his eyes hard. "Psyche, need I remind you that at your advanced age and without a dowry, this is the best you can hope for? Unless you have another prospect?"

Psyche glared at him. He knew perfectly well that she had no other offers.

"Not only will he dispense with your dowry, but Lord Amor offers a generous—*very* generous—sum as bride price," he continued.

Psyche winced. The widows' pension from the potters' guild was a paltry sum, and they were utterly dependent on it. Unlike the bold women of Khem or the shrewd female traders of Kreta, respectable Hellene women were not permitted to work outside the home.

Uncle Demetrios opened a small pouch made of soft leather stamped with an intertwining pattern of gold leaf and withdrew a small perfume bottle of brilliant blue faience. He thumped it on the table. "Lord Amor begs you to accept this gift of ambrosia and his proposal," he said stiffly.

"Daughter," her mother added. "If you accept, then your sisters will have a respectable dowry. And we could make many much-needed repairs." Her gaze went to the water-damaged ceiling.

Psyche swallowed, hard, staring at the little flask. Ambrosia was the rarest of scents, and fabulously expensive. It was rumored to be a powerful aphrodisiac as well. If Lord Amor could afford to gift her with this, then she could only imagine what he offered her mother and uncle. Her decision was made for her. She could not possibly refuse him.

At least she wouldn't be spending the rest of her life immured in her childhood home, living in genteel poverty, enduring her family's reproaches for declining this chance for a comfortable future for all. And she was intensely curious, if terrified, to find out what really lay beneath the cloaks and veils of the Erotes.

Psyche reached out and picked up the bottle. "Very well," she whispered. "I accept the offer."

When Psyche finally retired to her tiny bedchamber that night, her natural inquisitiveness drove her to open the precious vial. She inhaled the spicy, musky scent and fell asleep trying to imagine what being an Erotes' wife would be like.

Her late father had specialized in wares painted with erotic scenes, used for drinking parties and wedding banquets. Despite stern prohibitions, Psyche's insatiable curiosity meant she often crept into his workroom at night to gaze avidly upon the forbidden images.

These now came to vivid life in her dreams. Zeus abducted her in the form of an eagle, her naked limbs restrained in the firm grip of giant talons, feathers brushing her bare skin, raising shivers in their wake.

A satyr, fierce and bearded, ravished her on a sun-warmed rock, callused hands gripping her shoulders, hairy legs rubbing against the tender skin of her inner thighs, his huge phallus impaling her amid the tatters of her torn gown.

In the gray dawn, Psyche awoke, the place between her legs throbbing with a heavy, aching need, and wondered anew what the Fates had in store for her.

A few weeks later, the ship carrying Psyche arrived at the rugged island of Kupidos. From the deck, she could see many rich villas surrounded by terraced gardens on the rugged slopes rising above the harbor. To her disappointment, her prospective husband did not come to meet her ship. Instead, servants greeted her and escorted her to one of the villas overlooking the water. It was magnificently appointed, with an exquisite garden, inlaid floors of colored marble, and gorgeous frescoes of sea life on every wall.

It felt good to bathe away the grime and salt of her voyage in the villa's private bathing chamber, with its deep pool of heated water. Afterward, she was led to a suite of richly furnished rooms that opened on to the courtyard. There, a maid anointed her skin with ambrosia-scented oil, dressed her hair, and applied cosmetics. The scent of the ambrosia seemed to amplify the delicate touch of the perfume applicator at the base of her throat and the insides her wrists. She shivered at the feel of the kohl stick brushing her eyelashes and the rouge brush tracing her lips, the familiar sensations curiously intense now, sending her into a sensuous daze.

Unexpectedly, the linen bath sheet modestly draping her was pulled away, and the stiff-bristled rouge brush teased the tips of her breasts into points, the sensation shooting straight to her groin. The servant chuckled softly as Psyche gasped and squirmed.

"The master will be pleased," she said.

Psyche felt her face heat with a fierce blush. *What's happening to me?*

Servants dressed her in an indecently transparent russet gown of draped silk, fastened at the shoulders with gold filigree brooches and secured with a gilded leather girdle that clasped her waist like a lover. She scarcely recognized herself in the polished bronze mirror. Her mouth looked swollen, as if already thoroughly kissed, her hazel eyes were so dilated that they were nearly black, and her auburn ringlets were caught up with gold clips and a diadem, leaving her nape exposed and feeling curiously naked.

The light brush of the fabric against her rouged nipples proved a sweet torment as she followed the servant out of her rooms and into a large banqueting chamber overlooking the sea.

There, her bridegroom awaited her, reclining at a table set with a feast. She felt a pang of disappointment when she saw he was cloaked and veiled from his head to his feet. Even his hands were covered by finely worked leather gloves.

"Welcome, wife," he said in tones like spiced honey, leaving her weak-kneed. "I am Amor, son of Lilith, the high priestess of Aphrodite. I've been looking forward to this night since I first saw you in Aphrodite's temple on my last voyage to your fair city," he continued, gesturing her to sit.

She sank on a chair inlaid with ivory, and gazed over the myriad of dishes and bowls heaped high with delicacies. Was this her wedding feast? If so, where were the other guests?

Her bridegroom saw her glancing around. "Did you want to ask me something?" His voice held a hint of amusement.

She raised her gaze to the opaque blankness of his veil. "May I see your face?"

He shook his head. "It is forbidden . . . for now." She opened her mouth, intending to ask why, but he gestured toward the table. "Please, eat. How was your journey here?"

He continued to make pleasant, if trifling, conversation as she sampled the various delicacies—shellfish in a saffron broth, fish baked with lemon, crisp-skinned roast squab, chewy bread, rounds of goat's cheese crusted with herbs. While she ate, the sun sank behind the horizon in a blaze of orange.

The meal finished with a selection of ripe summer fruit. As she ate, her nose filled with the scent of ambrosia, making her unnaturally aware of the brush of her ringlets against her neck, of the slide of silk over her sensitized skin, and the velvety skin of sun-warmed apricots against her lips.

When she finished eating, Amor rose with a sweep of dark cloth. He picked up a pomegranate from the bowl of fruit and tore it open with a swift twist of his gloved hands.

"Come here," he commanded softly, holding out a section of the pale pith studded with ruby seeds like jewels.

This was the moment when her marriage would be sealed. It felt strange to do this without presence of witnesses or her family. She went to kneel before him, as was customary, and he raised the fruit to her lips. She obediently parted her lips and ate six of the seeds, their taste lingering sweet and tart on her tongue.

Then he raised her to her feet, and together they left the room. A servant bearing a lamp led them down a flight of stone stairs to a windowless underground bedchamber. The servant departed with a deep bow and left, taking the lamp with him.

Psyche was left in impenetrable darkness, terrified and aroused at the same time. She remembered her dream of the satyr and wondered if Amor would push her down and take his pleasure in the same way. She heard the whoosh of fabric dropping to the floor a moment before cold lips touched her nape and a cool fingertip lightly traced the line of her collarbone. She gasped and shivered and felt the throbbing ache kindle between her thighs.

"So responsive," he murmured, lips brushing delicately against the curve of her ear, raising gooseflesh. "Just as I'd hoped."

"Have you drugged me?" she asked.

He chuckled, a puff of air from his lips moving against her sensitized skin. "The ambrosia merely heightens certain . . . sensations. It does not create them."

"O-oh." With an intensity that left her heart pounding

and her mouth dry, she wanted him to continue touching her.

He obliged her, cool fingers brushing her shoulders, deftly unfastening the gown. The loosened fabric slid sensuously down, leaving her bare to the waist. His touch followed, echoing the caress of the silk over the slope of her breasts, featherlight and reverent. The teasing left her craving more, and she cried out when at last he gently plucked the very tips of her breasts, playing her like a fragile lyre.

He continued for some time, paying her compliments as he made slow love to her with fingers and mouth and what felt like the delicate brush of feathers against her skin, until she was trembling and begging him for something more. Each attempt she made to embrace him, to caress him in return, was gently rebuffed, until all she could do was stand there, her gown now pooled around her feet, utterly blind and at his mercy, intoxicated with desire.

She felt his cold mouth press against the base of her spine as he sank to his knees behind her, and the brush of feathers again, this time tickling the backs of her knees. He slid cold fingers between her thighs, and she swayed, crying out again at the blessed relief of that knowing touch, penetrating and caressing just the right places.

Her climax, when it burst upon her, arched her spine like a bow. She felt like a leaf caught by the wind and spiraled up to a great height before drifting down again, anchored by the fingers of his free hand gripping her hip. His mouth, pressed against the base of her spine was cold . . . so cold . . . almost numbing the skin it touched.

"I think you're ready now," she heard him say.

He rose, took her hand, walked two paces, and sat. He drew her down, languid and pliant yet still aching for something more, to straddle his lap. His hands on her hips, he guided her until she felt the head of his phallus pressing against her. It felt large and as unnaturally cool as the rest of him.

She pushed experimentally, feeling her desire-slicked tissues stretch around his tip, and heard him inhale sharply. The sound pleased her, as did the increasingly ragged breaths that followed. She lowered herself upon him by fractions, feeling a moderate burn of stretched muscles as her virgin body tried to accommodate itself to the invasion.

Forgetting his prohibition, she tried to embrace him when he was at last fully seated inside her. Her wrists were caught with unnatural swiftness, and he pinned them at the small of her back.

"Perhaps I should tie you up next time," he growled against her skin, his voice seductive and harsh at the same time. He turned his head and gently bit one of her nipples.

She strained involuntarily against his hold, squirming with the shock of renewed arousal. With a pleased laugh, he bent his mouth to her breast again and, using lips and teeth and tongue, continued the delicious torment until her movements, impaled as she was on his phallus, triggered a second climax, this one more intense than the first, wave after wave of a pleasure so intense she nearly fainted.

When the feeling finally subsided in a series of ripples, she found herself shivering with sudden cold, so tired she could scarcely move.

Amor kissed her mouth with a tender brush of lips and lifted her off his lap. She noticed his phallus was still rigid, which contradicted everything her mother told her about the wedding night.

"Thank you. You have pleased me more than I dared hope for," he said softly, guiding her stumbling steps to the bed she could not see in the darkness. "Sleep now."

She wanted to reply, to thank him in return, but sleep claimed her before he had even drawn the coverlet up over her shoulders.

And so began her idyll of sun-drenched days of luxury, of evenings spent in the company of her cloaked and veiled husband. To her surprise, the villa had no women's quarters, and Psyche was not expected to cloister herself.

They dined together every evening, though she never saw him eat. Amor told her of his travels around the Hellene city-states and to the ancient cities of Khem. Sometimes they walked together in the villa's gardens at dusk and discussed the books he gave her to read.

Psyche's nights were spent in the absolute darkness of his bedchamber, her senses filled with the scent of ambrosia and his caresses. The careful gentleness of their wedding night quickly gave way to bolder pleasures as he patiently tutored her in the many arts of love.

Her wrists bound behind her back, she learned to kneel and take the rigid length of him between her lips, ravishing him with mouth and tongue until he tumbled her down and returned the favor, not stopping until she shook with her release.

He introduced her to the exquisite torment of being tied to the bronze rings embedded in the marble slab of his bedchamber wall. There, the cool stone teased her breasts and belly as her back and buttocks were lashed by thongs of the softest leather, each touch of the whip more a caress than a punishment, until her skin was heated and painfully tender, and she was mad with arousal. He would penetrate her from behind, his hands caressing her hot skin, until pleasure and pain mixed like wine and water, intoxicating her with a dizzying climax.

He used erotic aids of polished marble and carved ivory, wire, and beads, and played every inch of her body like a master musician, drawing ever more intense responses from her.

It was bliss as sweet as honeyed pastries, yet it was not enough. She was forbidden to touch him, forbidden to see him, forbidden to do anything for him but submit to his pleasure. She was always shivering and exhausted when he finished with her. And she always awoke alone, in her own bed.

As the weeks passed, she found herself staring at him, noticing with unease how his cloak bulged and rippled in places that could not possibly be human. Driven by her insatiable curiosity, she questioned the servants relentlessly about what lay beneath those concealing garments. No one knew.

He treated her kindly thus far, but what was he hiding? Why was his skin always so cold? Why did his caresses leave her drained and shivering? Was he a monster, after all, for whom light was a burning brand, deadly and disfiguring?

Finally, she could bear it no longer, couldn't face the thought of another night spent blind and helpless, submitting to something possibly hideous and inhuman. Even if his touch was cool and gentle and his voice deep and pleasing to her ears, he was hiding something terrible. He had to be.

Trembling with nerves, her stomach sick with apprehension, she crept into the kitchen and stole a knife. Armed and carrying a lamp, she made her cautious way down to the underground chamber where Amor slept during the day. Her heart pounding, she pushed open the heavy door to his bedchamber and crept inside. There, she froze, staring with disbelief.

Sprawled nude on the bed was a beautiful young man with sculpted lines of muscle and bone and tousled hair the rich dark color of sable pelts imported from the frozen northlands. The reason for the odd shapes under his cloak became clear as she glimpsed his wings, feathered in the same shade as his hair.

The knife slipped out of her grasp, the blade ringing against the stone floor, and he came awake in an instant, springing out of the bed.

Speechless, they stared at each other. His eyes were the same startling shade of cobalt as the faience flask he had given her. When his gaze dropped to the knife, she saw emotions flash swiftly across his face—hurt, then betrayal, and finally, anger.

His wings unfolded and beat in agitation. "All I wanted," he said, his voice hoarse and almost unrecognizable, "was for you to love me."

"But—but I do!" Psyche cried. Inside, a voice was screaming, *Stupid! How could I be so stupid?*

"Love cannot dwell with suspicion. You had only to trust me," he whispered, his despair and sorrow stabbing her like the blade she had carried. "Did I not at least merit that?"

She stared at him, speechless with shame.

"We will not meet again."

"No!" she screamed. "No! Please stay. I'm sor—"

But he was already gone.

"Lady," said Mikion, the head servant. "You must go to him."

A week had passed. Psyche had waited futilely for Amor to return, prepared to humble herself and undergo any punishment in return for his forgiveness.

She was worried. They all were. The servants never said anything in her hearing, but she knew they blamed her for the departure of their beloved master. She blamed herself.

"I would, but I don't know where he is!"

"I have heard," Mikion began delicately, then stopped. "Lady, I beg of you—call upon his mother, the high priestess of Aphrodite."

With no other options, Psyche found herself in the sanctuary of Aphrodite as dusk fell, kneeling humbly on the cobbles of the temple's forecourt.

"So, it is you," said a cold female voice. "I wondered if it might be when the novice told me a human girl begged an audience."

"Yes, my lady Lilith," Psyche said, daring a glance at the veiled figure gliding toward her. "I beg for word of my husband. Is he well?"

"You dare ask me this, after what you did?" Her mother-in-law came to a halt, her voice dripping with contempt. "Didn't I tell him humans cannot be trusted? And yet he actually bound himself to you, the fool!"

"I have been thoughtless and selfish," Psyche said, her head bowed again. Her eyes stung with fresh tears. "But I do love him, with all my heart and soul. Please, my lady, can I just see him? I only want to apologize to him."

Lilith stayed silent for a long time, and Psyche, who remained kneeling, felt her intense scrutiny. "Well, then, girl," Lilith said at last, "come and see what you've wrought. He's dying, you know."

"Dying?" Psyche rose to her feet unsteadily. "Why? What happened?"

Lilith laughed bitterly. "I told you—he bound himself to you. While you live, he can feed from no other."

Psyche's eyes widened as much became suddenly clear.

Lilith continued, "I have watched my son slowly starve this past week, because he cannot feed from a woman who fears him. Complete trust and perfect submission is what we require of our spouses. Anything else is poison to us."

In chastened silence, Psyche followed her to the inner sanctum of the temple. There, the statue of Aphrodite presided over a garden with fountains that filled the air with the pleasant sound of splashing, beds of sweet herbs and flowers, a dovecote, and an altar strewn with petals.

Disrobed, Amor lay unconscious on the cushions of a

wide stone couch near the goddess. With a pang, Psyche saw how his wings wrapped protectively around him. Dark shadows smudged the skin beneath his closed eyes, and he was gaunt, his breathing labored.

"As you see, it's too late for him," Lilith said, her voice filled with pain. "He's too weak to feed." She stroked his hair with gloved fingers. "My poor son."

"What can I do?" Psyche pleaded. "Please, there must be a way to save him!"

The blank, veiled face turned toward her, as if measuring Psyche's sincerity. "There is a way, but it is dangerous," she said at last.

Psyche sank to her knees on the graveled path and bowed her head. "I'll do anything, my lady."

"Can you promise perfect submission? To me? To my attendants?"

Psyche nodded.

"If you can do this, then I will weave a spell to connect your souls. You must then submit to certain attentions to rouse your body. You must maintain that arousal for as long as possible, for only thus can you feed your husband and restore his life. But"—she raised her hand—"you absolutely cannot climax. In his weakened state, my son can only tolerate a measured flow of your life force. Your climax might overwhelm him and kill him. Do you understand?"

Psyche nodded again, feeling a mixture of hope and apprehension.

Lilith continued, "If he has not yet passed the point of no return, he will absorb the energy you feed him and

gradually become aroused in turn. Then, and only then,
may you have intercourse. But there is a risk. He may take
too much from you and kill you both. Should the fates be
kind, however, he may be able to complete the final step
of your union. If he spills his seed inside you, you will be
granted eternal youth as his soul-bonded spouse. Do you
understand, girl?"

"Yes, my lady," Psyche whispered, still kneeling. "I'll do
my best."

"See that you do," Lilith replied coldly.

A pair of veiled attendants, a youth and a maiden,
approached Psyche, and shortly thereafter, she found
herself nude and tied spread-eagle next to Amor on his
couch. A long scarlet cord connected her wrist to his. She
turned her head to where he lay beside her, watching his
rib cage expand with each labored breath.

Can I do this? Can I save him?

Lilith approached her, followed by a servant bearing a
tray laden with vials and brushes and erotic implements.
Psyche shuddered in mingled fear and anticipation.

Chanting in an unknown language, Lilith anointed
Psyche with drops of ambrosia on her lips, heart, and
navel. Next, she dipped a brush into a vial of fragrant ink
and began to write lines of tiny flowing characters that
scrolled across Psyche's abdomen, down her inner thighs,
and curved up under each breast. The delicate torment of
the brushes, mingled with the heady scent of ambrosia,
quickly set Psyche to squirming and gasping in delicious,
agonized suspense. She bit her lip hard enough to draw
blood when the brush moved to the apex of her thighs and

stroked, once, across the most sensitive place on her body.

"There," said Lilith, stepping back. "The rest is up to you if you truly have the determination to nourish my son and the strength to restrain yourself."

She reached out and tweaked Psyche's right nipple, sending hot pleasure coursing straight down to the hungry place between her forcibly spread legs. Psyche gasped and arched against her restraints as Lilith turned and walked away.

She felt the cord around her wrist grow warm. Turning her head, she saw Amor's blue eyes flicker open and watch her. He did not speak, and she saw that his phallus still lay flaccid against his thigh, but he had awakened. That had to mean something!

Her gaze never left his, as the attendants stroked every inch of her tender skin, first with feathers and then ivory wands with rounded balls at the end.

She didn't know how much time passed before sensation overwhelmed her and she arched and writhed against the unyielding net of the silken cords binding her. She moaned each time one of her tormentors brushed the aching tips of her breasts with a stiff feather or glided the ivory around the fringe of her painfully swollen labia, never quite giving her the intensity of touch she craved. The cord around her wrist grew burning hot and pulsed in time to her heartbeat.

Lilith returned, bearing a covered basket. The priestess drew back the concealing cloth, and something rose from the basket, thrumming with rapid wingbeats, and hovered over Psyche's flushed and straining form. She recognized it as one of the legendary winged phalluses, which allowed the Erotes to ravish whomever they chose. It was thick, with swollen veins, glistening with moisture in the torchlight, its wings pure white like a dove's.

Amor moaned, a low, needy sound, and Psyche noticed that he was now partially erect. Her heart rose with hope. The spell was working.

Working with deft fingers, one of the attendants slipped a gold ring engraved with foreign symbols around the base of Amor's phallus. It was connected, via a long scarlet thread, to the winged creature.

Psyche groaned with agonized pleasure as she felt the thing bumping its way slowly up her inner thigh. Finally reaching its destination, it pushed and wriggled between the slick, painfully engorged folds of her labia, slowly filling her, the thrumming vibrations of its wingbeats sending shocks of pleasure up her spine and curling her toes.

The attendants ceased their other attentions to her body, and Lilith watched her carefully as Psyche circled the edge of climax. Every fiber of her being burned for release as she held on frantically to what little control she had left. Finally, panting and sweating, she neared the critical point and cried hoarsely, "Stop! Please, no more!"

At that, the winged phallus abruptly shrank and slid out of her, leaving her empty and ready to scream with wanting.

Was it enough? Had she revived him?

To her relief and joy, Amor was now fully erect. His hands fisted in the cushions as their eyes met. "Please . . . now . . ." he whispered.

The cords binding her loosened and slithered away. She crawled to her husband, feeling feverish and aching with desire.

"I love you," she said, crouching over him, lowering herself upon him, and feeling that delicious, familiar impalement. Urgently, she began to ride him, bending to kiss and caress his face, his beloved body.

As she made love to him with every skill he taught her, cold spread from every place where they touched. At the same time, she saw color return to his face, and he began to move vigorously within her. When she finally climaxed, only embers of heat remained within her. Pleasure gripped her in icy tendrils, spreading in ripples that froze her blood.

It was worth this sacrifice to save him, she thought and fell willingly into darkness.

She woke in his arms at dawn, surprised to find herself alive. "Good morning, wife," he said warmly. Joy rose in her heart as he pulled her to him, and his kiss was heady as ambrosia.

Peter PumpKyn's Delight

By Elle Amour

There once was a savvy businessman named Peter "the Pump" Kyndill who savored all kinds of women. Age didn't matter to the towering, ruggedly handsome, broad-shouldered, and extremely fit Peter. He would take them young or old. Blonde? Brunette? Redhead? No problem. Tall? Short? Scrawny? Plump? Not an issue. From pale as snow to dark as pure chocolate, be they pierced, tattooed, or with skin au naturel, the female sex was a virtual smorgasbord to Peter, and he wanted to sample every tasty dish he could reach.

Peter enjoyed his life. Not only did he have a constant flow of women who pleased him, but business boomed as well. As the major investor in the venture capital group, Shell & Kwik Ltd., Peter had convinced his partner, Jack, a nimble fellow who'd been known to jump over raging business fires without a scratch, to keep Peter's position as CEO a secret. This allowed Peter to move incognito as he worked his magic over the primary aspects of the business. Pretending to be just a regular employee, Peter had been able to get some honest feedback from workers and clients, which helped him and Jack to make the firm more competitive in the cutthroat world they played in.

One day, while Peter was meeting with Jack in Jack's office, a brunette bombshell strolled through the door. "Mary!" Jack exclaimed and took her hand gently with both his palms.

Peter rubbed his jaw just to make sure his mouth didn't gape, then firmly pushed his chin in place. Peter eyed the sexy long legs that extended from the short hem of her skirt. When Jack released her, she turned toward Peter; then Peter got a good look at the perky breasts and nice cleavage, too.

"Like I was saying, Pete," Jack went on, "this is Mary Q. Contrary, our new senior analyst."

Had Jack said something? Peter closed his eyes a moment, shook his head to clear his libidinous thoughts, then extended his hand as he opened his eyes and gave the newbie his most professional, aloof look.

Her gaze returned as good as she got. Mary's soft palm slid nicely into Peter's, yet she clasped her graceful fingers around his much bigger hand with a firm grip. She was sure of herself. Peter had to give her that.

"Mary is the operator I told you about. She comes with experience and contacts that will really help broaden the firm. She trained with Humpty Dumpty and worked as a key investor in his firm until that accident he had a few months ago."

"Humph," Peter muttered, "always thought that egghead analyzed things too much."

Mary's dark almond eyes narrowed as she straightened, taking a defensive stance. "Humpty was an excellent strategist. One of the best."

Peter smirked. He loved women, but he wasn't about to be intimated by one. Standing closer so that he towered over her, he parted his suit coat and placed his hands on his hips. "No offense, but over the last few years his bloated liquid assets lay idle. He sat in his plush office and diddled with his investments so long I'm not surprised his crash happened on Wall Street."

Instead of backing up, she leaned into him, her eyes on fire. "Look, I know you're the prime analyst here, but don't expect me to stop doing what I do best just because you don't agree. There was a reason Humpty took that position."

"I'm sure." A whiff of her spicy perfume wafted to Peter as she jutted her chin upward, exposing the tender warm flesh at the base of her throat. Forcing himself not to take a bite, Peter stifled his smile as his thoughts wandered to what he'd like to do with the rest of her body with his now pulsing cock. He purposefully raised his brow, forced down his raging desire, and sent the woman a haughty look of disdain to make his point. Peter moved his head within inches of hers. Close enough so he could capture her lips with his if he wanted. "And what position was that?"

Surprised, Mary gasped. The sound was so quiet, the parting of her sweet pink lips so small, if he hadn't been this close, he wouldn't have recognized the familiar seductive response her body made.

She exhaled a ragged breath. "I'm under agreement not to discuss anything or anyone associated with Dumpty

Enterprises. The clients I bring over will be on the up and up. I won't breach any trust between Humpty, what's left of Dumpty Enterprises, or anyone else in that organization."

"I see." Peter appreciated her loyalty—and her other assets. He dipped his chin to gaze at her form. Her chest rose unevenly. Her eyes glowed with desire. She wanted him, too. He could tell. He straightened and released the unseen hold he'd created between them.

She scowled as she resumed her bristly demeanor. "Humpty was on the edge of making a huge plunge—in the right direction. Unfortunately, the accident happened first. There's still some suspicion around that. But now . . ." She shrugged. "He's getting out of the business. His wife doesn't want him taking any more chances." Mary glanced at Jack, then back to Peter, her eyes wary. "Not that it matters. If you don't mind, I'll get back to work." She looked at Jack again.

Peter's partner beamed as he studied Mary a brief moment, then shot a quick measuring look at Peter as well. "Don't mind at all. Have fun."

Her rigid body relaxed as she smiled and tossed a length of her brown-black hair over her shoulder. "Will do." She darted a final glare at Peter and strolled out the door, shutting it firmly behind her.

Jack chuckled and pushed himself off the edge of the desk—the observation post he'd taken while Peter sparred with the new analyst. "Well, that was interesting. Never saw you use that ominous tack of yours on a woman. Seen it on plenty of men, though, including myself." His friend and partner shook his head.

Peter cringed. "She's an employee. What did you expect?" He didn't want Jack to suspect the strange urges Peter had for Ms Contrary. Then a rogue thought hit him. "You don't have a thing for her, do you?" They had an unspoken policy not to mix business with pleasure, but that didn't mean they wouldn't change it if they wanted.

A light gleamed in Jack's eyes. "I like her, Pete, but she isn't my style. If I had to guess, I think she's more your type. The type you've been looking for, anyway. A woman to be reckoned with. One with brains and beauty."

Peter stared at Mary through the large glass window of Jack's office as she talked casually with L.B. Blue.

Jack noticed too. "She likes her men." He shrugged and shoved his hands in his pants pockets. "But from what I understand, she's kissing all those damn frogs to find her prince, so to speak."

Peter frowned. "Does she know L.B.'s gay?"

Jack snorted. "He's the one who brought her in. They're friends." Jack studied Peter a minute. "You know, we also have a policy to try something that looks promising, no matter what the situation. I'm thinking for you she's worth the risk."

It was as if Jack had read his mind.

Jack slapped him on the back. "Go for it, my friend. She doesn't know you own part of the company. As far as she's concerned, you're colleagues now. Although with such an auspicious start, you've certainly set yourself up for a challenge. For the first time, you could have a woman say no. You might lose."

Peter pasted on a wicked smile. "I don't play to lose.

Besides, you know what they say. The greater the risk, the sweeter the reward. This might be my best fuck yet."

Jack rubbed his jaw as he tried to cover the grin that spread from one cheek to the next. "Good luck. I think you're going to need it."

"If that's the case"—Peter yanked the door open and nodded to Jack with a shit-eating grin of his own—"then I'm all set. Luck never abandons me when I need it most."

Mary stood in L.B.'s cubical and eyed the arrogant, steely-eyed man who hovered in the doorway of Jack's office.

"Well, they say he got the nickname 'the Pump' from his power-lifting days in college," L.B. rambled on. "Guess he won some awards. Oooh, some sport that is. All that thrusting with those sweaty, powerful bodies." L.B. licked his lips. "But personally I think it comes from all the women he pleases. The women I've spoken to rave about the man after one night with him. 'Course, his main thing is play. Nothing serious, you know—at least not yet." L. B. sighed. "Wish he had some other, more wicked desires, but he doesn't."

"You can have him," Mary gritted out. "He's an arrogant prick."

"I wish, sugar. Like I said, he only likes women. So you don't want to know anything about him?"

Mary squirmed, wishing she could take care of the rampaging need that the encounter with Peter had caused. Her panties became wet as she thought about it.

She hated her reaction. To think a man like that would stimulate her to distraction. "Only the professional stuff." She lied to save herself. Having made the mistake before, she'd vowed to never date a fellow employee. Things at work got much too complicated, especially when your supposed "loving" partner only used you to get ahead. Still, the thought of Peter's sculpted body lying naked with hers kept teasing her mind—and her libido.

"Well"—L.B. rolled his eyes, unaware of the struggle within her—"if that's the case, the only thing I can tell you is he's been with the company almost as long as Jack. They're best friends."

"Great," Mary grumbled under her breath and plopped down in one of L.B.'s chairs. "Are you sure he isn't that silent partner you told me about?"

"Yes, my darling," L.B. tapped his fingers against his desk. "Although it's never been stated, it was made clear. Still, none of us really care who the other guy is. The company takes good care of us."

"It's curious, though. I'm not accusing Jack or his partner, but someone in the business upended Humpty. I'd like to know who."

"It wasn't anyone related to Shell & Kwik. I can assure you. These guys have too much pride in themselves and their success to do something like that."

As arrogant as Peter seemed, L.B. was probably right. She nodded. "Jack seems decent enough."

"He's a good man." L.B. leaned back in his chair. "So is that luscious Peter."

Mary screwed up her lips in doubt of that.

"L.B.!"

Both Mary and L.B. jumped at the deep commanding voice. "The Pump" loomed over the cubicle wall. "I need your assistance." His lips thinned as he shot Mary a guarded look with those steel-colored eyes of his.

Her breath caught again, and an intense tingle shot to her clit. Totally brushing her off, Peter marched to his office at the other end of the hall.

"Ooh," L.B. said, "I love it when he gets demanding."

Mary allowed herself a low growl. "L.B., what's the number for your kinky sex hookup business you've wanted me to try? After today, I need a release, and a stranger is probably my best bet."

"You're finally going to give it a try?" L.B. grinned lasciviously as if he suspected something more than she was willing to admit. "Well, what is it you want?"

"Something fresh. Something different." She threw her arm in the air in defeat. "I have no idea."

L.B. laughed again and planted his elbows on his knees as he leaned toward her. "I think I have an idea," he whispered. "I have all the health stuff on you which I'll forward over. Whoever you get will be clean. You can go without that little rubber cover if you want."

"L.B.!" The deep-voiced order came from down the hall. "Now."

Her friend's head snapped up. "Oh, do I love to be wanted. I'll give you the number when I get back."

Mary squinted and rubbed her temples to subdue the headache that threatened to grow. No matter how Peter excited and challenged her, the last thing she needed was to screw some wise-assed jerk in the office. Hadn't she learned her lesson yet? She would use the service L.B. told her about, and that would be enough.

That night Peter went to his preferred restaurant, a small, homey place that served his favorite dessert, Pumpkin Pie Delight. He needed sustenance to maintain his stamina for the evening. He smiled to himself, happy with the results so far. The stage was set. After grilling L.B. about Mary, first to ensure she had the company's best interests at heart, then to find out more about her personal life, Peter convinced L.B. to be a secret party to his plan. L.B. told Mary that her tryst with the unknown lover would be in the Castle Hotel, a place where, unbeknownst to her, Shell & Kwik had a nice penthouse suite.

Standing at the restaurant's door, Peter fingered the business card L.B. gave him and smirked again. *1-800-cum-play*. One of the more profitable investments L.B. had made. Peter was pleased. According to L.B., Mary's biggest weakness was sweets. Peter would ensure she had plenty.

Opening the door, he walked in. None other than Mary sat there in a booth, all alone, reading the menu. Mary lifted her head and looked right at him. Her gentle face turned bitter, but Peter would not be denied. He approached. "You're alone."

"Yes." She stared back at the menu as if to ignore him.

Needing to give this his best shot, he sighed for emphasis. "Look, we didn't start off well. My fault. If you give me the chance, I'll explain." He paused as she studied him with a wary gaze. "I'll even get the check," he added and threw her one of his more sheepish smiles, one that always worked when a woman was angry with him.

Her eyes narrowed. Her chest rose and fell with deliberation. She detested him, but the telltale signs were around her. She wanted him as well.

He bent to her and whispered in her ear. "We're going to work together, Mary. Very closely sometimes. It would help if we got our liaison off right."

Her tongue darted through her luscious parted mouth before she captured her bottom lip between her teeth. She gazed at him with a tentative yet demure lust in her look. The *L* word put her mind where he wanted it—on her sexual desires. Her long dark lashes fell over her intriguing brown eyes.

"L.B. said I could trust you." Her breathy voice was heady. "He's a good judge of people." She lifted her gaze again and studied him a moment. "Look, I don't want any enemies, not where I work." Her voice turned soft but it held power. She straightened and snapped the menu shut. "Fine. Have a seat. You can tell me why you dislike me. Just don't say it's because I worked with Humpty." She swallowed and that wary look took her again. This time, though, Peter suspected she was fighting herself.

"I won't, and I don't dislike you." He slid into the seat across from her. "I respect Humpty and what he'd built. Just didn't understand his strategy of late."

She swallowed. A small fear breezed through her eyes and disappeared. "You would if you knew what went on." She paused then lifted her napkin and placed it on her lap. Taking a deep breath, she leaned toward Peter. "Look, he was trying to protect the company. Someone had his grimy fingers on Humpty's piece of the pie. That's all I can tell you."

Pie? Peter suspected as much. Word had it some cunning jack-off was stealing opportunities from one investment firm at a time, only no one knew who. Shell & Kwik hadn't been hit yet, but Peter suspected it was only be a matter of time. "Would it help make amends if I found out who upended him?"

She huffed. "Sure. If you can, but whoever it was covered their tracks pretty well."

Peter had his resources. He'd already intended to find the person or persons. They posed too much of a danger to his and Jack's company, as well as the rest of the industry. Hell, the venture capital industry was ruthless enough as it was. They didn't need cutthroats like this.

"Well, well. If it isn't Peter 'the Pump' can eat her. And what tasty treat do we have here tonight?"

The voice from the past made Peter cringed. Knave O'Hartz, his nemesis in college, stumbled toward Peter and slapped him on the back. "Looks like a real sweet tart to me." He licked his thin lips and ogled Mary. Knave was drunk.

Mary's face turned stone-cold. "Excuse me." She glanced at her watch. "I forgot I have more work to do." She rose and left.

Peter cringed. Standing, he pushed Knave into Mary's now vacated seat. "Get some coffee. I'll buy." He pulled out a few bills and tossed them on the table.

Knave rubbed his one good eye and sneered. "You

think you're infallible because you're the king of the heap again." He fingered his black eye patch. "But you'll fall like the rest."

Peter made note of the comment. Knave worked for B.B. Wolfe. What did he know? Turning on his heel, Peter left. Tomorrow he would find out, but for tonight, he had his own, more pleasurable scheme to play.

This is crazy, Mary thought as she walked into the hotel lobby. She was a risk taker, but in business, not pleasure. Still, after the odd feelings Peter roused in her, she needed a release, and more of one than her vibrator could bring. She wanted a warm body to lying next to hers, skin to skin, a man's scent, something to stimulate all her senses.

She stared at the key for the elevator that would lead to the hotel's penthouse and steeled her resolve. Placing the key in the slot, she turned it and punched the button. When the elevator stopped, the door slid open—right into the room. The suite was one of the most luxurious she'd ever seen. The soft lighting, the spicy scent from low-burning candles, the burnished colors of ginger and copper, only enhanced an intimacy and comfort within the walls. She stepped inside.

L.B. had told her that, for reasons unknown, her partner in the tryst would be in disguise. The mystery unnerved her yet piqued her interest that much more.

When her eyes adjusted to the dim light, she scanned the room. The area was empty, but on a table centered in front of the elevator, a note leaned against a glass of wine. Strolling to it, she picked up the handwritten parchment.

Welcome. I'm looking forward to our acquaintance. Please make yourself at home. I'll be back shortly.

She checked the label of the wine bottle also on the table. A sweet red. Her favorite. L.B.'s company knew how to deliver. She sipped on the beverage as she strolled around the spacious area. Other than the elevator, she saw no doors. Only the large room. A kitchen . . .

And a bed. Quite a large one, even for a king. A shimmering amber coverlet lay as if tossed over the sumptuous reddish-orange cover, complementing the bed perfectly. She swirled the wine in her glass and compared the liquid to the decor. All the colors spoke of sexual energy. The thought stirred her even more. Excitement replaced some of her nervousness. "Well, here's to tonight." She gulped the wine and poured herself another glass. She needed as much false courage as she could get.

Peter watched from behind the curtained entrance to the staircase the hotel's service staff used. Mary was beautiful, but watching her, he knew something more fired his blood. How to capture her interest in return, get her to recognize what her body wanted—well, that was the problem. He slipped the black silk cloth over his head and tied the ends securely. His brown contacts were in place, and he'd downed some new formula from a business he'd invested in that would temporarily disguise his voice, giving it a husky rasp. He needed to be incognito to achieve his purpose.

When Mary had her back to him, he slipped behind her. Grasping the hand she had on the glass to ensure it didn't spill, he slid his other around her waist and tongued a slow hot kiss on the skin of her exposed neck.

She jerked slightly with the first contact, then released a deep sigh and molded into his torso as he suckled her skin. He'd suspected she hid a well of deep passion but her quick reaction overwhelmed him. As his penis rocketed into position, he worked to steady himself. He wanted this to last the night. "Thank you for coming," he whispered in her ear. Her body shivered with desire.

He wrapped his arms around her and slid her rear cheeks against his erection, nestling his hard cock in the valley between them.

Her eyes fluttered shut. Mary sighed as she released the remainder of her anxiety and leaned her head back against a hard set of pecs. *This is just what I need.* And the man smelled good. Spicy, like the room.

Moisture bloomed between her legs as callused hands slid around her waist and up her ribs to caress the underside of her breasts. The wine still on her tongue, she savored its flavor, letting the liquid trickle down her throat as the man behind her tugged her earlobe with his teeth. "Yes," she whispered as she swallowed the last of the drops.

The stranger turned her in his arms and held her flush against his hard body. His erect cock pulsed in need and thrummed against her abdomen through their clothes. The top of her head reached the underside of his chin. She exhaled and rubbed her nose against the few chest hairs exposed from the unbuttoned top of his black shirt; then she kissed the skin she found. She laughed softly.

"What amuses you, my angel?" His voice was husky

and deep. He hooked her chin with his finger and lifted her face, thumbing her lower lip as he did so.

She peered into brown eyes and a chiseled face that was half-masked with a black cloth. "Nothing really." She smiled. "I've never had a liaison quite like this."

A corner of his sensual mouth rose. "I didn't think you were a virgin."

"No, not that. I've never had a tryst with a total stranger before. Generally, I actually know the men I bed fairly well."

"Oh." He bent over and captured her lips in the most enticing kiss she'd ever experienced. "Which means you've played your sex safe. But you are here now."

His voice tantalized her. His scent filled her with heady anticipation. She suspected Peter's body was much like his. She gave herself a mental shake, trying to forget her new coworker. She was here now, and this man tempted her.

The dark stranger stroked his thumbs down the peaks of her blouse, swirling around the nipples that stood in salute through the thin silk. In the muted light she let her imagination run, thinking lascivious thoughts that kept returning to her challenger at work. "What should I call you?"

"Anything you like." His exhalations against her skin made her shiver with delight.

"Peter," she breathed and felt his body stiffen a little before his form eased against her once more. "You don't like that name?" She stood on her toes to reach the crook of his neck and tease the skin with her teeth and tongue.

He buried his face into her hair. "Peter is fine." Lifting

her, he wrapped her legs around his body. Holding her buttocks in his large, firm grip, he strode to the bed. "I understand from our friends you like to be in control, but tonight that will not be the case." He laid her gently against the coverlet, dangling her legs over the edge. His knowing fingers caressed upward against her ribs and then to the undersides of her arms. Pushing upward still, he guided her arms over her head and held them there with one hand in a comfortable but firm grasp. Slowly he unbuttoned her blouse, suckling her exposed skin on occasion. The tease tantalized her, let her know he was an experienced lover.

As he moved his lips lower, he raked the tips of his fingers down the undersides of her arms. When he had fully opened her blouse, her unknown lover pulled the ends of the cloth from the waistband of her skirt. His hands ran over her naked skin. His thumbs flicked her erect nipples through her bra as he moved farther upward. Sliding the shirt off her shoulders, he pulled the sleeves from her arms to her wrists, then used the ends of the shirt to tie her hands together. Before she could protest, he moved her lengthwise on the bed and put the loop he'd made with her blouse over a spindle in the center of the headboard.

"But . . ." Her logic wanted to reject his rashness, but it warred with her body.

"Hush, my angel. I only want to please you and make you come through the night." He grinned and his smile even reminded her of "the Pump." Her eyes fluttered shut and her pussy moistened even more. Why couldn't she stop thinking of him even when she had this hunk to please her?

He suckled her earlobe. "You don't know how much you stir me."

She could imagine because he sure was doing a job on her. Still, her business sense found it difficult to be at someone else's mercy. Mary closed her eyes. Her new "Peter" was right earlier. She was always in control because she had been hurt the one time she'd put complete faith in another partner.

Her pulse beat a rapid staccato as she worked to get a grip on her fear. Her mind wanted to protest, but there was something about this man she felt she could trust. A rarity for her.

"I won't hurt you. I promise." The warmth of his breath titillated her neck as his hands undid the front clasp of her bra. He nibbled on the upper curve of her ear as his fingers splayed against her body and slid underneath the cloth to her breasts to tug on the hardened tips.

A breathy moan escaped her again. Something about this risk made the tingling in her nerve endings surge into an erotic fire.

"You want this, don't you? Someone to take command. Someone you can believe in." A sincerity rang in his voice, and the sound of it intensified her desire.

"Yes," she said, although the word scared her. She opened her eyes to study him. The creased lines of what she could see of his face even reflected the truth. He cared about what she felt. For a moment, the thought troubled her, the remembrance of the pain of her past relationship. *Let it go. Take the risk.*

His mouth paused within an inch of hers as his gaze

scanned her face. Then he kissed her. Deeply. Captured her lips completely as their tongues shared a dance of passion. Somehow she knew he craved this too, the need to be wanted by someone who cared.

He pulled back, panting. His hands caressed her waist and, with the exception of her opened bra and blouse, made short work of disposing the rest of her clothes. From her torso down, she was totally naked for his inspection. His fingers raked the insides of her legs. Everywhere he touched felt like charges of sexual lightning. In turns, he took one nipple, then another in his mouth, licking, sucking, teething them. A moan left her lips. Her hips pressed upward with a will of their own, searching for the relief she craved. As she rubbed her mons against his body, her crease opened and the downy hairs on his lower abs tantalized her clit.

He slid down her, placing pecks along her nude frame as he eased her legs farther apart, licking and sucking on her until he reached her mound.

"You're wet," he whispered against her and lapped her pussy with the tip of his tongue.

Her body tingled. Wanting to strum her fingers against his hard frame, she tugged against her binding and moaned.

He rose and she felt the coolness of his departure. He strode to the kitchenette and pulled out a container from the refrigerator. "I'd been wanting to do this. A delectable cream such as yours deserves the right dessert for it, don't you think? And I haven't had mine for the night."

When he returned he lifted a spoonful of the sweet to her lips. "Try this."

She licked the creamy texture. "Mmm. What is it?"

His smile cocked to one side and spread. "Pumpkin Pie Delight. My favorite." Then he spread her legs again and spooned the cool concoction over her labia. The contrast of her heat and the chilled dessert caused her to squirm with a heightened need. He licked the length of her nether lips. "And with you, the treat tastes that much sweeter."

She groaned and lifted her hips to meet the tender onslaught of his mouth. Nips. Licks. And more. Along her clit, along her labia, his tongue thrust into her.

And his hands. They switched from caressing her bottom and her anus to fingering and tugging on her nipples. The shifting sensations intensified her need. "Please," she whispered. Whether he was the Peter her body craved or not, she wanted him.

"Patience, my angel. We have all night."

"You might, but I don't think I can wait."

"As you wish." He rose onto his knees. His torso was long, his waist lean. Slowly, he unbuttoned the black shirt, yet his eyes never left hers. "I want you, you know, Mary."

She swallowed. L.B. had told her that they only used first names. This man knew hers. Knew something about her, but to her, he remained an unknown. Although, at the moment, it didn't matter. She needed him to service her. But did she want more from him?

Finally, he tore off his shirt and tossed it to the floor. Mary swallowed. His sculpted body was more cut than she'd realized. He appeared broad-shouldered and lean, and the planes of his muscles went from dark to light as he moved through the candlelit room. Next came his pants. If she'd gone to a strip joint, the tease couldn't have been better. Slowly, he undid the zipper, then eased the waistband down.

Mary licked her lips. He'd gone without underwear. She savored the chiseled look of his lower abs, then his powerful legs and strong throbbing cock as he let the pants drop to the floor.

"You like to look, don't you?" He kicked off his pants after he heeled off his shoes, then, placing his hand on the edge of the bed, used it to balance as he removed his socks.

Her eyes flickered over his body. "Yes, and you look as yummy as that dessert you gave me."

"Glad you like." Now nude, he moved over her body and hovered. His erect penis dangled and pulsed against her vagina. "How do you want this, my angel? I can wear a condom if you want, but I can assure you I'm as healthy as you. The company made certain of that."

"I know," she whispered as the thought tantalized her. Naked skin to naked skin. The whole way. She'd never done that before. Had sworn she'd only do it with a man she could trust completely.

His brown eyes narrowed as he studied her, and in them she saw the same thing that she felt. She wanted to be loved, or at least experience the illusion of it. How better than with someone who would take the same risk as her? "Take me the way I am. No pretenses, no protection."

"You'll take the risk?"

She couldn't explain it, but something within her knew this to be right. "Yes. This one night."

She could sense his relief. He captured her lips again

with his, plumbed the depths of her mouth with the desperation of a lost man who had just been found. She returned his ardor with all that she had, understanding their unspoken shared need.

Balancing his upper body on one hand, her lover took his cock in his hand and rubbed the tip against her wet opening.

Mary closed her eyes as her hips rose to meet his.

He lay lightly on her, taking most of his weight on his forearms. His skin was soft, but underneath, his body was hard. The contrast stimulated and soothed. When he thrust into her, her body quaked with a searing carnal exhilaration.

"Mary." He whispered her name like a prayer as he thrust into her again, suckling her earlobe, then her neck, pulling himself out slowly, then plunging rapidly again.

She moaned with abandon, with the onslaught of pleasure. She'd never had anything like this before. Her nipples ached. She wanted to pull on them herself, but she couldn't. Not tied up like this.

"What is it?" he murmured. "What more do you want?"

"My breasts," she panted.

Keeping the sweet torturous rhythm pounding into her with his cock, he arched his body in response. His ragged breathing labored against her budded nipples. An arm came around her and pulled her chest to his mouth. He took one tip in his teeth and teased it gently.

Then the shirt twisted as he turned her so she was on top. "Move on me, Mary. Feel me. Pleasure yourself while I pleasure the rest of you."

"But," she protested again, this time for more, "I want to touch you."

He grinned that wicked, seductive smile. "You are, with your body." His rusty voice held power over her, mesmerized her into submission. She gyrated her hips, rubbed her clit over his pubic bone as he gripped her ass and held her steady against him. Lifting his hips, he positioned her well enough to suckle on her breast.

He thrust again. The sensations, the erotic pleasure, his touch, his breath, the scent of sex—it was everywhere, everything. All she could do was close her eyes and moan as her climax ascended to dizzying heights. In a split moment, lights seemed to appear behind her closed lids, and when she came, she came hard and cried with the sweet torment, the ecstasy of her release.

Spent, she collapsed on him, but he wasn't through with her yet. In a flash, he turned her yet again and plunged within her depths. His breathing hastened. She opened her eyes and watched his face. Even with the mask on, she could read him and knew he found the same intense carnal bliss she experienced. His deep groan signaled he neared his peak. One hard thrust, then another, and he wrapped his arms around her, gripping her to him. By instinct, she squeezed the inner walls of her vagina around his penis. His body shuddered as he shot the essence of himself within her; then he rested his forehead against hers.

Quiet descended, an intimate peace. His heartbeat thrummed against hers. Their breath intermingled. The conjoined sounds made a music of their own. And it was beautiful.

She gasped as reality returned, confusing her. She'd never had a lover like him. She peered in his eyes and he stared back at her with an intensity she couldn't name.

"Mary," he rasped. "You cannot leave me."

"We only promised one night."

"That doesn't mean we can't see each other again."

She swallowed. "But I don't really know you. I don't even know your real name."

"You can continue to call me Peter," he whispered against her lips, then kissed her. "And I promise that I will tell you more in time. Trust me."

"Trust is hard for me."

He ran his hands up her arms and relaxed his hard frame against her. "You felt it too, Mary. I know you did. Open up and take the risk, or you will always wonder where this would have led."

She bit her lip. He was right. Besides, wasn't that the type of business she was in? Except she'd never done it with her heart. Still unsure, she nodded. "I'm game, Peter. Take me then. And we'll see if this investment pans out."

He laughed. "Now, my sweet, we can get down to business."

"Business?" Her brows knitted.

"Oh, yes." He stood and strode to the kitchen area again. "The business of pleasuring you more than you ever have been pleasured before."

She laughed at that. Little did he know that he'd already accomplished that task.

From then on, Peter's days with Mary were cool, but the nights were hot. From their first bout of sex and the days of closeness afterward, Peter knew he and Mary were destined to be together. Each night he became the man in the mask, he worked to make their connection stronger sexually and emotionally, and in the confines of the penthouse, Mary turned from a calculating investor into a passionate fiery lover. Her sweet body would melt in his arms with his touch, and he would savor every moment, but he couldn't reveal himself. Not yet. He had made a promise to her, a pledge to find the person who'd pushed Dumpty. Peter needed to keep that before he could tell her more.

But now the day was finally here. He fingered the paper with the name of his contact, the one with the final link to the thief. He would tell her. Tonight.

And pray she would be accepting of his pretense.

He looked up and saw Mary slaving away on his latest project. He'd asked her to stay late to finish. He needed the extra time to complete his mission before he could confront her.

Rummaging through the bills on his desk, he found the directions he needed for the meeting; then, pocketing the paper, he left in a rush.

Mary puffed her cheeks, then blew the air out in an annoyed huff. Where did that guy go? She'd made sure the task was done as quickly as she could, and now the prick wasn't even here to get the results! She turned the light on to his dark office and walked around the desk to grab some notepaper and a pen. She wasn't waiting any longer. She had a date with her secret lover, and their meetings were something she would never miss.

Papers lay over the surface, and she pushed some aside so her file could be easily spotted, but when she went to put them down, a familiar logo caught her eye. "The Castle Hotel?" she muttered as she picked the invoice up and scanned it.

A bill for the penthouse.

"Oh, my God." Her hand shook as the reality of what she saw hit her. "You son of a bitch."

Slamming the file down, she stomped out. She would make her meeting tonight, but little did "Peter, Peter, 'the Pump' can eat her" know what kind of meeting it would be.

Peter struggled with his indecision. Should he begin this evening as usual, or should he come as himself, no pretense at all? He fingered the small box he had in his pocket as he closed his eyes and slowly exhaled, deciding.

This would be the biggest risk of his life. Telling Mary the truth.

And it was worth more than all the money he could get, because this time, it had to do with his heart.

Lifting his chin, he marched into the hotel and took the elevator to the penthouse. It was time to be real. He needed to give this his best shot.

When the elevator door opened, Peter slowly walked in. Mary lay on the bed dressed in a kitten outfit, mask and all, sipping one of the vintages he knew she liked. Even in the candlelight, he could tell her eyes narrowed, inspecting him.

He swallowed as a pang of fear shot through him.

"Mary." He spoke, but this time the hoarseness in his throat, not a potion, caused the raspy sound.

She sat up on the cover and eyed him up and down. "Well"—she slipped off the bed and sauntered toward him—"at least you decided not to lie to me tonight."

Her voice sent chills down his spine. "You mean you knew all along?"

She ripped off the mask. Her steely glare diced his heart. Then her shoulders slumped and she turned her back on him. "No."

Did she choke on the word? Peter rushed to her and wrapped her in his arms. "I didn't want to lie, but after what happened when we first met, I wanted you to get to know me without the baggage of our office roles."

"Why?" Her eyes teared as she turned within his arms to face him. "Why did you do it? I thought . . ." She bent her head and looked away.

"I don't blame you for what you thought," he whispered against her temple. "But meeting you the first time threw me. I didn't know what to do, so I royally messed up." He lifted her chin and stared into her beautiful watery gaze. "I love you, Mary. I think I knew that from the first." He placed a soft peck on her parted lips. "I'd never faced that before. It confused me." He thumbed away a salty droplet that slid down her cheek. "But after what happened, I couldn't tell you the truth. Not until I fulfilled my promise to you. Then I thought you'd forgive me."

"Your promise?" Her brows arched.

"To find the guy that upended Humpty."

"Did you? You must have. Otherwise you would have never come without the disguise." She threw her arms around his neck and kissed him. "I can't believe it. Who?"

Peter sneered, thinking about it. "Knave O'Hartz. I think B.B. Wolfe is involved too. Everything I have on him so far is circumstantial, but I'm determined to get what we need to make a case."

She cried against his shoulder. "Oh, Peter."

He held her tight. "There's something I want to ask you, Mary." He swallowed. "Now that you know who I am."

"What?" She rained kisses against his neck and chin.

He cleared his throat, hoping like hell she would agree. "Well, I want to suggest a special kind of merger."

"Merger?" Her brows knitted again. "You mean, something about the business deal you had me working on?"

"No." He knelt in front of her. "Not business." He pulled something out of his pocket. "Personal." Her eyes were glued to the box as he opened it. The diamond in the engagement ring sparkled with fire.

She gasped as a look of wonder and shock vacillated across her face. "Peter? Is this . . . ? Are you . . . ?"

Warmth grew inside him. He gave her his best smile to show her he meant business. "If you can find a way to forgive me, Mary, I want to spend the rest of my life making things up to you." He paused to gauge her response. "I love you. Please marry me."

She pressed her lips together. "I love you, too, Peter."

She paused and Peter's heart skipped a beat as he waited for an answer.

Then she circled her arms around his shoulders and kissed him deeply. "Yes," she murmured against his lips. "Oh, yes, Peter." She kissed him again.

Rising, he picked her up and wrapped her legs around his waist. "Good, then I don't want to waste any time. Besides"—he laid her on the bed—"you look too yummy in this kitten outfit."

She laughed and ran her hands up his chest. "I can't believe it. Peter, my hardened coworker . . . and Peter, the warmest, most heartfelt lover I've ever had."

"Believe it, Mary." He straddled her body and tossed off his jacket. "Oh, there is one more thing."

She stopped in the midst of unbuckling his belt. "What?" she asked with a breathy voice as dread shown in her eyes.

Placing his hands on the bed over her shoulders, he leaned in to her. "You're going to be a rich woman."

She looked at him and gave a cute little snort. "Right. I know you're a great analyst, but I didn't think you'd make a fortune at it. Not yet."

He chuckled. "Well, I have. You see, my sweet"—he caressed her lips with his—"I'm the silent partner for the firm. Jack and I are going to announce it tomorrow. We're getting too big for everyone not to know."

"What?" Her mouth gaped as the rest of her froze.

"It's part of my present to you, my angel. I want more honesty in my life." He straightened, ripped off his shirt, then proceeded to undo the tiny buttons on Mary's outfit. "For tonight, however, I have another type of merger, a more physical one, I'd like to suggest."

"I'm game." She laughed and ran her fingers up his forearms. "What was it O'Hartz had said? Peter, 'the Pump' can eat her. Well, lover, you can do that anytime." She licked her lips and shot him a serious come-on gleam as he undid her outfit completely, exposing her breasts and her nicely trimmed mons.

Peter grinned. "Careful. I might take you up on that. I think we should change that prose a little, though. How about, 'Peter, Peter, the Pump can eat her, but with his lover, he grew afraid he couldn't keep her.'" He hovered over her chest. "'So he put her in Pump's penthouse shell . . .'" He laved a nipple. "'And there he kept her very . . .'" He suckled the other hard nub. "'Very . . .'" He lowered himself to lick and taste her wet labia. "'Well.'" He pushed upward again and gathered her in his arms. "I love you, Mary. And I always will."

Wrapping her arms around him, she took his mouth with hers. "I love you too, Peter."

Then he plunged into her with his throbbing cock, savoring their newfound merger.

And indeed, he did keep her very, very well.

Also available from Black Lace:

Threesomes

Edited by Brit M

Two spicy novellas about red-hot threesomes

The Virgin Threesome

Marissa, a reluctant voyeur, becomes an eager participant
after her friend introduces her to the alluring world of
ménage. But can she overcome her inhibitions?

Three in Love

When Heather's two boyfriends move away to Nevada,
the sudden lack of a threesome in her life unsettles her.
So she follows them – but will this gamble pay off?

Black Lace Books – the leading imprint
of erotic fiction for women

Also available from Black Lace:

The Red Collection
Portia Da Costa

Step into the red collection...

From the *Sunday Times* bestselling author of *In Too Deep*, this collection brings you a stunning array of Portia Da Costa's short fiction – brought together in one volume for the first time.

As well as being the first collection of all of Portia's erotic short-stories, *The Red Collection* includes three new – never before published – hot short stories and two *Black Lace* novellas.

Discover why Portia Da Costa is the queen of erotic romance.

'Sizzling' *Cosmopolitan*